Sons of the Pope

Daniel O'Connor

BLOOD BOUND BOOKS

ISBN 978-1-940250-17-5

Artwork by Stacy Drum

Interior Layout by Lori Michelle

Printed in the United States of America

Second Edition

Visit us on the web at:
www.bloodboundbooks.net

Also from Blood Bound Books:

400 Days of Oppression by Wrath James White
Habeas Corpse by Nikki Hopeman
Loveless by Dev Jarrett
The Sinner by K. Trap Jones
Mother's Boys by Daniel I. Russell
Knuckle Supper by Drew Stepek
Sons of the Pope by Daniel O'Connor
Dolls by KJ Moore
At the End of All Things by Stony Graves
The Return by David A Riley
Fallow Ground by Michael James McFarland
The Black Land by MJ Wesolowski

THIS NOVEL IS DEDICATED TO ALL THE
KIND PEOPLE WHO INHABIT THE EARTH,
TO ANYONE WHO HAS EVER DONE
SOMETHING NICE FOR SOMEONE, AND
TO EVERY O'CONNOR AND RANDAZZO—
PAST, PRESENT AND FUTURE.

Though inspired by certain true events, *Sons of the Pope* is a work of fiction. Because, as many a New Yorker will tell you when asked about organized crime . . .

There's no such thing.

THANKSGIVING DAY-1989

CHAPTER ONE

E VEN HIS THOUGHTS were in Brooklynese.
Alls I gotta do is hope for a miracle. Not a Hail-Mary-catch-in-the-end-zone kinda miracle. Not even what they call the "miracle of childbirth." I need an actual freakin' balls-to-the-wall miracle.

And when the hell does it snow on Thanksgiving?

Peter Salerno grabbed a handful of socks from his drawer and tossed them into the open suitcase on the bed behind him. All the socks were black. Ham-fistedly digging through the dresser, he accidentally uncovered a black Smith & Wesson snub-nosed revolver. Once a gleaming prize of a weapon, it was now encased in a thin layer of lint and dust. Even so, it was still loaded.

⁓

The sun struggled to rise as the snow blew stronger in the Brooklyn dawn. Peter stuffed the final suitcase into the trunk of his worn beige Buick. He labored to fit it on top of the folded wheelchair. The fresh snowflakes melted on contact with his sweaty face.

No matter the temperature, humidity, or circumstance, Peter Salerno sweated. Now forty-one and heavyset with sprinkles of gray throughout his shiny black hair, he sweated no more or less than when he was a skinny teenager.

As he scraped the thickening frost from the windshield, he eyed Kathy waiting in the front passenger seat. Framed by the icy glass, she flashed the smile he fell in love with all those years ago. Shaking off the window scraper, Peter headed over to the driver-side door and barely dodged a

11

shopping cart that appeared from nowhere. The rusty wagon was pushed by an old man in a wool hat and tattered, layered clothing. The wheels of the cart battled the muddy slush on the old borough's pavement. An empty can fell from the mountain of aluminum and glass that filled the trembling buggy. Peter picked it up.

"Mr. Notoro, you dropped one."

A frostbitten hand reached out from the sleeve of an old New York Yankees jacket. The man never turned to face Peter.

"*Grazie. Dio vi benedica.*"

Peter handed the can over. He turned back toward the door, opened it, and then looked back at the man.

"God bless you too. Hey! When are the Yankees gonna get some help for Mattingly?"

No response.

Peter shrugged as he got in the car. Kathy was touching up her makeup when she asked, "He collects those cans in this kind of weather?"

"He don't seem to feel the cold no more, Kathy."

Kathy continued with her mascara while the car pulled away and headed down the snowy street. Peter drove slowly as his mind wandered. He wiped the sweat from his brow and from the burgeoning bags beneath his eyes. Kathy sensed his tension.

"You okay, Babe?"

No reply.

"Peter, don't worry. It's going to all work out. You'll see."

"I'm worried about my mother. What if nothin' changes? You know, most likely nothin' is gonna change."

⸻

It was a short drive and soon Peter Salerno's old sedan pulled up in front of his mother's home—just blocks from his own brick house—as Kathy was concluding her pep talk.

"Your mother is tougher than all of us. You know what? You can have General Patton, Jackie Robinson, Mother Teresa, and Superman on your team. I'll take Mama."

Peter smiled. "How can a woman her age be such a rock? You'd never know it to look at her. You'd swear the wind would knock her over."

He turned off the ignition and glanced up at his mother's house. He inhaled deeply; he never really knew what awaited him there. Conditions varied wildly. It was oddly similar to the shifting smells of the house. Sometimes the comforting scent of homemade sauce. Sometimes the cold, stinging smell of mothballs.

As Peter trudged from his car toward the snowy front stoop, two paces ahead of Kathy, he noticed that the front door at the top of the steps was wide open. The icy wind ushered the flakes right into his mother's home. Before he could process this information, there came a loud rattling noise, almost like a shaking box of screws. Then it came flying out of the doorway, bouncing as it tumbled down the snowy steps. It landed wheels over handle grips on the bottom step, propped against the sidewall of the stoop.

A walker.

Peter turned quickly toward his wife.

"Now what?"

He didn't wait for an answer. Instead, he bounded up the slippery steps and into his mother's home.

Mothballs.

From a room within came Mary Salerno's agitated voice. "I can't take it no more! Forty years of this! It's gonna change. It's gonna change now!"

Peter rushed into the kitchen to find his mother leaning on the table. Hung on the wall behind her, just above the stove, was a wooden crucifix.

"Ma, calm down. You sound like a crazy lady. What's wrong?"

Mary turned to face her son. No makeup, but her hair done nicely. Eyes moist and red. "So now I'm crazy? You gotta ask me what's wrong? Look in that front room."

Peter turned his attention to the darkened living room.

In contrast to his mother's hysteria, it seemed calm and inviting. The television was on, but the sound was very low. A portable heater, the size of a small end table, shielded the dim alcove from winter's chill. Someone was watching a very old cartoon. In the darkness, Peter could only see a silhouette bathed in shadows as the bluish halo of television light battled the crimson glow of the space heater. The figure didn't move.

Kathy entered the kitchen carrying the cold, wet walker.

"I don't wanna see that no more, Kathy," said Mary. "That was a brand new one, too."

Peter took a wrinkled handkerchief from the black shirt beneath his black overcoat and began to wipe his mother's tears. Mary took his hand.

"Peter. I'm old. I'm getting weak. I want this to be better. Better before I go."

Peter took his Mother into his arms. He looked over at his wife. Peter and Kathy then turned their attention to the shadowy living room. The television flickered. A bygone carnival tune was barely audible as the rudimentary animated credits rolled. The cartoon ended.

SUMMER-1945

Chapter Two

THE BOOGIE-WOOGIE SOUNDS of the Glenn Miller Orchestra be-bopped from a nearby radio as the new summer washed Brooklyn in sunlight. The bright rays streaked through the leaves of the tall, gangly sycamore trees, off the windshield of the Studebaker Commander, to the ragtop of the Ford Super Deluxe and down to the running boards of the Chrysler Saratoga. People darted in and out of the various mom and pop stores that lined each side of the street: the pork store, the candy store, the toy store. The sun shone like a spotlight on the glass door of Scotti's Barbershop.

The lazy serenity came to a crashing halt as the glass door shattered. A young man was ejected from the barbershop—right through the thick glass and splintering wood of the quivering front door. Three attackers streamed out after him. One slammed his bony back with a thick-handled baseball bat. Another added some powerful kicks to the rib cage of the prone victim. A third burly thug hoisted a metal trash can, full and heavy with rancid, baking garbage, and hammered it down upon the bloodied young man. The trash exploded like stinking confetti all around and on top of the semi-conscious prey. His blood ran serpentine down the sunny sidewalk toward the base of a rather sickly sycamore tree; the bloody motif eerily reflected the hypnotic spinning of the red and white barber poll that stood just a few feet behind.

"Get your hair cut someplace else," barked one thug. "This is my neighborhood."

17

"Clean all this shit up," yelled another. "And come back later to pay for the door."

Directly across the street from Scotti's Barbershop was Angelino's Bakery. The tempting aroma of his cookies and cakes wafted out of the open counter window, determined to fill the entire neighborhood. It was through that same wonderful window that Angelino would sell his deliciously thick Italian ices. At the moment, however, the baker's hand, still dripping with lemon ice, held a firm grip on the arm of a man who stood on the outside of the counter window. The broad-shouldered man was dressed in a perfectly pressed military uniform. The baker's grip deeply wrinkled the soldier's sleeve.

"Take your ice, soldier. *Ingorare*. Don't get involved. My boy's callin' an ambulance."

The baker loosened his cinch as the uniformed man lifted his lemon ice to his lips. His dress cap kept the sun from his wavy dark hair and deep brown eyes, but it shone brightly on his strong, thick jaw.

Salvatore Salerno, in his mid twenties, on his first day home from World War II, watched the three tough guys head back into the barbershop across the street. He then put three pennies down on the counter. Two copper, one steel.

"Not a chance, Sal. It's on me, *paesano*. Welcome home."

"Go 'head, buddy, let me pay you for it."

"No can do. The Krauts are finished. Hitler's dead. Yous guys are heroes!"

"Well," replied Sal, "Japan says they'll never surrender."

"You believe that crap?"

Sal Salerno flashed a wide grin as he licked his frosty treat. "Nah."

Sal pointed at the square, walnut-colored RCA AM radio on the counter playing big band music. "Say there, is that Glenn Miller?"

"Yeah. God rest him," Angelino replied.

"What a shame."

"He's another hero, ya know; he was flying his airplane to France to play for the soldiers."

"I know. Flying to France."

"Some people will tell you that God took him," said the baker. "Reached His hand down from Heaven and took Glenn Miller and his plane right out of the sky."

Sal paused, then tapped the counter and began to walk down the street. Directly across, two women rendered aid to the beaten man as he coughed, spat, and struggled to sit up.

A horn blared as a mustard-yellow 1942 Packard Clipper ambled by. "Jumpin' Jesus! Is that Sal Salerno? Welcome home," the driver yelled.

"Thank you," he replied with a salute.

As he walked on, Sal heard another yell from across the street behind him. "About time you got back, cuz! I ain't hit on a pony since you been gone."

Sal turned to see his cousin Vito Salerno. He opened his arms.

"Vito! Your pimples cleared up!"

Sal's cousin was a few years his junior, but appeared even younger. The light-gray felt fedora he wore was too big for his head. His eyes were wide, and he gleamed with nervous energy.

"Wise guy," replied Vito. "You look good, too. You're home just in time. Your cousin Vito is gettin' married next week!"

"Married? Not you, you skirt chaser!"

"Yeah. You're gonna flip your wig over Francine! I didn't send you no invitation bein' that you was in the service, but—"

"I'll be there. Absolutely."

"Great!"

"But, Vito, I don't got a steady girl or nothin'."

"Not to worry. I'm way ahead of ya. Francine's got this friend—"

"Vito . . . "

"A girl she works with. A seamstress."

"I'm no good on these blind dates."

"Just show up," replied Vito. "We'll introduce yous at the wedding. Wear them snazzy army duds. With you togged-to-da-bricks like that, you'll have a girl by the time we cut the cake."

Sal laughed. Then his jaw tightened as he saw the three thugs re-emerge from the barbershop across the street. They stood proudly—like hunters by a fresh kill—as they watched the women attend to the beaten man. A siren wailed in the distance as one of the assailants, Nicky the Zipper, gave his victim a reminder. "Don't forget, clean it up and pay for it."

Sal looked back at his cousin.

"Vito, why do you pal around with those fellas?"

"What? They're good guys. Regular Joes. Come on over to the barbershop, Sally."

"Why? So I can get thrown through a glass door?"

"You don't know what happened there, cuz. This Irish fat-head didn't like his haircut or somethin', so he starts jawing at ol' Mr. Scotti. That old man's been there for forty years."

"They didn't have to beat the kid like that."

"That fuckin' mick called Mr. Scotti a greaseball. He was real tough because he didn't know the boys was there in the back room."

A white ambulance huffed to a stop in front of the barbershop.

"You ever wonder," asked Sal, "how none of them guys ever had to serve their country?"

"They gotta take care of things here at home. They was just playing with Mr. Scotti's little grandson. Pushing toy cars with the kid. Those Irish punks need to know that this ain't Hell's Kitchen or somethin'. They don't run South Brooklyn. Fuckin' criminals. Besides, I seen worse beatings. Come on over, Sal. You'll see that they're real good guys."

"Maybe some other time."

"You know," said Vito, "I remember a time when you spent a night in the pokey for crackin' wise to a copper."

"Seems like a long time ago. Listen, Vito, you be careful around them guys."

"Relax, Sally Boy. Your ice is meltin'."

Sal's hand was a sticky, yellowing mess. It dripped onto the sizzling sidewalk, then dried like the blood on the other side of the street.

Chapter Three

THE WEDDING HALL was packed; everyone stood by their appointed circular table. Each table was draped in a thick Victorian rose-print cloth. The tuxedoed bandleader approached his microphone and cleared his throat.

"Ladies and gentlemen, for the first time as husband and wife, Mr. and Mrs. Vito Salerno!"

Cousin Vito and his new bride, Francine, bounded into the ballroom to boisterous cheering, applause, and Italian music. The hall was ringed with the stars and stripes. Equally conspicuous was the red, white, and green of the many Italian flags. After a moment, the crowd simmered down and the new couple began dancing to a lovely ballad. They danced alone in the dimming light.

Midway through the song, the bandleader invited all the guests to join the Salernos on the dance floor. The seats began to empty as the floor filled with couples.

In a remote corner, Salvatore Salerno, in full military dress uniform, stood alone. His eyes moved toward a table of five women in their early twenties. A couple of them glanced his way, whispering and giggling. His eyes focused on a third young lady. A dark-haired beauty with soft features and long, fluttering eyelashes. They locked eyes for an instant—then it was over. She looked away. Sal nervously adjusted his necktie as an elderly man meandered toward him. The man rested on a threadbare cherry wood cane.

"My eyes ain't so good," said the old fellow, "but, nonetheless, I've been watching you."

Sal smiled as the man continued. "You had the *coglionis* to stare down Hitler, but you're afraid of that pretty girl?"

"Hitler didn't have peepers like those."

"Well, you think you're the only single fella in the room? Next thing you know, she might be hoofing it with some other gent. Worse yet, one of these *spivs* might sweep her off her feet."

Sal spotted several of the local gangsters lazily approaching some of the women seated at various tables around the room. He quickly turned to the old man.

"Wish me luck."

The man rubbed Sal's shoulder. "*Vi auguro buona fortuna.*"

The soldier headed toward the ladies' table. They saw him coming. Four of them smiled anxiously. The dark-haired beauty avoided eye contact. Sal blurted out the first thing that came to mind. "Nice wedding, eh? So, do you ladies work with Francine?"

"We're seamstresses," replied a redhead.

"Sewing. That's nice," stumbled Sal. "You probably have nerves of steel. You know, to maneuver that tiny thread through that little hole there."

Silence.

"Ah, I'm just needlin' ya." He paused. "Get it? Needling?"

She tried to hold it in, but couldn't. An outburst of laughter. Only one girl laughed at Sal's feeble pun—the one with the eyelashes and dark hair. She looked up at him now, and she was smiling beautifully.

"I'm Sal. Would you care to dance?"

"Yes, I would, Sal. I didn't come here to sit all night. I'm Mary."

As they headed toward the dance floor, one of Mary's friends called out, "You should really tell Sal about your relationship with the singer."

Mary stopped and looked into Sal's eyes.

"Sal, it's only right that I tell you about me and the singer."

He froze, then looked over toward the singer on the stage. He returned his eyes to Mary.

"I spend all day," she continued, "with the singer—the Singer sewing machine!"

All the girls laughed as Sal exhaled.

"See," said Mary, "we got some jokes just as bad as yours!"

They reached the dance floor and joined all the other couples. Mary's seamstress friends were now being approached by other men. Salvatore Salerno made it just in time.

While dancing, Sal and Mary crossed paths with the newly married Vito and Francine. A puzzled Vito tried to mouth something to his cousin, but Sal didn't understand. They were separated in the crowd of dancing couples just as the music ended. Sal was escorting Mary to her seat when Vito intercepted them.

"Excuse me, Sal. Can we talk a minute?"

"My married cousin! You and your lovely bride look fantastic!"

"I'm going back to my table," interrupted Mary. "Will you come by later, Sal?"

"I'll be there more often than your waiter."

Mary smiled as she turned away. Sal returned his attention to Vito.

"What are ya doing, Vito? Why are you steppin' on my toes like that? How am I supposed to get anywhere with Mary if you do things like that?"

Vito looked down at the parquet floor. Then he looked up at his taller cousin and gently cupped both sides of his smiling face.

"Cecilia," said Vito. "We were fixing you up with Cecilia."

"What's wrong with Mary?"

"There's nothin' wrong with Mary, but Cecilia would be better. You shoulda waited for Fran to introduce you to Cecilia. She's Nicky's sister. Nicky the Zipper."

Vito tilted his head in the direction of a table occupied by several hoodlums and their dates. Nicky the Zipper raised a shot glass from the table and gulped it empty. As Nicky's head turned, Sal got a better look at the zippered scar that ran down the left side of his face. A jagged, pinkish slice that marred his olive complexion. Sal had not seen him since his first day home from the war—when Nicky was dumping a trash can on that patsy by the barbershop.

"Sorry to mess up your plans for my life," Sal told Vito, "but I'm sure you can fix 'Cecilia the Zipper' up with someone else."

"Shhh! You crazy or what? You can't say nothin' like that."

A hand thumped on Vito's shoulder. He turned to see a handsome, dark-featured man, about thirty years of age. Thick eyebrows. The well-dressed fellow was accompanied by a lovely blonde. She was sodden with jewels. Vito's nervous system took it up a notch.

"Oh, Mr. Falcone . . . and Mrs. Falcone. Thank you for coming. It's truly an honor."

Vito clutched the hands of the Falcones as he turned to Sal.

"Sal, I don't think you know Mr. Biaggio Falcone."

"No. Nice to meet you, sir."

"And you, soldier."

"That's my cousin, Sal Salerno," Vito interjected.

Sal shook hands with Biaggio Falcone as Vito continued, "And this is Mrs. Falcone. She's Norwegian."

"Olga," she offered as she touched Sal's hand.

"I haven't seen you around the neighborhood," said Biaggio.

"Been here most of my life, except for the last few years. There's been a war going on."

Vito winced at the sneering remark.

"Yeah," said Biaggio. "There's always a war someplace. I'll be seeing you around, Sal."

The Falcones moved on.

"Sally, are you nuts? That was a wise-ass remark."

"Yeah?"

"Mr. Falcone is a real up-and-comer. They say Don Campigotto has big plans for him. We've got to show him respect."

"Where is Don Campigotto? He didn't come to your wedding?"

"No. He's almost ninety. His health ain't good. I'm sure he sent a gift. I'm sure."

Sal pinched Vito's cheek.

"Go take care of that new wife of yours, okay?"

Later that evening, Sal was walking toward Mary's table with a drink in each hand. The elderly man with the cane approached him again.

"Hey, G.I. How goes it with the brunette dish?"

"Her name's Mary, old-timer. I think I'm goin' belly up. Fumbling over words, being clumsy. I think I'm gonna strike out."

Loud applause exploded as the wedding cake was wheeled in. Sal watched with the old man as the bride and groom happily approached the oversized pastry. Vito and Francine both grasped the lustrous cake knife. They held it tightly as they plunged it into the fluffy, four-tiered confection. Sal glanced at the old man. He was smiling broadly and nodding. His salty grin featured two glistening gold teeth. They were side-by-side.

CHAPTER FOUR

THE WEDDING CAKE was cut. A different wedding cake. A different wedding—a much smaller, more provident affair. The beaming groom fed an oversized chunk of cake to his new bride.

"Aren't they a lovely couple? Let's hear it for Mr. and Mrs. Salvatore Salerno," a cherubic bandleader barked into his microphone.

The small group of revelers broke into applause for the newly married couple as Sal wiped the sugary icing from Mary's smiling lips. Three steamy summer months had passed since Cousin Vito and Fran's grander nuptials. Vito made his way over toward Sal as the cake-cutting ceremony concluded, winking at a pretty waitress en route. The wedding guests applauded as the band began their version of Doris Day and the Les Brown Orchestra's recent hit "My Dreams Are Getting Better All the Time." Sal immediately embraced his new bride.

"Did you request this one?" he smiled.

She didn't need to respond. The elderly man that Sal met at Vito's wedding did his best to keep pace in the grasp of a robust matron. He tapped his weathered walking stick in near-perfect time as the female vocalist purred about the moonlight and the man of her dreams.

"Sally Boy," said Vito, "I told ya Mary was the gal for you! But three months? Wow!"

Sal raised an eyebrow as Vito continued, "Being hitched for the whole summer, I can tell yous that married life is A-okay!"

"That's not what Francine told me," laughed Mary.

"Ah, she don't like that I hang out with the fellas so much."

"She's right," said Sal. "You don't even have time to go to the track with me no more."

"That's because you need to come to the racetrack with me and the fellas. And you should've invited them to the wedding—at least Biaggio Falcone. He should be here, Sal. He's important."

"I don't run with that crowd. Nothing personal."

"I don't want my husband mixed up in all that," said Mary. "Now, if you'll excuse us, I'd like to dance with the fella I married."

She put her head on Sal's shoulder and quietly sang along to her favorite song. It was all about being in the arms of her love.

Sal shooed Vito, "Look over there at your wife. She misses you."

Fran stood—arms folded—on the other side of the room; her eyes fixed on her husband.

"Ah, jeez," sighed Vito. "How's that new job, Sal? You like delivering that soda? Sounds like back-breakin' work liftin' all them bottles."

"No complaints. It puts food on the table. I like driving the truck. It's quiet."

Vito yelled out to Francine, "Comin', sugardoll!" He turned back to Sal and Mary. "Let me give yous the envelope now because my brain blacks out now and again. Have a great life and lots o' healthy little babies."

Vito kissed them both and placed the white, gold-trimmed envelope into Sal's hand.

CHAPTER FIVE

THIS ENVELOPE HAD no gold trim. It was stuffed thick with cash, though. It was placed into a hand by Angelino the Baker. The calloused palm in receipt of the bulging paper pouch belonged to Biaggio Falcone. He leaned inside the counter window of the bakery, thick eyebrows tilted down toward the envelope. This was the window where Sal had stood months before as he witnessed the beating outside the barbershop. The New York air had chilled since then. The leaves turned brown and were falling from the trees above. The counter radio was tuned to the second game of the 1945 World Series. Biaggio stuffed the envelope into his pocket as the baker presented him with a large white cake box, neatly secured by red and white string.

"Please, Mr. Falcone," said Angelino, "take this cake to your lovely wife. I made it myself."

Biaggio pointed at the box. "I'll take this generous gift to Mr. Campigotto with your respects. Please don't ever offer anything to me without giving it to him first."

"*Perdonami, per favore,*" stuttered the baker. "I get another cake."

"Don't worry about it, Angelino. Mr. Campigotto is very ill. I'll bring the cake home to Olga with your compliments. This time, anyway."

He tapped the counter radio.

"How's the ball game going?"

"The Tigers are winning. Greenberg hit one out."

"Who you pullin' for?"

"I like the Cubs. The National League, same as the

Dodgers. Plus the Cubs ain't won a World Series in thirty-seven years."

"I don't follow the games much. That Greenberg, he's the Jew, right?"

"Uh, yeah," said Angelino. "He was a G.I. Signed up after the Japs bombed us."

"Hmm. Well, we showed them some fuckin' bombs, eh?"

An eight-year-old boy hurried up to the window. His mother kept a watchful eye from the doorway of the nearby hair salon, her hair meticulously structured in soft pink curlers, as she sucked on a Chesterfield.

"Can I have a chocolate ice?" asked the breathless child.

The boy laid his three cents on the cold counter top.

"I give it to you this time, young fella, but the ices went up a penny. Remember for next time, okay?"

Biaggio dropped two crisp dollar bills onto the counter.

"The ices are on me. For the rest of the year!"

The little boy's eyes widened as he retrieved his three pennies from the counter.

"Wow! Thanks, Mister. You're the tops!"

Biaggio patted the boy's head, then left the counter, cake box in hand. He glanced at the child's mother. She smiled broadly as she ground out her cigarette beneath her reptile-skinned shoe. He walked briskly down the street, yet whistled a somber tune. Biaggio Falcone stopped abruptly by Marcello's Pizzeria and walked inside.

Across the street, in front of Scotti's barbershop, sat a 1940 Pontiac Special Six—a rich dark blue, but mostly wood-bodied. Lots of wood. Seated quietly, nearly motionless, in the front seat, were "Little Jimmy" and "Chicky the Termite," both in their mid-forties. Jimmy, despite the "Little" moniker, was a full six feet four inches and easily 300 pounds. His share of the front bench was nearing 75 percent. He wore thick black eyeglasses, which, despite their enormity, still appeared too small for his colossal head. Chicky, slight of frame, with a dollop of red hair plopped on his head like a scoop of gelato, sat at the wheel behind the woodgrain dashboard, beneath the woodgrain top. He whittled away with a small, curved knife; he was carving a figurine out of a rectangular chunk of basswood. One might expect this vehicle to have the warm redolence of a kindling log, yet any trace of such was stripped by the antiseptic sting of Little Jimmy's thick, oppressive aftershave. Chicky dug into his wood block, cleared his sinuses and spat through the open car window.

"Biaggio Falcone," he mumbled. "What does Don Campigotto see in this bastard, Jimmy? I was a made guy when he was still shittin' yellow."

"I've heard this song before, Chicky."

"I mean, how many bums you think we rubbed out for the old man?"

"Between the both of us . . . I dunno . . . ten?"

"Twelve," said Chicky. "Twelve—counting that one time I blasted the wrong guy."

"I'd omit that one."

"A body is a body. Alls I'm sayin' is we done twelve more than Biaggio ever done."

Little Jimmy lit a Camel as Chicky the Termite whittled away.

Biaggio tucked another weighty envelope into his pocket as he emerged from the pizzeria. He still held the large cake box under his left arm. As he resumed his dirge-like whistle, he encountered a ruddy-faced beat patrolman. He gave the cop a sturdy handshake, then whispered something that drew a snort and a snicker from the rubicund lawman. Jimmy and Chicky continued to observe from the Pontiac woodie.

"Well, scratch my ass with your mother's toothbrush," said Chicky. "My blood ain't even dry on his billy club and Keegan the Cop is makin' like Fred and Ginger with Biaggio."

"That's the difference between you and Biaggio Falcone. You can usually be found on the wrong end of a bloody truncheon; he is a slick businessman. Don't take offense, but if he sneezed on you, your I.Q. would increase."

"Jeez, are you in love with this guy? Maybe you should send him some flowers."

Jimmy leaned toward Chicky. His aftershave fumes stormed up his friend's tightening nostrils. "I'll send the flowers," whispered Jimmy, "to Biaggio Falcone's funeral."

Chicky chuckled as he dug his knife deeper into his wooden slab.

"As soon as the old man goes," Jimmy continued, "so does he."

Smack! Something crashed down upon the windshield.

"What the hell?" yelled Chicky.

They left the car to get a closer look at the thick, ant-covered tree branch that split from the tall, sickly sycamore outside Scotti's and dropped to a rackety rest atop Chicky the Termite's hardtop.

"*Va fangul,*" whined Chicky. "Help me get this shit offa my car, Jimmy."

A bevy of crisp, brown leaves floated lazily down in the wake of the fallen tree limb. They came to soft landings all about Chicky's car. More foliage settled on both men as they hoisted the heavy, insect-ridden wood from the Pontiac.

"Oh, look at this," said Chicky as he examined the damage. "I'm gonna need body work on this here."

"Absolutely," said Jimmy. "But you needed a paint job anyway.

Chapter Six

T HE PAINTBRUSH WAS thick with yellow. As it ran down the kitchen door molding, the amateur house painter spoke up. "You're sure you like this color, baby?" asked Sal Salerno.

"It's perfect," replied Mary. "But I'd like it a whole lot more if you'd let the landlord do it."

Their new apartment was coming along nicely. The kitchen had a nice four-burner Magic Chef stove, a relatively new G.E. refrigerator and even a washing machine, albeit a wringer-styled Maytag, not one of the newer automatic models.

"I don't want any rush job by the landlord," said Sal. "If we're gonna live here, we're gonna do it right. I got some good paint at Pintchik's, I've got a steady hand, and we're gonna have a nicely painted home."

"Not if you keep getting it all over the ice box."

Mary grinned as her finger wiped an errant yellow drop from the refrigerator.

"Maybe you can do a better job," smiled Sal.

"I can!"

Mary approached her husband and placed the tip of her finger on Sal's nose, leaving a bright yellow smudge on the end of it. Sal calmly dipped his brush into the paint bucket.

"Oh yeah?"

His wife let out a scream as he chased her with the dripping bristles. He caught her just past the living room, a trail of wet yellow dots on the tiles behind them. Not bothering to douse her in paint, he pulled her close. Their eyes met as she caught her breath. He swept her dark hair aside and rested his face next to hers. She liked the feel of the grainy stubble as his cheek grazed her lips.

"I love you, Mary Salerno," he whispered.

He kissed her softly as they embraced by the open door of a small, stark bedroom.

"What color should we paint that room?" she asked.

Sal coughed before responding.

"You mean . . . as in pink or blue?"

She nodded.

"You're not . . . I mean you're not sayin'—"

"Oh, no! No! I just mean that maybe we should start thinking about our future."

"Already?"

"I'm just talkin' is all. I think you'd make a great pop."

"Well, um, I'm still the new guy at my job. I'd like to maybe get some seniority and save a little money. I'm working as many hours as they'll give me—"

She put her finger, still yellow, to his lips.

"I'm working, too," she whispered. "Maybe between us, we can save up some money and see if, sometime not too far down the road, the Lord will send a little miracle our way."

Sal cast his gaze into the barren room, the paint drying on the tip of his nose.

"Well, you shouldn't choose the color until the baby arrives, anyway," he said.

Mary beamed as she pressed closer against her husband. He leaned in to kiss her once more. The paint brush fell from his grip and slopped onto the tan floor tiles. The jaundiced, leaden enamel oozed slowly in all directions from the abandoned whisk.

CHAPTER SEVEN

THE STREET WAS dark, but it was still only a little past six on this windy fall evening when two men entered the toy store. A woman watched her young son happily sample a brand new, shiny silver novelty. They were the only customers in the rather bare-shelved emporium. The place was oddly dim, and its musty cardboard smell was briefly interrupted by the chilled zephyr that invaded via the front doorway. The dangling door chimes sang until the entry closed with a thud.

The woman took the toy from her son's hand and led him briskly toward the door. More lilting chimes as the mother and child bolted. Little Jimmy flipped the window sign to "Closed" as he and Chicky the Termite sauntered toward the counter. The owner, a Puerto Rican man in his mid-fifties, was kneeling, his back toward the front door. He stopped unpacking a carton and turned around.

"Good evening, Hector," said Jimmy. "It is Hector, right?"

"Y-Yes. Hector."

The anxious proprietor wiped his hands across his apron as he glanced toward the back of the shop. A light, yet hurried, scratching echoed from a distant corner. Chicky walked slowly in the direction of the scraping noise. Little Jimmy leaned his ample frame over the counter.

"The kid that just left—I saw he was playing with one of those new spring toys that Mr. Falcone kindly gave to you as a welcoming gift."

The store owner nodded but had his head turned toward the back, where Chicky was headed.

"What do they call those springs?" Jimmy continued.

"It's . . . Slinky," replied Hector, still not looking at Jimmy.

"That's right. You do know that those toys are not in stores yet. Even Gimbel's don't have 'em. They won't be in stores for weeks, but Biaggio Falcone gave you a case of them, Hector."

The slim Puerto Rican took a few steps toward the back of the store.

"Hey! I'm talking to you," shouted Jimmy.

Chicky closed in on the noise. He thought perhaps it was a dog clawing against a door.

Then he saw her.

She sat silently at a small desk. Her hair in pigtails. Soft, angelic and small, she was no more than seven years of age. The clamor came from the scraping pencil in her small hand. There were several more awaiting her in a nearby cup. She ran the pencil with surprising velocity across the drawing paper. Her head held in stony stillness as her hand vacillated with eerie precision.

"Leave her be—*por favor*."

Hector was now beside the young girl. Her eyes did not leave her artwork. Little Jimmy was a step behind the proprietor.

"Hello, sweetheart. What's your name?" asked Chicky as he crouched beside her.

The frenetic penciling continued.

"Her name is Annette. My granddaughter. She won't answer. Please understand," said Hector.

Chicky stood up. He nodded.

"Can she hear?"

"*Si*. She hears, but no answer. Let her be."

"But she makes such nice pictures! Look at these here, Jimmy."

Jimmy gazed at the newly completed artwork on her desk. It was an astonishingly detailed likeness of a young child holding a toy. It was the boy with the Slinky.

"We need to go up by the counter again."

Little Jimmy put his large hand on Hector's shoulder, nudging him toward the front counter.

"C'mon, Chicky. Up front."

The red-haired Termite followed Jimmy and Hector. He glanced back at Annette more than once. Her head never moved. Her eyes fixed on the paper. The pencil wouldn't cease.

Jimmy looked Hector directly in his eyes.

"Listen, we just saw some punks hanging around outside. We chased them away."

"I saw no one," replied the store owner.

"They cause trouble. They smash windows. They burn things. Know what I mean?"

Hector nodded.

"We keep them away. That's what Mr. Falcone explained to you when he welcomed you to the neighborhood, right?"

"*Sí.*"

Chicky kept looking back at Annette, even as Jimmy grabbed a Slinky.

"Then he gave you this exclusive toy to help you get your Christmas sales started."

"I tell him, 'No, thank you.'"

Jimmy played with the new toy, letting it drop from one hand to the other. The pencil scratching continued from the back.

"Hector, the toys are on your shelf, so you must have accepted Mr. Falcone's gift."

The merchant sighed as he rubbed the beads of sweat from his forehead.

"Do you have the tribute?" asked Jimmy.

"I don't understand 'tribute.'"

Jimmy looked over at his partner. Chicky still peered toward the back, fixed on Annette. Her eyes focused intently on her rapid sketching.

"Chicky, wake up. This guy is dancing with me here."

"Listen, Hector," snapped Chicky, "Biaggio Falcone makes sure that your store is kept safe. *Capisce*? Don't play stupid with us and don't try that 'no speaky English' shit either. You are late with your payment for his protection services."

"No, *señor*, I cannot afford this. I try to start new business here. I make no money yet. I still have shelves that are empty. Maybe after Christmas I can give something."

"Maybe after Christmas?" retorted Jimmy, biting his lower lip.

The Slinky fell to the floor.

As Annette repeatedly slashed her pencil across the paper, she could hear the noises that came from the counter area. Grunting. Breaking glass. Items, large and small, crashing to the tiles. Voices were muffled. Sounded like a muzzled medley of cursing and pleading. The pencil ran faster. Annette's deep brown eyes ascended from the artwork. Her hand never slowed. She cast an empty gaze toward the front of the store as her feverish work continued.

"Gimme a cigarette, Chicky."

That's all she clearly heard as the ruckus settled. Her pencil slowed as the racket faded. Her new drawing was complete. The paper was awash in grays and blacks. The illustration detailed two men, one clearly larger than the other, as they stood over a third man. That individual, robed in an apron, was depicted as being sprawled before them. A thin river of light gray spilled from his head to the bottom of the page.

Little Jimmy's cigarette lighter sparked a glow just as Annette laid her pencil on the desk.

"I'm gonna take two Slinkys for my kids."

One year later
Fall 1946

Chapter Eight

"**T**HIS IS CRAZY," said Mary. "I was all ready to buy some things for the baby's room."

She stood on the sidewalk casting a shadow in the late morning sun. Her head rested on Sal's burly pea coat. The hefty mass of her rounded belly left no doubt as to her approaching motherhood. They stood in front of what was once Hector's Toy Store. It was now a wet, black, smoky shell. It stank of scorched wood and melted plastic. The street was still damp and oily where the fire engines had stood. Cousin Vito hurried up toward the couple, a black and chrome camera in his hands—a brand new 1946 Ensign Commando foldout.

"Aw, don't tell me yous were goin' to buy toys," yelled Vito.

"What is this? Three stores burned to the ground in two days?" asked Sal.

Vito leaned in, pulling Sal away from Mary.

"A Sicilian barbeque," chuckled Vito.

Sal didn't laugh.

"Sally, maybe these people didn't cooperate, ya know?"

"Hector is a nice man, Vito."

"Nobody got hurt. He's fine. Listen—between you and me, Don Campigotto had a soft spot for him on account of that little girl. He's lucky the old man held on for so long. Hector ain't paid up in over a year. But now that the Don has passed on, Biaggio made all accounts payable."

"So half the neighborhood burns to the ground two days after Campigotto dies?"

"Do you two think I'm deaf?" interrupted Mary. "Is that little Annette okay?"

"Yeah, everybody's fine," said Vito as he kissed her cheek.

Sal's jittery cousin raised the camera to his eyes.

"C'mon, help me test out the new camera. I wanna make sure it works so as I can get good pictures of the funeral procession on Monday."

"You make like it's a president's funeral or something," said Mary.

"Just gimme a smile, you two. Sal, you rub the *bambino*, eh."

Sal placed his hand on his wife's belly. The daily *Racing Form* was still rolled up in his mitt.

"Lose the scratch sheet, Einstein," suggested Vito.

Stuffing the horse-racing paper inside his coat, Sal smiled broadly with his wife as Vito snapped the photo. The skeletal remains of the toy store simmered behind him. Vito grabbed his pocket watch.

"The wake starts in less than an hour. You'd better get a haircut and get dressed."

"Relax," replied Sal. "I'm going over tonight, about seven-thirty."

"If I had my way," said Mary, "Sal wouldn't be going at all. Rest in peace, but the truth is that Campigotto was nothing but a hoodlum. An embarrassment to the Italian people."

"Jumpin' Jesus, Mary! Don't say nothin' like that out in public! *Femmina pazza!*"

An agitated Vito clasped his hands, as if in prayer.

"Can I go get my haircut now?" joked Sal.

"Get that neck shaved nice, will ya? I'm gonna go shopping with my sister," said Mary.

Sal embraced his wife before he and Vito headed across the street toward Scotti's barbershop. Two trucks were pulling up as they arrived. Their side panels read: One Two Tree - Tree Service.

Vito was still mumbling. "Hoodlum? What a thing to say. That man had some will to live. What a fighter."

Two men exited the trucks and began to examine the distressed sycamore in front of Scotti's.

Old man Scotti sat reading the Italian Tribune as Sal and his cousin entered. Standing by the mirror was Nicky the Zipper, trimming his nose hairs.

"Good morning, Mr. Scotti," said Sal.

"Hello, son. *Come stai?*"

Vito interrupted as he spotted Nicky. "Nicky, you remember my cousin, Sal? He's a good guy. His parents are from Palermo."

The Zipper never turned from the mirror. His reflection gave a slight nod in Sal's direction. The nod was reciprocated. A handful of men were clamoring in the back room. Some telephones rang as others were dialed.

"Did you get all the cars washed?" Nicky asked Vito.

"Sure did. They look beautiful."

Sal got into the chair that Mr. Scotti readied for him. He darted a look at his cousin.

A large, breathless man emerged from the back room; the button fastening the dark suit jacket around him fought a valiant battle to hang on.

"Sally," asked Vito, "you ever meet Tommy Box o' Cookies?"

"Huh?"

"These guys call me that. Tom DiRocco. Nice to meet you."

As Sal shook his puffy hand, he couldn't help but think that this guy was rather square-shaped, yet bulging in spots, not unlike a stuffed bakery box. Tommy went over to the register and grabbed some cash.

"I'm going out for some sandwiches," he barked.

"Salami, provolone, and mustard," was Nicky's response. "Send Vito."

Again Sal looked at his younger cousin. Tommy handed

43

the cash to Vito, who waved sheepishly to Sal as he stuffed the money in his pocket and headed for the exit. On his way out, he held the door for two men who were entering—Little Jimmy and Chicky the Termite.

"Here they are," said Nicky the Zipper. "I was starting to think you guys maybe woke up dead or something."

"Never happen," replied Chicky. "You finally got some guys for that tree outside?"

Mr. Scotti looked up, a fluff of Sal's hair in his grasp.

"They rip it out, Chicky. Rip it out."

"Good riddance. Chop it down so it doesn't mar the funeral," said Jimmy.

"Yeah, that's the goddamn eyesore that dented my car last year," added Chicky. "About time."

"All the time fall apart, that tree," said Scotti. "Sap leak out. Lotta bugs. No good."

Clippers hacked away at Sal's wavy brown tuft as he joined the conversation.

"Can't they treat it? Spray it or something?"

"Ah, lotta money," replied the old barber. "Lotta time. Even then—who knows? I call these men. They cut it down. Rip it out."

"You should nurture it, Mr. Scotti. That tree might be around for a long time. It could look real nice out front there."

"No. Too sick. I tear it out," sighed Scotti. "*Piena di guai.*"

"Um," Sal said, "isn't that tree owned by the city? I mean, are you permitted to just tear it down?"

Silence.

All at once, Nicky, Tommy Box o' Cookies, Little Jimmy, Chicky and Mr. Scotti all burst into laughter. Another lock of Sal's hair fell to the tiles. It rode across the floor in a gust of wind as the front door opened. Biaggio Falcone walked in as the laughter died down.

"A lot of laughter in here for such a sad day."

All smiles faded.

The somber-faced boss walked slowly toward the back room.

"Nice job with the numbers last week, Jimmy."

"Thank you. It is a very sad day, Mr. Falcone," Jimmy replied softly.

"After the funeral, things will start to get back to normal," offered Nicky.

As Biaggio disappeared into the back room, he responded, "I hope so. Monday will be a new day."

Chicky the Termite leaned his rosy head into Little Jimmy and whispered a virtually silent, oddly tranquil assertion for Jimmy's ears only, "Not for you, Biaggio."

Thump!

Chicky the Termite winced as the air escaped from his lungs. Jimmy's size 15 shoe smashed down like a lumbering barbell onto his size 8. Message received.

As the rest of the crew looked toward the discordant duo, Biaggio yelled from the back, "Somebody get rid of those freakin' lumberjacks out front. The wake is starting soon for God's sake; and Scotti—close up when you're done with this guy."

Sal Salerno—this guy—swallowed the remark without expression as he felt the cold steel of the straight razor that Scotti dragged through the shaving cream on his neck.

Sal stepped out into the daylight rubbing his smooth face, still feeling the spicy tingle of aftershave. The "Closed" sign was already hung on the door behind him. A small mountain of limbs, twigs, bark, and sawdust was piled high on the edge of the sidewalk, over the curb, and into the street. A short, fat stump—only three inches tall, but as wide and round as a pizza pie—remained stubbornly anchored, its adamant roots entrenched beneath the concrete sidewalk.

Tommy Box o' Cookies emerged as Sal strolled into the distance. He addressed the landscapers. "Whoa, what a mess this is!"

"We'll have it all cleaned up," replied a worker. "We just need a little more time to get this stump out and get everything cemented over nice."

"Forget the stump for now. Time to abort your mission, fellas. Clean all this up. There's a wake today and tomorrow for a very important man. We can't have crap all over the street. Clean it up and come back Monday, after the funeral procession, to finish with the stump."

"But you don't want—"

"Abort mission. Put up some kind of sign and come back in two days, *capisce*?"

One of the workers fetched a sign from his truck.

Caution.

∽∽∽

Mary toted a few small packages as she navigated the long stairway in the four-story apartment building. The yawning hallway snatched its minimal light from a couple of lackluster bulbs, its ossified air stale and dank. She knocked on the door marked 3-B. Then a second knock. The expectant mother leaned closer to the door.

"Ma, are you in there?" she yelled.

From behind her, and behind door 3-A, came a reply in a voice that sounded like Ellis Island.

"In here, Mary. *Qui*."

As Mary pushed open the door to her own apartment, the light rushed out into the cavernous hallway. Mary's home bled Technicolor into the ashen corridor behind her. All four feet eleven inches of Mama stood there on her tippy toes, balanced atop a kitchen chair, her back to her daughter.

"What are you doing now, Mama?"

The middle-aged immigrant was intently cleaning the inside of a cabinet; a red and white apron was neatly tied around her floral house dress.

"Your closets, Mary. Very messy."

"You're right. *My* closets. Do I go across the hall and snoop around your apartment?"

"Now you will be a mother. You gotta be more neat. Make a nice place for Sal and the baby."

"If I wanna please Sal, I give him a bag of peanuts and

46

send him to the racetrack. Come down from there; I wanna show you something."

As Mama stepped down, she saw her smiling daughter holding up a small, yellow cotton ensemble.

"Isn't it adorable, Ma? I got the yellow one because—"

Mama instantly rendered the sign of the cross as she mumbled something or other in Italian.

"Oh, don't get all holy on me now," protested Mary.

"Take it back. I go with you now. *Per favore.* Buy nothing before the birth. Buy nothing."

"You are so spooky you should have your own radio program. Put your head back in the cabinet, Ma."

CHAPTER NINE

THE ICY THOMPSON M1 submachine gun was as dark as the bleak night that surrounded it. The weapon rested like a sleeping baby on the lap of Chicky the Termite, seated in the passenger seat. Wood shavings floated down upon the gun like so much bedraggled snow. Chicky was carving some kind of animal from his timber block. Little Jimmy's ample frame was squeezed in behind the steering wheel of the haggard, decade-old 1936 Chevy sedan delivery. The auto belonged to neither him nor Chicky and was, as intended, bland and nondescript. The two men waited silently in the vehicle, parked diagonally across from Scotti's barbershop and just down the street from the funeral parlor. It was the first night for the viewing of Don Campigotto's body.

Chicky halted his knife. "When I'm done with this, I'm gonna carve me a whole chess set. Piece by piece."

"You play chess?"

"Hell no. I ain't got the patience." The knife resumed digging. "I feel like we been here all night. The wake ended almost two hours ago."

"That part was for the general public. Not the inner circle," replied Jimmy.

"So you and me are general public?"

"Guess so."

"How can you be sure he'll be alone?" asked the sculptor.

Jimmy dragged deeply on his Camel. "It'll be just like this afternoon. You know Biaggio Falcone. Everyone leaves the funeral home, then he appears a few minutes later with the

48

don's widow and family, puts them in the car, has a word with the driver, and watches them drive off."

"The ol' man's a corpse and Biaggio is still kissin' his cold ass," said Chicky.

"It's called loyalty, Chicky. Quiet. Here come the boys."

The hitmen drew their heads back into the shadows of the Chevy's interior. Nicky the Zipper, Vito Salerno, and Tommy Box o' Cookies exited the funeral parlor and were walking toward Scotti's. Chicky placed his half-born wooden animal on the floor of the car. The boys reached the barbershop and Nicky slid his key into the front door lock. Once they were all inside, the light from the back room could be seen briefly, and then the door to that meeting room was pulled tight. Inside the old sedan, Chicky closed his carving knife. As if blowing an odd, unnatural kiss, he heartily puffed the arboreous shavings off the Tommy gun.

"I'll teach you," whispered Jimmy.

"Huh?"

"How to play chess. I'll teach you someday."

The dull thud of a closing car door echoed down the quiet street as Biaggio Falcone assisted the widow Campigotto into her limousine. He said a few words to her driver and tapped the trunk of the car as it drove away. Little Jimmy snuffed out his cigarette by crushing it in the palm of his hand. He and Chicky placed fedoras on their heads and began to tie dark scarves around their faces—just below the eyes. The footsteps could be heard by then, growing closer.

Somber whistling filled the crisp night air. Biaggio strode briskly toward the barbershop, drawing closer to the hit car. Chicky tightened his grip on the gun. The target was now directly across the street from Chicky and Jimmy. Once he passed and was a few paces in front of them, Little Jimmy stepped gently on the gas pedal. The Chevy crept out toward the middle of the street. Biaggio Falcone treaded quickly as his whistle echoed down the dark street. Chicky the Termite was halfway out the car window, Thompson gun at the ready.

Jimmy was about to slam fully on the gas when the sedan delivery ran over a small fallen branch that had come to rest on the blacktop.

Crack.

The whistling stopped.

Biaggio turned his head. He could focus only on the gun barrel as it began firing.

He ran like hell as the bullets hit all around him. They slammed into some parked cars, which acted as shields between him and his assailants. They bounced off the bricks on the storefronts behind him. They shattered glass all around. He heard them sizzling past his ears. Then he felt a piercing hot sting by his left shoulder. Then another.

That was when he tripped.

Something caught the toe of his shoe, and he fell, like a sack, to the hard sidewalk. Bullets ripped into the bricks above him. Debris rained down on him as his heart raced. He heard the vehicle slow down but couldn't see it due to the parked cars between him and the rolling Chevy. Biaggio regretted his decision to eschew a handgun of his own. His shoulder pain quickly intensified. He was expecting the gunman to walk up and finish him off when he heard more shots—different-sounding shots. Then screeching wheels and the beautiful sound of the hit car speeding away.

The boys burst out of the barbershop, blasting away at the Chevy. They continued firing as it disappeared into the night. The air was filled with gunpowder as people who lived above the stores began to open their windows. They saw Nicky the Zipper and Tommy standing in the middle of the street, guns still smoking. Vito Salerno was kneeling beside Biaggio, near the curb.

"Mr. Falcone, you're hit," yelled Vito.

"No, shit, Vito. Remind me to send you to medical school."

Nicky and Tommy ran over to Falcone.

"We gotta get you to a hospital," said Tommy.

"It's only my shoulder, I think. Just get me over to Dr. Messinio."

Biaggio felt Nicky pulling something out from under his legs. He strained to look back. Nicky tossed the object aside. It rattled as it settled against the barbershop wall. A small metal sign. It stared back at Biaggio as he read it.

Caution.

Biaggio Falcone had tripped over the small tree stump. The last piece of the diseased sycamore.

The boys helped the wincing victim to his feet. They ushered him to a nearby parked Ford and helped him into the back seat.

"Vito, close up the barbershop. Then disappear," barked Nicky as he tossed the shop keys to the shaken Salerno. Nicky got behind the wheel of the car. Tommy Box o' Cookies plopped down in the back seat beside Biaggio. As Nicky sped them toward the local doctor's home, Tommy removed Biaggio's jacket, revealing the bloodied shirt beneath.

"I was running toward the barbershop," grunted Falcone. "My mind was racing. I wasn't thinking straight. Then I tripped."

"Let me get a hanky on that wound," said Tommy.

"Listen, Tommy. I tripped and fell over that tree stump."

"Damn it. That's my fault, boss. I sent those tree cutters away before they finished the job."

"Because I told you to. If I didn't fall over that, I'd be Swiss cheese right now. I'd look like the front wall of Scotti's."

"The Lord works in strange ways. I'll make those guys take that stump out in the morning instead of waiting 'til Monday."

"We just saw a miracle, Tommy. That little tree stump stays where it is! Don't let anybody touch it."

∽

Back by the barbershop, people began to emerge, many in bathrobes or pajamas. They chatted quietly amid the broken glass and shattered brick. Some examined the bullet holes in

Scotti's storefront. The smell of the gunpowder lingered. Vito Salerno was long gone.

Not too far away, in a dark, grassy wetland just off the parkway, stood Little Jimmy and Chicky the Termite. Chicky's Pontiac woody sat waiting for them, but they stood beside the old Chevy. Jimmy inhaled a smoke while Chicky emptied a gas can all over the sedan.

"I don't think you got him," said Jimmy.

"Maybe I did. Who knows? You knew I wasn't the best with that gun."

"Yeah, but you're even worse as a wheel man. You would've crashed as soon as I started shooting."

"You're a riot, big boy."

Jimmy smiled as he tossed his Camel into the Chevy.

They motored away silently, sans headlights, in Chicky's Pontiac. The bleak marsh behind them glowed brilliantly as the abandoned hit car burned.

Chapter Ten

THE CRACKED BRICKS and bullet holes were illuminated by the afternoon sun. Police officers were removing the yellow crime scene tape and dismantling the wooden barricades outside of Scotti's barbershop. A large group of curious onlookers whispered their own theories to each other, safely out of range of the detectives' ears. Some took photos of the scene. As the police barriers came down, the locals moved closer to the shooting scene. Two plainclothes investigators conversed as they packed away their notepads.

"What a surprise," said one. "Nobody knows nothing."

Another detective addressed the crowd.

"You people should muster up some nerve. If there was a shooting on my doorstep . . . "

He could only shake his head as he turned to his partner.

"This is the first time I've seen this shop without a handful of those two-bit gangsters milling about."

"Well, maybe there's one or two less of them today."

"We can only hope."

Turning the corner with a hefty grocery bag covering her burgeoning belly, came Mary Salerno. Her expression changed as she saw the commotion. She stopped by a cop as he rolled up some tape.

"What happened, officer? I thought this might've been the crowd from the Campigotto funeral procession, but that's not today, is it?"

"That circus ain't 'til tomorrow, lady. Sure as shit, this is connected to it somehow, though. Forgive my language, please. Looks like some local hood maybe took one for the team here."

Mary slowly walked closer to the barbershop. She spotted the bullet holes and the broken glass. As she stood there, more bystanders began to squeeze between her and Scotti's. She took a step backward, away from the elbowing of the zealous congregation. Her mind began to race as she retreated farther.

Vito. What if Vito got shot? I'd better try to get in touch with Sal.

One more rearward step. Then she clipped it. Not more than a glance, but enough to turn her ankle. As she toppled backward, she let go of the grocery bag. She reached out to grab for something—anything—to stop her fall. She twisted, hoping to grab a parked car or a wooden barricade.

There was nothing.

The twisting motion caused her to fall face first into the street. Her torso slammed onto the rigid curb. The grocery bag landed beside her, minus a glass bottle that shattered on the street. Fresh milk oozed back toward the curbside. Beneath Mary's legs was the tree stump that induced her fall. Police and civilians alike rushed to her aid.

"Oh, God," yelled a woman. "*Avete bisogno di un ospedale!* She's expecting!"

"I'll be fine. No hospital. Just help me up, please."

The officer she spoke with earlier was now beside her.

"No. Don't move. We'll get you to a hospital. How far along are you?"

"Six months. I'm fine, really. If I don't feel good later, I'll go to my doctor. I don't trust a lot of these butchers."

Against his better judgment, the cop assisted Mary to her feet. People were scooping up her fallen groceries and putting them back in the bag for her.

"At least allow us to drive you home," pleaded the cop.

Mary smiled as she tried to brush some of the street filth

off her coat. She glanced over at the displaced sign that still rested against Scotti's wall.

Caution.

∽

Mary held onto the officer's arm as they climbed the apartment building stairs together. He clutched her grocery bag in his other arm. Mary's mother was at the top of the landing, mopping the floor.

"Mary! What happen? You all dirty!"

"I'm okay, Ma."

"Why the policeman?"

The officer placed the bag outside the apartment door.

"You sure?" he asked Mary.

"I'm sure."

The cop headed down the stairs as Mary turned to Mama. "I just had a little mishap. Nothing to call the newspapers about."

"You look like you get hit by a truck, Mary. Tell me what happen."

"I just need to lie down a little. Wake me at four o'clock so I can make Sal's supper."

Mary bent to pick up the groceries, but her mother beat her to them. They left the mop and bucket on the landing as they entered Mary's apartment.

CHAPTER ELEVEN

INTENSE PAIN DRAGGED her from her dreams. Mary's eyes opened to darkness. The clock hands told her it was almost 1:30 a.m. She heard Sal's snores beside her. The pillow was nearly stuck to the back of her head as she tried to get out of bed. So much sweat that her hair was glued to her face and neck. Her foot reached the floor but couldn't support her. She dropped to one knee with a thud. Sal's snoring stopped.

"Oh, sweetheart, what's wrong?"

He jumped to his feet.

"I'm sick. I think maybe my water broke."

"I'm calling an ambulance. Mama told me you didn't look good, so we let you sleep."

As Sal went to the telephone, Mary adjusted herself to sit on the floor.

"Did you eat supper, Sal?"

"You need to stop worrying about me."

"I'm scared. I don't feel right, Sal. Our baby can't be born this soon."

ᔕ

The hospital delivery room was white and cold. Mary couldn't hear the doctor's instructions, as they were drowned by the sound of her screams.

"That's it, Mary. Push for me!"

Her teeth were clenched, grinding in pain.

"Almost. Almost. Give me . . . one . . . more . . . push!"

A final scream rang out as the baby exploded from her trembling body. In the time it took the new mother to gather

her thoughts and come to her senses, the baby was gone from the room, engulfed by the medical staff and whisked away.

"My baby," stammered Mary. "Where's my baby?"

A nurse clutched her sweaty hand.

"We took the newborn for some urgent care. You need to rest now, Mrs. Salerno."

"Oh, those comforting words will lull me right to sleep. Please! Is my baby alive?"

"It appeared to be a live birth. The baby is in good hands. The doctor will be right back in to get you all set, okay? Let me get your husband for you in the meantime."

"Yes. Get Sal. I want Sal."

The nurse turned to leave, but Mary stopped her.

"Nurse? What is it?"

"Excuse me?"

"My baby. What is it? A boy?"

A blank expression.

"It was all so fast," said the nurse. "I—I don't even know. I'll try to find out. Sorry."

That nurse left, but another remained in the corner of the room, tidying up for the next delivery, apparently. Mary stared up at the ceiling. She thought of the future. She thought of the past. Each happy fantasy of her future family ended in horror. Every rainbow led to Hell. All she heard was her own breathing, mixed with the occasional tap or clatter from the clean-up nurse. She just wanted to see Sal, but it was taking forever. Then he nearly broke down the door. The wind from the swinging ingress tossed her hospital gown aside and felt like it gusted right up into her aching womb.

"He's alive, Mary," yelled her husband as he raced to her bedside.

"Oh, thank God. He?"

"Our little boy. He's alive. I knew it."

"What did they say? Will he be okay?"

"They won't say much yet. He's in God's hands."

"Did you see him?"

"No. They're watching him closely. They said these first few minutes and hours are very important. But you know what? One of the nurses told me that he's just beautiful."

Mary managed a smile through all of her fears.

"He's here, Mary. I can't believe it. Joseph Salerno, right?"

Her smile faded.

"Don't name him yet, Sal. I'm not going to name a baby after your father and then have to bury him."

She broke down in tears as Sal placed his head down upon hers.

CHAPTER TWELVE

THE DARK CLOUDS hung low in the sky. It was a windy late morning at the cemetery. The mourners braved the chill in their heavy black coats. They ringed the grave site en masse, like a grand, shadowy horseshoe. The priest concluded his sermon, and the anguished congregation began to approach the open grave one by one. A woman, face hidden by a black veil, was first.

"May God keep you forever," she said quietly.

"*Riposi in pace*," said the man beside her.

After waiting his turn, Vito Salerno approached the grave. Beside him was Nicky the Zipper.

"Rest in peace, Don Campigotto."

As the first mourners began to leave the service in their limousines, they drove past the unmarked police cars that sat on the outskirts of the graveyard.

The shades were all drawn at Scotti's barbershop. Biaggio Falcone sat in a barber chair, his arm in a sling and a wrap on his ankle. Nicky, Tommy, and Mr. Scotti were in various stages of removing their overcoats. Biaggio was the only one not wearing a suit.

"It wasn't a sanctioned hit," said Nicky. "Tommy and me was at that meeting in Queens for three hours last night. It wasn't the Verengia family. There's no need for a war because whoever took a pop at you did it on his own."

"I don't know if this is better or worse," replied Biaggio. "It could be anybody now."

"See here, who could benefit most if you wasn't around?" asked Nicky.

A brief pause as Biaggio Falcone rubbed his face.

He looked into Nicky's eyes as he quietly said, "You."

All movement ceased.

Then Biaggio allowed a smile to cross his face. "I had ya, didn't I?" he laughed.

All the others joined in the amusement as the laughing grew louder.

"I nearly shit myself over here," said Nicky the Zipper.

"There's a load of jealous young Turks around," offered Tommy. "Maybe somebody thought they'd move up in the ranks if you were gone. Maybe somebody thought Nicky would be a better boss for them. There are plenty of local merchants who kiss your ass but talk evil behind your back. Maybe it's someone you took candy from in second grade. Either way, we got to hide you until we sort this out."

"That's why we had to keep you from Don Campigotto's funeral," said Nicky.

"Yeah. That bothers me."

"And," continued Nicky, "that's why we brought in Staten Island Lou. He's gonna shadow you until we get to the bottom of this."

Nicky turned his attention toward the closed bathroom door.

"Lou! What'd ya fall asleep on the bowl?"

The washroom door opened. Staten Island Lou came forth. Bald head like a timeworn wrecking ball. The anatomical frame of an iron worker.

"You guys got a plunger?" he asked.

"Lou, there's a plunger in there," replied Mr. Scotti.

"Not no more."

Lou showed it to them. Both pieces.

"They make these things like toothpicks," he grunted.

"Nicky," said Biaggio, "I don't really need a bodyguard."

"Not our call, Boss. At the meeting it was determined. You got Staten Island Lou."

Biaggio glanced back toward the bathroom. The door was

open, and Lou was back inside, sloshing away with the half-plunger.

"Wonderful," groaned Falcone.

"Oh, and you gotta leave town," added Tommy.

"What?"

"You heard him right," said Nicky. "You're the new head of the family. The commission don't want nothing to happen to you now."

"Where am I going? Can I bring my wife?"

"You bring Staten Island Lou. We'll make sure Mrs. Falcone is looked after."

Biaggio swiveled his chair a few times. Lou continued to battle the toilet.

"I haven't told you guys yet because of all that's gone on," said Biaggio. "Olga's expecting our firstborn."

Everyone shouted their approval. Biaggio Falcone received a hearty round of handshakes, including a wet one from a smiling Staten Island Lou. As he dried his palm on a barber towel, Biaggio's jaw tightened.

"I want to be here for the birth of my child."

"Without question," said Tommy. "We'll get whoever did this. It might take a little while, but scum eventually floats to the surface."

A bang on the front door. Lou's handgun materialized instantly. Tommy, closest to the entrance, peered through the shade and unlocked the door. It was Vito Salerno. Tommy let him in.

"Hello, fellas. Sorry I'm late. Hey! It's Staten Island Lou! How ya doin'?"

Lou nodded his wrecking-ball head.

"Close the door, Vito," said Nicky.

"How you feelin', Mr. Falcone?"

"A little pain and a lot o' pissed off. Where you been?"

"Oh, listen, you know my cousin Sal? His wife had the baby last night. Three months premature."

"*Caro Dio*," sighed Mr. Scotti. "How they do, Vito?"

"Okay, I guess. I still didn't get the whole story, but I think she fell down or fell outta bed or somethin'. Next thing—she's having the kid."

"One of my kids came early," offered Lou. "It's okay. They're tougher than we think."

"I hope so," replied Vito.

"I should know. I got eight of 'em," said Lou.

"You got eight kids?" shouted Tommy.

"I happen to be very productive."

"Yeah. The only productive thing about you is your cough."

"Very funny."

Tommy turned to the other boys.

"I'm just wonderin' what dame is gonna screw this grisly bastard eight times," he laughed.

They all cracked up. Even Staten Island Lou.

"Hey, that's my wife you're talking about, you fat fuck. She says I look like Clark Gable."

"Clark Gable? Look in that mirror. You have a big swollen egg over your eye, two raspberries on your cheek, and a giant cauliflower ear. You're like a fuckin' salad with ugly and vinegar!"

"Get lost. I get in a lot of fights, is all."

"Next time try winning one of 'em."

"Tommy," said Lou, "I win every one of them."

"Enough already," said Nicky. "We gotta get going. Boss, we need to get you on your way."

Biaggio stuffed a cigar into his mouth and managed to strike a match despite the arm sling.

"You know, the bullet I took didn't really hurt. You know what hurts? I wasn't able to attend the funeral."

"That was for your own safety," offered Nicky.

Biaggio lit his stogie and held the burning match in the hand of his good arm.

"Mr. Campigotto lived here since the time of Abraham Lincoln. Now some asshole takes a shot at me during his wake. Makes me unable to pay my last respects. Turns his funeral into a circus with cops everywhere. Now I might not even be here for the birth of my child. Whoever did this is gonna wish their father never stuck it to their mother."

The match burned down toward Biaggio's fingers. He turned to Vito.

"Your cousin Sal and his wife, tell them I'm gonna pray for them, and their baby too."

He snuffed out the flame.

ONE YEAR LATER
OCTOBER 1947

Chapter Thirteen

A PUFF OF smoke rose as the flame flickered out. A single birthday candle rode proudly atop the cake. Mary Salerno blew it out with the one-year-old guest of honor in her arms: Joseph Salerno—Joey. Gathered in the homey kitchen with the boy and his parents were Mama, Vito, Francine, and a handful of other relatives. The group cheered loudly as the last of the thin strand of smoke wafted away. Mary handed Joey over to his father.

"He's a load, this kid," she said.

"That's my boy! Whatta the doctor's know, eh?" added Sal.

"God bless," said Mama. "More beautiful every day. I wish you luck."

She kissed her hand and rose it toward the Heavens.

"He's gonna be in center field for the Giants one day, Mama," said Sal.

"The Giants?" blurted Cousin Vito. "We just had the greatest World Series between the Yankees and the Dodgers, and you wanna talk about the Giants?"

"You gotta stick by your team, Vito."

"Who's the team with that colored fella?" asked Francine.

"That's the Bums! The Dodgers! Now you're talkin'. He's gonna be somethin' else, that rookie. Jackie Robinson. He's as fast as Assault, that kid. I swear to God."

"Fast as what?" wondered Francine.

"*Assault*. The Triple Crown winner! *Mamma Mia*! Don't you know nothin' about sports? Why'd I marry you?" kidded Vito.

67

He gave his wife a big kiss on the cheek. Sal placed Joey down on a blanket where he could sit and play with some toys. Vito watched his nephew as his thoughts turned away from sporting events.

"Jeez, I can't help thinkin' about Mr. Falcone. He's got a five-month-old son that he still ain't seen."

"That's a shame," replied Sal. "You'd think they could sneak him back from wherever he is just to see the boy. Or maybe take the baby to him."

"No way. That got a firm No from the commission. Too risky. Nobody knows who to trust no more. Nicky's the only one who even knows where he is. Nicky and Staten Island Lou."

On the blanket, Joey put down his toy. He tried to stand up but fell quietly back onto the soft quilt. Sal and Vito were oblivious to this as they continued conversing.

"How 'bout a piece of that cake, Vito?"

"Huh? Oh, yeah. I mean it's been a whole year and still nothing. I thought for sure they'd know who put the hit on him by now."

"You need some other interests," said Sal. "You're spending too much of your life all caught up in those guys from the barbershop."

Vito's mouth was now full with cake as he mumbled, "You gotta stick by your team, Sal."

Mama's attention never left Joey. He struggled again in a vain attempt to stand. Fran Salerno caught Mama's eye. She noticed it too.

CHAPTER FOURTEEN

HE LONG WALL of the apartment living room held shelf after shelf of his hand-carved figurines. They were meticulously aligned: sports figures, pirates, automobiles, sea vessels, animals, saints, and soldiers—a multitude of soldiers. These wooden creations were the centerpiece of the otherwise modest home. Chicky the Termite was happily transferring the contents of a bottle of scotch into a bright red thermos. A car horn blared from the street. Chicky took a swig from his bottle and meandered toward the open second-floor window. Standing in the street below was Vito Salerno. The heads of other men could be seen in the idling car beside him.

"Hold your horses," yelled the Termite. "I'll be right down!"

"C'mon, we don't wanna miss the kickoff," replied Vito.

Vito drove with Little Jimmy seated beside him. In the back seat, next to Chicky, sat Sal Salerno.

"You gotta start being on time, Chicky," said Vito. "Now I gotta drive like a lunatic."

"Chicky's problem is that he lives alone. He needs a wife, this guy," said Jimmy.

"Yeah, no thanks."

"Marriage ain't so bad. Right, Sally?" asked Vito.

"Right," he murmured from behind.

"I finally get my cousin to come out with us and alls he can do is mumble back there."

"Give him a break," offered Little Jimmy. "He's got to get accustomed to us. I still get uneasy when I have to sit next to Chicky."

69

They started laughing. Even Sal cracked a smile.

◦◦◦

The football was kicked into the chilled wind that swirled around the Polo Grounds. Vito, Jimmy, Chicky, and Sal made their way down the stadium steps toward their seats.

"Hey, at least the Giants ain't losin' yet," cracked Vito. "I don't see none of the fellas here."

Sal was checking his ticket stub. "We're supposed to be here," he said.

Four other men occupied the seats. Jimmy placed his ample frame beside the men.

"Excuse me, gentlemen. You appear to be in our seats."

One of them gulped a beer as he replied, "You're mistaken, pal."

"Sal, you've got better eyes than me," said Jimmy. "You said these are our seats, right?"

"That's what my ticket says, anyway."

"You heard him, gentlemen," said Jimmy. "Can we please have our seats?"

"You know where your friend needs a seat?" replied the man. "At the eye doctor's office."

Little Jimmy sighed. He glanced at his friends. Sal checked the ticket again and offered it to Jimmy. He glanced at it, then looked around the stadium. Chicky the Termite's blood pressure rose along with his blood-alcohol level. He decided to interject.

"How 'bout this? Get your stupid asses outta our seats."

The men put down their beers and stood as one.

"How 'bout this?" was the reply. "Fuck yous all, and your families too."

Chicky mustered up some warm mucus and spat into the man's face. Before the Termite could appreciate the accuracy of his phlegm marksmanship, a fist smashed into his left eye. Jimmy promptly decked the assailant with an elbow to the bridge of his nose. Beer spilled everywhere, and the brawl was on. Vito Salerno was no fighter and found himself on the bottom of a pile, fallen men above him, sticky puddles of beer below. Sal struggled to drag the men off his cousin as Chicky chewed the ear of his combatant. As security arrived, Sal had two men in headlocks—one under each arm. Little Jimmy had one bent over a seat, smashing his thick elbow onto the man's skull. The small army of Polo Grounds security began to separate the adversaries.

"Let's go!" shouted a guard. "Everybody out!"

Hurrying down the steps came Nicky the Zipper and Tommy Box o' Cookies.

"What the hell did you guys get into over here?" yelled Nicky.

"They're all out of here," responded the guard. "Stay back or you go too."

Nicky put his arm around the guard and whispered into his ear. He slipped something into the security man's hand. "These four can stay," the officer said to his troops. "They're in the right."

"You gotta be kidding me," yelled one of the ejected men.

They were escorted from the seating area as Sal, Chicky, and Jimmy dusted themselves off. Vito squeezed his nose as blood poured from it, dripping to the ground and mixing with the spilled beer. Nicky handed him a handkerchief.

"So you guys decided to start a little riot? What were they, Steelers fans?" asked Nicky.

"Man alive! Even Sal Salerno is throwing punches over here," said Tommy. "I thought you were some kind of saint or something, Sal."

"One of 'em punched my cousin," replied Sal.

The bloodied Vito started laughing.

"It's all Sally's fault anyways. He found them jokers sittin' in our seats."

"Really?" asked Nicky.

"They were in our seats and things got out of control," replied Sal.

"Sal," offered Nicky, "our seats are two sections over. Where do you think we were sitting?"

Sal held the ticket up to his eyes, examining it closely. "Section . . . D . . . row . . . seven."

"Turn around and look at the sign, Salerno," said Nicky.

The crowd rose with a loud cheer as the Giants completed a long pass against the Steeler defense. Sal turned to see the section sign. Section B.

"Holy Moses," he muttered. "Those guys were in the right seats."

"I realized that after I asked them the first time," said Jimmy as he rubbed his elbow.

"You knew?" asked Sal. "How come you didn't—"

"Hey, to hell with those guys. I wasn't gonna let you look bad in front of them."

Sal glanced over at his cousin. Through the bloody hanky, Vito winked.

"Can we get over to our real seats now?" asked Tommy. "Maybe we can see the Giants win a freakin' game."

As the boys headed over to their section, the Giants fumbled the ball. It was recovered by the Pittsburgh Steelers.

Vito's nose had stopped bleeding by now. He sat between Sal and Chicky the Termite. Chicky was hitting his thermos pretty hard. Seated in the row in front of them were Jimmy, Nicky, and Tommy. On Tommy's lap was a white cookie box.

"C'mon, Giants," yelled Vito. Then he turned to Sal. "I got a fifty on 'em."

"You're nuts. They haven't won a game yet this year."

"I got a good feelin' about today, Sally."

Chicky, growing more inebriated by the minute, leaned in.

"You know, Sal, it's good that you finally came out with us. You can't just go to work and then stay home all the time. You'll go batty."

"He's worried about little Joey," said Vito. "Some people think the kid ain't standing right."

"He's okay," Sal replied. "Don't worry about it."

"Sure he is. For sure. Glad you could come out with us, cuz."

Touchdown, Pittsburgh. The crowd began to boo.

"I wish I could get Mary out a little," said Sal.

"Soon Joey will be playin' with Mr. Falcone's boy," suggested Vito. "They'll be runnin' all over the place, right Chicky?"

"What, Biaggio's kid?" slurred the Termite.

He turned away, almost in disgust, and guzzled some more booze. Nicky turned around and looked at the boys.

"Vito, go get everybody some hot dogs."

Obediently, Vito Salerno stood and accepted some cash from Tommy.

"I have to hit the men's room anyway, Nicky. I'll get the food," Little Jimmy offered. "Let Vito rest that nose of his."

"Make sure you wash your hands before you touch my frank, ya dipshit," joked Nicky.

Jimmy chuckled as he took the money and headed up the steps. Vito sat back down to see Chicky staring right at him. The crowd exploded as the Giants returned the kickoff deep into Pittsburgh territory.

"Why do you like him so much?" came riding out of Chicky's mouth on a cloud of alcohol.

"Who? Jimmy?"

"No, not Jimmy. I'm talking about Biaggio Falcone."

"What? He's the boss. He's a good man. I don't understand."

"He wasn't always The Boss," laughed Chicky.

The drunk Termite took another potent swig.

"Well, he deserves to be," replied Vito. "He was always very good to Mr. Campigotto."

"There's a fine line between loyalty and ass kissin'."

As the crowd noise died down, Vito leaned in to whisper, "Chicky, don't talk like that. You know what Nicky would do if he heard that?"

Chicky waved a hand and shrugged.

"And what would Little Jimmy think?" continued Vito. "He's your best buddy."

"Jimmy? Ha!" laughed Chicky.

Nicky and Tommy turned around.

"What? You talkin' some shit behind Jimmy's back?" asked the Zipper.

"Nah, Nicky," offered Vito. "Chicky's pickin' on me 'cause I got money on the Giants."

"He should," blurted Tommy. "The crowning achievement of their season is a fuckin' tie for Christ's sake."

Nicky continued to stare at Chicky.

"He's just drunk, is all," said Vito

"*Che cosa e nuovo*?" sighed Nicky. "This guy's drinking is gettin' outta hand."

As Nicky and Tommy returned their attention to the football game, Chicky accorded them with an Italian hand gesture—to the backs of their heads. Vito looked over at Sal, who had a pair of binoculars raised to his eyes, intently focused on the game. Then Vito turned back to Chicky.

"Why don't you put away that sauce?"

"Now you're gonna be my boss too? Biaggio, Nicky, Tommy—you might as well give me orders too."

"Shh. Relax, Chicky."

"I'm everybody's pal when they need me to whack somebody. Other than that, I'm just a drunk piece of shit, right?"

"Quiet down. You want me to take you home?"

Chicky just stared out at the field for a moment, but he wasn't watching the game. Then he leaned into Vito, stinking like a barroom toilet.

"What would you do," he whispered, "if someone beat you down all the time? If they stole something that was rightfully yours? What would you do if someone treated you like a fuckin'clown?"

"Well, maybe I'd try to find out—"

"Find out? My ass. You're a man, Vito. You'd put him under."

Chicky glared into Vito's eyes. A smile loomed on his clammy lips. He leaned even closer.

"You've always been okay with me," burped Chicky. "I respect that. There's something I want to tell you, my friend."

The Termite was in Vito's ear now, furnishing a slurred, malodorous undertone. The crowd noise began to grow. Sal leaped from his seat, as did Nicky, Tommy, and most of the New York Giants' faithful. Vito's eyes widened as he absorbed Chicky's tale. He began to tremble. The Polo Grounds was alive with excitement. Touchdown, Giants! Vito didn't even notice. As Nicky and Tommy applauded their home team, it hit them both from behind. A warm, chunky cascade of vomit drenched their backs.

"Holy shit!" yelled Nicky. "You sonofabitch, Chicky."

The two men spun around to see that the retch was supplied, not by the intoxicated Chicky but by Vito Salerno. Sal was attending to his cousin. Vito sat motionless as Chicky continued to drink. Nicky and Tommy were removing their soiled jackets as Little Jimmy returned, bounding down the concrete steps, his mission complete.

"Okay, who wants hot dogs?"

Chapter Fifteen

THE MANHATTAN DOCTOR'S office was much larger than the ones they'd been to in Brooklyn. There were paintings on the walls and the seats were very comfortable. Sal and Mary sat across the desk from Dr. Irv Schatzman. Little Joey sat quietly on his mother's lap. Attending to some business in one corner of the office was a younger physician, James Mangano. Sal watched closely as Dr. Schatzman looked through his notes. Mary clutched her husband's hand.

"Mr. and Mrs. Salerno, we've studied your son closely and administered quite an array of tests. I'm sure you have heard the term cerebral palsy."

Mary's breathing grew stronger. She tightened her grip on Sal.

"I believe this to be Joey's affliction," said Dr. Schatzman.

"What can we do about it?" asked Sal.

"Well, cerebral palsy is a very imprecise term that is applied to various motor disorders. It is usually the consequence of prenatal trauma, sometimes even occurring during the birth itself. It can be caused by obstructed delivery, lack of oxygen or, as likely in your case, trauma within the womb.

From behind them came the voice of young Dr. Mangano. "Originally, it was called Little's Disease after William John Little, a British doctor who studied this intrapartum asphyxia and came to—"

"Please," interrupted Sal, "I don't care who discovered it. How can we cure my son?"

Dr. Schatzman glared at his junior partner. Mangano quietly left the room. The bearded M.D. turned his attention back to the Salernos.

"There is no cure, Mr. Salerno."

Mary began to sob. She struggled to stifle her tears as Joey played with the shiny religious medal that dangled from her neck.

"We can help you to make his life more comfortable," continued the doctor. "There are treatments that can help him to be his best."

"Doctor, will he ever walk?" asked Mary quietly.

Schatzman took a deep breath.

"We can hope," he said. "But I wouldn't expect it."

"He'll walk," said Sal. "You know, when he was born the doctors thought he might not even live. Might not ever leave the hospital because he was so premature. You're all so quick to dismiss. Just needs a little nurturing."

"I'd dearly love to be incorrect here as well, sir. But I do need to tell you that there is a very strong possibility that Joey will not reach adulthood. I'm so sorry."

Mary pulled her son closer. Both arms were around him now. Sal tried to say something but couldn't. Joey grunted the way he always did and slid the small silver medallion across Mary's slender chain. The harsh office light flared back off the image of Saint Jude Thaddeus.

CHAPTER SIXTEEN

C HICKY THE TERMITE'S black and white wingtips sloshed through the puddles as he dashed toward the front door of his apartment building. A soggy copy of the *Racing Form* acted as his umbrella on this particular dreary afternoon. He was thrilled to find the front door unlocked as he burst into the stuffy vestibule. The floor was muddied from those who had come before. Chicky shook himself off like an unwanted stray as he took to the staircase and climbed two steps at a time to the second-floor landing. He let the wet newspaper fall to the hallway floor as he turned the key in his front door lock. He entered his home and muttered to the small painting of Jesus Christ that hung in his tiny foyer, "Is Heaven pissin' on New York lately or what? Jake LaMotta gets beat by some stiff last night and now this."

He hung up his coat and hat, leaving his soaking shoes by the door. He glanced at the white tiled kitchen floor.

Mud.

Chicky arched an eyebrow as he felt around for his handgun.

Inching in closer, he saw his kitchen table. An open bakery box. Crumbs. Cookies. Chicky relaxed.

"Tommy?"

The Termite crossed into his kitchen and made a right turn toward the living room. His nose nearly drove into the capacious chest of Tommy Box o' Cookies. The imposing gangster wasn't smiling.

"Whoa! You nearly scared the balls offa me, Tommy. Did Jimmy let you in?"

No response. Chicky's face began to tighten. It felt harder to swallow. From behind Tommy's ample frame, emerging from the living room, came another figure.

"Shitty day, eh?" was all he said.

Biaggio Falcone returned.

Chicky went pale. He tried to regain composure.

"B-Biaggio. Welcome back. You . . . You look good."

Chicky moved to embrace the man he tried to murder. Tommy put a hand on his chest to keep him away. Then he found, and quickly removed, Chicky's revolver from his waistband.

"What? Whatsa matter, Tommy?"

"Come sit down," said Biaggio.

They entered the living room. Chicky slumped into a chair and Biaggio continued, "Is there something you want to tell me?"

Chicky's mouth opened, but nothing came out.

"I've always been up front with you," said Biaggio, "I expect the same. Listen carefully. Honesty can only help you now."

"Biaggio, please," pleaded Chicky. "You don't think that I . . . Biaggio . . . *So nulla.*"

"*Silenzio,*" screamed Falcone.

Biaggio turned to Tommy.

"He insists on lying to me. I don't want to hear anything if it's not the fucking truth."

"Admit what you did," grunted Tommy.

"Who's trying to pin this on me—that fuckin' Vito Salerno?" spat Chicky as he wiped his face on his sleeve. Biaggio turned back to face his terrified underling.

"I was testing that fuckin' canary," continued the Termite. "To see if he could be trusted. I made it all up to test Salerno."

Biaggio Falcone pulled up a chair right beside Chicky's.

"You're right, Chicky. Vito Salerno told Tommy about your confession. You see, you should have given your confession to a priest instead. That said, we did have to verify it. I wouldn't take something like this lightly. So Tommy, Nicky, and Staten Island Lou had an interview with Little Jimmy."

Biaggio grinned. Chicky gazed at his shelf of wooden figurines and the small carving knife that lay beside them.

Biaggio yelled into the room behind them, "Isn't that right, Jimmy?"

They came from the bedroom. The first thing that Chicky saw was Nicky the Zipper, smiling and covered in sweat. Then came Lou, with something very business-like about his manner. His big right hand held onto the rope that bound Little Jimmy's hands together. Jimmy's feet were also secured, and his mouth was gagged. As he was shuffled closer to Chicky and his face came into the light, the heavy bruising and caked blood on his tired scowl became much clearer.

"It took some doing, but Jimmy finally volunteered that you were the triggerman, Chicky," said Biaggio. "Now, you'll note that Jimmy is certainly not dead. That's a plus, right? Honesty has kept Little Jimmy breathing. Now you face the same dilemma, my old friend."

"You want me to say that I tried to kill you?"

"I want the God's honest truth. You will be severely punished. I won't lie. But your honesty will permit you to see another day. Just like him."

Biaggio pointed to Chicky's bloodied partner.

"Jimmy will get to see his children again," said Falcone.

Chicky glanced around the apartment. He eyed his figurines, the knife beside them, the painting of Jesus, then Jimmy.

"Well," he sighed, "I ain't got no kids, Biaggio. I've given almost that same little speech you just gave, many a times, too. It's like an old song by now. You can't sell horseshit to a horse. I'm supposed to look you in the eye and admit guilt. Just so you can sleep better after you whack me."

Across the room, Little Jimmy began to cry. His breaths came heavy through the tight gag in his bloody mouth. His knees buckled and he collapsed onto them. He may have been in prayer.

Chicky saw this but continued anyway. "You never killed nobody, Biaggio. At least not by your own hand. But you were a 'good earner' for your boss, I guess. Maybe I should be honored to be your first kill. I'm not. Why not let Nicky or Tommy do me in? At least they done it before."

"I will be the one to settle this," replied Falcone. "I owe this to the memory of Don Campigotto. I owe this to the son I still haven't seen."

Nicky handed Biaggio a small pillow from the sofa.

"It took me six months to find pillows to match that couch," yelled Chicky. "Now you're gonna ruin one with a bullet hole?"

"Let's not drag this out, Chicky," said Biaggio.

"What? I'm supposed to turn around and drop to my knees? I'm dragging this out? You're the one with the gun, asshole."

Like a launched jack-in-the-box, Chicky catapulted from the chair and onto Biaggio. In one motion, he grabbed the wood-carving knife from the shelf. Tommy and Nicky bounded to Biaggio's aid. Lou stayed with the kneeling Jimmy. Chicky was wild-eyed as he tried to force his pointed tool deep into Biaggio's left eye. He was extremely powerful for a man of his slight stature. Falcone grimaced as the cold blade came within an inch from his soft, moist eyeball. They crashed into the shelves of figurines.

Two muffled shots.

A scanty splatter of blood landed on the small wooden effigies. The body of Chicky the Termite collapsed onto the shelving, bringing it all tumbling down. Various figurines fell to rest on his corpse—horses, pirates, and saints.

Chicky was sprawled there with the anger still on his face, only now with raw, crimson holes in his neck and forehead.

Biaggio dusted himself off and gave Nicky a nod. Nicky turned toward Little Jimmy. As Biaggio Falcone headed for the door, he too looked at Jimmy.

"You have a boy and a girl, right?"

The huge, sweaty mess that was Little Jimmy nodded feverishly.

Biaggio exhaled.

"We'll look after them."

He and Tommy left the apartment. Nicky grabbed the pillow. Jimmy squealed through his gag as he tried to stand. Staten Island Lou forced him back to his knees. Jimmy hurriedly shook his head as he tried to plead.

"*Si disgusto*," said the Zipper. "At least Chicky had some dignity."

Jimmy wept like a newborn after an ass slap.

"You turned out to be a rat bastard," continued Nicky. "We rough you up a little and you sell out your best friend. That was worse than trying to take out Biaggio."

Nicky dropped the pillow to the floor, beside Chicky's oozing remains.

"It don't seem right that you should check out as painlessly as Chicky. You were always pretty book-smart, Jimmy, but Chicky had something you ain't got: a pair of balls."

The Zipper reached down to the bloody floor for Chicky's razor-sharp carving knife.

"You know what I got a good mind to do?" said Nicky.

Chapter Seventeen

TWO RED BALLS landed with a thud. An oddly warm November day in Brooklyn spurred many of the locals to play some bocce at the neighborhood park. Nicky, Tommy, and Lou were accompanied by Vito Salerno as they chose sides.

"Me and Tommy are red," said Nicky. "You and Vito can be green."

"How come you and Tommy are always on the same team?" griped Vito.

"What, you got something against having Lou on your side?"

Staten Island Lou stared menacingly at Vito. Then he smiled.

"No. *No*. Lou, you know I love ya. It's just that you ain't the best bocce player, is all."

"And you're so good?" asked Lou.

"That ain't it. I'm just tired of losing money to these guys. They even cleaned up on the LaMotta fight. How did they know he'd lose to a palooka like that?"

Nicky and Tommy laughed.

"You mean you *didn't* know?" chuckled Lou.

"We playing or what?" asked Tommy.

"Let me see if Sal wants to be on my team, okay?" asked Vito. "Lou, you can play next game, all right?"

"*Non importa*," shrugged Lou.

Vito turned and yelled toward the outer edge of the park, toward the swing sets.

"Hey, Sally, wanna play some bocce?"

Sal was seated on a wooden bench, having a little lunch with his wife and son. Joey tried to pick at the peeling paint on the bench rail. Mary gently pulled his arm away as she fed him—not with a spoon, but a dropper.

"Not right now. Maybe later," answered Sal.

Sal saw Vito throw his arms up in disgust, then drape one around Staten Island Lou.

Mary said, "It's all right if you want to play."

"Go 'head? You pulling my leg, sweetie?"

"I'm not exactly in love with those characters," replied his wife, "but you need to relax. You work so hard all week."

"Hmm. But why would I play bocce when I could be teaching our boy to walk?"

Sal picked his son up and placed him on the walkway. He held tightly onto both of Joey's frail hands as the boy struggled to stay upright.

"I got more doctor's bills in the mail this morning," said Mary.

Sal's attention was devoted to his son's struggle to stand and walk.

"That health insurance from your job only covers so much, Sal."

"Don't worry. We'll get by."

"I was late with the rent this month."

"Make sure you pay the rent, Mary. The doctors will let us pay over time."

"Not according to the bills I've got. Joey looks tired. Let's put him in the carriage."

"He ain't tired."

"Come on," said Mary. "Let the boy rest. Besides, he didn't finish his lunch."

Sal gently placed Joey in the carriage. Mary resumed the dropper feeding. The bocce balls could be heard clacking in the distance.

"I'm gonna get that second job for sure," said Sal.

"Then you'll have no time at all to spend with Joey. He needs you around, Sal."

"I've gotta pay the bills."

"Listen, why don't you go over and play that game with your cousin while I feed him," said Mary. "Please?"

"You really don't mind?"

"As long as that Biaggio Falcone isn't there. These dopes are just followers. He's the one who thinks he owns Brooklyn."

⌘

A green bocce ball came to rest just beside the *pallina*. Vito gave Sal a pat on the back.

"I told them you could play, Sally."

"Nice one," said Tommy.

"Thanks."

Staten Island Lou squatted on a nearby bench, downing his third onion-laced hotdog.

"How's the boy doing, Sal?" asked Tommy.

"Good. He don't give up. He's fighting hard."

"He'll be fine. You'll see. My wife, Eleanor, says that God takes care of guys like you."

Tommy rolled a red ball.

"What do you mean?" asked Sal.

"You know, a family man like you. You don't carouse. You go to work. You're straight and narrow, *paisan*."

"Yeah. My cousin the priest," hollered Vito.

"Priest?" asked Lou as he wiped the mustard from his lips. "Yous make him sound more like Pope Pius."

Silent until then, Nicky the Zipper began to laugh.

"Sally the Pope. That's a fitting name if ya ask me," he chuckled.

"Yeah, that's good," said Tommy. "Right, Lou?"

Lou took another mouthful of frankfurter as he mumbled, "The Pope."

"Please," said Sal, "you're talking about the Holy Father."

"Hey, a nickname is a sign of affection," said Tommy Box o' Cookies. "Don't complain about 'Pope.' I'm named after a fucking dessert."

85

"There's a lot of '*Sals*' around; it gets too confusing," added Lou.

Tommy said, "We got Big Sal, Little Sal, Sally Eyeballs—"

"That guy is uglier than a hatful of assholes," said Nicky.

"There's also Happy Sal," offered Lou.

"They found Happy Sal floatin' in the Gowanus Canal," said Tommy.

"Oh. Rest in peace."

Tommy continued. "There's Sally Crowbar, Big Sal—Holy shit! There are two Big Sals!"

"How come you guys never gave me a nickname?" asked Vito.

"Vito, these things just happen on their own," answered Tommy.

"They give birth to themselves," said Nicky the Zipper. "They come from a person's whole aura. Their very emanation."

Tommy stopped in his tracks, bocce ball in hand. Lou ceased to chew. They both just stared at Nicky for a moment.

"What? I know some big words too," said the Zipper.

"I like the horses," blurted Vito. "I could be Racetrack Vito!"

"Nah."

"Or maybe Vito the Jockey?"

"Forget about it," said Nicky. "You can't name yourself."

"Take me for instance," said Staten Island Lou, "you know how I got my name?"

"I dunno I guess you was born in . . . Staten Island or somethin'?"

Nicky and Tommy were already laughing.

"I have never set a fucking foot on Staten Island," answered Lou.

"I don't get it."

"Nothin' to get, Vito," said Nicky. "He ain't never been to Staten Island, so he's Staten Island Lou."

Even Sal couldn't help but laugh by this point.

"I guess it's sometimes the reverse, Vito," said Sal. "That's why, even though Jimmy is so damn big, they call him 'Little Jimmy.'" Salvatore Salerno was now the only one laughing. Vito took him aside.

"Don't mention Little Jimmy no more. Or Chicky."

"What?" asked Sal quietly.

"As far as we're concerned, they never existed. Okay?"

Sal appeared shaken and confused.

"Biaggio wants to see you, Sal," interrupted Nicky.

"Huh?"

"Yeah. Tomorrow. Come to the church carnival."

It's called a feast ✓

Chapter Eighteen

A COOL RAIN pelted the cola delivery truck as it huffed to a stop outside the Catholic school that sat beside the church. Colorful balloons danced in the angry wind as the "November Charity Carnival" sign rippled like a sail in the stormy Atlantic. Salvatore Salerno walked a steady pace from his double-parked rig to the main entrance. Walking through the doors in his work uniform, he followed the signs to the school basement. As he descended the stairwell, he could hear the sound of fun—music playing, children laughing, bells ringing, water splashing. Then he smelled the popcorn. The school basement was cavernous and filled with food stands and carnival games: ring toss, frog leap, lucky cups, and shooting gallery. Kids and adults alike shared in the festivities. The first person he noticed was his cousin Vito, happily standing behind a counter, pouring lemonade for a line of children. Francine was beside him, scooping ice cream.

"Here he is," shouted Vito as he spotted Sal.

Sal approached with a smile.

"If you want lemonade, ya gotta get in line," joked Vito.

"You'd better not be spiking these kids' drinks."

"Boy, some impression ya got of me, cuz," replied Vito. "Sally, where's little Joey? You shoulda brung him to the carnival."

Sal pointed to his uniform. "I'm working!"

"Then Mary should have come over with him."

"He's still too young for this kind of thing, Vito."

"Nah. He'd love it. The balloons. The clowns. You kiddin' me?"

Sal leaned closer.

"Vito, to tell you the truth, Mary would never set foot in here. You know how she feels about Biaggio Falcone and these guys."

"What?"

"She thinks they're a disgrace to her parents, her grandparents, and all of the real Italians."

Vito looked at his wife.

"Francine, can you pour for a couple o' minutes?"

Vito stepped aside and grabbed his taller cousin by the arm.

"Sally, the fellas are doing a wonderful thing here. They run this whole shebang for the parish. The money goes to the poor. How do you think the church will feed the needy come Thanksgiving?"

"I guess. Well, I'm supposed to see Falcone here—"

"He's down that end by the ring toss. Come on, I'll take ya."

Vito led his cousin through the crowd, toward the other end of the festive basement. They passed a frankfurter stand.

"How 'bout a hot dog, Sally? They're straight from Nathan's!"

No reply. Sal was watching a small pocket of people as they encircled one of the carnival games. It was a pool of murky water with a flimsy seat suspended above it. Beside that was a large target, fixed with a bull's-eye release button. The seat was occupied by a black man. Soaking wet. He was dressed in a variety of rags that were intended to pass as African tribal garb. His face was festooned with some hastily-applied makeup—war paint.

He yelled out at the laughing crowd. "Me cook you for dinner! Me eat white man tonight!"

The crowd jeered as a young boy threw a ball and missed his target.

"Me like tasty white boy stew," smiled the black man.

"What is this?" asked Sal.

"Huh?" replied Vito. "Oh, that's African dip! You never seen that? The kids love it. You know, they hit the target and the cannibal falls in the water."

"I get it. Who's the guy?"

"The cannibal? That's Mack . . . or Mike or somethin'. He's the school janitor."

"That ain't right, Vito. Cannibal?"

"It's all a game! He does it for charity. He's doin' a good thing."

"Then how come you ain't in the wet seat, Vito?"

"It's freakin' African dip, Sally. How am I gonna be in that seat?"

"He volunteered to do this?"

"Yeah. Nicky or Tommy asked him."

"Oh. Like he's gonna say no to them, right?"

"He's having fun. Look at him!"

"Your legs tastes like chicken!" bellowed the grinning janitor in his best savage voice.

"Vito, I saw people like him on the battlefield. They fought Hitler, too."

"Hitler? What are ya talking' about? We're at a charity carnival for Christ's sake. Look, there's Biaggio over there."

As Sal turned to look for Biaggio, the black man hit the water. Most everyone cheered.

"Look at him with those kids," stated Vito, proudly.

Biaggio Falcone stood near the ring toss game, handing out cotton candy to a throng of excited children. Beside him, almost clinging to his pants, were a little boy and girl. They didn't appear as jovial as the other kids. A few feet away stood their mother, dressed in black.

As Sal walked closer, Vito filled him in with a whisper. "Aww. Sally, those are Little Jimmy's kids there. God bless them. That's his wife, Angie."

Biaggio knelt beside Jimmy's son and daughter.

"C'mon, why don't you try the Ring Toss game? It's so much fun."

He glanced at their mother, who forced a slight grin. The children did not answer.

"Here, I'll show ya," said Biaggio as he stood up.

He tapped the counter and was quickly handed some rings by the attendant. His first toss missed, as did his second.

"You want to try this one?" he asked the children. "You're probably better than me."

The little boy hesitantly stepped forward. The girl didn't move. Biaggio handed the ring to Little Jimmy's son and picked the child up. He leaned him over the counter, closer to the pegs. The boy hurled the ring. It hit against the side of the peg and fell to the floor. No good.

"Oh! That was closer than any of mine," yelled Biaggio.

He reached over the counter to grab a prize for the boy. A stuffed toy animal. A tiger.

"This is for you because you are a little tiger. You're already better than me at this game."

The boy took the toy and flashed a hint of a smile. Biaggio then turned to the little girl.

"You sure you don't want to prove you're better than either of us?" He laughed.

She looked at her mother. Then her eyes returned to the floor.

"Okay then," said Biaggio. "I've got a special one for you, sweetheart."

He reached over the counter again and pulled out a stuffed toy for Jimmy's daughter.

"This one reminds me of you, angel."

Biaggio handed her a beautiful white lamb with big blue eyes and long eyelashes. Complete with a crisp pink bow around its neck. The girl took the lamb and stared into its wide, azure irises.

Behind them came a yell from Vito Salerno. "Now that's some *silver-neer!*"

Biaggio turned to see Vito and Sal.

91

"It's *souvenir*, Vito. Not *silver-neer*. There's no precious metal involved at all." Biaggio laughed.

"Really? You sure it ain't silver-neer?"

Falcone could only shake his head as he extended a hand to Sal.

"Glad you could make it, Sal. I'll be with you in a minute. Vito, show your cousin where that little office is. We'll meet there in ten minutes."

Biaggio released Sal's hand and ushered Little Jimmy's children over to their mother. The young girl held on tightly to her soft, white lamb.

Brushing quickly past Sal and Vito came Tommy, holding an open box of bakery cookies. Crumbs fell from his lips as he spoke.

"Hey, fellas."

He sidled up to Biaggio and took him toward an empty corner.

"I heard from Nicky," he whispered. "Him and Lou are down at the docks. The Diabolist is there with them. You sure you wanted that?"

"That's exactly what I wanted. There was a little disagreement down there. Some bunking of heads. I want to send a clear message, one they won't forget."

Sal and Vito casually left the area as the whispers continued. Tommy bit into another pignoli as he mumbled, "We ain't never hired the goddamned Diabolist before . . . "

⚇

The rain hit hard on the South Brooklyn docks. Seemed the only colors for miles around were varying shades of gray— the sky a dead ringer for the river. Inside a particularly rundown brick building, nearly twenty men sat in carefully positioned rows of folding chairs. It almost appeared as though some type of lecture was about to commence. Save for the perspiration, petrified stillness and the echo of one or two weeping dock workers, this could be an adult education classroom. A classroom with a machine-gun-toting faculty member at the head of the class and another at the rear.

The rain pounded the filthy windows as Staten Island Lou lit a smoke. He looked toward the front of the room at Nicky the Zipper. Lou just wanted it all to be over, but Nicky had the slightest hint of a grin on his face. The long scar on his swarthy cheek quivered ever so slightly.

About fifteen feet from Nicky, at the very front of the room, sat a steel table. It rested on a large, worn tarp. Strapped tightly to the metal slab was a twenty-six-year-old longshoreman named Bud Reilly.

Bud envisioned his wife, Della, and how over-the-moon she had been to spot Bing Crosby in the audience of *Finian's Rainbow* over the summer. He mostly thought of their son, Arthur. His third birthday party was to be two weeks hence. Bud Reilly was blindfolded, and silenced by a thick, dry, chewy gag. Swallowing was laborious and painful. Occasionally, one of the seated onlookers tried to look away or lower a head. Each time, Nicky would say the same thing. "You. Eyes front."

Bud Reilly fought hard in an internal struggle to accept his fate with dignity.

Just be quick and painless, he thought.

Despite his prayers, that was not to be. Not today.

From behind a row of metal lockers he came. Traipsing slowly, his long, wrinkled hooded cape dragged on the cold floor. Its hemline amassed a growing cluster of hair, crumbs, and assorted filth as it traversed the front of the room. The onlookers produced an audible gasp as he approached the table. The flurry of sound caused Bud Reilly to move as much as he could. His head jerked slightly from side to side, despite the taut strap across his sweaty, benumbed forehead. His blindfold became a godsend as it prevented him from seeing what the others saw. Beneath the black hood was something of a face. It was perceptively disfigured from Lord knows what type of accident . . . or incident. The entire area that was once a face was painted heavily in a purplish-black makeup, save for a white circle around each eye. The eyes themselves appeared yellowed when contrasted with the pale paint around them. The figure spoke nary a word as it handed a piece of paper to Nicky. Leaning on a wall at the back of the room, Lou just shook his head as he watched Nicky begin to read the note.

"I was sent to you by Mr. Biaggio Falcone," read Nicky. "I am known as the . . . the . . . Debal . . . Dayobla . . . "

"The Diabolist," yelled Lou from the rear. The machine gun rested against his ample thigh.

Nicky continued to read. "The man who lays before you has betrayed the trust of Biaggio Falcone. He made a sworn commitment and ren . . . ren . . . reneged on it. He stole from the people who gave him a means to support his family."

As Nicky read on, the Diabolist began to lift Bud Reilly's shirt, exposing his abdomen. This initiated more futile movements from the supine victim. His hairy midsection pulsated like a beating heart.

"When asked about his ind-indiscretions, this man lied and attempted to contact the police."

The Diabolist strode back behind the lockers and returned with a wooden box filled with various items.

"It is most important that the rest of you gentlemen understand the seriousness of this situation," continued Nicky's scripted monologue.

The Diabolist tapped the table to get Nicky's attention. Nicky paused his reading as the hooded being raised a gloved finger to his gnarled purple lips. From somewhere within his flowing cloak, he quickly produced two small wax plugs and shoved them into Bud Reilly's ears. As the doomed longshoreman grunted and squirmed, the Diabolist motioned for Nicky to continue.

"The man on the table is nothing but a filthy, worthless rodent," continued Nicky. "He's the worst kind of rodent. Gentlemen, Bud Reilly from Canarsie shall, from this day forward, be remembered as a rat."

The Diabolist then produced, not without some flair, an

old, rusty cage that housed what might be the biggest, dirtiest Norwegian rat that ever prowled the sewers and subway tracks of New York. The rodent marched around the cage, which wasn't that much larger than the beast it restrained, pausing occasionally to tear at the bottom of it. Even Staten Island Lou, in the back of the room, could hear its hard, razor-like claws attempting to lacerate the cage bottom. Those closer to the front had a clear view of the rat's two long, yellow incisors.

"You! Eyes front."

The Diabolist placed the cage on top of Bud Reilly's bare abdomen, strapping it to the table below him. The iciness of it caused the blindfolded victim to lurch against his own straps.

"You should be aware," read Nicky, "that a brown rat's teeth are stronger than copper, lead, or iron. They can chew through concrete. Their knife-edged claws might be of even more interest than their teeth. They are natural diggers. This particular specimen has earned its appearance today by killing my cat."

Nicky looked up from the paper. The hooded assassin nodded his approval.

"It killed your fuckin' cat?" asked Nicky the Zipper.

The Diabolist did not respond, but motioned to Nicky to continue while he reached down into the wooden box.

"Um," said Nicky as he searched for his spot on the typewritten note. "Just as Bud Reilly had a choice to make, so shall our other rat."

The Diabolist ignited the blowtorch that he'd removed from his box.

"The caged rodent shall choose between burning to death or engineering an escape."

Placing the scalding hot torch down momentarily, the hooded menace quickly slid out the bottom of the rat cage. Now the cage and the rat stood in direct contact with Bud Reilly's shivering flesh. The victim—now without sight, sound, or speech—shuddered violently at the odd, prickly sensation scurrying on the softness just below his restrained rib cage. The Diabolist placed the torch flame directly onto the top of the metal cage. It wasn't long before the entire enclosure was broiling. The bottom corners of the cage began to sear Reilly's flesh. Soon, he would no longer notice the burning sensation.

"The rat's only escape is straight down. Through Bud Reilly." Nicky folded up the paper.

Then, louder than ever, "Eyes front, motherfuckers!"

The rat first scurried to all sides of the cage. Then it lowered its prickly whiskers to sense the surface beneath its feet. Bud Reilly's flesh. The two-pound, cat-killing rodent began to dig. A high-pitched squeal came from the victim's gagged mouth. As a mound of torn skin and fat began to accumulate beneath the rat, it used its hind legs to push the bloody excavated material farther rearward—to make room for more. As the terrified animal tunneled deeper, only its hindmost leg was visible, and it was drenched in the fresh, warm blood of a Judas.

❦

Balloons were popping at the charity carnival when Sal Salerno knocked on the office door. Vito stood behind him in the school hallway. After a moment, Tommy Box o' Cookies opened the door.

"Hey, Pope! He's inside."

As Sal stepped through the door, Tommy took Vito with him back to the carnival.

"Let's get some of them candy apples."

Sal spotted Biaggio Falcone seated at a desk in the corner of the makeshift office. He was just hanging up a telephone.

"Come on in, Sal. The boys tell me to call you 'Pope,' but—"

"Oh, I don't know how they came up with that."

"Can I offer you a drink?"

"No, thank you. I'm still on the clock."

"Right. Delivering the sodas," said Biaggio as he eyed Sal's work clothes.

"Yeah."

"You should be offering me a drink!"

"Excuse me?" asked Sal.

"Soda. Maybe some root beer. You got it all in the truck, right?"

Sal laughed politely as Olga Falcone emerged from the lavatory. Nodding at her husband's guest, she headed over to the far side of Biaggio's desk.

"Hello, Mrs. Falcone."

She returned carrying her one-year-old son. She placed him on her husband's desk.

"Your turn, honey. I'm going out for a while."

"Hey," replied Biaggio. "At least leave him in that playpen while I speak with Mr. Salerno. I'll keep my eye on him."

Olga returned the boy to his wooden enclosure and promptly left.

"Nice looking boy you've got there," offered Sal.

"That's Frederico. My pride and joy. I like for Olga to leave him with me whenever she can. I wasn't able to see him when he was born."

"I know," replied Sal. "That's a shame."

Biaggio Falcone inhaled deeply.

"I don't know how to say this, Sal . . . Pope . . . but I'll try. I'm so sorry. I sincerely beg the forgiveness of you and your family.

Sal sat silently, waiting for more information. It did not come. "Sorry for what, Mr. Falcone?"

Biaggio stood. He stepped over to the playpen and lifted Frederico. As he returned to his seat, with his boy on his lap, he mustered up his answer.

"Dear God. That tree stump out in front of the barbershop. Your wife would have never fallen if I let them remove it when they should have."

Frederico let out a grunt as he played with his father's

97

shirt pocket. Biaggio continued, "Odd as it sounds, that tree stump saved my life. I felt it was lucky, but now I hear that your son—"

"It's not your fault."

"I want to help you, Pope."

"There's nothing you can do. Say a prayer for my Joey. Put a new tree out in front of the barbershop."

"I want to help Joey with his future," said Biaggio as he produced a thick envelope. "I know this can never alter what I have done to your life, but maybe—"

"With all respect, I have to decline your offer. My wife Mary would never accept charity."

Biaggio grabbed the hefty black Western Electric dial phone and placed it down in front of Sal. It gave off a slight hint of its ring as it landed.

"Get Mary on the telephone. I'll talk to her."

Sal swallowed hard as he dialed. He stared at the white plastic after-market dial ring that displayed the characters on the whirling rotary. It was an ad for Al's Plumbing. He looked over at Biaggio Falcone.

"Let me talk to her first," said Sal.

Frederico bounced on his father's knee as Mary answered the telephone.

"Hi, sweetie," said Sal. "How are you? How's Joey doing? Good, that's great."

Sal smiled nervously at Biaggio, hoping he wouldn't be able to hear the words he knew Mary would soon be saying.

"Listen," continued Sal, "I'm over here with Biaggio Falcone—"

"What?" came loudly through the receiver.

"That's right, dear," responded her husband as he placed his hand over the earpiece.

"She says, 'Hello,'" said Sal to Biaggio, smiling. He removed his hand from the earpiece and continued his conversation with Mary. "Anyway, Mr. Falcone has been kind enough to offer a gift to Joey."

"What is it, somebody's head on a cake stand?" yelled Mary as Sal winced. Sweat beaded on his forehead as he prayed that his wife was inaudible.

"You're right," Sal responded loudly. "He is too generous. But I told him I'd have to ask you first."

"You tell that criminal that the Salernos don't need any dirty money. Tell him that real Italians are hard working, God-fearing people."

"I certainly will thank him for you."

"Let me speak with her," asked Biaggio with a grin. Sal couldn't tell if Falcone heard Mary's ranting.

She kept right on going. "Come home right now! You play one game of bocce and you think you're Al Capone."

Biaggio was reaching across the desk for the phone. Sal thought as quickly as he could.

"Whoa, is Frederico spitting up?" blurted Salerno.

As Biaggio turned his attention to his boy, Sal quickly hung up on his wife.

"No, he didn't throw up," replied Falcone.

"Oh, it must have been . . . maybe . . . uh, I dunno."

Biaggio just stared at Sal.

"Anyway, Mr. Falcone, Mary says she's very appreciative, but she just couldn't accept your very generous offer."

"I didn't get to tell her why I made such an offer."

"You're very kind, but—"

"Listen. The envelope will be here when you need it. How do you like being a papa?"

"I like it very much."

"Me too, Pope. Me too," replied Biaggio as he rubbed his son's head. "So, how'd you like a second job?"

"Well, I . . . "

Biaggio smiled. "Not breaking legs or anything like that."

Sal exhaled a little as Falcone continued, "I notice that you play the numbers every now and then."

"I think the whole neighborhood does," replied Sal.

"Sure. If they can gamble in Las Vegas, then why not

Brooklyn, right? I'm short a numbers guy. I could use a trustworthy neighborhood guy."

"Can I ask what happened to the prior guy? You know, the one I'll be replacing."

Biaggio leaned closer. "No."

Sal sat in silence as Biaggio looked deeply into his eyes.

Then Falcone burst out in laughter. "He moved to Florida. Retired just like everybody else. Ran numbers part-time. He drove a grinding truck. I bet he sharpened your kitchen knives and scissors. He was a regular Joe, not some kind of murderer. As far as I know, he never put a head on a cake stand."

Sal's blood ran cold.

"I'm sorry . . . " he began.

"Hey, forget about it, Pope. How 'bout the numbers gig?"

"Well, it's not really legal . . . "

"True enough. But neither is double-parking that soda truck in front of the school."

Sal smiled. He watched little Frederico play with the gold watch on his father's wrist. A head popped in the door behind Sal. It was Nicky the Zipper. He was gnawing at a stick of pink cotton candy.

"Rodent problem solved," he said through a full mouth.

"Thank you," replied Biaggio, and Nicky was gone. Falcone turned to Sal once again.

"Don't decide now," he said. "Think about it. I'm sure you have some hefty bills for Joey's medical care. If you don't take the envelope, at least think about taking the job. Then it's not charity."

"Thank you. I'll discuss it with Mary."

"Uh-oh," joked Biaggio.

Sal laughed. "She don't mean anything by all that talk."

"Not to worry. Not to worry."

Biaggio stood up with his son in his arms.

"Say good-bye to Mr. Salerno, Frederico."

Biaggio put an arm around Sal and guided him toward the door.

"I want more kids. I told Olga already. How 'bout you, Pope?"

"Well, one doctor told her not to have any more. Said her womb is too small."

Biaggio listened intently as Sal continued. "But a different doc says to have another baby right away. He thinks it'll be good for her state of mind."

"That's a difficult choice, my friend."

"Naturally, I told Mary the decision is hers."

"Hmm. Let me ask you, what would your choice be?"

EIGHT YEARS LATER
SEPTEMBER 1955

CHAPTER NINETEEN

J OEY SALERNO SAT at the kitchen table being
spoon-fed his breakfast oatmeal by his mother. He was
nine years old. Mary put the spoon down and wiped his
mouth. She stood and extended a hand. Joey slid his hand
into her comforting grip and began to stand. He looked up at
Mary and grinned. Joey's smile, though somewhat more
crooked than the norm, was at least as endearing as a
physically perfect one—maybe more so. Mary returned a
cheerful smile to her son as she kissed the top of his head.
She bent to deliver the kiss to her stunted child. Once
standing, Joey was able to walk slowly on his own. His gait
tilted to the right and his stride was short. He devoted full
concentration to each step because he desperately wanted to
walk. And walk he did.

"Let's get washed up," said Mary. "Your father is off
today. He wants to take you to the club with him. How's that
sound?"

Joey grunted as he tugged on his thick, black hair.

"Yes," replied Mary. "The barbershop. Club, barbershop—
in Brooklyn they're the same thing, Joey."

As Mary and Joey slowly ambled toward the bathroom,
they saw Joey's brother standing half-dressed in a schoolboy
uniform. He appeared anxious as he lingered under the
archway between kitchen and living room. He was six years
old.

"What about me?" asked Peter Salerno.

"What's the matter, Peter?" responded his mother as Joey
continued toward the bathroom.

"Well, it's my first day of school."

"I know that, honey," replied Mary as she approached.

"I can't find my school shirt."

"What? I thought I laid it out on the couch for you. Where's your father? I thought he was helping you get ready."

"Um, he was . . . "

Peter looked toward the bedroom. Although three years Joey's junior, Peter was already taller and broader than his brother. His face was round and full, but there was an emptiness to his expression. Mary looked toward the couch— no shirt, just Peter's Lone Ranger lunch box. Then came the footsteps. Sal was hurrying from the bedroom, Peter's white Catholic school shirt in hand.

"Where were you, Sal?" asked Mary.

"I ran the iron over Peter's shirt to get it just right. First day of first grade is a big deal!"

"Boy, I don't think I've ever seen you go near that iron."

"Well, it's not every day that my son starts school, right, Peter?"

"Right, Pop."

"You nervous, honey?" asked Mary.

"Nah. I wanna be smart."

"That's my boy," said Sal. "You're already smart!"

"But I'd rather go to the club with you like Joey does."

"Joey's older than you. I'll take you there soon."

"Joey's lucky; he doesn't have school." Peter sighed.

"Lucky?" asked Mary, her voice getting higher. "Go take a look at your brother, Peter. He can't talk. He can barely stand up straight. You think that's lucky?"

"Mary," interrupted Sal. "He's a kid. He doesn't understand."

"He's got to understand. There'll come a day when you and I won't be here for Joey. Who'll care for him then?"

Both parents looked at Peter, who stood shirtless on this first day of school. Sal leaned in toward his youngest.

"In a few days Joey is going to go to a special school that will help him learn a lot of things. So both you and Joey will be schoolboys. Okay?"

Peter smiled as he put on his shirt. He inhaled deeply, enjoying the warm aroma that lingered from the steam iron. Behind him, filling the 21-inch screen of the faux-mahogany GE Black-Daylite television was NBC newsman Dave Garroway and a little chimpanzee.

Tired of waiting in the bathroom for his mother, Joey drifted over to the living room. He grabbed his father's arm.

"Hmmm. Hmmm."

"Sure. You can bring your shoeshine box," said Sal.

Many wondered how Sal and Mary could almost always understand what Joey was trying to say. There was no formal sign language used, just Joey's grunts and some raw hand signals that he devised on his own. Although his "grrr" or a "hmmm" might always sound the same to others, Joey's family could pick up the slightest inflection and differentiate it from another "grrr" or "hmmm." Peter was picking up quickly with regard to his brother's "language" as well.

"You look so handsome in your school uniform, Peter," said his mother. "Let's go, we don't wanna be late."

Mary kissed Sal and Joey as Peter put on his light jacket.

"Sal, don't let Joey out of your sight at that club. It's enough that he pals around with those characters down there."

"They treat him like one of the boys," said Sal.

"That's what I'm afraid of."

"Hmmm," bellowed Joey through his unique grin.

❦

The black-leather, wingtip Florsheim shoe was getting shined quite professionally. The buffing almost seemed in time to the music coming from the nearby Philco radio. As Bill Haley and the Comets' "Rock Around the Clock" filled the air inside Scotti's Barbershop, Tommy Box o' Cookies admired the shine on his lace-ups. He could just about see his reflection in the glossy hide. His hair was graying on the sides and thinning at the top. He was as hefty as ever, and the puffiness in his cheeks helped keep the wrinkles at bay.

"You are the tops, Joey. I couldn't get a better shine at any price."

Joey chuckled in his special way as Tommy dropped some change into his Boscul coffee can. Tommy headed toward the barber, who was giving a haircut.

"How's this for a shine, Punch?" asked Tommy.

The young barber, whom they called Punch the Pedal, gave a smiling thumbs-up before returning to his work.

"Look at you. All business," said Tommy. "You take your work seriously. Good for you. Your grandpa would be proud. God rest him."

Punch lifted his eyes from his patron's head to look briefly at a picture on the wall. It was a photo of old Mr. Scotti standing by the same chair in an erstwhile decade.

Out of the back room came Sal Salerno. "I hear Joey button-holed you for another shoeshine, Tommy."

"He's good, Pope. I cannot decline his offer."

"I hope you didn't give him any money."

"Hey, you don't work for free. Why should he?"

Tommy took out a small paper and handed it to Sal. "My sister-in-law is in from Sicily. She wants to try the numbers in America."

Tommy walked past him and into the back room. Behind his desk, on the telephone, was Biaggio Falcone. He gazed across the room at his large, metal-framed tropical fish aquarium as he spoke.

"I understand your concern, Mr. Davis," he said. "I know the IRS has a job to do."

Tommy rummaged through a day-old cookie box on Falcone's desk as the conversation continued.

"I've told you twice already—I sell and install carpeting from my business in Queens," said Biaggio as he waved a dismissive hand. Tommy bit into a pizzelle as Falcone continued.

"I already sent those records. Okay, I'll send them again. Gimme a couple of days. What? Within the hour? How am I supposed to do that? I know you've got a job to do but you're really breakin' my balls over here . . . Hello? Hello?"

Falcone hammered the receiver down and opened his desk drawer. He shoved some papers into an already-thick folder. "How can I get these papers out to the IRS within the hour?" he asked Tommy.

Crumbs dropped from Tommy's lips as he answered, "Punch the Pedal."

Falcone jumped from his chair and hurried past Tommy, out of the back room and into the barbershop.

"Punch! I need you."

Biaggio grabbed the scissors from Punch's hand.

"Why do we call you Punch the Pedal?"

"Some of the boys think that I drive—"

Biaggio put the folder into his hands. "Go!"

Punch dashed for the front door. "The address is on the front. Don't even stop for the cops," Biaggio Falcone yelled as Punch left.

Mere seconds after the barbershop door banged shut came the sound of a slamming car door, then screeching tires. Joey laughed as he arranged the items in his shoeshine box.

"Punch is a good kid," said Biaggio. "I just don't know how he ever got a license."

"License?" replied Tommy. "The only license he has is hanging on that wall."

The abandoned customer in the chair looked up at the framed barber's license. His haircut was about 50 percent complete.

Sal put away his numbers log, put on his hat and took Joey by the hand. They headed for the door. "I'm gonna get Joey some air," said Sal. "Maybe he can do some business outside."

The fellas nodded and waved. Tommy turned his attention to the barber-less patron's partial haircut.

"Looks good."

Tommy walked over to the radio that was still playing Punch's rock 'n' roll. As Fats Domino pounded out "Ain't That a Shame," Tommy adjusted the dial until he settled upon the smoky sound of Frank Sinatra's "Learnin' the Blues."

"That's better."

∽

Outside Scotti's, Joey was placing his rattling can of coins on the sidewalk.

"You hungry, Joe?" asked his father.

"Hmmm."

"Stupid question, eh?"

Around the corner came cousin Vito, his walk as brisk as ever. His olive '55 Fedora sat snugly atop his head, almost glued there via Brylcreem. The brim on his new hat was noticeably thinner than those from a decade before. His hairline had waned along with the rim of his topper.

"Hey, Vito!" yelled Sal. "Can you watch Joey for a few minutes? I wanna go get him some lunch from the pork store."

"Jeez, that kid eats like a gorilla," answered Vito as he rubbed Joey's head.

"He burns a lot of energy just walking. Takes a lot out of him."

Vito pulled his cousin a couple of steps to the side.

"Listen, Pope, yesterday I was at the doctor's office. My stomach ain't been so good. So I took a couple of them there waitin' room magazines into the toilet with me, see."

Sal wondered where this was leading as he watched Joey arrange his shine kit.

"Anyways, I was flippin' through that Look Magazine, y'know? They had a bunch o' pictures and a little story about . . . "

Vito pulled Sal another couple of steps away from Joey.

"There's this place in France, you see. Almost a hundred years ago a girl seen a vision of the Virgin Mary—"

"Lourdes," said Sal.

"Yeah! You know about that?"

"It hasn't exactly been a secret, Vito."

"They cure people, Sally. Miracles."

Joey was trying to neatly fold his buffing cloths. They were white but covered in black polish residue. Each one its own Rorschach test.

"That's good," replied Sal. "God bless them."

"So? Why don't you take him there?"

"Who? Joey?" whispered Sal.

"Yeah. There's been over fifty confirmed miracles there."

"Nah. That's for sick people. People that are dying, Vito. Joey's doing fine. Leave the miracles for those who really need them. Let me go get him some lunch, okay?"

Vito just shook his head as Sal headed down the street. Joey looked up and offered a loud grunt that stopped Sal in his tracks. As his father reversed course, Joey put out his hand.

"I'm just going around the corner, Joey. I'll be back in five minutes with salami and provolone!"

"Rrrr!"

Sal sighed as he reached into his pocket and produced his key ring. A handful of worn metal latchkeys that dangled from a round chain emblazoned with the same blue and red emblem that adorned the side of Sal's cola delivery truck. He handed the jingling clump to his son.

"Where do ya think I'm gonna go, kid? Don't lose 'em, okay?"

Sal turned to his smiling cousin.

"Still with the keys, this kid. He thinks if he's holding 'em, I have to come back. Like I'm not gonna come back? Sheesh."

"Don't complain," said Vito. "He loves you. Those keys are like a security blanket or somethin'."

The door chimes rang as Biaggio popped his head out of the barbershop.

"Vito, have you seen Nicky around?"

"He went to the Yankee game with his nephew."

"Nicky and those Yankees. You'd think they were paying his salary," huffed Biaggio. As he shook his head, he took note of Joey prepping his shine kit.

"Oh, yeah, Joey—hang on one second, pal."

Biaggio ducked inside the barbershop. Vito looked at Sal with a shrug. As Joey lined his brushes up in size order, Falcone reappeared carrying a shopping bag. He knelt down beside Joey Salerno and systematically removed six pairs of expensive shoes from the bag. He held up a pair of wingtip Oxfords. "Joey, I've been meaning to get these spruced up for the longest time. I also got a pair of white gators here. I don't know what you can do about them. So let me pay you in advance for your service," Biaggio said.

Falcone stuffed a wad of cash into Joey's Boscul can.

"Biaggio—" said Sal.

"Excuse me, Pope. This is a transaction between Joey and myself. You know to show me some respect when I'm talking business. When does he start that school you were telling me about?"

CHAPTER TWENTY

THE RAIN FELL heavily as Sal and Mary brought Joey through the front door of the old brick schoolhouse. Sal began to remove his son's raincoat beneath the peeling paint of the sign that read: The Dandridge School. Somehow the place smelled cleaner than it looked. As Mary closed her umbrella, she was greeted by a statuesque woman with thin lips and a gummy smile.

"You must be Mr. and Mrs. Salerno! I'm Roberta Lucas. We spoke over the telephone."

"Yes. Nice to finally meet you," said Mary.

"I don't want to appear immodest, Mrs. Salerno, but you couldn't have chosen a better environment for Joseph," announced the schoolmarm in the dark wool Hattie Carnegie suit.

"I'm not sure that we have chosen it yet," said Sal. "Do they get enough to eat at lunchtime?"

"Sal!" snapped Mary.

"It's just that he's got a big appetite," said Sal.

"We've got quite a varied menu," said Mrs. Lucas, smiling.

"He can't feed himself," replied Sal.

Mary interrupted, "Sal, I've gone over all of this on the telephone with Mrs. Lucas. Taking care of these children is her specialty."

"More importantly, it's my pleasure."

Her smile grew wider as she crouched to address Joey.

"Joseph, would you like to come and see the activity room?"

He grunted as the school administrator clasped his cold, damp hand. He walked with her, albeit hesitantly, toward the long hallway. A janitor was mopping at the far end. Young voices echoed in the distance. Sal took a step to go with them, but Mary clutched his arm.

"He needs this. Let him go."

Joey stopped walking. He struggled to turn around and look back at his parents. Still holding on to Mrs. Lucas, he reached out with his other hand. Sal fished through his pockets for his key ring. He removed his car key and went to hand the rest to his son. Roberta Lucas stepped between them.

"Mr. Salerno, we cannot permit our students to have any sharp objects on their person. Please understand."

Sal winked at his boy as he returned the keys to his pocket.

"Grrr."

"We'll be back soon, Joey," said his mother. "You have fun with the other children. You're a schoolboy like Peter now!"

"If you'll have a seat in my office," said Mrs. Lucas, "I'll be right back to finish everything up with you."

Sal whispered to his wife, "She means to collect the rest of the tuition."

"Quit being so negative, Sal. Anne Marie Pesta from Union Street has a nephew in this school and she—"

"Swears by it—I know. You've told me a hundred times."

"They do activities that are good for him. There's a lot of pressure on his bones and organs. They do things to help that, so his body don't age too fast. They help with his . . . his mental condition too. Give the place a chance."

∽∾

Whack!

The black leather belt slammed down on the bare buttocks of eight-year-old Frederico Falcone. He was face down on his father's lap as the punishment concluded in the backroom office of Scotti's Barbershop.

"There. Get up. Pull up your pants, Frederico. I hate doing that," said Biaggio. "You must start behaving in school."

Olga Falcone sat across the room, gazing at a small mirror as she retooled her makeup.

"He beat up two more kids today. What a treasure," she uttered.

"Tell me, Rico, why do you do this?" asked his father.

Frederico controlled the tears that fought to emerge. He sniffed as he answered. "I dunno. They get me sore."

Biaggio pulled his son closer.

"Don't make me do this anymore. You should get along with the other children like those fish in my aquarium. You see how they coexist, all the different kinds of fish?"

"But you said not to take any shit—"

"Watch your language," barked Biaggio. "That doesn't mean you pound every kid who walks by."

Olga sighed as Biaggio turned to her.

"Honey, can Rico stay here for an hour or so? I want to play with him a little."

"He has homework to do," she replied.

"He can do that after dinner."

"Fine. Take him. I'll get my hair done."

"Go out front," smiled Biaggio. "Punch the Pedal will give you a nice haircut."

"I'd rather stick my head in a propeller."

Biaggio placed a kiss on Olga's freshly blushed cheek as she left the room.

"So," he said to his son, "what do you feel like playing?"

The boy thought for a moment. "Korea!"

"Again? What, you're gonna be General MacArthur?"

"Yep!"

"That's fitting. He's good at giving orders, but not so good at following 'em. And me? Who am I?"

"The Koreans."

Biaggio rubbed his face.

"All of 'em? I think I'm gonna need a bigger office."

Through the door came Nicky the Zipper, his cigar smoke wafting up under the brim of his Yankees cap. "You do need a bigger office. Every other family head has a big office, a big house, fancy cars—"

"Yeah, and most of them are gonna die in the slammer," replied Biaggio. "All of that showing off does nothing but bring the heat. I got enough trouble with the IRS now. Imagine if I lived in some mansion somewhere."

"Who's the IRS, Daddy?" asked Rico

"Nothing, buddy. The IRS is nothing."

Frederico positioned his toy soldiers as his father continued with Nicky.

"Besides, if you haven't noticed yet, we are the smallest of all the families. I'm not ready to be compared to the big guys."

Nicky pulled Falcone away from Frederico and his plastic army.

"Understood. Listen, the D.A. is screwing Staten Island Lou. What started out as a two-bit assault pinch suddenly don't look so good. He's gonna do some real time."

"They're gonna try to sweat him, make him sing," said Biaggio.

"They could cut his legs off. He wouldn't talk."

"Probably not. Listen, Nicky, lose that ball cap. What did they ever do for you?"

"For me? Nothing. They're good for the kids, though. Mickey Mantle. Yogi Berra."

Nicky removed his cap and tossed it to Frederico.

"You should take the boy to a game, Biaggio."

Both men looked over at Frederico. He ignored the Yankees hat, but he was knocking down soldiers at a feverish pace. He mowed them down with his imaginary machine gun. "Die, Koreans. Die!"

⚭

In the bright Salerno kitchen, a beautifully tall, homemade

chocolate layer cake sat proudly on the chrome and Formica table. Sal, Mary, and their two boys were joined by Mama, now nearly sixty years old. She sat at the table in smiling repose as young Peter rested his head on her shoulder. Mary gathered some utensils from a drawer near the sink. At the end of the kitchen, just outside the entrance to the living room, sat Joey on the cold red-and-white linoleum. His shoeshine kit stood beside him, atop several scattered pages of the *Herald Tribune*. One after another, he buffed the footwear that Biaggio entrusted to him. In order to shine them in the manner he knew best, Joey needed someone to stand in the shoes and keep one planted firmly on the iron footrest. He would complete a shine, grunt, and then grin as Sal Salerno stepped into the next pair of Biaggio's shoes. As he stood, Sal read whatever pages of the newspaper that weren't in use as a temporary floor cover.

Just when the aroma of the freshly baked cake reached its peak, Mary called out, "Okay, time for dessert! Joey gets the first piece because he's a real schoolboy now."

Peter gazed up at his mother. She didn't notice as she pulled out a chair for Joey.

"It looks as good as it smells," smiled Sal as he stepped out of Biaggio's shiny wingtips.

"You're a good mother, Mary," said Mama. "Beautiful family. I wish you luck. God Bless."

"Pop, did Nashua win his race today?" asked Peter.

"Look at this kid." Sal chuckled. "He knows the horses! Yeah, Pete, Nashua won again."

"Oh, great," said Mary. "Don't raise your son to bet the horses."

"No," laughed Sal, "Maybe he could pick 'em for me, though!"

"Peter, you can't win on the horses," said Mary. "Same thing with those numbers."

"Mary, eat your cake," said Mama. "I win fifty dollars on the numbers last month!"

Sal and Mama laughed as they tasted Mary's delicious confection.

"Grrr!" yelled Joey as he grabbed at his chest. He tried to tear his shirt off.

"Not this again. What's wrong, Joey? You itchy?" asked his father.

"Rrrrr!"

"Mary, what's this?" cried Mama. "Maybe he hurt from the shoe shines. Hunching on the floor—no good."

"No. I can't figure it out," yelled Mary as she removed his shirt, "I checked him for a rash, for hives. It comes and goes. He's been this way for a couple days."

"Since when, Mary?" asked Mama. "Since he start that school?"

Mary glanced at her husband. He stopped chewing his cake.

"Oh, God," she uttered as she rubbed Joey's contorted back. "You're right, Ma. But he's got no bruises or nothing, thank God."

Sal rushed over to inspect his son.

"Maybe we're jumping to conclusions," said Mary.

"Rrrrrrr!" growled the boy, as he slammed his fist onto the chocolate cake, destroying it.

"Send him to the school tomorrow, like usual," said Sal. "I'm gonna go up and see him . . . unannounced."

Peter made his way over to his father.

"Is Joey okay?" he whispered.

"He'll be fine, Pete."

"Oh. That's good," replied the boy as he leaned in toward his father's ear. "How come Mommy didn't bake a cake when I started school?"

Sal was rubbing Joey's back as he looked in Peter's eyes. He had no answer for him.

∽

Lots of wood. Everywhere wood. I feel like a fucking squirrel in a hollow tree.

Those were the only thoughts Staten Island Lou had as he stood in the nearly empty Brooklyn courtroom awaiting his sentence. His mind wandered as he sort of heard somebody read an official-sounding statement.

" . . . not less than ten years in a federal penitentiary . . . "

He was shackled and led away from the wood panels and into a stark-white hallway.

∽

The low rumble rolled down the street in a pulsing wave. The charge of its thunder seemed to shake loose the last grasps of the brown leaves above it. They floated down in a laggardly, terminal dance. Each of them permitting, in their vacancy, another drop of fall sunshine to filter through the trees. The droning finally ebbed as Sal Salerno killed the engine in his cola delivery truck. He bounded—in work clothes—from the huffing rig just as it spit a final cloud of black smoke. He strode through the gassy haze and into the Dandridge School.

A security guard tried to intercept him, but Sal brushed past him without a word.

"Hey, there," yelled the guard.

Sal kept walking. The guard headed for a telephone. As he marched down the hall, Salerno stopped to peer in each room that he passed. One had a small group of children seated on the floor, a young female teacher at the head of their circle. Another room contained a few students sound asleep on a group of cots. No Joey. Sal stopped dead at the next room; he'd almost walked past it, thinking it was empty.

The room was dark. It was cold and sterile, but not empty. He almost missed her as she sat at a desk in the shadows. Her dress was a pretty light blue, but the lap and hemline were stained. Black stains. He wanted to race to find his son, but he paused here for a few seconds. She was maybe fifteen or sixteen years old. Sal moved closer to her, to see if she was okay. He saw that her hands were covered in some kind of black soot—same as her dress. Then he saw the

119

artwork scattered about the floor. He didn't have time to study the pages, but they seemed angry and dark. Maybe even evil. He thought he saw images of serpents.

Demons?

As she turned toward him, he looked at her soft face. Her sad eyes. He knew her from somewhere.

Annette?

Indeed it was. The little Puerto Rican girl from the toy store. He hadn't seen her in maybe eight or nine years. She ignored him as she picked up a piece of charcoal and blackened a sheet of paper. Her desktop was covered in blank paper, pieces of coal and a large eraser.

Of course. No sharp items. No pencils.

"Annette?" he asked quietly. "Are you okay?"

The charcoal slid back and forth across the paper gripped tightly in her soiled black hand.

As he thought of what to say next, Sal heard the muffled cries from down the hall.

"Nnnahhh. Grrrrr!"

He vaulted from the room, yelling, "Joey! Joey!"

The grunting grew louder.

"I'm here, Joey!"

Sal flew down the hallway toward his son's voice. Then he found the room. Their backs were to the door, but Joey was among them. Three boys, all facing a blank wall, strapped tightly into their hard-backed chairs. Not a teacher in sight.

"Jesus Christ," he muttered. "It's okay, Joey. It's okay now."

Sal removed the belts that held his son. Then he did the same for the other two children. One freckly lad ran screaming from the room; the other child remained in his seat. Sal embraced his boy.

"You doing okay?"

"Hmmm."

"Yeah. You're a tough guy. I know."

Sal heard a sobbing from the doorway behind him. It was the boy who fled the room. Standing beside him, with a hand on his shoulder, was Roberta Lucas. She was accompanied by the uniformed guard and a burly male nurse in a white shirt and pants with a black bow tie.

"I know what you must be thinking, Mr. Salerno," she said quickly. "But this is a technique we employ, only for brief periods, during the acclimation process."

Sal stood and took Joey by the hand.

"We'll be leaving now."

"You only witnessed the first part. You didn't see the 'reward' phase. Have you seen our other students learning and playing?"

"I saw a young girl trying to draw pictures in the dark," he replied.

"She can have light at any time. She revels in shadow."

Sal and Joey were at the doorway now. The three staffers were in their way. The freckled boy sniffled and sobbed.

"Out of our way," said Sal.

"Those restraining bands are not affixed tightly," said Mrs. Lucas.

"I've never raised a hand to a woman," replied Sal, as he looked into her eyes. "Don't be a trailblazer."

Mrs. Lucas stepped aside, as did the guard. The burly male nurse was the last to move. He tried to stare down Salerno. Sal eased right up to his face. "You got something to say, candy striper?"

The nurse moved back. Sal and Joey walked slowly down the hall toward the exit.

"In the morning, I'll be back for our tuition."

Thick, fresh, homemade pizza sauce. The scent of that heavenly creation filled Mary's warm kitchen this September evening. She gently stirred the pot as she spoke.

"No. I'm going up to get that tuition. I also might knock that woman's sonofabitchin' teeth down her throat."

"Hey," said Sal as he caressed her back, "Settle down. It's over. Joey's home. Did you call the cops? The newspapers? Your friend Anne Marie? What about Annette's family?"

"Yes. Yes. Yes. And yes," replied Mary as she let Sal taste the tip of her wooden spoon.

"Then it's done. We keep Joey home from now on. He's gonna learn about life. What this kid needs is the love of his family."

Peter tugged on his father's pant leg.

"Can I make the pizza now, Pop?"

"This kid!" laughed Sal.

Joey grinned at his younger brother. Mary stepped away from the stove, wiped her hands on her apron, and took something from on top of the ice box. She put it behind her back and crouched in front of Peter.

"Before we make the pizza, can you guess what I got today?"

Peter didn't blink as he replied, quite matter-of-factly, "The grape wax moustache candy."

"Not exactly." His mother laughed. "We can get some of those tomorrow. Today, I got this."

She produced a small, shiny decorative plate.

"A plate?" asked Peter.

"A very special plate," she replied.

She held the dish out for him to see. There was a hand-painted schoolboy in the center of it. Just below was some writing.

"It says 'Peter starts first grade,'" said Mary. "Then just below that—do you know what these numbers are?"

"Sure," he said, smiling. "It says, '1955.'"

"That's right."

"Can I eat my pizza out of it?"

"It's a little small for that. It's for decoration. It's to show how proud we all are of you, Peter. But you know what we can do? Come Christmas we can hang it on the tree."

"And Santa Claus will see it?"

"Sure will."

"Neat! Can I throw the pizza up in the air now?"

"Oh," sighed Sal, "give him the ball already."

Mary gave her son a hefty slab of dough. She sprinkled some flour onto his hands. He carefully stretched the soft concoction out on the table. His mother helped him to knead, pinch and form it, then placed it on his little fists, awaiting a toss. He moved it around in a circular motion.

"Very nice," smiled Mary.

Joey grinned broadly as he watched his brother give the wobbly base of the future pepperoni pizza a high heave toward Heaven.

TWELVE YEARS LATER
SUMMER 1967

CHAPTER TWENTY-ONE

GRAVITY PULLED THE fresh pizza dough back down onto the fists of the young man who'd tossed it. Peter Salerno finished high school and was working at his Uncle Vito's pizzeria—though not actually an uncle, that's what Peter called his father's cousin. He stretched out the dough and ladled a thick layer of sauce onto it. The lunch crowd was gone and it wouldn't get busy again until the dinner hour. A small handful of people were scattered about the eatery on this bright summer day.

Peter perspired as he toiled in the domain of the hot ovens behind him. The whirring fans above and beside him did little more than push the heat around. The customers were comfortable, but the air conditioning was no match for the swelter behind the counter. It didn't help that the walk-up window was positioned there as well. For much of the year, that window would usher in a nice breeze. Not during the New York summer, though. Now the humid boil from outside would saunter in to fuse with oven fire.

This could be what Hell feels like.

Apart from the glorious aromas that wafted from the pizzas, calzones, and strombolis, maybe Peter's thoughts weren't far off.

Outside the corner shop that was Vito's Pizzeria, the streets were alive with activity. It was virtually impossible to pass one block without seeing children of all ages playing one of the many city games. Boys were sprawled on the steamy blacktop, flicking bottle caps around a hand-chalked game board. They would dutifully stand to let a car pass, only to immediately return to their skully match atop the hot, sticky tar. If you'd asked those boys the name of the game they were playing, some might refer to it as "skelly" or "skelzies," or even "corksies." A similar response may come from the group who competed in ace-king-queen. Or was it kings? Or aces? Some even called it "Donkey." Whatever the name of that handball game, the loser had to deal with "Asses Up." Hands on the wall, bent over, as the other players took turns firing a hard rubber spaldeen ball at his posterior. This could often lead to a marathon game of ringoleavio. This was basically hide-and-seek but involved a makeshift "jail" that was usually just a fence, stoop, or a group of garbage cans. Kids would be captured and freed well into the night. A much faster, exciting game was hide-the-belt. One, kid hides belt. Two, other kids search for belt. Three, one kid finds belt. Four, kid with belt chases remaining kids and hits them with belt until they reach home base.

A rail-thin boy with a crew cut was doing just that as he galloped after his screaming buddies. His olive-hued Boy Scout belt whipped in the wind, its solid brass buckle searching for the soft skin of slow-footed prey. In stark contrast to the hurried violence of the hide-the-belt gang, a small group of musicians in front of the pizzeria performed some peaceful anthems for the passersby. The band consisted of two men, two women, acoustic guitars, bongos, and a tambourine. They were draped in robes and flowers, patches and peace signs. They harmonized about groovin' on a Sunday afternoon. They displayed a couple of handwritten anti-war signs. An open guitar case accepted all manner of coins.

Their music wasn't audible inside the pizza place. There was, instead, a small radio that tried to be heard above the din of the oscillating fans. From its speaker came a powerful female voice that did manage to lift above all the extraneous sounds. She sang out, "R-e-s-p-e-c-t."

Peter was on the telephone.

"Sure thing, Mrs. Clune. I'll have that ready in fifteen minutes."

As he hung up, he saw an elderly female customer struggling to get out of her chair and grab hold of her walker. She just enjoyed a late lunch with her pre-teen granddaughter. Peter hurried from behind the counter to offer assistance. He wiped his sweaty hands on his apron.

"Let me help you there, Mrs. Aceto."

"Oh, thank you, young man. You're very kind. I need to clean up our mess here."

"Don't worry about that. That's what they pay me for. You trying to have my job eliminated?" He smiled.

"Thank you. God bless," she said as he helped her to the door.

"How was your pizza?" he asked the little girl.

"Good," she shyly replied.

"Was it the best you ever had in your whole life anywhere in the whole world?"

"Hmmm," she said, thinking. "Maybe so far."

"Well, that's really boss!" he shouted as he opened the door for them. The sounds of the street musicians could now be heard. They were going on about a place where nothing is real. Peter wished he could stay outside and listen to the music, or maybe find some buddies for a game of stoop ball, but he had to run his uncle's restaurant. At least he had his radio.

As he wiped off the red and white table cloth and put the chairs neatly in position, Peter thought about how he hoped his father could get him a job working the cola delivery trucks. Even the loading dock would be fine. It sure paid better than Vito. There were only two diners left in the place now, two women who'd stopped in for a bite after shopping. As the British voice on the radio bid adieu to Ruby Tuesday, the door opened behind Peter Salerno. The teenager tossed a couple of cups into a trash can and headed behind the counter.

129

"You let those cryin' hippies pollute the front of your store like that?"

"Excuse me?" asked Peter as he looked up to see a man with a huge, monolithic head like an Easter Island statue.

"What? I gotta repeat myself?" replied the stone-skulled thug. "Who are they to shove their fairy beliefs down my throat?"

"People seem to like them," replied Peter. "I like them. They're nice people."

"You're a Salerno, right?"

"That's right," answered Peter as he wiped his brow. "And who might you be, sir?"

The visitor placed his hands on the counter.

"They call me 'Pinky.' "

Peter glanced down to see the fellow's right hand was missing the very digit for which he was named.

"Vito Salerno. He your uncle or something?" asked Pinky.

"He owns the place," answered Peter. "Before you ask, he's not here and I don't know where he is or when he'll be back."

"Is that so?"

Without taking his eyes off Peter, Pinky slowly waved his four-fingered paw. The door opened. The singers roared about Alice feeding her head. In walked Ruddy and Pino. They stood just behind Pinky. He leaned a little over the counter.

"We're gonna take a look in the back."

"You can't do that," said Peter, the ovens seeming hotter than ever before.

"Listen, kid, if you wanna die young, get your ass to Vietnam. Don't check out over a tray of zeppoles."

Ruddy and Pino bolted into the back room. The two diners headed for the exit. After a loud crash, Vito Salerno came running from the back. He had a step on his pursuers. Pinky grabbed a tall, wrought-iron coat rack and slammed it into Vito's midsection. As he collapsed to the tiles, the forty-five-year-old Salerno yelled out to his nephew. "Get out of here, Pete!"

Ruddy and Pino were on him now, like lions on a warthog. Peter reached beneath the counter and grabbed an old baseball bat. It was wound in a bit of cobweb, entwined with a bottle cap, a penny and two long-dead cockroaches. He whipped the bat to his shoulder, only to see Pinky standing beside him, a cold, cocked revolver pointed at his head. Pinky slowly pressed the barrel into the young man's forehead. Peter could only wonder if his sweaty head would cause the gun to slip and fire. Pinky stared wildly into Peter's eyes but yelled at the writhing Vito Salerno.

"You're a punk, Salerno! You're gettin' too old for this shit. Next time you stick it to a broad, you'd better be sure she's either single or a fuckin' mute."

With his left hand, Pinky took the heavy Louisville Slugger from Peter's moist grip.

"Ruddy," he yelled, "scrub him with his own soap."

Pinky tossed the lumber to his accomplice while Pino continued pounding Salerno. Ruddy took a firm grip of the bat and stood there like a flush-faced Carl Yastrzemski.

"Back up, Pino," was all he said as he prepared to swing.

Just outside the pizzeria, a broom handle was swung. A teen boy had a tight grip on the black electrician's tape that was wound around the base of it. He made contact with a white pimple ball. It was launched far into the afternoon sun.

"Holy shit," yelled a teammate. "That's gotta be three sewers!"

The stickball game was in full swing. People watched from their stoops as they devoured snow cones straight from the street vendor's rackety cart. The quartet of flowered performers offered a harmonized warning about an eve of destruction.

∽

The backs of the street musicians could be seen through the window from inside Vito's pizza joint. A tambourine jiggled high as the sun's rays bounced from it in all directions. A final kick was applied to Vito's blood-soaked, unconscious head. Pinky lowered his gun from Peter's brow. A small red circle remained—like a brand. The young man's mind raced.

He's probably dead. Holy shit! Are they gonna kill me 'cause I'm a witness?

Pinky wandered over to the motionless Vito Salerno.

"You're lucky you still got a dick in your pants."

As Ruddy and Pino dusted themselves off, Pinky headed back to Peter's counter.

"Gimme a slice. Not too hot."

It was just past the dinner hour and most of the families were sitting outside, hoping to catch a cool evening breeze. Salvatore Salerno sat on his front stoop reading the *Racing Form*, a cold Rheingold beer by his side. He was handling his mid-forties quite well. He appeared strong, fit, and confident. Mary sat beside him, with a tall iced tea in one hand and Joey's ice cream pop in the other. Though her son was twenty years old, he still had to be fed, bathed, and clothed by his mother. Mary was destined to care for a needy tyke for as long as he lived. Joey hadn't grown much in stature and still tilted to one side. His face was no longer that of a child, though. His features looked the part of a young man, and Mary let his hair grow a little longer to keep up with the style of the day. His happiest moments almost always centered around shoeshines, music, or car rides. Today he was pointing at another kind of ride. It sat right across the street. It was huge, noisy, and surrounded by screaming kids.

"Hmmmm," he said, pointing.

Joey wanted to go on the "half moon."

The ride was mounted on the back of a rusty old truck, and it rocked back and forth, launching its riders higher and higher, one end of the "moon" at a time.

"You really want that?" asked Mary.

"Hmmm!"

She knew that meant either she or Sal would have to go with him. Neither relished the idea of the half moon, but at least it was better than the other ride that drove around their neighborhood: the whip.

"Okay," she said. "Let's finish your ice cream, digest a little bit, and we'll go."

Mary found herself tapping her toes to the music that bounced from a speaker jutting from the second-floor window of the building next door. The salsa sounds of Bobby Cruz and Richie Ray jumped down into the sunken areaway that hosted an almost nightly game of dominoes. Pedro and Diana Loperena would have their cousins over to pass the hot summer evenings with a little music and beer while their children played games like red-light-green-light or stoop ball. Some intense baseball-card flipping could also transpire. On really hot nights like this one, the kids would join dozens of others running in and out of the cool gush of water coming from a fire hydrant that had its cover removed illegally. It was great fun until the police or fire department would show up and temporarily end the party. Mary thought she might have a way of avoiding the half moon.

"Joey, how 'bout you and I run through the johnny pump? Looks nice and cool."

He thought about it for a moment, weighing the pros and cons of the fire hydrant spray and the thrill ride.

"Naaah."

She turned to her husband. "Who's taking him, you or me?"

Sal turned the page of his horse racing paper. "Well, I did take him on that smelly donkey cart that came around last week," he said.

"That was nothing," laughed Mary. "You're comparing a donkey ride to this?"

The riders screamed as they were swung from side to side.

Sal laughed as he glanced over toward the Loperena

family next door. Two of the men saw him and quickly looked away. One hurried into the house and lowered the music.

"Oh, look at that," sighed Mary. "I told you they were afraid of you."

"Afraid? Go 'head, Mary—I never said nothing to any of them other than 'hello.' I never even bitched about that loud racket every night."

"It's the people you hang around with, Sal. Everyone's scared of them, so everyone's scared of you."

"They have no reason to be."

Mary put down her glass and laid her head on her husband's shoulder.

"What if you get that promotion? What if you supervise the loading dock?"

"That would be real good."

"Would it be good enough to stop running numbers?"

"Sweetheart, we've talked about this. My numbers work doesn't hurt anybody. That money is a big help to us. You know that. I know you wanna go up to the Catskills before the summer ends. What about the Jersey Shore? Don't we try to do right by our boys? We give 'em the best life we can. Why would I throw that away?"

Mary stared off into the distance. She listened to the gush of the hydrant, the yelps of the half-moon riders. They drowned out the salsa music that was now barely audible. Joey was pointing toward the rusty truck.

"Hmmm!"

Mary took his hand as she turned to Sal. She pointed at the thrill ride.

"If those kids on the high bench spit down on us this time, I'm gonna want you to hurt somebody. Got that, Legs Diamond?"

Sal smiled as Mary led her son toward the thrill he craved. As they disappeared behind the creaking truck, Sal peeked over at the Loperena family. They were laughing as they enjoyed their dominoes. He could smell the *pollo frito* that

Diana just brought out. Though he finished dinner less than an hour ago, Sal was hungry again.

That chicken looks damn good.

Pedro placed a tile down and looked up to see Sal peering over. He quickly returned his attention to the game. Sal recognized this.

Maybe Mary was right.

Sal put down the *Racing Form*. He took a swig of his now lukewarm Rheingold. He fixed his shirt as he stood and slowly ambled toward the short wrought iron fence that divided his building from the one beside it.

What if they won't talk to me?

They might not even speak English for Christ's sake. Should I say, "hola?" Don't be stupid.

As Sal cleared his throat, he heard a familiar voice from behind him.

"Hey, Pop."

He turned away from his neighbors to see Peter standing by the stoop. He looked pale and tired.

"Pete? What are you doin' home so early?"

"Something happened at the pizzeria."

Sal rushed over to him. "You okay? What happened? Is Vito all right?"

Peter sat on the steps. "Pop, it's not cool, man. Things happen and I can't call the cops. I can't call an ambulance. I have to dial some mysterious number on the wall—"

"Tell me what the hell happened, Peter."

The shaken young man gazed out into the street. He watched his mother and brother swinging on the half moon.

⚬⚬⚬

The sun had been gone for a few hours as the neon lights flickered in the window of Henley's bar. Two large men stood at the front door. Several others milled about the nearby parked cars much like the moths drawn to the neon Schaefer Beer sign.

The large, smoky main room of Henley's was packed.

Maybe fifty men seated around several tables. Five others sat at a dais with a podium. There were no women. The gentlemen at the dais were gray-haired and neatly dressed. One appeared to be almost twenty years the junior of the others as he strode to the podium. Biaggio Falcone was a distinguished fifty-one years of age. His hair and eyebrows were as thick as ever, though now a duel between black and gray.

"Welcome, my friends and associates. I am honored to finally have a meeting in my territory. You all know my underboss, Nicky, and my capos, Tommy and Lou."

From their table, Biaggio's three closest confidants nodded at the others in attendance. A voice yelled out, "Welcome home, Staten Island Lou!"

Lou cracked a weary smile and waved to a smattering of applause.

"You said it," said Falcone. "Lou did more than a decade in the joint without complaint. He had many opportunities to sing his way out, but chose the path of loyalty and respect. This is a man of honor."

The place erupted in cheers. Tommy Box o' Cookies put his big arm around Lou. As the cheers subsided, Biaggio continued.

"Some years ago, I was in my office feeding my fish when I heard a tremendous blast. I didn't know what the hell was going on. I thought maybe the Russians really were coming or something."

Some laughter.

"Well, it wasn't that. I know you all remember what it was. Two planes collided in the sky and came crashing down on New York. I went over there and saw a United Airlines tail section sitting right in the middle of Seventh Avenue. Now, we've all seen a lot of ugly things, many of us have done a lot of ugly things, but I've never seen anything worse than that. People just out on the street Christmas shopping, shoveling snow, walking their dog, whatever—just killed like that. They were minding their own business, and a plane comes down and kills them. The butcher shop there—I used to take my son there when he was small. They'd give him the tail of the bologna. Then the place is just destroyed. Not to mention the poor souls on the planes—all dead."

The elder dons puffed on their cigars.

"It could all end at any minute, for any of us. Yet we continue to spin our wheels and go with the flow. We sit by when they say everything we do is wrong. Most of us remember Prohibition. No alcohol. Some of my associates up here might've sold a little to keep up the spirits of the people."

Biaggio looked at the older family-heads on the dais. They grinned through their cigar cloud.

"Now, I'm not calling you fellows old or anything, so don't get sore at me."

Laughter.

"But selling it was 'wrong' until the government said it was right. In other words, it's all good when they can collect their take. Jesus, the state of Mississippi was still dry until last year! Now they've thrown us another curveball. Selling numbers is wrong. It's illegal gambling."

The crowd listened intently.

"But now they've come up with the New York Lottery! Are you kidding me? Once again, it's just dandy as long as they get their cut. I've seen a big drop in our numbers play. I'm sure you all have experienced the same in your neighborhoods."

Nods and grumbles.

"How do we rebound from this? The people of our territories, the people we protect from outsiders and predators, now they play numbers with the government. When they go on vacation, they pack up and go to Las Vegas to spend the rest of their gambling dollars. You think the pennies they play in our backdoor rooms compare to what the casinos rake in out in Nevada? The real money in any enterprise seems to be when it becomes legal. I suggest to you that we need to be involved in that way. Forget Las Vegas. If you're not a crazy fuck named Howard Hughes, you've got no potential out there with all the *puttanas.*"

Outside the bar, a white 1965 Ford Falcon screeched to a halt, smoke drafting from its tires. Sal Salerno jumped out of the hastily double-parked car. He shot toward the door of the bar. He still smelled of burnt tire rubber when he was intercepted by one of the men who lingered by the parked cars. It was Punch the Pedal. Now in his mid-thirties, Punch still had a youthful air about him—and a bit of a thicker midsection.

"Pope! Pope! Where you going? You know people like you and me can't go in there tonight."

Salerno ignored him and was now steps from the door. The two imposing figures by the entry stepped in his path.

"Outta my way," he growled.

They didn't budge. Sal tried to force his way between them. One of them grabbed him by the throat. Sal thrust his hand onto the man's face like a vise. Punch raced over with another man to break it up. They managed to get between Sal and the goons.

"What's got into you?" asked Punch. "That meeting is for made guys only."

Sal stormed the doorway once again, only to be grabbed as he was before. This time the door opened as the struggle continued. Out came Tommy Box o' Cookies.

"What the hell is . . . Pope?"

"I gotta see Biaggio" was all Sal could say through the clutches.

"Let go of him," said Tommy. "He's all right."

The enforcers hesitated.

"I told yous to let him go. Do I need to go inside and tell your boss?"

They loosened their grasps, and Sal pulled away. Tommy put an arm around his friend and took him just inside the doorway.

"Who are those monkeys?" asked Sal. "Shouldn't your guys run security here?"

"Listen, sometimes concessions have to be made to make things happen. Why do you suddenly give a shit about things like that? What's got into you?"

Sal didn't respond. He quickly ditched Tommy and headed toward the main room.

"Pope! Come back!"

As he bounded closer, Sal could hear Biaggio's speech.

"What seaside town did we all used to go to before it turned into a dump?" asked Falcone of the attendees.

"Atlantic City!" was the response.

"Damn right," he replied. "Now it's a shithole. Who runs the place? People that are too inept to oversee anything. The men at this dais know plenty of powerful people, and we all know who can be bought in New Jersey. The feds are tearing that place to shit as we sit here. We need to make our own Vegas right next door, gentlemen."

In came Sal Salerno. He moved right for the podium. Biaggio spotted him as several men moved to protect their bosses.

"Relax, everyone!" yelled Biaggio. "Sit down. I'll handle this. He's an associate of mine."

Sal reached the dais and leaned into Falcone's microphone.

"Who the fuck is Pinky? Stand up, coward."

Biaggio pulled Sal aside as Tommy hustled up behind them. Nicky ran to unplug the mic.

"I am very, very surprised and disappointed in you," growled a wide-eyed Biaggio Falcone. "I'm hosting some very influential people here. They are not known for their patience."

Sal continued to scan the crowd as he answered, "You know what this Pinky scumbag did?"

Sal spotted the rock-faced button man advancing toward the dais with a grin on his face.

"You Pinky?" he yelled.

From the middle of the room came a slow, sneering nod.

"I am gonna stack you up, campfire girl," snarled Salerno. "Outside. Let's go!"

Pinky calmly waved him on. Sal didn't hear Pinky quietly mutter to Ruddy, "I hear he got another son even stupider than the one we danced with."

As Sal was held by Tommy and Nicky, Biaggio whispered in his ear. "I know about Vito."

Sal finally looked into Biaggio's eyes.

"You know?"

"Come here," said Falcone as he and his boys hustled Sal into the nearby restaurant kitchen.

Two cooks were there when they entered, but they quickly vanished.

"Not that they needed it, Pope," said Falcone, "But I gave them my permission to tune your cousin up."

"What? After all he's done for you? He'd take a bullet for you, Biaggio."

"I know that. Do I look like some fucking asshole to you, Salerno? I just saved your cousin's life."

Tommy and Nicky loosened their grip on Sal.

"Don Verengia is sitting in that room you just invaded. They say when he was younger he killed some jackass right in the Paramount Theatre because the guy farted near his mother. He's over seventy now, but he has a thirty-year-old blonde wife named Betty or Betty-Jean or some shit—"

"A thirty year-old wife that your cousin was drillin' like a fuckin' Gulf Coast oil well," Nicky the Zipper interrupted.

"Shhh!" cautioned Biaggio. "Not so loud."

"The Verengia family asked permission to whack Vito," continued Nicky. "They got an okay from the commission. Doing a made guy's wife is a death sentence. Now you're talking about the head of the family— forget about it! He's lucky they didn't make a long weekend out of his extermination."

"Biaggio gave a lot of favors to save Vito's life," added Tommy. "Pope, it took all we could do to keep Vito alive. He'll be fine. Hell, they didn't even break his legs, I don't think."

"Vito gave me the people who tried to kill me all those years ago," said Biaggio. "Now I consider us even."

Sal thought briefly about Little Jimmy and Chicky the Termite, then took a breath. "Vito is a grown man. He chose this life for himself. That's not why I'm here."

"Well, what would make you disrespect my meeting in this manner?" asked Falcone, as Staten Island Lou joined the group.

"He put a gun to my son's head, this Pinky jerk. What does Peter have to do with any of this? He's just trying to make a few dollars making pizza for God's sake."

Biaggio paused. He ran a hand through his hair.

"That's not called for," he said. "They should not have involved your son in any way."

"Let me go out there and settle it," said Sal.

"I cannot permit that. You're not even supposed to be in here. I'll talk to Don Verengia. Maybe he'll discipline the guy. I can't promise you, though."

Nicky, Tommy, and Lou ushered Sal toward the back door as Biaggio returned to the meeting hall.

"Listen, Pope," said Nicky, "if the Verengias don't take care of this internally, I will. The feds are close to dropping a pile of shit on me. I can smell it coming. I'm facing some time. Before I go away I'll settle this for you, if it comes to that."

"Nicky, you can't start a full blown war over this," said Lou.

"I don't mean to, you know, kill the guy," said Sal. "I just wanna square off with him."

They all laughed at Sal's comment.

"Come on," said Lou, "let's go outside. I'm tired of this meeting anyways."

Staten Island Lou took Sal out the backdoor of the bar. Nicky and Tommy returned to the gathering within.

Sal and Lou emerged from the back alley to the street in front of Henley's and headed toward Punch the Pedal. He stood by Biaggio's shiny black 1967 Cadillac Eldorado, right beside Johnny the Beatnik, a younger associate of the crew.

"So Nicky's really looking at some hard time?" Sal asked.

"Shit yeah—I kept the bed warm for him," laughed Lou as he nodded at the Beatnik. Lou had only met Johnny recently, when the young man came with Tommy to pick Lou up on his release day. He seemed a decent enough guy, but Lou couldn't come to grips with the longer hair and sideburns, much less the odd Fu Manchu moustache. He didn't really like having a hippie in his crowd, but the boys told him Johnny was very loyal and would do whatever was asked of him.

"I don't know if I could handle prison, Lou," wondered Sal.

"That's why you shouldn't mix it up with guys like Pinky. They say he once killed a guy in church."

Sal laughed. "I don't buy any of these stories. Killed a guy in church, killed a guy for a fucking fart. Gimme a break over here."

"I dunno," said Lou. "I think those stories gotta come from somewhere."

"Who killed a guy for farting?" asked Johnny the Beatnik.

"That was Don Verengia," whispered Punch.

"No shit," said Johnny. "I heard of a guy in Mill Basin who cut his own brother's throat over a jar of Nutella."

"See what I mean?" said Sal.

"Trouble comes to a *cucuzza* like Pinky like moths to an asshole," said Lou.

"To a flame," said Punch. "'Moths to a flame' is the saying."

"What are you talkin' about?" asked Lou as he lit a cigarette.

"You said 'moths to an asshole.' That ain't a saying, Lou."

"Yes it is."

"It don't make sense. Did you ever see a moth around an asshole?"

"Well," responded Lou, "what about when they say someone 'drinks like a fish'? I never seen a drunk fish in my life."

Silence all around.

"You see," continued Lou, "these sayings come from years ago, maybe the Middle Ages. Over time they get twisted around, like the stories about killing guys for farts and burps, maybe."

Lou returned his attention to Sal.

"Pope, what I'm saying is some guys always have trouble around them. Pinky is one of those guys. So was I. This life has caused me a lot of trouble. That trouble led to prison. Then the prison led to cancer."

"Cancer?" asked Sal.

"Yep. Got it in the big house. I think it's in the food there. Maybe the water."

"Oh, Louie," said Punch.

"Cancer of what?" asked Sal.

Lou dragged deeply on his Camel. "Just about everything," he sighed.

"Can they do anything for you?" asked Sal.

"Nah. I ain't gonna be a guinea pig. We all gotta go sometime."

Sal looked at Punch. Punch looked at Johnny.

"Have you ever heard of Lourdes?" inquired Sal.

"Yeah. Mother Mary. The bathtubs."

"Well," said Sal, "supposedly, there's been a load of miracles there. Real cures."

"What's that?" asked the Beatnik.

"The Virgin Mary," answered Sal. "She came to a girl. A girl named Bernadette. Sound familiar?"

Johnny shook his head.

"They even made a movie picture about it," said Sal. "Who's the girl who played in that movie?"

Lou coughed. "Jennifer Jones."

"Good movie," added Punch.

"So tell me more," said Johnny.

"Well, Mary asked Bernadette to unearth a spring. You know, water. They say that very water cures people to this day."

"Ah, I don't know," wondered Johnny.

"What, you believe a guy kills his brother for a can of chocolate, but you can't understand this?" asked Sal.

"Not sure," said Johnny. "It's spooky."

"Years later, after Bernadette passed away, they exhumed her body," Sal continued. "Thirty years after she was buried, her body still hadn't decomposed."

"Holy smokes," said Johnny.

Lou made the sign of the cross.

"She's a saint now," added Punch. "Even skeptics have admitted to witnessing some of the miracles of Lourdes. It's officially recognized by the church. My mother talks about it all the time."

"You believe, Lou?" asked Sal.

"Absolutely."

"There might be a miracle there for you."

"There just might be a miracle there," said Lou, "but I'm sure God ain't saving it for me."

"My mother says, 'we all share one God.' She means Catholics, Jews, whatever. She always tells me that he's a forgiving God, Lou," Punch responded.

Lou sucked on his smoke, and then he answered. "I hope so."

"Go to confession, pal," said Salerno. "Punch is right. The Lord is forgiving."

Sal glanced at his wristwatch.

"You know who isn't forgiving?" Sal asked. "My wife." He laughed. "*Marone*! I gotta call her. I left the house like a lunatic, and I told Peter not to tell her anything about what happened. She'd never let him outta the house again. I'll be back in a minute."

A couple of the flying insects that hovered around the neon Schaefer sign drifted over and circled Punch's head. He tried to swat them away.

"See?" smiled Staten Island Lou. "Moths to an asshole."

They all laughed as Sal crossed the street, passing the small groups of men who waited by the various cars outside the bar. He spotted his unconventionally parked Ford as it sat at a thirty-degree angle to the other vehicles.

I gotta park the car right, too.

༤

The phone rang in Mary's apartment. Joey ambled over and lifted the receiver.

"Hmmm."

"Hi, Joe," said Sal's voice through the handset. "How you doing? Okay?"

"Hmmm."

Joey glanced over his shoulder, smiled and emitted the unique sound that was his laughter.

"Nnnnn!"

"What's so funny, you joker?" asked his father.

Joey's laughing grew stronger.

"All right funny guy, put Mommy on."

A grinning Joey held out the telephone as Mary came over, a dust mop in her hand. Joey gave her the receiver and turned his attention toward the object of his delight. Across the room, his brother sat on the hard clear plastic that covered all of the living room furniture. Peter sat on the plastic that sat on the sofa. Beside him was a pretty, petite brunette. A long-lashed seventeen-year-old by the name of Linda Fazio. Seeing his brother sitting with a girl had Joey nearly doubled over and almost in a wheeze.

"I hope you're entertained," deadpanned Peter.

Mary was ready for the phone call.

"Sal? Why'd you run out like that? Where are you? Peter's got a nice girl here. The one I told you about, Linda."

"Everything's okay. There was something I had to do. Tell

145

Peter I'm sorry I didn't meet the girl. Make sure he's got a few bucks for the movies."

Joey wandered over by the sofa. He began to stroke the plastic covering as he stared at Linda. Mary saw this and yelled over toward them.

"Don't worry, Linda. He won't hurt you."

Peter rubbed his face as he tried to shoo his brother away. The combination of Joey's stare and his mother's booming holler was becoming too much. He didn't want Linda subjected to too much of his family on her first visit.

"We're gonna miss the start of the movie, Ma. I can't wait for Pop much longer."

Mary relayed the message to Sal—quite loudly. "He says he can't wait for you. He got ants in his pants."

"Ma, we don't wanna miss the start of the movie."

"What movie you gonna see?" asked Mary as Sal listened in.

"She wants to see *Barefoot in the Park*," replied Peter.

"Yeah?" asked Mary as she looked at Linda.

The nervous girl nodded with a smile. Joey stood beside her, grinning. Peter felt the perspiration coming on.

Mary yelled into the phone, "They're gonna see Barefoot Park, Sal."

"What's that?" he replied. "Tell 'em to see *The Dirty Dozen*."

"It's *Barefoot in the Park*, Mrs. Salerno," offered Linda.

"Tell 'em *Dirty Dozen*," yelled Sal.

Peter led Linda to the door.

"We're going now."

"Okay," said Mary. "Have a nice time."

"Hmmm," said Joey.

Linda waved to Joey as Peter closed the door behind them.

"Tell Pete to get her home on time," yelled Sal into the phone. "Lemme go, Mary. I'll be home soon. I love you."

"I love you too," she said, much more softly than the rest of the conversation.

Before Sal hung up in the phone booth, he had one more question. "They gonna see *The Dirty Dozen?*"

It was too late, so he put the receiver back on the hook. He opened the door to the phone booth in time to see a young man pass by in quite the hurry. Sal knew this ambitious fellow with all the sculpted muscles and overdone tan.

"Hey, Pope," he mumbled as he sped by without eye contact.

"Hello, Rico."

As Biaggio's son continued toward Henley's, Sal couldn't help but feel a little disrespected that the younger man addressed him as a peer, and not as one would speak to an elder. He didn't care for the lack of eye contact either.

Frederico Falcone reached the doorway of the bar and encountered the two large thugs who had scuffled with Sal earlier. One of them placed his meaty paw square on Frederico's chest. The young man looked down at the goon's enormous hand.

"You wanna start wearing a hook, fuckface?" was all Rico said.

The second bouncer intervened, and he advised his partner. "He's okay. That's Falcone's kid. He's in the books now."

Chapter Twenty-Two

THE SAND FELT good between Peter's toes. The Atlantic would splash over his feet to claim its grains, but a fresh batch would quickly embrace him as he ran. Rockaway Beach was just perfect on this day. Much of the extended Salerno family was there. The sun shone brightly, humidity was low, and homemade sandwiches were the fare of the day. The air was salty and fresh as the seagulls danced overhead. As Peter caught the red Frisbee thrown by his pigtailed, pre-teen cousin Joanne, the ocean cleansed his feet yet again. Not far from the shoreline was a row of half a dozen bed sheets and blankets, all weighted down by sneakers and sandals at their sandy corners. At each end of the sheet train were transistor radios. Both were set to the same station: WMCA. "Good Guy" Harry Harrison introduced the number-one song in New York: Frankie Valli's "Can't Take My Eyes Off You."

Joey sat beside a radio and used a tiny plastic shovel to smooth out the hilly sand before him. His father was snoring on the nearest blanket. Mary stood at Sal's feet in a blue floral one-piece bathing suit and white bug-eyed sunglasses. She smiled, watching her two sisters dance through pointy, broken shells and raggedy seaweed as they haltingly penetrated the icy Atlantic.

Two fingers with long, red manicured nails spread some Coppertone tanning lotion over Vito's forehead, down his nose and then very carefully around all the purple and black facial bruising that covered his eyes and cheeks.

"Easy there, sweetheart," said Vito to Francine, and his

wife sighed with desperation. "I don't need no more pain than I already got," he said, grimacing.

"Well, you want the tanning butter or not?"

"Yeah, I want it. Bad enough I'm gonna have one brown arm and one white one," he replied as he looked at the full-length orthopedic plaster cast on his broken right extremity.

"Gimme that freakin' hanger again."

Francine handed him a metal clothes hanger that had been bent into a straight rod. She laid back and opened her autographed Jacqueline Susann novel. Vito grabbed the makeshift tool with his left hand and shoved it under the cast, violently scratching away at the sweaty skin beneath.

"Gonna cut yourself to ribbons with that," said Fran from behind *The Valley of the Dolls*.

"I'd rather do that than go crazy itchin'."

As Vito Salerno clawed away at his encased flesh, he spotted Joey calmly flattening the sand around him as others ran past, playing games and charging into the waves.

"Hey, Joey, c'mere," yelled his father's cousin.

Vito's bellow woke Sal as Joey slowly stood.

"Don't think for a minute," said the groggy Sal, "that you're gonna use my son as a personal arm-scratcher."

"What? Nice to know how yous think of me. Jeez."

As Joey ambled over, still carrying the little yellow shovel, Peter ran by with little Joanne and her older brother, Michael. The three were doing their best to get a kite airborne.

"Pete," yelled Vito. "Do me a favor. Fill this here bucket with some water for me and Joey."

Peter took the blue plastic bucket and ran toward the water as Michael and Joanne fumbled with the kite. Joey grinned as he sat down next to Vito.

"Listen, kid," said Vito. "You can see I only got one good wing right now."

"Hmmm."

"So, the thing is, how am I gonna make a big sand castle by myself? No can do."

149

"Hmmm."

"Maybe you and me together can make a good one, eh?"

Joey studied "Uncle" Vito's discolored and contused face as he spoke. It reminded him of the world map that his father would show him on occasion.

"You think you feel like helpin' me with the fortress or castle or whatever," asked Vito.

Peter returned with a bucket of seawater. He placed it beside his brother and returned to his cousins. Joey looked at the wet, sandy bucket and slowly dipped his fingers in.

"So you push some sand toward my hand and I'll push some toward you so as we can make a pile."

"Hmmmm."

Vito smiled, revealing the empty spaces where three of his teeth once dangled.

Further down, a refreshed Sal Salerno joined Peter and the two younger cousins.

"Peter, I forgot to ask you to invite that girl. What's her name? Linda?"

"No sweat."

"Oooh! Peter has a girlfriend!" teased Joanne.

"No, he doesn't," responded Peter as he took his father aside.

Sal was still smiling and sipping beer from a plastic cup. Jack Spector had taken over for Harry Harrison on the radio and was talking over the twinkling piano keys that opened the WMCA's "Sure Shot" pick as a future hit: the Young Rascals' "A Girl Like You."

"Pop, Linda has a new boyfriend," whispered Peter.

"What?"

"Yeah. So let's not bring her up anymore."

"But just last week—"

"I know," replied Peter. "Things happen."

"What happened, Pete?"

Several feet away, Peter's cousins were adjusting strings on the kite's bridle.

"Nothing."

"Listen. You need to tell me. I'm your father."

"She just probably decided to go with a guy who's got less . . . baggage. I don't know."

"What baggage? You mean us? Your brother?"

"I just mean that, y'know, Joey was staring at her all night; standing right next to her. Mom was screaming all that 'he won't hurt you' stuff that she tells everybody. Then I mentioned about Uncle Vito and the pizzeria . . . "

His voice trailed off as Sal was watching Mary standing near her sisters by the shore. The breeze tossed her hair around as she laughed with her family. The sunlight diffused around her soft skin and she looked very much like the girl Sal met at Vito's wedding over two decades ago. Sal put a hand on his son's shoulder and leaned closer. Peter could smell the beer, but knew his father was stone-cold sober.

"Then Linda isn't the one," was all Sal said.

His big, calloused hand gave Peter's back a strong, reassuring pat as he walked off toward Mary. Peter turned back to Joanne and Michael. The kite had finally taken flight. It launched quickly as they ran down the beach. Peter squinted as he looked up at the diamond-shaped flyer. Vibrant images of the Green Hornet and Kato gazed back down from the fluttering dirigible, becoming smaller and smaller against the bright, blue Rockaway sky.

Opening the door to leave the salumeria, they unleashed the scents of a thousand delicacies onto the street before them. Mary, Mama, and Joey walked into the afternoon sun, leaving behind the cheeses and cured meats that hung from the ceiling like bats in a gluttonous cave. Mama pulled the rusty, two-wheeled folding shopping cart behind her as Mary held hands with her son.

"If I let Sal buy the meats, he gets fennel seeds in everything," said Mary.

"That's good," replied Mama. "The seeds help Joey to—*come si dice*—digest."

"Always siding with Sal." Mary laughed. "I thought you were my mother!"

"*Ho mal di testa.*"

They turned the corner and came upon Scotti's Barbershop. Plopped on folding chairs out front were Sal, Staten Island Lou, Tommy Box o' Cookies, and Punch the Pedal. Sal stood and smiled as he saw his family coming.

"Here they are! Thanks for bringing Joey down, sweetheart. Hello, Mama."

Sal kissed his wife and mother-in-law. Mama was smiling; Mary, not so much. Joey rubbed his father's pant leg. Though a young man, Joey was under five feet tall and quite thin, in contrast to his burly pop. Sal's three friends politely stood to greet the women. "When four guys stand outside a barbershop, they're supposed to sing," said Mary.

"Mrs. Salerno." Punch smiled. "How about I give Joey a nice haircut, eh?"

"No, thank you. His hair is fine the way it is."

Hustling across the street came Nicky the Zipper, looking more tan than ever. He tipped his most recent Yankees cap at the ladies. At least Sal was happy to see him.

"Nicky! Where you been? These guys don't tell me nothing."

"Nothing too thrilling, Pope. I was in Florida a couple o' days with Johnny the Beatnik."

TAMPA, FLORIDA. ONE DAY EARLIER.

Nicky the Zipper stood over him. All the man could see from his position below—on the wet Gulf Coast grass—was Nicky's scarred scowl, dark Ray-Bans, and a white fedora. The barely audible, jaunty sounds of a Tijuana Brass instrumental taunted the victim from a long distance. A single palm tree swayed behind him as the Zipper raised a dirty iron pickaxe above his head. He slammed it down so violently that snot flew out of his own nose. Nicky raised the axe tip again, now covered in blood. A red drop landed on his hat brim. Expelling a feral grunt, he slammed the heavy weapon down a second time. This time he left it in. He picked up a shovel and handed it to Johnny the Beatnik, who stood beside him in a wrinkled red tie-dye.

"Here. Dig, hippie."

∽

As Joey continued to rub his father's leg outside Scotti's, Tommy gave him a pat on the head.

"So, Mary," said Tommy, "are you gonna let Sal and the boy come with us to the track today?"

Sal winced as Mary walked over to Tommy and ran her finger down the front of his ultra-tight shirt.

"You know, if you insist on always buying your shirts three sizes too small, I could at least move the buttons over for you. You might find it easier to breathe."

"Pretty ladies can say anything they want," said Tommy, grinning. "So when are you gonna meet my wife, Eleanor? You two would be pals. I know it."

Mary looked at Nicky, "Are you the one who takes him shoppin' in the boys' department?"

The Zipper smiled as he addressed Mary's mother. "*Signora*, you raised a strong daughter."

The door to Scotti's opened, and Biaggio emerged with the still-bandaged Vito Salerno by his side.

"Okay, fellas, my little meeting with Vito is done," said Biaggio. "Now how 'bout a little help inside?"

Biaggio spotted Mary.

"Good afternoon, Mary. Looking lovely as usual." He bowed slightly toward Mama. "And you as well, ma'am. The beauty is in the bloodline, no?"

Just as Mama smiled, two teenage girls awkwardly ran up to Falcone. One carried a shiny black-and-white Polaroid Swinger camera, while the other mustered the nerve to speak.

"Um, excuse me, please, Mr. Falcone," she stuttered. "We

are big fans of yours and we love your Fourth of July parties so much! Could we please take a picture with you?"

As Biaggio turned toward them, Vito already had them sized up and wondered when they'd be legal.

"Well, girls, I thank you for the compliments, but I am so camera-shy you wouldn't believe it. I don't think I've been in a picture since my wedding," he smiled.

"See, I told you," said the girl with the camera to her friend.

"Then, could we have an autograph, please?"

Mary Salerno just shook her head as Falcone responded.

"Tell you what . . . I'll sign two papers for you girls, and you take them down to the dress shop and tell them I said for you each to pick out a nice outfit on me. That's better than some crummy picture, right?"

The girls happily produced some papers and a pen for Biaggio to sign. Vito was looking at the groceries in Mama's cart.

"Did you get some nice *panforte*, Mama?"

Mama playfully slapped his good hand as Joey made a laughing sound. As the teenagers dashed happily toward the dress shop, Vito batted his eyelashes and asked Biaggio in a squeaky voice, "Would you autograph my arm cast, Mr. Falcone?"

"Yeah, I'll put you in a full-body one, too." Biaggio smirked. He addressed his crew, "Guys, I need someone to help me out with the fish tank. Vito would do it, but since he's outta commission..."

"What's with the fish tank?" asked Nicky.

"Ah," sighed Falcone. "I asked my son to put a new heater in it for me, but he set it all wrong. My fish don't look good. I don't like when my fish are stressed."

"I'll take care of it," offered Punch the Pedal.

"Thanks, Punch."

The barber smiled at Mary and her mother as he headed inside.

"Sal, we're gonna be going now," said Mary.

Salerno embraced his wife.

"So, Joey can stay, right?" he asked.

She nodded as she took hold of the cart that Mama had been pulling. The fellas smiled politely as Mary kissed Joey and the two women walked away. Mama was still looking at Biaggio Falcone as she whispered to her daughter, "He remind me, Mary. He remind me of your father."

Mary shot her mother a look of horror.

"God forbid."

⌒⌒⌒

The black 1967 Buick Skylark convertible blasted through the streets of Brooklyn with Punch on the gas pedal. Joey Salerno was enjoying every minute of it from the front passenger seat. He seemed to live for times like this. He was one of the boys as his hair danced in the wind. Just behind, in the long back seat were his father, Vito, and an uncomfortably wedged-in Tommy Box o' Cookies. The men would gladly forsake their comfort so that Joey could ride shotgun with Punch.

"Just a little slower, okay?" Sal reminded the driver.

"Sure thing. Sorry there, Pope."

"Nyaaah," complained Joey. He cherished the speed.

Sal adjusted his position and grimaced as he grabbed his lower back.

"You too, eh?" asked Tommy.

"Yeah. It's lifting those soda cases. I'm gettin' too old for that crap," laughed Sal.

"My back's like a fuckin' house of cards," replied Tommy. "I could lift you over my head and I'd be fine; then two days later I sneeze and it's like Cassius Clay punched me in the ass."

"Look at you two ballerinas complainin'," said Vito. "I'm squeezed between yous gorillas with my own broken arm diggin' a hole through my ribs and I ain't said nothin'."

Sal leaned forward toward Joey. He had to yell because of the wind whipping around the drop-top Buick.

"You excited about going to the track, Joe?"

"Hmmm."

Punch interrupted as he eyed the rearview mirror.

"Oh, shit."

"What?" hollered Sal.

"Cops. We're gettin' pulled over."

"I told you to slow down," said Sal.

"*Va fangul*," moaned Punch to nobody in particular.

The Skylark pulled over to the roadside, an NYPD Plymouth with spinning dome light directly behind it. The tall officer approached the driver's side. Punch leaned over toward Joey.

"Joey, remember what to do?"

Instantly, Joey shot both hands to his crotch and began to writhe around in his seat, making as many disturbing sounds as he could muster. The officer reached the driver door. He first glanced at the back seat and noticed Vito's bandaged, shit-eating grin. He saw the two larger men who sandwiched the broken-armed, cigar-chewing pixie. Sal paid no mind to the officer; he was more concerned about Joey squirming in the front seat.

"License and registration, please."

"Certainly there, officer," replied Punch, one eye trained on Joey. "Sorry I was going a little fast there, sir. My brother here has to go to the toilet real bad."

Joey got louder. The cop gave him a good long look as he accepted Punch's paperwork.

Punch continued, "He's got that cerebral *Paulie*."

"Palsy," said the cop. "You mean cerebral palsy."

"That's exactly what I mean."

"You okay, young fella?" asked the officer.

"Nyaaaaaaah!" screamed Joey as he squeezed his groin and bent over. The policeman paid more mind to Joey's physical abnormalities than his staged wriggling and writhing.

The license and registration were returned.

"Go on. There's a bathroom in the diner on the next corner. Just ease up on that gas."

"God bless you, officer," replied Punch.

Just as he began to stride back to his idling green and black Fury, the cop had a question for Vito Salerno. "Do I know you?"

Vito flashed his remaining teeth as he shook his head. New York's finest continued to his squad car.

"What the hell was that?" blared Sal. "You use my son's handicap to get out of a ticket?"

"Don't get sore at me, Pope," replied Punch. "You know who taught him that?"

"Who?"

"His brother."

"Peter?

Sal looked at the grinning Joey and repeated himself, "Peter?"

"Hmmm."

Sal sat back, slamming into Vito's plastered arm.

"Holy Moses," said Sal. "That's not a good thing to do, Joey."

"Yeah, but it is fuckin' funny," laughed Vito as he returned his cast to its original rib cage-digging position.

As Punch hit the gas, Tommy tapped him on the shoulder. "You'd better stop at that diner the cop was talking about. Just to make it look good."

"Make it look good? You mean so you can stuff your face, *gavone*."

"Maybe they got some nice cookies for me."

Vito glanced beside him. He gave Tommy the once-over. "One day, you are gonna explode."

⚯

Sal knew that the air conditioning was particularly strong in George Wong's grocery store. It was more than welcome on this humid summer afternoon. It hit him in the face as he opened the door, and felt as though his sweat evaporated on contact. As always, he was accompanied by his hand-truck and his stacked cases of twelve-ounce soft drink bottles. This time he brought along someone else to help him stock Mr. Wong's refrigerator. Young Peter Salerno looked very spiffy in his blue delivery uniform. He appeared as nervous as might be expected of a rookie, only with more perspiration.

"Hello, George." Sal smiled. "How's things today?"

"Very good, Sal," replied the gray-haired Chinese-American from behind the counter.

"I'd like you to meet my son, Peter."

"This your son? Nice looking boy!"

"Thank you, George," replied Sal as Peter shook hands over the countertop.

"He's gonna work with you now?"

"I'm showing him the ropes a little. He won't be working with me on the truck, but he's getting an overview of the whole delivery system, you could say."

George Wong knocked his hand on the counter precisely eight times. "Good luck to you, Peter."

"Thank you, sir."

Sal took Peter and the hand truck toward the back of the store.

"You'll like this job, Peter. Even the loading dock will be a lot better than working at that pizzeria. You don't need to be anywhere near Vito and his problems."

"Okay. We've been over this before."

"You'll make better money, too. It's a good job. You can start a savings account."

"Yeah, unless I get drafted."

"You cross that bridge when you come to it."

"Bobby DeFrancesco got drafted."

"Yeah? He's a good kid. He'll make a strong soldier. How 'bout that fat kid—what'd they call him, Chubby Anzalone?"

"Law school. Harvard."

"Harvard? Chubby? Who does he know?"

"Dunno. He's a smart cat, though."

As they reached the refrigerators, Sal began to explain the procedures. "First we're gonna fix up these bottles that are already in here."

Sal opened the glass door.

"Whoa, that cold air feels good, Pop."

Up front, Mr. Wong rang up some customers while he greeted others. His wife, Zhi, made sandwiches for the lunchtime customers. As he tapped the green and yellow buttons on his bulky brown cash register, Wong was startled by the sound of a breaking glass bottle. Then another. Then, quite loudly, two more.

"Zhi!" he yelled.

Mrs. Wong took over the register while George ran to the back. He found Sal steadying a stack of bottle cases while Peter tried to pick up some broken glass with a rag. The soda was spreading in all directions on the tiled floor. Peter was beet red.

"How many break?" was all Wong asked.

"Four, George," replied Sal. "I'll take care of it."

Wong studied the mess on his floor. Then he reached into the top crate on Sal's load, lifted a bottle of cola, raised it as high as he could and let it fall to shatter with the others on the floor.

"I'll pay for that one," he said. "Mop is in the backroom."

George Wong hurriedly returned to assist his wife at the front counter. Sal had his cases in order and turned toward the back room. Peter looked up from his kneeling position.

"What was that all about?"

"Superstition, Pete. George does not like the number four. I don't even say it around him."

"Huh?"

"It's a Chinese thing, he tells me."

Sal grabbed the dirty mop as his son rounded up the glass shards. Peter stood to take the long-handled swab from his father, slipping once on the sticky mess before regaining his balance.

"I hope every day isn't like this." Peter sighed.

"My first day on my own I had six missing cases. They were all over my ass about that. I still don't know where they went. Don't sweat it."

Sal went about stacking the new cases in the fridge while Peter cleaned up. The mop head hit one of the broken bottlenecks and it rolled slowly, almost casually, down the aisle. Its cap was still attached, but its bottom half was gone. It was an empty shell that resembled the jagged head of some rejected medieval weapon. It rolled in an awkward half spin—leaving behind a thin trail of sticky refreshment—until it came to rest against a calf-high white go-go boot. A drop of the dark, sugary cola landed atop the smooth, pearly plastic, like a tire track in fresh snow. Peter took note of the boots, then the pink Mary Quant miniskirt above, not missing the composition and contour of the slim legs between the two. There was a matching pink top with a bright white collar, then a smoothly tanned neck tickled by her loose blonde hair. As Peter found her face, he found her smile. Glittering, glossy, and genuine, it caused the slightest ripples around her big brown eyes.

"So sorry," huffed Peter. "Let me get that for you."

He produced a wrinkled, worn rag from his back pocket.

"Not with that dirty thing," replied the girl as she supplied her own clean, frilly handkerchief and handed it down to Peter. He wiped the soda off her boot and attempted to neatly fold the hanky to return it to her.

"You can use it if you want," she said, pointing to his sweaty forehead.

"Oh, no, I wouldn't think of it," he said as he handed it back and hoped she'd say her name.

"Kathy," she said, and smiled.

"Kathy? That's nice." He smiled as he dried his forehead with his dirty rag. "Listen, let me give you a soda. They have the new twist-off caps. Have you seen those yet?"

Peter reached for a cold bottle.

"I drink Tab," she said apologetically.

"Oh," he replied, using the unwanted bottle to cool his brow.

Sal continued to load the refrigerator as he eavesdropped.

"I told you my name," she smiled.

"Peter Salerno," he blurted. Then he offered a more tranquil, "Pete."

Sal was done with the loading, and he coughed loudly to get his son's attention.

"I'll be up front, Peter," he said. "Sorry about those broken bottles. My fault."

Peter smirked at his father's attempt to take the blame in front of Kathy. Sal headed toward the counter near the store's entryway. George Wong again left the cash register in his wife's hands and headed toward Sal. He placed some paper slips into Salerno's hand, turned his back to count out some money and handed that over as well.

"Also, wish good luck to your son. Tell him breathe deep and go slow. He'll be good."

"Thank you," replied Sal. "I'll see you in a few days."

"Sure thing. Maybe I win again?" Wong laughed.

"Wouldn't surprise me," said Sal as Peter came up behind him.

"Sorry, Pop. Ready to go. The floor is all cleaned, Mr. Wong."

"Almost clean, young man," said Wong. "I need to use soap or customers stick to the floor."

"We'll soap it up for you," offered Sal.

"No, no, I take care of it." Wong laughed again.

Sal stuffed the money and slips of paper into his pocket and pulled his empty hand-truck as he and Peter left the store. As they approached their truck, Peter asked about the money and paper.

"What's all that? Mr. Wong plays the numbers?"

"Yeah. He's good at it, too. Don't ask me how. He's won more than a few times."

"He probably plays 7-7-7 or something like that, right?"

"No. First of all, 7-7-7 is a cut number. The payout is low because half of Brooklyn plays that. Smart players wouldn't touch that. I don't know Wong's system, but I know he never plays the number four."

"Well, at least people are still playing, right?" added Peter. "You'd think with the new legal lottery—"

"Old habits die hard, Pete. But enough about me collecting numbers. The real mystery is did you collect any numbers in there? Specifically, I'm referring to seven of 'em from that Barbie doll."

Peter leaned against the back of the truck. He couldn't control his grin as he pulled out the clean, frilly hanky from his back pocket. It had some handwritten numbers on it. His smile grew wider as he gently dabbed at a few beads of perspiration on his right temple.

⌒∽⌒

Peter Salerno was dressed in his best, and only, suit. It was dark brown, with a matching necktie over a freshly pressed white shirt. He was standing in front of his mother, right by the stove, in their kitchen. A pot boiled behind her as he quietly pleaded, his face just inches from hers.

"Please, Ma. This is our third date. I don't know how to say this other than, 'Please don't act crazy.' I really like this girl, and I didn't even want to bring her here, but she wanted to meet you."

Mary smiled. "You worry too much. Does she know that your brother is handicapped? Did you tell her he won't hurt her?"

"Oh, Jesus. That's just it, Ma. Nobody thinks he's gonna hurt them. You need to stop with all that. Just let her meet Joey like she meets everybody else."

"I don't know when your father will be home. You know how it is with him."

"I can't worry about that. I want her to at least meet you and Joey."

"I can't wait," replied Mary.

"Okay, then," said Peter.

He walked slowly toward the door that led from the kitchen into the hallway of the apartment building. As he opened it, Kathy was waiting there patiently, in a powder-blue skirt set and those shiny white boots. She seemed relieved because standing beside her was a man of about twenty-five, well over 300 pounds and wearing a filthy plumber's overall. With a leashed German shepherd beside him, he just stared at her as he gnawed on a cold chicken leg.

"What are you doing, Mahoney?" asked Peter of the plumber.

"Nothin', Salerno. Just trying to make some conversation here."

"Go back upstairs, okay?"

Peter took his maiden by the arm and led her inside, slamming the door as Mahoney dropped the chicken bone to his dog. Mary Salerno adjusted her apron and approached with a wide smile.

"Kathy! I have heard so much about you! Look how pretty you are! What a fancy outfit. What are you, a Rockefeller?"

Still recovering from the Mahoney encounter, Kathy tried to get her bearings as Mary shot toward her.

"Ha! Rockefeller? I wish. Thank you, Mrs. Salerno. You're so kind."

"Peter's gonna need some more suits if he's to keep up with you and the style and all."

"Ma."

"I'm hoping Peter's father will be here soon to meet you too."

"That would be so nice," smiled Kathy.

"Did Peter tell you he's got a brother?"

"Yes, he did."

"If he explained to you—"

"Ma."

"Come, sweetheart," said Mary to Kathy, "let's sit at the

table. I made a nice chocolate cake. You're so skinny. I hope you eat cake."

"You kidding?" Kathy smiled as she sat. "I love it!"

"I got Italian coffee. You like that? Peter told me you're Italian," said Mary, smiling as she placed the cake on the table.

"Oh, I am! Milk is fine though—if you have it."

"You kids with the milk. Nobody drinks coffee no more!"

From behind Kathy came a loud roar. "Nnnayyyh."

The growl startled her as Joey came ambling in from the living room.

"That's my Joey. He's a milk drinker, too."

"Sit here, Joe," said Peter as he tried to direct his brother to a chair across the table from Kathy.

"Nnnayyyh," was the reply as Joey sat right beside the pretty girl.

"Hello. I'm Kathy." The nervous guest smiled.

"Hmmmm."

She began to feel a little uncomfortable as Joey silently gazed at her, offering only a grin. His eyes drifted down to her white boots. His grin grew wider as he became fixated on them.

"He likes your boots," said Peter.

"Oh, my. Well, thank you, Joey."

"Hmmmm," he replied as he lifted his right hand and placed his thumb and forefinger half an inch apart.

"Not today," said Peter.

"Nyahhhh!"

"No, I said."

Joey waved his hand around, making a pinching motion. Peter turned to his new girlfriend.

"He wants to shine your boots. That's his thing. He shines shoes."

"Oh."

"Not this time, Joey. They're shiny already," said Peter.

As Joey continued to stare, Peter sensed Kathy's discomfort and slid his chair between them.

"I'll feed you your cake," he said to his brother, as Mary silently poured the milk, emptying the last of it into Joey's glass.

"Nyaaaah," howled Joey as Peter sat between him and Kathy. The girl flinched from the loud roar.

"Don't worry, he won't hurt you," Peter blurted to his date, and he immediately felt the fool.

He looked at his mother; she pretended not to notice. Kathy readjusted herself in her seat and tasted her cake. Peter raised a fork to feed his brother. Agitated, Joey pushed the fork away, knocking over his glass. The cold milk doused Peter's suit pants. He leapt from the table.

"Dammit!"

His mother quickly grabbed a kitchen hand towel.

"Here's a *mopina*. It'll be all right, Peter."

"I can't believe this." Peter sighed, not knowing whether to wipe his wet pants or sweaty brow.

"Joey's sorry. Look at him there," said Mary.

Joey sat without expression as Peter dabbed at his clothes.

"Now my boy's got no milk and I'm all out. Gimme a minute so I can go and see if they got some upstairs, okay? He needs milk for his cake. He eats like a teamster, this kid."

"He can have mine, Mrs. Salerno. I haven't touched it," offered Kathy.

"No, honey, I wouldn't think of it. I'll be right back," said Mary as she headed out the door.

"Sorry, Kathy," said Peter, "I'm just gonna go in the bathroom so I can take these off and use my mother's hair dryer on 'em."

"I'll do them if you want."

"It's okay. You need the bathroom, Joey?"

"Naaayh."

"Are you sure?"

"Hmmmm."

Peter disappeared into the bathroom. He was gone only

ten seconds when Joey calmly stood up and supported himself by leaning first on the table, then the chair back, then nothing. He came toward Kathy and reached out his hand. Not sure how to respond, Kathy smiled and slowly put her hand on his. Even her petite palm was larger than Joey's.

"Hmmmm."

He began to walk, leading her to the living room. She stood.

"Pete?" she yelled.

No response, save for the noise of the hair dryer behind the bathroom door. They ambled slowly—at Joey's pace—to the living room. He brought her directly to the far corner of the room, right by the avocado-paneled wall. There was one small chair in the corner next to a folding table. On that table was a light blue box. It could have been a small piece of luggage, save for the electrical cord that ran out the back of it and into a wall outlet. Joey let go of Kathy's hand and motioned to the box.

"Hmmmm."

"That's nice. Does that belong to you?"

He pointed at the box again and pulled her hand toward it.

"Hmmmm."

She got the idea and lifted the hinged top. She saw the enclosed record player and its stack of 45 rpm singles, with their yellow center-hole adapters wrapped around its shiny spindle.

"You like music," she said, more of a statement than a question.

He guided her hand to the records.

"You want me to look at your records?"

"Hmmmm."

One by one, she lifted them off the spindle and examined their labels.

"The Monkees, Supremes, Beatles, Beatles, Beatles," she rattled off. "Guess you dig the Beatles?"

"Hmmmm."

"I like this one! 'Paperback Writer'!" she held up the record. "Can we play it?"

Joey reached out for the record and Kathy handed it to him. He promptly flipped it over and handed it back.

"Hmmmm."

She examined the flipside. "Not sure I know this one. 'Rain'?"

"Hmmmm."

Joey tapped two fingers on the turntable. Kathy placed the vinyl platter down and started it up. She smiled as Joey started bobbing his head the instant Ringo Starr attacked his snare drum. She watched as her new friend closed his eyes and listened as John Lennon droned about the effects of inclement weather on one's psyche, or quite possibly about how he saw much of the human race as uptight, uncaring, and oblivious. Regardless, Joey liked the drums. He sat silently in his chair, with Kathy standing beside him, for over two minutes as the sound of the Beatles washed over the shrill din of the hair dryer behind the bathroom door. Then, as the song continued, he stood, turned and strode toward the bathroom. He moved a little faster than he did on the way in. Kathy half-watched him as she was examining the paper sleeve cover of the 45 that played. The top third of it was blue, the word "Beatles" printed in white and "Paperback Writer/Rain" and the Capitol Records logo in black. The bottom two-thirds featured a photo of each member of the band.

"Nyahhh," said Joey as he reached the bathroom door. He pushed on it and tried to turn the knob. The dryer blew loudly from behind the door. Joey banged the door, then hunched over and grabbed his crotch. The dryer stopped. Peter opened the door just as "Rain" stopped dead for precisely one beat, then resumed with John Lennon's vocal running hypnotically backwards.

It was at this point that Joey urinated in his pants.

"Oh, no," screamed Peter, who stood frozen in his white briefs with a hot dryer jutting from his right fist.

Kathy came rushing out of the living room and saw Peter—sans pants—and Joey, with a warm, expanding piss stain on his.

"I asked you if you had to go before I went in there," yelled Peter.

Joey stared straight ahead, at nothing in particular. Peter turned to Kathy.

"I gotta get him in the bathtub. My mother's gonna go nuts. This has happened before and I got blamed for being in the bathroom."

Kathy listened intently, but she kept her eyes off both Salerno brothers.

"You don't have to do this," said Peter to his dapperly dressed, distressed date. "But do you think you could help me get his clothes off?"

∽∞∾

Inside the sterile warmth of a Brooklyn courthouse, a judge bellowed long and hard about something or other while Nicky the Zipper stood with an attorney at each shoulder. As he was shackled and led away by court officers, Nicky thought he heard some yakking from the bench where Tommy Box o' Cookies was seated with Johnny the Beatnik, young Rico, and a sickly and thin Staten Island Lou. He turned his head just enough to see additional court security rush over to contain and eject a screaming, cursing Rico Falcone. As Nicky wondered what the Yankees needed to do to improve on their recent ninth-place finish, he didn't notice the goodbye salute from Staten Island Lou.

Chapter Twenty-Three

THE PLASTIC VIRGIN MARY stood high atop the aluminum Christmas tree, arms wide and welcoming. Her hue changed from white to red, dependent upon the flashing lights below. Then she tipped over and fell, plummeting toward the living room floor. She landed safely in the hands of Peter Salerno.

"You owe me one, Mary," he laughed.

"Peter," barked his mother. "Don't speak that way to the Madonna."

"Don't get all bummed out. It's just a joke," replied Peter as he reattached the treetop. He then flopped on the couch beside his father as his mother and Joey looked through the ornament boxes on the floor by the tree. Mary's mother sat in a big, comfortable chair across from the couch. She watched as a burning yule log glowed from the television screen. It was accompanied by a series of musical holiday standards.

"We're always the last to get the tree up," said Peter. He knew what the reply was going to be.

"The tree goes up on Christmas Eve," said Mary. "That's the way it is."

"Doesn't have to be," said Peter.

"Everything else is just people trying to commercialize. Buy the tree early. Buy your ornaments the day after Halloween. Buy this. Buy that," moaned Mary.

Peter began playing a card game with his father as Joey handed the ornaments to his mother, one by one.

"Mary," said Mama, "the tree looks crooked."

"Sal will straighten it out whenever he decides to get off his rear."

"Hey," Sal said laughing as he threw a card down, "didn't I set it up and put all the lights on it? Besides, you're doing a fine job, sweetheart."

"Grrrrrrrr."

"You too, Joe. Just be careful with those hooks."

"Here it is. My favorite ornament," chirped Mary as she lifted the small plate that read, *Peter starts first grade—1955.* "Can't believe it's been twelve years already. You remember this one, Peter?"

"How can I forget?" the teen said and smiled. "You show me every year!"

Peter tossed a red queen onto the table as the doorbell rang.

"I'll get it," he said as he hustled toward the door.

Sal stood to help straighten out the tree. He stopped in front of the television to "warm" his hands at the image of the flaming fireplace, sharing a laugh with Mama. He adjusted the shiny aluminum tree just a bit while eyeballing the trembling virgin effigy at the summit. Through the corrosion-resistant foliage, he saw Peter return to the living room. Standing beside him, in Christmas red and holding a neatly wrapped gift and a thin package, was Kathy.

Sal joined the others in greeting her with a hello, but he really wanted to say, *You keep coming back? You've seen Joey wet himself; you helped him get—naked—into a bathtub. You've sat here as he stared at you for an hour straight. You've helped him play his records, and he's shined all of your shoes. You've sat at our table while Mary shoveled food into his mouth and he digested like a boa constrictor, and unlike the other girls, you keep coming back?*

"Hey, Joey," said Kathy. "I got you something."

She knelt beside him and took the brightly colored album jacket out of the thin bag. The first thing Joey noticed were the colors and the images of all the people. He recognized W.C. Fields because Peter would always watch his movies, but he didn't immediately connect with anyone else—except for the four lads in the kaleidoscopic military garb. They held brass and wind instruments instead of guitars, and though Joey could not read what was spelled out by the red flowers at their feet, he knew.

Beatles.

Kathy helped him remove the shrink-wrap. She had already taken off the Woolworth's price sticker.

"Ooooh," yelled Mary. "He's gonna love that! We buy him the little records, but those big ones are expensive. You shouldn't have done that, Kathy."

"I know he loves the 'Strawberry Fields/Penny Lane' single; this album is like that."

Joey's grin was wide as he stared at the record cover. He opened the gatefold and got a closer look at his favorite band in their vivid garb.

"Let me lower the television set. Put the record on for him," said Mary.

As Kathy placed the record on Joey's portable turntable, Mary turned down the Christmas music. The yule log still burned, though—a constant loop that reset every twenty seconds.

"He loves that music, and it's okay 'cause he's always with me and can't do any harm to himself, but I think this music can lead kids to bad things. You know, the drugs and all," said Mary.

"Maybe, but it doesn't have to. I don't think drugs are needed to expand the mind," replied Kathy. "I think a needle in the groove beats a needle in the arm any day."

The family sat there as the recording began. They eventually met Billy Shears and Lucy. Mama left her chair to make some coffee, but the rest remained. They were taken away to a color-splashed circus. Kathy flipped the record over and they arrived in India, only to be quickly transported to a

1940s dance hall. It was at this time that Sal began thinking of the old music that he loved so much. Mama returned in time to hear a chicken cluck morph into a guitar pluck. The military band that unleashed this animal were now trying to get it back in its cage. There came an incredible crescendo that sounded as if all the music they'd ever heard was being played at once. Then it stopped—but not before a thunderous piano chord that seemed to echo into eternity. Mary wanted to speak but wasn't sure when to start, fearing another explosion of sound. Peter beat her to the punch.

"Wow!"

"These are the same fellas that sang 'I Want to Hold Your Hand'?" Mary asked.

"Hmmmm," replied Joey before another could answer.

"What did ya think, Ma?" asked Mary.

"Nice boys. But I like the Italian music. I wish them luck."

"All well and good," said Sal as he disappeared into a hallway closet. "But now it's my turn at the Victrola."

He dusted off an old dog-eared record sleeve and slipped out the slab of scratchy vinyl. He winked at his wife as he took Joey's record off of the player and replaced it with his own. As the phonograph needle began its roundabout, Sal walked to Mary and put out his hand.

"What the heck are you doing now, you nut?" laughed Mary as she stood, dropping some tinsel she'd been holding.

She recognized the music of the Les Brown Orchestra immediately. She giggled at first as they danced slowly in the heart of their living room. The song they danced to on their wedding day played for well over a minute before Doris Day told of the mysterious man who'd smiled at her in her dreams.

"It's as beautiful as it was over twenty years ago," whispered Mary, her head resting on Sal's ample shoulder.

He held her closer, oblivious to the rest of the room. "So are you."

The dance continued as Kathy sat beside Peter. Joey

studied a sheet of cutouts that came with his new album. The lights on the aluminum Christmas tree danced along with the Salernos, bouncing brilliantly off Peter's 1955 first-grade plate. Mama sipped her coffee as she watched her daughter dance as if it were 1945. Sal and Mary floated in front of the television, shrouding the view of the burning log. Peter almost didn't feel it, as it arrived so softly—Kathy's head was settled on his shoulder.

∽∾

The snowflakes poured down from the moonlit sky, and those that landed on the warm window panes of the Hotel Dixie quickly melted away before their brethren could float down to Times Square below. Inside this particular room on the twenty-third floor, a man and woman lay fully clothed on the bed. They had just returned from a performance of Burlesque '67 in the Bert Wheeler Theater on the first floor of the same building. She rested her head on three stacked pillows; his head lay on his folded arms, down at the foot of the bed. His eyes were fixed on the color television as a news reporter informed viewers that many thousands braved the storm to converge on Times Square and bid *adieu* to 1967 on this cold New Year's Eve. As if the folly of his ways had only now become evident, the man turned his head to face the pretty blonde who was nearly twenty years his junior.

"I gotta be insane. If your husband knew that we was here..." said Vito Salerno, trailing off.

"Oh, be a man," replied Betty-Jean Verengia, as if Vito hadn't been almost beaten to death a couple of months earlier for a similar transgression on their part. "Besides, you haven't touched me since we got up here."

"We've only been here fifteen minutes."

"Yeah, fifteen minutes of television watching."

"It's color. That's the sign of a good hotel."

Betty-Jean left her pillows and crawled over beside Vito.

"Why bring me here? Why risk your neck if you don't want to make love to me?"

173

"I risked my neck going to that show with you downstairs. Us right out in public. What's wrong with me?"

She began to nibble on his ear.

"Maybe you love me?"

"I ain't never been too good with promises, but I'm tryin' to change. I promised you I'd never just dump you like it meant nothin' to me. I also promised Biaggio that I'd never do no funny business with you no more on account of he saved my life when your husband wanted my balls hangin' off his cuckoo clock."

"Mmm," purred the blonde as she ran her nails down his neck.

"So I think this is a nice way for us to say good-bye. We saw a good show, we'll order up a nice dinner from room service, and we'll watch the ball drop and welcome in the new year together. Then we can both have a fresh start as we go our own ways. A new year, a new start."

"You know we won't be able to do that," she teased. "And we can't really see the ball drop from this crappy view."

"That's what the television is for. We can see a lot of the people from the window, though. Let them freeze out there in that shit hole. Times Square sure ain't what it used to be. We got it just right in here."

"What a gallant way to dump me."

"What am I gonna do, wind up in a dozen pieces? Besides, don't think he wouldn't whack you too."

"Where would he find another girl like me to fondle that soggy noodle of his?"

Vito Salerno was about to tell her that there might be a line of women stretching across the Brooklyn Bridge, but he was rudely interrupted by the sound of their hotel room door being smashed in. Vito and Betty-Jean saw the handguns first, then they saw the men holding them. It was Pinky and Ruddy. Don Verengia's goons. Again.

"Ain't love grand?" was how Pinky announced his entrance.

Ruddy lifted Vito's sport coat off a chair back and found the shoulder holster he knew would be there. He took the pistol and tucked it into his waistband.

"This is the type of dump you bring her to?" asked Pinky of Vito.

Salerno didn't answer, but Ruddy didn't seem to fully concur with his cohort.

"It's got color TV," he mumbled.

"We didn't do anything, Pinky," said Betty-Jean, perhaps feeling a little too safe. "We just came here to—"

"Save it, blowjob. One more word and you die an inch at a time."

Pinky had never spoken to Betty-Jean that way—in fact, nobody had. Not since she became Mrs. Verengia, anyway. She felt her body go cold as she realized that Vito was right about her precarious mortality. Ruddy produced a thick roll of dusty, heavy-duty duct tape and grabbed Vito Salerno, tossing him into the chair that held his coat. As his mouth was being wrapped tight by the sticky restraint, Vito couldn't help but wonder how old this duct tape was and where it had been all these years. It was army green, you see. Commercial duct tape had long been sold as silver, to match duct work. Vito hadn't seen this green tape in twenty years. He guessed they might still make the green variety for military use, but this batch, with all the dust that was funneling up his nostrils, was an old ring of tape.

How could it still be so fuckin' sticky?

It was Betty-Jean's pleading that snapped him out of his duct-tape fixation.

"Please, Pinky," was all she could manage as she wept.

Vito could only watch, as he was now tightly taped to his chair back, his sport coat at his feet. Ruddy ambled over toward Betty-Jean on the bed—the tape roll still clenched in his salmon-like paw. She brought her knees to her chest as he leaned in. His breath was right on her, like a damp cigar at the bottom of a drained glass of warm beer. His severe case of rosacea had never been more evident. The engorged pimples and blisters that littered his flaming cheeks, nose, and forehead crowded her vision like a hot, leaking volcano.

This cannot be the last thing I ever see.

Just as she finished her thought, the tape was on her mouth and a hotel pillow case came down around her head. She tried to scream, but it only forced air and moisture out of her nose, and made her ears hurt, too. She could still smell Ruddy, and she heard Pinky begin to ramble at the foot of the bed.

"Salerno," he grunted, "if it was up to me, I'd also enjoy paying a visit to that punk cousin of yours. He had the balls to try to embarrass me at a meeting of the families?"

A grinning Ruddy tucked his gun behind his back and produced a thick, rusty pair of diagonal cutting pliers. He walked toward the window, craning his neck for a glimpse at the New Years ball. It was starting its slow descent.

"You know why your cousin has Biaggio Falcone's protection, right?" asked Pinky. "Because his kid is a fuckin' retard. That's the only reason."

Vito made an attempt to charge at his assailant. He hopped a few feet with the chair strapped to his back before Ruddy kicked him square in the face and slid the other pillow over his head.

"Ruddy, let's start by taking off his thumbs," commanded Pinky.

Ruddy knelt behind Vito's chair and tried to decide which of the thumbs would be easiest to get at first. Betty-Jean snorted and bounced around on the bed, trying to shake off her head cover. Vito's whitening hands hung down behind the chair and under the duct tape; his cold fingers like dead roses awaiting the pruner. Ruddy made his choice. The icy, dirty steel cutter engrossed Salerno's left thumb like a pit bull's jaws on the neck of a kitten. Ruddy's gin-soaked brain sent the message down to his scaly right hand.

Squeeze.

Ruddy's forearm bulged ever so slightly as his grip began to close.

"Don't go doin' somethin' like that," came a winded voice from the doorway.

Ruddy looked up to see Tommy Box o' Cookies standing beside the broken door. Almost completely out of breath, he leaned against the door jamb pointing a gun directly at the kneeling Ruddy. Beside Tommy stood Johnny the Beatnik. He had two guns pointed at Pinky. Vito's head began to jerk under his pillow case as he recognized his friend's voice.

"Back away from him," said Tommy. He was wearing a lobster bib. It looked like a postage stamp against his huge, tight shirt. His buttons were almost at a breaking point. "Relax, Vito. It's okay. These *cuccios* had to ruin the nice New Year's dinner we were havin' down in the restaurant."

"Back off, Tommy," said Pinky with his gun still in hand and pointed at the Beatnik. "This is a sanctioned hit."

"Number one," answered Tommy, "it was a sanctioned hit last time. Then it was agreed it would be a beating. You never submitted anything for a second approval. Number two, you made me run down this long hallway and I can't freakin' breathe."

"Submitted approval?" laughed Pinky. "What are you, a fuckin' mortgage banker? This guy's humpin' the don's wife!"

Vito mumbled as he vigorously shook his pillow case No. Behind him, Ruddy dropped his wire cutter, but his left hand, hidden by Vito's chair, searched his back waistband for his handgun.

"I don't think they were doing it this time," said Tommy. "They were breakin' it off. I think we should all put our guns away—starting with you—and we can all go sort this out at the club."

Pinky had been inching toward Vito's chair, Ruddy and the window, looking for a better angle on things trajectory-wise. His gun was now trained on Tommy and vice versa. The Beatnik had one pistol pointed at each of Verengia's men.

177

Ruddy's left hand was on his weapon now, waiting for Pinky's cue.

If I drop fast, I can use that mattress for cover. Me and Ruddy can. That would leave these two jerks exposed like two trees waiting for the lumberjack, thought Pinky.

Tommy walked slowly toward his adversaries. "Listen, Pinky, our guys have been tailing Vito for a while now. Biaggio wanted to know if there was still any funny business goin' on. You know he ain't stupid. My hand to God, this is the first time Vito has been with this woman since you threw him a beatin'."

On the television, and down below in Times Square, the final countdown had begun. The ball was nearly at ground level.

"Ten," yelled the crowd.

Pinky's mind was racing. He hadn't heard a word Tommy said.

"Nine!"

"I think they came here to end it in a nice way and go their separate ways," offered Tommy as he inched closer to Pinky. "Look, I can't let you ice him, so let's not start a war over this, okay?"

"Seven!"

Pinky sighed. Tommy was five feet away now. Ruddy looked for a sign.

"Six!"

Just as Pinky relaxed, it happened. Tommy's shirt popped. A button exploded off his groaning midriff, just below the bib. The round projectile hit Pinky smack in the right eyeball.

"Ahhhhh," Pinky screamed as his left hand instinctively reached for his eye. His right hand simultaneously squeezed the trigger and send a bullet into Tommy's left bicep.

"Four!"

A puzzled Ruddy was immediately cut down by a barrage from Johnny the Beatnik. He was dead before he knew what happened. A hooded Betty-Jean flopped around on the bed like a striped bass on the Brooklyn docks. Hearing the gunfire, Vito toppled to the floor, still taped to his chair. He landed partially on Ruddy's fresh corpse.

"One!"

With one eye closed, Pinky's shots went everywhere and hit everything but flesh. Tommy and the Beatnik riddled Pinky with lead. He and the large window behind him were basically fragmentized together. Pinky fell back into it, then out of it, and began his plunge from the twenty-third floor of the Hotel Dixie.

"Happy New Year!"

The cold air blasted in from the shattered window, helping to clear the gun smoke from the room. Down below, the ball landed just before Pinky. People danced in the snowy streets as Pinky's body came to an ugly rest on the roof of a three-story extension. He bled out amid pinkish snow and wet glass shards. Up in the room, Tommy yanked the hood off Vito's head but left the tape over his mouth.

"I'll get you outta that chair in a minute," he said as he eyed the bullet wound in his arm. The blood was beginning to spread on Tommy's shirt sleeve. He looked back to see Johnny removing the pillow case from Betty-Jean's head. Her hair was a mess, and soaked with sweat. He left the tape on her mouth as well.

"Over here, Johnny," said Tommy.

As the Beatnik reached him, Tommy handed him the lobster bib. "Do me a favor, tie this around my arm. We gotta scoot from here."

Johnny wrapped the bib around the bloody wound, and then Tommy suddenly bent over.

"You okay, big fella?" asked the Beatnik.

"Oh . . . yeah. I thought maybe I seen my button on the floor."

THREE YEARS LATER

Chapter Twenty-Four

THE BREEZY CALM of the late April afternoon was about to melt under the buttery Sunday sun. The folks strolling lazily on the avenue sidewalks arched their necks as a distant hum blossomed into a deep, low rumble. They all instinctively looked upward at first, searching the azure sky for an airliner, but it was not to be found.

Ever so slightly, the storefront windows began to rattle, like dominoes falling from behind. The heads turned to look down the street. Now it was really loud. One might think it would produce an impressive cloud of smoke, but it left just a trail of semi-opaque haze. Sundry papers and street litter took flight as it charged past like a pauper's ticker-tape parade. Sun rays bounced off the streaking white Trans Am as the locals grabbed their fleeting glimpse. They could tell it was white. Looked like a blue hood scoop. All manner of vents and spoilers. Then it was gone, blurring into its own haze. A discarded coffee cup abandoned the trash tornado and flicked teasingly against the windshield of the first of the wailing police cars behind. As each approaching cross street was quickly devoured, the NYPD vehicles lagged further in the distance, no match for the beastly Pontiac. Punch the Pedal did just as his nickname suggested; his hands held so tightly onto the steering wheel that it felt like an anatomical extension growing from his fists. Somehow, to Punch, the world seemed to slow down when he was careening through the streets of New York. As he approached the age of forty, his hair was thinning, his walk was slowing, but he could drive faster—and with more control—than ever before. The

183

Temptations did their soulful best to come through the car radio with "Just My Imagination," but they were no match for the engine of the powerful hellion.

Punch loved the shiny guzzler that he called his "1970-and-a-half Trans Am," due to a delay in its production. It had not the powerful Ram Air IV engine that all his car-loving buddies raved about, but the ultra-rare, monstrous Ram V furnished him with 500 horsepower to unleash upon Brooklyn. Many refused to believe that the Ram V engine even existed. But Punch had one.

With each successive squealing turn, it took longer for Punch to find the cops in his mirror. With the sparse Sunday traffic, even the red lights were a piece of cake. Too easy.

His passenger seat was empty, and there was a stack of brown blankets piled in the backseat. Punch blasted up onto the Brooklyn-Queens Expressway, then was off it just as quickly at the next exit. He thundered down back alleys, causing all manner of cat and pigeon evacuations. He knew of shortcuts through parks and graveyards, but avoided the former due to the number of children present on weekend afternoons. He knew a handful of streets that weren't even found on maps. Most importantly, he knew he'd never be caught.

The radio jockey boasted of a brand new song from the just-released album Sticky Fingers. "Here's 'Brown Sugar' by the Rolling Stones on WABC!"

⌒∞⌒

Peter Salerno always felt a little out-of-place in a fancy suit—much less a freaking tuxedo. He may have reservations about his monkey threads, but he was rock-solid on the commitment he'd just made. Kathy had been his wife for a scant few hours and he was elated to share his joy with their closest family and friends. He escorted his radiant new bride table-to-table to chat and laugh with those they cherished most. The six-piece band played everything from Frank Sinatra and Louis Prima to Three Dog Night and Marvin

Gaye as the dancing revelers brought the Brooklyn wedding hall to life.

Sal watched from a distance as his son and daughter-in-law settled in to sit with some of the younger guys from the cola company. Peter held a portable AM radio up to his ear as he laughed with Larry and Ben. Honestly, Sal wasn't sure if they were Larry and Ben or Barry and Len. Now in management, Sal didn't know the junior guys that well.

"Not gettin' any scores on your radio," Peter nudged Larry. "Alls it is is reports from that march down in Washington."

"Told ya," added Ben.

"Can we be married one full day before we have to find out how the Mets are doing?" Kathy sighed.

"Kath, I heard you say it with my own ears," Larry said and laughed. "For better or for worse!"

∽∞∾

Punch barreled around a residential street corner and deftly guided his roaring machine onto the driveway of a two-story brick home and into the waiting two-car garage. A lanky, bearded gib-cat of a man in an oil-stained jacket pulled down the garage door behind Punch, further muzzling the already-distant police sirens. As Punch cut the growling Ram V and exited his Trans Am, he eyed the rather pedestrian vehicle that awaited him, parked front-facing the garage door. As he inhaled the rubberized smoke still wafting from his baking tires, he couldn't help but grin at the green 1965 Volkswagen van before him. A little rusted and dented, it actually had a peace sign on the front of it, replacing the usual "VW" logo. Punch the Pedal was going to be tooling around town in a hippie mobile.

"Thanks for the swap-out, Carbone. I'll have it back to you in an hour or two."

"No hurry," replied his oily associate as he chomped a piece of jerky. "We can make it a permanent trade if you want."

"If that beatnik bus is carrying a load of diamonds, gold bars, or Raquel Welch, you might have a deal." Punch chuckled. "My real plates are under my front seat," Punch added as Carbone handed him the keys. "Think you could put 'em back on for me while I'm gone?"

"Sure."

"*Grazie*," replied Punch as he pulled the Pontiac's driver's seat forward. "Gimme a hand with my blankets and payload, would ya?"

Punch tapped twice on the roof of his prized ride. "Did you have a stroke back there or what?" he yelled.

⟨⟩

Mary Salerno had several thick cloth napkins on the lap of her fancy light-blue dress. There were even more napkins on Joey's small spiffy tuxedo. They sat at a large table with Mary's sisters and brothers-in-law. Though Joey was now in his mid-twenties, feeding could still be a messy proposition for him. He gulped food from the spoon in his mother's hand like a baby bird, while he tapped his shiny left shoe as the wedding band offered up "That Old Black Magic."

Across the room, his father stood with his big hands on the shoulders of Peter and Kathy as the happy couple continued to mingle with the young delivery men from the beverage company. The newlyweds sat smiling as Sal stood, towering between them.

"Hey, Pop," shouted Peter over the song that he knew as a Louis Prima/Keely Smith classic—though his father heard a Glenn Miller standard. "Larry has already been to that new off-track betting joint."

"Go 'head? The one in Grand Central? Were you in line behind Mayor Lindsay?" Sal asked and laughed.

"No sign of him when I was there." The young delivery man smiled.

Ben leaned forward. "They say that 'new game in town' might put the traditional bookie right outta business, Mr. Salerno."

Larry kicked him under the table.

"Imagine that," was all Sal replied.

"Well," interjected Peter, "time for the missus and I to move on and make the rounds a little. Can't spend the whole reception with my friends!"

Sal departed the table along with the new couple. He had a question for his son as he watched Mary at the far end of the room. Through a screen of dancing couples, he could see her wiping Joey's mouth.

"What did he mean with that 'bookie' remark?"

"Nothing. He was just making conversation, Pop."

"Hmm. That's probably it, I guess. Boy, there's almost nobody here from the neighborhood. So many guys from work and lots of people I don't even know, Pete."

Peter turned to Kathy, and her face hardened.

"Sweetheart, can I have a minute with my father?"

She forced a smile and turned away, walking toward her family's tables.

"Pop, Kathy has friends too, and a lot of family that you haven't met yet. You also are not familiar with every friend in my life. This is our wedding. Please don't start again about me not inviting all your *paisans*. That's your crowd, Pop. Not mine. Not Kathy's."

"I know that." Sal sighed. "But maybe at least Biaggio should be here. Out of respect, Peter."

"Why? So I can have detectives sitting outside in cars taking pictures of who comes and goes at our wedding? Go look outside. No cops."

"I did already."

"I guess they know I'm not part of that life. I'd like to keep it that way."

"You act like I'm Dillinger. All I do is—"

"I know the song, Pop. You just do a little numbers. You don't hurt nobody. You just dip your toe in the pool. Guess what? When you do that, you still get wet."

"I do what I have to do for Joey. You're the lucky one. The healthy one. Don't judge me like that."

"Pop, I love you. I just don't like that life. I don't like what comes along with it. Look at cousin Vito. He's not here at my wedding. I've known him my whole life. He was at my first communion. He was at my confirmation. He was at your wedding. Now, he might as well be dead."

"Come on, Pete. You know his situation. Even I haven't seen him in three years. If he came to Brooklyn now, it would be a death sentence."

"Well, that makes The Life sound great, doesn't it?"

"That's got nothing to do with it. In fact, without the friends he has, he'd be buried in some Jersey swamp right now. His *paisans* have kept him safe and alive."

Peter paused. Then he put his hands on his father's face, feeling the stubble that always seemed to reappear the minute Sal laid down his razor.

"Let me get back to Kathy. Why don't you go sit with Mom. Maybe ask her to dance?"

As his son walked away, Sal reached into his jacket's inner pocket. He acquired some pricy Cuban cigars for the occasion, brought in by way of Canada. He figured now might be the time to enjoy one in the crisp evening air.

∽

The sun skedaddled to points west as a quiet darkness took the reins of this Sunday night. The streets surrounding the wedding hall were nearly deserted, the stores all closed. Sporadically, a few teenagers or kibitzing old men would wander past the front of the wedding hall. A lone city bus echoed like a tank as it growled by with only two riders aboard.

Sal smiled as he thought about all the pricy fare being served inside the manor behind him. Why then, did he yearn for a hot dog from the Coney Island Nathan's that he knew was just a few blocks south? Surely he couldn't smell those smoking grills from this distance? Must be all in his mind. He carefully clipped the head off the thick, handmade Cifuentes Altezas Reales that he imagined came from

Castro's own backyard. As he lit his prized cigar, he allowed himself a moment of serenity and closed his eyes. As the medley of smoky flavors filled his mouth, he took comfort in knowing that Peter was fully a man now, with a wonderful young bride, a secure job, and a happy life ahead of him. Upon exhaling his warm Cuban cloud, however, Sal's thoughts returned to normal. As his premium smoke wafted toward the stars, he had Joey on his mind again. He knew his elder son would certainly never marry, never have a fulfilling career, and never be able to care for himself. An eternal child, dependent on others for as long as he should live.

From the front door behind Sal emerged a balding, middle-aged priest, smiling as he zippered his light spring jacket halfway, his black shirt and white clerical collar still quite visible. Father Lazarro ran a hand through the thin silver locks that remained atop his crown.

"Getting breezy, eh, Sal?"

"Turning a little nippy, Father. How'd ya like a nice cigar?"

"Much appreciated, but no, thank you." He smiled.

"I can't give these things away."

"You doing okay, Sal? You seemed a little lost in your thoughts. Anything you need to talk about?"

"Oh, I'm fine. Thank you for a beautiful service today. Thank you for your blessings to my son and his wife."

"My pleasure. You have a wonderful family. If you ever need to talk about anything—"

"You'll be the first to know."

"I tell people not to waste money on some shrink; all I ask for is maybe a fresh cannoli and we can talk all day," the priest said and laughed.

"Sounds good."

"You know, you're always welcome to come to mass with Mary—"

The exhaust huffed and puffed as the green Volkswagen

van ambled slowly toward the wedding hall. Sal knew he had seen it before; he remembered the peace sign that took the place of the VW logo. The van didn't turn into the valet lot but pulled up right beside the fire hydrant directly in front of Sal and the priest. He and Father Lazarro tried to discern who the two occupants were. Then the passenger-side door opened and a slightly statured fellow in a nicely tailored suit hopped onto the curb.

"Hey, cuz!"

Sal nearly dropped his hand-rolled smoke as he laid eyes on Vito Salerno for the first time in three years.

"Holy shit," he mumbled before remembering he was in the company of a man of the cloth. "Sorry, Father."

The priest said nothing, as he too couldn't believe his eyes. He watched as Vito ran up to Sal and gave him a big bear hug.

"What?" asked Vito. "You think I was gonna miss your son's wedding?"

Vito turned toward the priest.

"Hey, *Padre*."

"Hello, Vito," whispered the astonished clergyman, then uttered in an even lower voice, "holy shit indeed."

Father Lazarro quickly placed his hands on the backs of Sal and Vito. "Well gentlemen, I have to get back to the rectory for some business. Wonderful wedding, Sal."

With that, the priest left, disappearing into the valet parking lot. Sal and Vito couldn't help but chuckle at the nervous Father.

"What are you doing here? You nuts?" asked Sal.

"This freakin' *chooch* kidnapped me and dragged me over here," Vito laughed and he pointed at the van. Sal dipped his head and spotted a smiling Punch behind the wheel.

"Enjoy your day, Pope."

"Get outta that hippie wagon and come inside. Have a drink."

"You sure?"

"Park it."

Sal turned to his cousin.

"No kiddin' around, you're crazy to come to Brooklyn. You shouldn't even be in New York State."

"Sally Boy, you got one of those fancy cigars for me or what? You gimme one and I'll tell ya all about it."

⟨◦∞◦⟩

Punch the Pedal sat there in his casual, open-collared shirt. He hadn't dressed for a wedding. He lifted a cold beer to his lips and he found himself making conversation with Peter's friends from work.

"So, you had to sneak Pete's uncle in here?" asked Larry.

"Pete's cousin. That's neither here nor there, though. What I was trying to say is that I got the idea on how to transport him from that movie they were making around here."

"What movie?" asked Ben.

"I dunno. *French* something-or-other. Anyways, I couldn't freakin' escape that movie. I seen them three different times runnin' that brown LeMans into the ground."

Vito Salerno was savoring every bit of the expensive cigar as he hugged Mary tightly. She frantically waved the smoke away from her face. Then he leaned down and whispered something in Joey's ear. The young man smiled broadly as he made his fingers into a V and stuck his nose between them. This caused Vito to double over with laughter as Mary took Joey's fingers away from his face.

"Stop telling my boy your Italian curse words. You get him all crazy that way."

Vito gave Mary a smoky kiss on the forehead as a group of other relatives surrounded them, many rubbing Vito's shoulders and patting him on the back.

⟨◦∞◦⟩

"I think maybe this new movie is trying to be like *Bullitt*," Punch said.

"Now that was a movie," yelled Larry.

"I think I seen it seven times," said Punch. "I wanted to see it with Vito, but he . . . "

Punch took another drink.

"That Mustang," offered Larry.

"You ain't kidding," replied Punch. "Well, this LeMans in the new movie. I seen a guy in the back seat with a camera in his hands, and they had him all wrapped up in blankets and mattresses and stuff."

"No shit."

"That ain't the best part. I got a buddy who was leaving his house to drive to work and sure as shit they crashed right into him. Right on 86th Street."

"The movie car?"

"Yeah. The LeMans. A big crack-up with my buddy."

⟨∞⟩

Vito's cigar was down to a nub as Sal pulled him away from the rest of the family.

"So, how did you pull this off?"

"Calm down, Sally Boy. I'm gonna be gone before anyone even realizes I was here. I wasn't gonna miss your boy's wedding. You got another cigar?"

"What about Biaggio?"

"He knows. He sent Punch to get me. I only got an hour. Well, maybe two." He smiled.

"But if Don Verengia finds out—"

"He won't. We dodged some cops who might or might not be in his pocket, but they were no match for Punch. Do you even know what happened that night in the hotel?"

Sal lit a cigar for his cousin.

"No."

"Good," said Vito. "Neither does Verengia. Not for sure, anyway. He ain't seen me since. He ain't seen his wife since—"

"His wife?"

"Oh, she's fine. If he ever sees her again...*morto*, but she's safe. He ain't seen those monkeys he sent to off us, either. Biaggio sent in some cleaners, you know? Within hours that

192

hotel room was ready to go with a mint on the pillow. So as far as Verengia knows, his two button men never came back, and me and his missus disappeared too. Let him try and figure it out."

"But if he ever knows you're here—"

"He's old. Not much time left for him. When he goes, I come home. Biaggio will work it out."

⌒

Punch continued talking movies with Peter's friends, a cigar and a beer in his left hand, right hand in constant motion for emphasis.

"I got friendly with some go-fer on the movie, a nice kid. Anyways, he hooked me up to be in a big Hollywood picture myself."

"No way."

"Yeah. Well, I got no lines, but I'll be in it. Like in the background."

"An extra?" Larry laughed.

"Whatever. There's free Italian food and who-knows-what."

"So, you're going to California for this?"

"Hell no. It's on Staten Island, next week."

They all laughed.

"Another car chase movie?"

"No," replied Punch. "A big gangster picture. I'm actually sort of rehearsing right now because I'm gonna be in a big Italian wedding scene."

They chuckled as Punch downed his beer and drew deep on the handmade Cifuentes.

"I dunno if he'll pass as a *paisan*, but Marlon Brando will be in the same scene as me."

"This one is dedicated to the parents of our wonderful groom," announced the bandleader. "Can we please have Sal and Mary to our dance floor? Sal and Mary Salerno, please!"

The guests all applauded as Sal walked briskly toward his wife, Cousin Vito following just steps behind. Mary tried to smooth out her pretty gown as she stood, her cheeks growing rosy with all the unwanted attention. The band launched into the tune just as her husband reached her. The years melted away from Mary's face as she heard her song—their song.

"My Dreams Are Getting Better All the Time."

As Sal took her hand, Mary turned to her younger sister Janet, who was seated nearby with her husband, Tony. "Keep an eye on Joey for me."

"Baaaaahhhh," grunted Joey as his aunt sat beside him.

Sal held his wife tightly as Mary lost herself in the song and the moment. Much as in the lyrics, she found the man of her dreams, and though life was far from easy, he was still there, and she was safe in his arms. At the invitation of the band, other couples began to join the Salernos on the dance floor. Mary drifted into her thoughts, distracted only by the thought that though the wedding band's female singer was talented, she was no Doris Day.

Cousin Vito was playfully trying to get Joey up to slow dance with him.

"Grrrrrr."

"He's been moody since the Beatles broke up." Peter laughed as he swayed with Kathy on the edge of the dance floor.

"The Beatles?" said Vito. "That ain't real music."

He leaned down and whispered some more Italian curse words into Joey's ear. That got the boy into a full grin and he stood and began to amble slowly about with the older cousin he loved so much. Sal and Mary. Peter and Kathy. Joey, Vito, and all their family and friends.

My dreams are getting better all the time.

TWELVE YEARS LATER
FALL 1983

Chapter Twenty-Five

AGAIN IT WAS Vito Salerno dancing with Joey, but the sickly young man was slower, more brittle than in years past. Joey was closing in on forty years of age. Cousin Vito had been back for several years now. Just as he had hoped, Don Verengia passed on from natural causes and Biaggio Falcone initiated a deal with his successor. Vito had no particular liking for this "Billie Jean" song by Michael Jackson, but Joey loved it, and the party DJ wasn't going to play Dean Martin and Frank Sinatra music all night. Vito also preferred Joey's relaxed dancing to that of his latest girlfriend, Brenda. She was half Vito's age and behaved as half of that.

Once again, the extended Salerno family, friends, and co-workers found themselves at a celebration. Though not as formal as a wedding, and in a smaller Knights of Columbus hall, this was a night to honor Salvatore Salerno. But he had to share it with two other men whose families were also at the event. The room was basically divided into three sections of tables, but they all shared the dance floor and buffet tables. Three gold watches were handed out, along with three framed retirement proclamations. Sal's was spelled correctly, but Greg O'Halloran's had an additional G added to the end of his first name and no apostrophe in his last. Wali Chattopadhyay's last name was spelled perfectly, but his first name was written as Wally.

The guests in Sal's section of the room did include the fellas from the neighborhood, unlike when his son was wed a dozen years before. Some came with wives or girlfriends, some alone. They were all a little grayer and some a little thicker, as many were over sixty years of age. They still ran the show, though there were more than a few younger up-and-comers waiting in the wings. Biaggio Falcone could probably oversee things for at least another twenty years, if health permitted and if he could still control his thirty-seven-year-old son, Frederico. A decade younger than the others, but still several years the senior of Johnny the Beatnik, was Punch the Pedal. He was quite happy to be with the boys and in the company of his new Puerto Rican girlfriend, Inez. She was middle-aged and quite stunning; unlike Vito Salerno, he wasn't one for the younger girls. Inez sat smiling beside Punch as he dipped into his favorite party stories once again.

"Then, in the middle of everything, Marlon Brando dropped his pants and mooned the whole crowd. Don't even get me started on Jimmy Caan."

"*Jimmy Caan*? You're in a scene with five hundred people and you make like you're his best friend?" The Beatnik laughed.

Punch looked at Inez, closed his eyes for a second, then slowly replied to the Beatnik, "*Metete un palo por el culo.*"

Inez giggled.

"I know you said something about my ass but that ain't Italian." Johnny laughed.

"It's his Spanish," Inez said and smiled. "He's trying hard to learn for me."

"Shove a stick up your ass," translated Punch.

"Spanish and Italian are very similar, right?" asked Johnny.

"Sometimes," answered Punch.

"I think Portuguese is in the middle of them," said Inez.

A hand was placed on Punch's shoulder.

"Got a minute, Punch?" asked Biaggio Falcone as he smiled at Inez.

"Sure, sure. Excuse us," said Punch as Falcone led him to a quiet corner of the room.

Waiting for them was Tommy Box o' Cookies. He was as voluminous as ever as he bit into his Linzer Tart—or "Bullseye" as they were called in the neighborhood. A dab of raspberry jam hit the floor as Biaggio and Punch arrived.

"We need you to be honest with us," whispered Biaggio to his driver.

"Of course," responded Punch, not showing any nerves.

"Seems there was a little bunking heads, whereby you drove my son to the scrap yard?"

Punch knew he was fucked. How do you say that in Spanish?

"Biaggio, I think it might be best if you spoke to Frederico about something like that."

"He'll lie to me, Punch. I'm ashamed to say that. I know I'll get the truth from you."

"He's my boss, sir. I'm in a bad spot here."

Tommy listened in as he wiped the crumbs from his lips.

"I'm his boss. I'm his father," replied Biaggio.

"I did drive him to the scrap yard. Yes."

"Good. Then what happened?"

"Maybe if you just asked Rico—"

"Punch. This could be a very serious matter and I'm starting to feel like a marionette's asshole over here."

Punch the Pedal breathed deep.

"Rico told me to drive him to the scrap yard. I just did as I was told. He said he got a call from somebody there—a friend of his—that some guys were causing trouble. Making threats and gettin' violent. The guys at the yard were scared because the two punks were saying they were connected."

"They are connected. Very much so."

Tommy brushed some powdered sugar from his chins but said nothing.

"What did you and Rico do at the scrap yard?" asked Biaggio.

"Do you really want to hurt me?" pleaded Boy George as Culture Club's hit blared from the sound system.

"What I did was I drove there, and then I kind of tapped one of the guys with the front bumper of my car."

"Tapped?"

"Uh-huh."

"You broke both his legs with your car, Punch."

"Oh."

"Rico? What'd he do exactly?"

"He . . . uh . . . he dealt with the second guy himself. I stayed in the car."

Tommy chose to speak to Punch. "He beat that fucker with every piece of scrap metal he could find, didn't he?"

"In a way."

Biaggio soaked in what he already knew.

"Those guys—the boys that you and my son practically crippled—are very close to Don Sacco. They're made. Frederico's friend at the scrap yard is a nobody. He's just a guy my son knows from around Brooklyn. So to impress this scrap guy, Rico makes ugly with Don Sacco's men. Do you see what I'm getting at, Punch?"

"Holy shit," groaned Punch. "I swear to my mother I didn't know."

∞

Sal's co-retiree, Greg O'Halloran, approached the party DJ as Donna Summer's "She Works Hard For the Money" had the dance floor moving. The disc jockey left his turntables and navigated over a few plastic milk crates that were filled with records. He was a dark-haired Italian cobra in his mid-twenties, skin like an egg cream and as taut and wiry as the gold chain around his neck. He had the voice of a Coney Island sideshow barker.

"What's up?"

"Hey, buddy, you wouldn't happen to have any Irish music would ya?" Greg shouted over the pounding bass.

"Say again?"

"Irish music?"

The DJ thought for a minute as he tapped his hand on the table that separated him from Greg.

"I could spin somethin' from U2. You fancy that?"

Greg appeared puzzled.

"I might have the Boomtown Rats, but I dunno . . ."

"I was thinking about the Clancy Brothers or perhaps Christy Moore?"

The DJ leaned in closer to aid his hearing.

"Dinty Moore?"

Greg felt a familiar bear hug from behind him. Sal Salerno.

"Go 'head, Greg. You asking to make the music louder?" Sal laughed.

"Just asking for some Irish songs, Sal." O'Halloran chuckled.

"Any luck?"

"Not too much."

"I don't think I got what he wants, Pope," shouted the DJ in his thick Brooklyn accent.

"With all those records?" asked Sal. "I think I've heard the same song about twenty times tonight. At least they all sound the same."

"Ah, gimme a fuckin' break over here, Pope," said the DJ with a smile.

"You played Italian music. I heard Jerry Vale and Al Martino before," said Greg. "How come nothing Irish?"

"Hey, I ain't exactly gettin' paid for this here. I'm doin' it for Pope and his friends. Now I'm gonna get worked over by all yous lorry drivers?"

Greg turned to Sal. "Lorry drivers?"

Sal just waved it off.

"Yous get all mullered and gang up on me over here."

"Mullered?" asked Greg.

Sal took his former co-worker aside.

"Sometimes this kid uses British phrases. Don't ask me why. He's my friend, Tommy's nephew. We call him 'Winnie.'"

"Vinny?"

"No. 'Winnie.' He's a good kid and a good barber. He does this music on the side, and tonight he's doing it as a favor," said Sal over the din of the speaker system. "You think the company was gonna pay for music? Hell, they crammed three of us into one party."

"I hear ya."

"I'll work it out for you, Greg."

The third retiree, Wali Chattopadhyay, sauntered up beside them. "I'm guessing there's not much hope in hearing some Ganasangeet then?"

⟡

Punch the Pedal sat alone in the corner, warm drink in hand. He studied the final meager ice cube in his glass as it melted to nothing. Gone was the smile he'd brought to every other party.

Biaggio stood several feet away, chatting with Tommy and Punch's longtime friend Carbone—the bearded, string bean gear head who helped Punch switch cars so many times, including when he brought Vito in for Peter's wedding a dozen years before. Carbone's loyalty and quiet manner earned him the trust of Falcone and the boys, and he had recently been welcomed to the inner circle.

"What, they didn't have no overalls to match that tie?" joked Tommy, finding the sight of Carbone wrapped in a tailored suit quite whimsical.

"I got nice clothes. I'm supposed to work on cars dressed like fuckin' Liberace or something?"

Over Carbone's pointy shoulder Tommy could see a rather ruffled, burly yeoman striding toward them. He was coming fast. Tommy quickly got his large frame between the stranger and Biaggio.

"Where you going, boss?" asked Tommy with his hand on the man's chest. Carbone began to walk Falcone backward toward Punch's chair. Punch shook from his trance and hurried to join his friends.

Winnie was spinning a track from a brand new artist who

was about to make her debut in the Top 100. "Holiday! Celebrate!" urged Madonna over the throbbing bass.

The robust stranger was sweating as he spoke. "Forgive me, please. I just wanted to speak with Mr. Falcone, if I might."

"Does he know you?" Tommy asked, his meaty hand still just above the man's rib cage.

"No, sir. My name is Travis. Travis Greenwood. I'm here as a friend of Greg's."

"Who?"

"Greg O'Halloran. One of the retirees."

"Don't know him. We're here for somebody else."

"I know. I . . . I just was hoping to maybe offer my friendship to Mr. Falcone."

Tommy was straightening the man's tie now.

"You need something," he said.

"W-Well," stammered Greenwood, "I would like a favor. But I'm willing to repay."

"You're in a jam, eh?"

"Yes, sir. I am. I think I could help Mr. Falcone as well, though," Greenwood said as he lowered his tone to a whisper. "I'm a CO, a corrections officer. I'm about to be made a captain."

"Good for you. Listen, Mr. Falcone will be taking meetings with community members next week. He's always willing to help if he can. I will give you a business card. You call and make an appointment, okay?"

"But I—"

"That's the end of it, Mr. Greenwood. Next week. No off-duty weapon either, *capisce*?"

Vito Salerno led the cheers, nearly jumping up and down as his cousin approached the makeshift podium. It was Sal's turn to make his retirement speech. This was the moment he dreaded. Public speaking was not his favorite pastime. Though he knew most of the gathered revelers, there were many strangers as well. He approached the table and microphone setup uneasily as Winnie faded the music from his nearby DJ area. Waiting for Sal was a small, bespectacled fellow from the cola company—some fourth- or fifth-level VP. He handed Sal a velvet case, opened to reveal the gold watch for the photos that began snapping almost immediately.

"Uh, thank you very much," mumbled Sal. He could see cousin Vito clearing the way to make sure Joey had a view from his seat. "I think I only talked into one of these microphones once in my life, and they unplugged it on me."

The crowd laughed, but only a select few caught his reference. Punch smiled at Tommy as they realized Sal meant the time he crashed a sanctioned meeting in the summer of '67. He was looking to tear the head off the guy who'd put a gun to his son's head in Vito's pizzeria.

"I'll be quick because my wife is more superstitious than her eighty-seven-year-old mother. She thinks retirement celebrations seal your fate for an early death."

Laughter.

"That's why I calmly explained to her that this is Greg and Wali's party."

Louder laughs.

"But I have been working here since 1945, and I'm happy to say this job gave me much more than just a bad back and some hemorrhoids. It gave me the chance to work outside most of the time. I'm not really an office guy. It gave me a means to take care of my family, and it gave me a sense of pride and responsibility. Also, a shitload of free soda."

Mary just shook her head as everyone howled. Joey sported a huge grin as Vito held his hand. He was happy that his "uncle" was with him and not spending the whole night across the room with the fellas from the barbershop.

"To my wife Mary, I would like to say, most of the 1940s I gave happily to Uncle Sam. The 50s and 60s was the time to raise our wonderful boys. The 1970s, well, Peter married Kathy, they gave us two beautiful grandkids, and I won $200 because Secretariat won by more than twenty lengths."

"Comedian," muttered Mary as she tried to hide her smile.

"Well, sweetheart," continued Sal, "from 1983 onwards belongs to you."

All at once, the women let out an audible sigh. Mary smiled as her eyes welled up.

"Uh, well, thank you all and God bless," concluded Sal as he exhaled.

He was mobbed as he stepped away from the table, shaking hands and getting pats on the back. Flashbulbs flickered as Winnie got back to the music. He was about to spin "Celebration" by Kool and the Gang, but, as he saw Sal approach Mary, he dug out a recently popular slow dance number. Peter held Kathy's hand as he watched his father walk into retirement. He saw him march directly toward his wife of nearly forty years.

"So, the eighties belong to me?" asked Mary with a raised brow.

"You heard me."

From the turntable, Lionel Richie promised to always have her heart and to be there forever.

Truly.

"Can I come with you tomorrow?" Mary asked her husband as they began to dance to the unfamiliar ballad.

"Where?"

"You know. When you visit your friends."

"You don't mind?"

"No. I want to be with you, Sal."

⚮

On the first Monday morning of his retirement, Sal didn't sleep a minute later than usual. He awoke, dressed Joey, fed him breakfast, and took him over to his aunt's house. He made Mary promise to sleep a little later. He wanted to use his new free time to give her a little break.

She'd been caring for a child for four decades. Upon his return from dropping off Joey with his aunt, he found his wife awake and dressed, with hot coffee on the kitchen table.

They walked arm-in-arm through the crisp morning air. The only sounds being an occasional sparrow chirp and the constant crunching of dead leaves beneath their feet. Far off in the distance might be the faint rumble of a truck, or a car horn that sounded no greater than the tweeting bird. The dirt below them was hard and cold. They'd already knelt and prayed at the grave of Sal's parents. Mary had done that with him many times before. But on each cemetery visit, she would sit in the information center while Sal continued on his journey alone. True to her word, that would no longer be the case. She crossed herself while her husband placed a small bouquet on the grave of Luigi Scotti. His headstone was well-worn, as he had passed on in 1949. Sal remembered him as both a kind old barber and as Punch the Pedal's grandfather.

Mary saw him in a different light. The same light that shone on all of those from the barbershop. They were a disgrace to hard-working Italians across the world. Phony and blasphemous, taking communion with blood on the soles of their shoes. No matter to her that Mr. Scotti had never injured or killed anything more than a housefly or the sickly tree he had removed from the front of his shop. He knew what the others were doing, and he harbored them and lied on their behalf. Worst of all, her own husband had become some version of Mr. Scotti right before her eyes. She knew Sal would never cause harm to anyone, but how much did he really know about the activities of Biaggio Falcone and his minions? Sal and Mr. Scotti were one thing, but Mary swallowed hard as she and her husband took the short walk to the next tombstone. Sal's eyes welled up and his face changed, but Mary felt nothing. She knew she stood at the crypt of a killer. Sal stood at the grave of a friend. He knelt and placed the flowers in front of the cold, hard stone.

"Staten Island" Lou Romano
B: 10-15-1909 — D: 07-02-1968

"I just wish they'd let me see Nicky in prison before I wind up visiting him here."

206

Chapter Twenty-Six

THE FORTY-STORY, black-aluminum-and-darkened-glass Bankers Trust Plaza building was quite impressive and somewhat intimidating against the lower Manhattan skyline. That is, until one turned around and looked up at the two buildings across the street to the north. Nearly three times the height of the Bankers Trust structure, One and Two World Trade Center were wondrous giants that dwarfed even the mighty Empire State Building since they were completed roughly a dozen years prior to this day that brought Tommy and Punch into their majestic shadow.

Lower Manhattan was bustling around lunchtime, but there was serenity, space, and balm among the benches in World Trade Plaza. The sun shone directly upon them and warmly illuminated the twenty-five-foot gleaming bronze sphere that sat proudly atop the lush water fountain. The fountain provided a soothing, natural soundtrack that almost drown out the rest of New York City if the wind was just right. Riding on that same breeze would be the enticing scents of the various foods offered by the vendors conducting business under their brightly colored umbrellas.

"I think it's stupid that we had to come all the way down here. Parking's a joke," mumbled Punch.

"We're not in a position to complain," responded Tommy.

He knew that Don Sacco had some type of business with Bankers Trust and that his top underling, Jackie "Moose" Musumeci, spent a lot of his time in the area. Since the don often fled to Florida as soon as New York's air turned chilly, he wouldn't be at the meeting himself—just Moose. Accordingly, Biaggio decided to send Tommy in his stead; he felt he might be demeaning himself to meet with the subordinate of another family head.

"I was in a movie right here," said Punch, the smoky scent of hot pretzels filling their noses.

"Another movie? *Madone.*"

"Yeah. King Kong."

"You're crazy. That movie's from when I was a kid."

"No, Tommy. The remake. I was here about eight or nine years ago. There was an ad in the paper. They wanted a crowd here for when Kong fell off the Twin Towers. They broke up fake concrete shit all over the floor and the big, fake monkey layin' right on top of it."

"I never saw the remake. What's the point?"

Punch spotted a barrel chest in a long black coat approaching from the direction of the Bankers Trust building. All Punch knew about that particular skyscraper was that he sat in one of its highest floors on July 4, 1976 to take in the beauty of Operation Sail. His girlfriend at the time knew someone who knew someone who invited her and a guest to the celebration. He fondly recalled the parade of sailing ships that skirted the Statue of Liberty on their way up the Hudson that sunny day. Oddly though, his greatest recollections of that time were the painted footprints of King Kong that had been stamped around the area to promote the release of the film in which he had appeared. He remembered how eager he was to see if he could spot himself on the big screen. No luck. He now had a VHS player but still hadn't been able to find a tape of the movie.

The black-coated sparkplug of a man grew closer, like a tall ship on the Hudson.

"I guess this is him," said Punch.

Tommy turned to see Moose pushing back his greasy hair. He stood to greet the man who was nearly thirty years his junior.

"Hello, Moose."

He received a nod in response. Moose arrived along with the warm smell of honey-roasted nuts.

"No Falcone?" were the first words from his mouth.

"No," said Tommy. "He was going to come, but he received word that Don Sacco was unavailable."

"What about the kid? Rico? Where's he?"

"Not here. I brought Punch. He was there on the day in question."

"Well, that's not too good. No Biaggio and no Rico."

"You and I can make this work, Moose. Let's talk."

"My don wanted to hear from Rico. At least he deserved that respect, no?"

"I apologize for my part," interjected Punch.

Moose ignored him and stood toe to toe with Tommy. From Punch's seat on the bench they towered above him, like the north and south towers behind them.

"What can we do to square this all away with you?" asked Tommy.

"Maybe you and I can go down a back alley and face off," spat Moose. "I heard you're a tough guy."

Tommy just smiled as the man continued yapping.

"You're old now, Tommy. I bet you'd have tangled with me twenty years ago."

"Damn right," said Tommy. "You'd have been about fourteen then, Mr. Wizard."

Moose bit his lip as he replied, "I don't know if we can do much, to be honest. Rico didn't even show up. Now there's a guy I'd like to take down an alley. This princess here wouldn't be much of a challenge." He glared at Punch.

"What is this, junior high?" barked Tommy. "Did Don Sacco send you here to jerk me off or to work out a deal? We came here in good faith."

"I'll tell you what the don wanted. He wanted apologies from Rico Falcone, from Biaggio Falcone and from whoever this *chooch* is. He also wanted some concessions in business terms. He needs a bigger slice. He needs some of Biaggio's pie. It's gonna take a lot to make things right."

"Well, I think for something like that to be on the table, my boss and your boss need to meet nose to nose. I have no power to arrange any of that."

"So I should tell my don that you wasted our time here today?"

"No. We came. Punch already made his apology. Let me arrange to try and get Rico to a meeting. We'll set it up when Don Falcone and Don Sacco can both be present."

"The two men that your guys practically disfigured, they need to be considered too."

With neither nod nor handshake, Jackie the Moose Musumeci turned and headed back toward the blackness of the Bankers Trust building. The scent of roasted nuts was also gone as the breeze shifted. In barged the meaty essence of boiled frankfurters, mustard, and sauerkraut. Punch gave an inquisitive gaze up at Tommy as the fountain beneath the lustrous sphere clamored like a rainstorm.

⌒⌒⌒

One after another, the cold waves of Jamaica Bay would settle onto the marshy grasslands of Floyd Bennett Field. The early morning wind was picking up as Salvatore Salerno stared into the eyes of his accuser.

"You're about to become a murderer."

Sal came prepared, and his readiness became evident as the allegations continued.

"Do you want to lose your soul?"

"No," answered Sal.

"Then don't do it."

It was time for Sal's backup plan.

"I'm not gonna do it. Okay?" He sighed.

"You made the right decision. I'm proud of you, Grandpa," said Lisa as Sal moved the fishing hook away from the slick, bristly eight-inch pile worm.

Lisa was eight years old, all ponytail and tenderness. She

sat, bundled in layers, beside her brother Joseph, who was two years her junior. Peter and Kathy named their son after his uncle Joey, but it was the child who was referred to as Joseph while the uncle retained the more adolescent moniker.

"We're not gonna fish now?" Joseph hollered as if his entire early morning preparation had been wasted. He was slim and spirited, and he had come to the edges of this once-bustling airport to catch a fish.

"We are gonna fish," replied Grandpa Sal. "We just ain't gonna use this here bait worm."

Sal dropped the squirming annelid back into the container, right atop several others.

"You should say a special prayer tonight, Grandpa," suggested Lisa.

"Yeah? But I didn't kill the worm, so my soul should be safe," Sal said and smiled.

"Probably," said Lisa. "But you bought those worms, so you helped keep the people who kill them in business. Just maybe tell God you're sorry."

Sal reached into his tackle box and grabbed a large rubber lure.

"This here is a fake worm. How's that?" he said, smiling as he shook it at the kids.

"At least it don't bite like the real ones," Joseph said, then laughed.

As Sal rigged his lure, he enjoyed how much better it was to spend some time with his grandchildren than to break his back at the cola company. He had his transistor radio with him so he could listen to the horse races later in the day, and he promised the kids some hot sandwiches from Roll-n-Roaster for lunch. Retirement was good. He still had the other job of running numbers, but he thought of that as a hobby with some extra income. He knew that Mary wanted him completely retired, though. "Let a younger man handle those numbers" was how she would phrase it. Years ago it was, "Let some other jackass handle those numbers."

211

Sal's eight-foot pole was all set.

"Now you guys are gonna hold the fishing rod with me."

"We can't hold it ourselves?" asked Lisa.

"Not just yet. Stripers can be big and strong. Each time we come you'll get more used to it." Sal paused for an instant. "Lisa, even if I use the fake worm, wouldn't I still be a murderer once we catch the fish?"

"No," she said as she brushed a strand of windswept hair from her rosy cheek. "Because we will throw him back in the water to be with his family."

The kids grabbed onto the pole and waited for about ten seconds.

"Nothing," yelled Joseph. "Put that real worm on the hook."

Chapter Twenty-Seven

TODAY, BIAGGIO FALCONE would be hearing requests from the denizens of his community.

Two blocks down from the barbershop, Sal and Vito emerged from the salumeria carrying loaded brown paper bags. The darkly tanned ends of freshly baked Italian bread jutted teasingly from the top of the sacks. One of them brushed repeatedly against the small gold crucifix that swayed from Vito's neck. Storm clouds brewed above them as Vito, his head level with his tall cousin's shoulders, rambled on about his latest young girlfriend.

"So I says to her, 'How come in the furniture store you keep callin' it a sofa, but once I pay for it and you get it home it becomes a freakin' couch?'"

"Leave that poor girl alone, will ya?"

"Hey, Pope," came a yell from behind them.

They turned to see a scruffy, curly-haired fellow rolling up behind them. The double amputee sat not in a wheelchair, but atop a flat wooden dolly with a piece of mildewed carpet serving as its seat. His hands were tucked into a pair of withered, leather driving gloves.

"Hey, J.J.," said Sal with a smile.

"What's cookin'?" added Vito.

"Just wanna get my number, Pope. I got a good feeling today."

"Sure thing."

Sal handed his grocery bag to Vito, who was now practically hidden behind the sacks of cold cuts and breads.

As Sal went about the business of recording the man's three digit lottery pick, Vito's nose was almost touching the soft, toasty loaves.

"Listen," said the legless man as he finished his transaction, "tell Joey that he owes me a shoeshine, okay?"

Sal almost said "sure thing" again, but he caught himself.

"Get outta here, J.J." He laughed. "You better get inside before it pours over here."

Vito handed a bag back to his cousin as J.J. wheeled away. The top of the bread had been gnawed off.

"Who told you to eat the bread?"

"I like plain bread. You get everything with seeds. Bread, bagels, sausage . . . "

"Seeds are good, Vito. Almost everything starts with a seed. Even you, you jackass."

Vito spotted a lanky man slipping a bag over the top of a parking meter rather than dropping a coin into its slot. The fellow turned—rather nervously—revealing two colossal, protruding eyes. They locked with Vito's.

"Whoa! Long time, no see, Sally Eyeballs," yelled Vito as crumbs dropped from his lips.

"Oh, yeah. How's it hangin', Vito?" Sally twitched.

"You remember my cousin, right?"

"Yeah. The Pope. The numbers guy. Good to see you again, Pope."

"Doing well. How's life treating you?"

"Why don't you come down to the barbershop and see the fellas?" interrupted Vito.

"No time. No time today. I'm running some errands for . . . " Sally Eyeballs finished his sentence by merely touching the tip of his nose.

"Oh," nodded Vito. "How's he doing?"

"Fair. But he's been feeling some heat, y'know? What do you hear from Nicky the Zipper?"

"Eh. He's still got some time to do. I got to see him a few weeks ago. He ain't the same."

"That's a shame. Well, next time you see him, give him my regards. Tell the boys I was asking for them too."

"Will do," said Vito. "Give my best to . . . " Vito touched the tip of his nose.

"I will. Take care. You too, Pope."

Eyeballs was gone. He walked briskly toward the Jewish deli with the "Hebrew National" poster in the window. Though the deli had been here for years, at one time it was probably the only non-Italian food shop on the avenue. There had been a Chinese restaurant around the corner for quite a while too, but now there was also a Russian establishment and a couple of Korean businesses with signs that weren't in English. Truth be told, Biaggio could have final say over these things, but they didn't bother him in the least—as long as the proprietors acquiesced to long-standing neighborhood protocol, and did so promptly, in cash. His son, Rico, harbored very different feelings on the matter.

"Sally Eyeballs," mumbled Vito to himself as his thoughts turned to the mozzarella and tomato he was going to pile on that tasty Italian bread.

They walked side by side down the avenue as they had done thousands of times before. Sal and Vito, like a tall and short comedy team from days gone by. If not for a few more pounds and facial lines, and a few less hairs to comb, this could have been that summer day in 1945 when Sal, still in his military garb, saw the beating outside Scotti's barbershop. He could remember the lemon ice and the Glenn Miller tune on the radio. It was the day that cousin Vito ran up behind him and breathlessly announced his upcoming wedding. It could be that day today. Except that day was sunny, and today, thunder could be heard over the East River. The cars were very different too; and there were no Russian or Korean storefronts back then.

"What's this?" asked Vito, chewing more bread as Scotti's barbershop came into view.

Several people stood in line outside the shop. That was to

be expected as they all probably had something they wanted from Biaggio Falcone. But there was a television camera with a big light on it. A young news reporter was trying to interview Rico as he walked from his car to the shop.

"Mr. Falcone, do you have a response to those who claim you are next in line to head up the Campigotto crime family?"

"You're mistaken. I'm a working man just like you. I sell carpeting."

"The FBI describes you as acting underboss. Is that an accurate description?"

"Can I get inside?"

"Is it true that you've angered other crime families by what they perceive to be arrogance?"

Rico stopped and looked into the reporters eye's as Sal and Vito were almost at the shop.

"I sell carpets."

"It's impressive how your father has avoided prison for so long. Has he given you any tips on how to stay one step ahead of the law?"

His face turning just a little red, Rico calmly placed one of his strong hands over the microphone in the reporter's hand. He pushed the hand down by the questioner's side and leaned in toward his ear.

"You know what kind of carpets I sell?" whispered the angry Falcone.

The reporter, his bravado waning, shook his head ever so slightly.

"The kind your whole family could be wrapped up in."

The reporter was pale now. Rico sported a grin normally found on a Halloween mask.

Giving the "cut" sign to his cameraman, the newsman turned away just as the camera light was terminated. Vito handed his grocery bag to Sal. An empty white paper sleeve, that once wrapped a full loaf of bread, took flight in the heavy breeze, leaving a trail of breadcrumbs in its wake. Sal lugged all the bags into the barbershop while Vito remained outside with Rico. They watched the local news van drive away, as did several of the queued residents.

As Sal entered the barbershop, he was greeted by that familiar scent: a welcoming cocktail of talc, tonics, and Barbicide. It splashed him in the face like some phantom aftershave. There was Joey, propped up in the barber chair, raised high off the floor. He was getting a trim, not from Punch the Pedal but from Tommy's nephew Winnie, the barber/DJ who had helmed the wheels of steel at Sal's retirement party. Joey's shiny shoe tapped along to the radio as John Lennon warned the world of instant karma. It had been three years since the former Beatle was taken away by some cowardly monster in a bizarre quest for his own immortality, but his songs were being played now more than ever, and Joey adored them. Today was the day that Biaggio was taking requests from the neighborhood, yet over the years Joey had only one real request. He would raise his left hand, pinch his fingers together and point afar. Most, including Biaggio, laughed and assumed this indicated Joey's normal desire to accompany the boys to the bar and have the one cold beer that Sal would permit. It was Peter who had his own opinion on what Joey's request of Biaggio Falcone truly was, and he kept it to himself. You see, Joey had always used his right hand for the "drink" signal, and he offered it to all. This left-handed variation had only appeared a few years ago, and it normally presented itself when there was mention or evocation of anything Beatles-related. It was only brandished in the presence of Biaggio. Peter was almost certain that his older brother, who had never solicited anything more than a shoeshine in his entire life, wanted desperately for the omnipotent Biaggio Falcone to rid the planet of the one who murdered John Lennon.

Peter never told a soul about his theory, as most assumed Joey knew little, if anything, about Biaggio's actual position or the fact that cutting hair was not the most pressing issue in Scotti's barbershop. Peter knew his brother had substantial physical challenges, but he had the gift of sight and sound, and was vastly more intelligent than a glance would reveal.

Sal nodded to Tommy, who stood just inside the door. He was waiting for the okay to let those who wanted their moment with Biaggio inside—little by little. There were three chairs along the wall that would serve as the indoor waiting area; then, one by one, the local residents would be granted their few moments in the back room with the don.

"He's just about done, Pope," said Winnie as Sal rested the grocery bags on a counter top.

"Looks good," yelled Tommy from his position by the door. He smoothed his dark-blue pullover across his bulging midsection. He had taken to wearing sweaters not long after the Times Square button-popping incident.

The shop was crowded, but Joey was the only one there for a haircut. Buzzing between the front and back rooms, in addition to Winnie and Tommy, were Johnny the Beatnik, Carbone, and Biaggio himself. Right behind Sal came Vito and Frederico through the front door.

"Nice, Joey," said Sal. "You look like John Travolta!"

"Hmmmm."

As Johnny and Carbone meandered around near the barber chairs, Winnie gathered them and stood them behind Joey, who sat up regally on his elevated throne. There they stood on either side of Joey's freshly cut grin, maybe the only two in the neighborhood with such majestic beards.

"Look! It's ZZ Top," Winnie said and laughed as Joey sat, clean-shaven, framed by the hairy duo.

"Who?" asked Sal.

"Ah, never mind," shrugged the young barber as he kiddingly waved his scissor at Carbone's facial hair.

"I still can't believe my father lets you two walk around like that," huffed Rico.

"He understands that Jesus had a beard," answered Johnny the Beatnik.

"Yeah," replied Rico. "When you walk on water you should have one too."

Biaggio appeared from the back room just as John

Lennon was exalting the masses to shine on like the sun. The song was nearly over and Joey afforded Falcone his special left-handed plea.

"Nice haircut, kid. We'll get that drink later, okay?" promised Biaggio.

WNBC then segued into a new song by Prince. Biaggio didn't mind when Winnie played the popular music AM station, and even brash-talking radio personality Don Imus was fine, as long as the station was changed when Howard Stern came on in the afternoon.

"No Punch yet?" whined Falcone. "I need him here."

Thinking for a moment, he turned to Carbone.

"Can you do me a favor? I need you to go down to the garment district and meet with Murray Carr. We've been bunking heads a little bit and I want you to relay a message for me."

"Of course."

"Has anyone tried to call Punch?" asked Falcone as Sal was taking his ring of keys back from Joey.

"I tried," said Carbone. "He's probably got those headphones on listening to that "Learn Spanish" junk again. How 'bout I go over to his place. I got a key."

"I need you to go meet Murray Carr."

"I could take a walk over there," offered Sal. "I gotta collect some numbers down that way anyways."

"Great. Thank you, Pope. Give him that key, Carbone."

Sal accepted the keys to Punch's building just as he returned his own keys to Joey—a token of his continuous vow to return to his son.

"Vito, keep an eye on Joey for me, okay?"

"Where's there a safer place for Joey?" Vito asked with a laugh. "Maybe he'll give us all some nice shines, right Joe?"

"Hmmmmm."

"Maybe I'll be on the TV tonight, Sally," continued Vito to his cousin. "If they show that Rico thing on the news, they'll say, 'Here he is with his bodyguard, Vito "the Jockey" Salerno!'"

"Bodyguard?" Rico chuckled as he surveyed the much smaller and older Salerno.

"You're still trying to give yourself that 'Jockey' nickname," Tommy chimed in. "Ain't gonna happen."

"I don't get no respect around here," Vito said with a laugh.

"You'll have the respect of an old bluesman," added Winnie as he dusted the hair from the towel on Joey's shoulders.

"Eh?"

"I mean like Muddy Waters or Robert Johnson," replied Winnie. "They were underappreciated for decades. Then their songs were played by Clapton, Hendrix, and the Stones, and the world loves them. One day, it will dawn on everyone how important you are and, well, Bob's your uncle."

"My uncle? Muddy Waters? What the fuck are you talkin' about?" Vito smiled and pointed at Winnie. "Even he's got a freakin' nickname!"

"You want my nickname? You can have it. You think I like going around being called Winnie? What am I, a storybook bear? I look like I got a bowl of honey on me?"

"You know it ain't the bear," added Tommy Box o' Cookies. "It's cause you talk like Churchill."

"Well," muttered Winnie, "Winston woulda been a better name."

As Sal headed out the door, he heard Biaggio ask Rico if the TV news had been out front and what they had wanted.

The clouds were moving quickly now as Sal passed the line of people awaiting their invitation to see Falcone. Some were staring into space while others practiced their pleas to themselves. He had the key to Punch the Pedal's building gripped firmly in his palm.

⌒⌒

Biaggio stood to greet his first well-wisher. It was in the back room, which was Falcone's large, functional office; not all leather and fine wood as one might expect, but more like the brightly lit workspace of the finance manager at a car dealership. On either side of the room stood Johnny the Beatnik and Vito Salerno. They were there for Biaggio's safety (Johnny) and to get drinks and napkins and silence all distractions (Vito). After being patted down at the front door by Tommy, three of the guests would sit in the front room amongst the barber chairs, listening to Winnie's radio and thumbing nervously through magazines. Occasionally someone would come in for an actual haircut. Those customers weren't frisked because they were not there to enter the back room to meet Biaggio. A haircut is a haircut.

The first one in to see Falcone was a young man barely into his twenties. He wore a clean suit that needed some pressing and there were some nicks on his neck from a hurried shave.

"Hello, Mr. Falcone. Thank you for seeing me," he said.

Biaggio directed him to his chair and then went around to sit behind his desk across from the youthful fellow. The room was quiet, save for the bubbling of Falcone's prized aquarium.

"Would you like a drink? Are you old enough to drink?" smiled Biaggio. "We can get you a soda."

"No, thank you, sir."

"Well then, what can I help you with?"

"I am here to ask for an entry-level position," said the man as he cleared his throat.

"A job?" asked Falcone as he looked at Johnny the Beatnik. "So you have experience in the carpet business?"

"No, sir."

"Well, I don't really have any openings right now. We don't run a large business."

"With all respect, Mr. Falcone, I'm not talking about carpeting."

"Okay," said Biaggio as his face hardened just a little. "But please choose your words carefully."

"The Campigotto family," replied the young man.

Biaggio began to stand, which would mean that the meeting was over.

"Please listen, sir."

Johnny began to walk toward the guest.

"The Campigotto blood family . . . "

Johnny had his hand on the guy's shoulder as Vito approached as well.

"Mr. Falcone, my great-great-grandfather was known as Don Campigotto."

Biaggio put his hand up to pause Johnny and Vito. The fresh-faced man continued. "I am told that you once worked for him. That he treated you well. That you were his hand-picked replacement. My name is Mario Campigotto. I want to work for the family that still carries my surname."

Johnny took his hand off the fellow's shoulder. Biaggio stood frozen for a moment, then slowly returned to his chair. He stared into the man's youthful brown eyes.

"Did you say great-great-grandfather?"

"Yes sir."

A deep breath.

"I am fucking old."

∽

Sal headed quickly up the avenue as the storm clouds darkened. He shot into a gas station on the corner to get some numbers and scratch from the workers inside. While there, he used their phone to ring Punch once again. Still no answer. He grabbed a box of Cracker Jack that he would feed to Joey later. Mary said it made their son cough, but Sal knew his boy loved the sweet caramel popcorn and was always thrilled to discover his prize. Sal tucked the box into his outer jacket pocket. The gaming numbers and cash went to the inside pocket.

∽

Biaggio was personally escorting the young Campigotto out of his office and into the front of the barbershop. He had his arm around the young man's shoulder. The next three guests looked up as they passed.

"So, I want you to come back with your father. Is your father's father still alive?"

"No."

"My regrets. Just set up a meeting between your father and me. Tommy here will tell you when."

"I'm not sure if my father—"

"He'll come. Tell him it's a favor I ask of him."

Before stopping by the front door to make arrangements with Tommy, the ambitious tenderfoot grasped Biaggio's calloused right hand between his palms. He leaned in and placed a kiss upon the gold ring on Falcone's pinky. He then looked up and gave a slight bow.

"I thank you, Don Falcone."

"Very dramatic," said Biaggio. "You watch a lot of movies."

Behind them, by the barber chairs, Winnie was entertaining Joey. As Rico sat near them leafing through a copy of *Guns & Ammo*, Winnie had both of his hands covered with black socks. On each sock were two cotton balls that functioned as eyes. Joey laughed almost uncontrollably as Winnie had the sock puppets engage in a war of Italian curse words. The two men and one woman in wait for Biaggio offered little reaction to the disconcerting scene of an aspiring gangster kissing the ring of his desired family head while a vulgar puppet show transpired in their wake.

⤬

Sal reached the front steps of Punch's building. He climbed them with the keys in hand. There were three labeled doorbells, but he knew the middle one belonged to Punch. He pressed it twice and waited. He knew it would be fruitless to see if Punch's car was parked on the street because he kept it secure in a windowless garage around the corner.

⤬

Johnny the Beatnik led the next visitor into the backroom. Tommy patted down the first in line to come in from the street, as he did with all the other men. For the female, he

223

politely asked her to open her bulging purse, which he went through quickly and cordially. Embarrassed by the presence of some tampons, he saw nothing that wasn't soft, fluffy, or feminine.

Rico simmered in his seat as his father now had the sock puppets on his hands, entertaining Joey. How mortifying for the younger Falcone to watch his father dancing with puppets on the day the neighborhood came to see him.

"Hey, I'm Vito. Somebody gimme a nickname for Christ's sake," said Biaggio as he held an unlit cigar in the mouth of the puppet.

"You gotta earn your nickname," replied the other puppet. "I'm Tommy Box o' Cookies. I got my name because I eat like a lion in a zebra cage."

Everyone laughed loudly, save for Rico and the guests awaiting the backroom.

As Biaggio slipped the black socks off his hands, Vito yelled out from the doorway to the back.

"Very funny, but you'd better wash your hands good, Boss."

Biaggio looked down to see Winnie standing barefoot.

"*Vaffancul*," Biaggio said with a sigh as Joey laughed even louder at the obscenity. Joey made his right-handed "drink" request.

"You're a good kid, Joe," said Biaggio. "All you ever want is that half a glass of beer. God bless you."

Almost immediately, Joey shot up his left hand, pinched his fingers together and growled his other request. Biaggio smiled as he washed his hands in the barbershop sink. Sal's key ring rested on Joey's lap as Biaggio headed back to meet with his next visitor. Rico's face was a fevered vermilion.

∽

Sal got no response from the third and forth bell rings. Just as he was about to use the key to enter Punch's building, he was interrupted by a gaggle of umbrella-toting housewives— a slight, but icy, drizzle began to swathe South Brooklyn.

"There's the best and handsomest numbers guy in town! Hey there, Sal," bellowed one of the women as they all had their chosen digits at the ready.

∽

Leaving the back room was Travis Greenwood, the man who approached Biaggio at Sal's retirement party. He was wearing his newest and best suit, but he didn't wear a smile. He said nothing as he passed Tommy, who held the front door for him as he left the barbershop. A misty rain washed in the front door as those in line outside huddled under umbrellas or folded newspapers. They all eyed Greenwood and saw the disappointment in his face. A meeting with Biaggio Falcone was not an ironclad guarantee of help.

Next up to meet him was the woman. As with Mr. Greenwood, she was impeccably dressed for the occasion. She looked quite lovely in her dark blue, knee-length skirt and matching blazer. Her olive complexion complemented her big dark eyes. She appeared to be in her late thirties, but could have easily been forty years of age.

Vito noticed the lack of a wedding band. Biaggo noticed the lack of a smile. The handbag that Tommy ruffled through was fashioned from fine Italian leather. As Falcone stood and approached her, she finally flashed something of a grin. Perfect white teeth framed by full, healthy lips. Not much makeup at all.

"Hello, young lady. Welcome. I'm Biaggio Falcone."

She said her name was Lucy; she appeared a little uneasy, or perhaps intimidated.

"You can relax, Lucy. We don't bite." Biaggio said with a smile as he looked at Vito and Johnny.

∽

Sal recorded all the ladies' numbers and sent them happily on their way. They chatted and giggled as they moved swiftly down the avenue. Sal wanted to get in from the rain. Even if Punch wasn't home, maybe he could make a cup of coffee, warm up, and wait a little while for him to show. He turned the key and opened the door to a shared hallway. There was an apartment door to his left, but Punch's place was above that one, up the flight of stairs. The hallway was dark; the single bulb was missing and any sunlight was suffocated today by the immense cloud cover. On the second or third step, Sal slipped on something that coated a small area of the staircase.

Dog shit?

No. Maybe it was grease or something, but he couldn't smell anything and it was too dark to inspect closely. It didn't seem to be on all the steps, just here and there. Maybe someone dragged in something on their shoes. He got to the top landing and knocked on Punch's door.

No response.

He thought he heard something behind the door.

"Punch," he yelled.

He put his ear close to the door. Maybe it was the TV or a radio. Sounded like a man's voice. He pressed tighter against Punch's door. Ever so slightly, it opened.

⟨∽⟩

With the rain coming down a little harder, some of the folks lined up outside the barbershop were asking Tommy if they could come inside and wait in the dry warmth of Scotti's. He explained that he had to pat down each person and that there wasn't enough seating inside for all. Most didn't want to ruffle feathers and were very compliant. A couple of men, while remaining respectful, wondered aloud if they were to get a haircut while they waited would they be permitted inside as paying customers were.

Biaggio heard the commotion from the back room and waved Johnny to go out and help Tommy with the situation. Carbone left for the garment district, Winnie was cutting hair, and Rico was likely to go overboard with unnecessary violence. Joey was shining the shoes that Winnie removed for the puppet show, though the barber had his socks back on. "Instant Karma" still rang in Joey's head while he buffed the leather footwear.

Johnny left Biaggio and Vito in the back with the woman. She sat across the desk from Falcone. Vito soaked in her elegance as he leaned on a cabinet eating a quickly prepared sandwich. The woman politely declined an offer of food and drink.

"It has taken me a long time to build up the courage to come see you," she told Biaggio, oblivious to the activity in the front room behind her. Falcone was taken by her comeliness, but even more so by her posture. She sat straight in her chair like some resplendent drill sergeant.

Her delicate, ambrosial perfume captivated Biaggio as she continued. "I have battled with myself for many years before deciding that I had to come here. This is the only way to solve my problem, if it can be solved at all."

"Well, I hope I can help you. I'll certainly try."

"You knew my father, Mr. Falcone," she said.

∽

Sal slowly entered Punch's apartment. In the kitchen, he slid on another patch of the greasy substance. He heard a droning male voice resonating from another room.

"Deaf," stated the deep, dispassionate voice as Sal reached for the light switch.

Rain tapped on the windows as the kitchen light came on. The slippery substance on the floor was a thick golden brown. *At least it's not blood.*

If Sal carried a gun, he may have taken it out at this point, but it remained stuffed in the back of a drawer at home, and he had been meaning to give it to Peter anyway.

"*Sordo,*" announced the voice in a cold baritone.

"Deaf. *Sordo,*" it repeated.

Sal realized he was listening to a recorded Spanish lesson, but he didn't call out to Punch. He wondered if maybe he shouldn't have turned the kitchen light on in the first place.

"Death."

He walked cautiously in the direction of the voice, sidestepping some more grease where the kitchen met the living room.

"Death. *Muerte*."

Sal didn't look for a light switch in the living room; the kitchen's glare flickered benignly to the corners of the carpeted roost. He was drawing closer to the voice.

"Demon."

⌒⌒

"It's like ancestry day here," said Biaggio, smiling at the woman who sat like a sleek arrow across his desk. "You say I knew your father, Lucy. Well, at least that makes me feel better than the kid who said I knew his great-great-grandpa!"

By the far wall, Vito snickered into his sandwich. He watched a black molly peck at some algae on the aquarium glass.

"*You* knew him as well," offered the woman as her head swiveled toward Vito like some posturing owl. She turned back toward Falcone as Vito's smile faded.

"My childhood was not happy," she continued. "We were taken far away to a cold, cold place. My brother and I were told we needed a change of scenery. Turned out, our new scenery featured miles upon miles of nothing."

The story seemed a little off-point to Biaggio, but he let her go on.

"In time, we got accustomed to the desolation. I got older and less prone to feelings—bad or otherwise. Then, as a teenager, I met a boy who made me smile. He introduced me to rock 'n' roll music, which was very new at the time."

"Ma'am," smiled Biaggio.

"I'm rambling, I know. Just another minute, please. That music made me happy. For the first time since I was very small, something brought me joy. Well, the boyfriend did, but it was more the life—and the youth—in the music."

"Good." Biaggio sighed, trying to show compassion.

"Ever hear of the Surf Ballroom?" she said, her voice raising slightly.

"I don't . . . "

"My boyfriend took me there. It's in Iowa, where we were forced to live."

228

"Miss Lucy—"

"It was the best night of my life. We danced like you wouldn't believe. Such sheer pleasure. Youthful, innocent joy. The place was filled with the wonder of something new. It was our time. We were right there with our idols. They stood on the stage smiling, sweating, and being with us in the moment. Then my favorite, Buddy Holly, sang "Rave On" while we all danced like hellcats. We went home so happy. Then I awoke to find out that Buddy Holly was dead. So were Ritchie Valens, the Big Bopper, and their pilot, Roger Peterson. Nobody ever remembers his name. They were all smiling with us the night before and then they were gone. Stone cold dead in a plane crash out in the middle of my nowhere."

Though seldom at a loss for words, Biaggio wasn't sure how to respond to this.

"Like Glenn Miller," offered Vito, only to be ignored.

"May I?" she asked Biaggio, as she placed her gleaming purse on his desk. She undid the burnished clasp and reached inside. Biaggio thought she might be retrieving an old photo of her father, but instead she pulled out something soft and white. Off-white, really. Furry and old.

~∞~

"Demon. *Demonio.*"

Sal continued in the direction of the deep drone. The rain pelted the windows as an old, black cable from an aerial antenna whipped noisily against them in the wind. He wanted to call out to Punch, but something told him not to. The bedroom was just past the living room and off to the side. Sal could tell the door was ajar, and there seemed to be some dim light filtering through. The voice was coming from that bedroom.

"Devil."

There was a heavy trophy on a table in the living room. Looked like some kind of replica from an auto race. Sal picked it up and was pleased with its heft. Could make for a formidable bludgeon if need be.

"Devil. *Diablo.*"

Gripping the trophy tightly, Sal inched toward the open bedroom door. As he reached it, he slowly eased his head toward the doorframe, allowing just one eye to peer into the room. He saw the cassette player and could even hear the tape hiss as it played. Tilting his head just another inch, he saw Punch the Pedal seated in a folding chair by a cheaply made pressed-wood desk. He was bound with heavy rope. A sea of the thick, light-brown gunk surrounded his chair.

"Diabetic."

The word nearly distracted Salerno as it blared from the tape player. As he stepped into the room, he was able to see more. The greasy substance was all over Punch and dripped from his pants to the floor below. Empty cans were scattered around the chair and within the mess that seeped into the carpet. Punch's head was back and looking straight up at the ceiling. His eyes were wide, and there was something protruding from his mouth. Something quite large.

"Diabetic. *Diabetico.*"

His mouth was ajar, held open by a filthy metal funnel. The goo was all over his face and neck. Standing right in it and being able to identify the cans made Sal's heart race. Punch had been force-fed, and drowned in, motor oil.

"Diabolic."

Sal stared into his friend's lifeless eyes, still gripping the replica trophy. His thoughts were spinning like tires on an icy road.

"Diabolic. *Diabolico.*"

He dropped the trophy and placed his shaking hand on Punch's cold, oil-soaked neck. He pressed two fingers just beside the Adam's apple and felt for a pulse from the carotid artery. Sal had no clue if this was the correct way to check, but he'd seen it done in movies. He pulled the funnel from deep in his friend's throat and let it fall to the floor. He didn't feel any type of pulse, but he already knew, from appearance alone, that Punch the Pedal was dead.

"Diagnose."

He thought about grabbing the phone, but he knew Biaggio wouldn't want that. Maybe he shouldn't have even removed the funnel. There would probably be no police involvement anyway. Falcone would take care of it all.

"Diagnose. *Diagnosticar.*"

Sal decided to close his friend's eyes, more for reasons of dignity than in fear of the old adage that the dead left with eyes agape choose someone to take with them. The lids did not shut as easily as he'd hoped, and they remained slightly ajar at the base of the irises. Looking down at Punch's body, Sal quickly made the sign of the cross and bounded for the exit. His shoes were now covered in oil, and once he huffed through the living room and landed on the kitchen tiles, he slipped across the floor like it was some kid's first day on ice skates.

"Diagonal."

Out the kitchen door and onto the hallway stairs, clutching the banister tightly, Sal took the steps two at a time, hoping his feet wouldn't slide out from under him. He blasted through the hallway door and out into a hailstorm. The sharp pellets fell from the sky as if someone had taken a bat to Heaven's windshield. The ice particles stung as they pounded Sal's face. He managed to get down the front stoop despite the mix of ice and oil on his shoes. He ran hard toward the barbershop, down the desolate avenue, all the while being stoned from above.

᷐

Biaggio's puzzled smile greeted Lucy's woolly novelty on his desk.

"My brother was killed in Vietnam, and our mother is now gone too, so this is left to me," she said blankly.

"Your brother left that to you?" asked Biaggio, glancing over at Vito.

Vito Salerno stepped a little closer for a better view at the furry lump on the desk.

"Not the toy," replied the woman. "The deed."

Vito had the toy in view. A small stuffed animal. Old and dirty. One of its eyes was gone, and the one that remained was bright blue. A tattered pink ribbon cloaked its neck like a noose.

"Does this help you to remember my father?" whispered the woman to Falcone.

Assuming she was somewhat unstable at this point, Biaggio looked to make eye contact with Vito so he could politely escort her out. Vito was staring at the toy. It was a lamb. From a place deep in his memory, it manifested itself like an old image from a slide projector. He saw a vision that his brain recorded nearly forty years before.

As the woman stood from her chair, Vito was lost in memory. He saw the church carnival. He saw a young Biaggio Falcone handing a snowy-white stuffed lamb toy with bright blue eyes to a little girl. Now three black mollies picked feverishly at the tank glass beside him.

"You had a name for my father," she said as she reached behind her erect back. "You called him Little Jimmy."

Biaggio's eyes widened as he stood. Vito shook off the image of Little Jimmy's widow clothed in black at the carnival, and he moved toward the woman.

"Then you murdered him!" She screamed like some exorcized demon. She now brandished the cause of her perfect posture. It was nearly two feet in length. A stainless-steel dagger in the shape of a lightning bolt. Its handle was configured from finely carved wood—quite possibly by Chicky the Termite, who went to the grave with Little Jimmy. It glittered like the tip of the Chrysler building as Vito closed in on her. The boys in the front room had heard the scream and were running back to Falcone's office. As Vito charged nervously to protect his boss, she swung her serrated blade deftly at his midsection. As she had trained herself to do, she drove more than a foot of the knife into Vito's belly and back out in one motion. It was covered in warm blood as she raised it to attack Biaggio Falcone. Vito collapsed to the floor, his hands covering his torn shirt as blood poured through it. He raised his knees to his chest in a fetal position, turning pale as he stared blankly at his half-eaten sandwich on the linoleum beside him.

The woman met Falcone at the side of his desk; he came at her rather than retreat for his safety. She had one chance to shred his intestines before the boys reached her. She was keen to go for the stomach area because she'd read that a mortal wound to the heart would be considerably less painful than eviscerated intestines, with the burning digestive acids and all. Lucy drove the jagged, bloody dagger at Biaggio's abdomen. He swung his left hand in defense and caught enough of the weapon to deflect it past him—slicing open his palm in the process. The woman began a backhanded attempt to drive her blade up into Biaggio's neck, but Rico and Johnny the Beatnik plowed into her back like two linebackers at the goal line. The crimson-soaked lightning bolt was fumbled to the floor and slid away as Lucy landed with a thud and two men upon her. Tommy and Winnie headed directly for Vito as he writhed and kicked in a growing pool of his own blood.

"You fucking cunt," screamed Rico as he repeatedly drove his fist into her face. Just as she was about to lose consciousness, Biaggio Falcone's hand was on his son's muscular right arm.

"Stop it, Rico," he said as his own blood drizzled from his left palm to the floor.

Rico stopped beating her, but he reached into his ankle holster and produced his Smith &Wesson snub-nosed. He pressed it against her eye.

"You really did bring a knife to a gunfight, bitch."

"No," yelled his father, not knowing if Rico was actually going to pull the trigger.

After a moment, Rico moved the gun from her eye socket. Her face was raw and her nose shattered. Vito's blood was soaking through Winnie's stocking feet as he stood in the pool trying to help Tommy lift their screaming friend.

"We gotta get him to a hospital," yelled Winnie.

Tommy looked back at Biaggio but already knew the answer.

"Can't do that, Winnie. Let's get him in a car and take him to our doctor."

Biaggio leaned over Lucy, some of his blood landing and mixing with hers on his office floor.

"Can you hear me?" he asked, not waiting for a response. "We are going to drop you outside an emergency room. Your purse was stolen and you were mugged by some coloreds. You understand me? That's the only way you live through this. You're very lucky I knew your mother. Your father tried to kill me as you did, but I wasn't as forgiving in those days."

"You're fucking kidding me?" responded Rico. "You're gonna let this bitch breathe? Look at Vito over there, Pop."

Tommy and Winnie had Salerno by his arms and feet and were headed toward the front room of the barbershop, on their way to the street. He was now ghostly white and unresponsive. Biaggio turned to his son as Johnny handed him a towel to wrap his hand.

"Take her to a hospital. Leave her outside."

A crowd gathered in the barber shop.

"Make a hole," yelled Tommy.

Moments ago Joey Salerno had been shining Winnie's shoes while "Instant Karma" continued to play in his head despite whatever else was on the radio. He still held one shoe in his hands as he sat high up in a barber chair and watched his cousin—de facto uncle, in fact—being rushed, like a wounded battlefield soldier, to the front door. As Joey saw the fresh blood, he let Winnie's shoe fall to the floor and clutched his father's key ring that sat on his lap.

"Nnyyaaaahhh!"

"Grab us some towels," yelled Tommy to nobody in particular.

A man who had been in line retrieved a stack of barber towels and dropped them onto Vito as he was hurried past. Another fellow opened the front door, and the hail storm blew inside the shop and onto Vito, Tommy, and Winnie.

"Nnyyaaaahhh!"

Some local men went over to tend to Joey, but they were unfamiliar to him and brought no real comfort.

"Open that Caddy for us," yelled Tommy as he nodded toward Winnie's parked car. A man opened the unlocked rear door as the ice pellets ricocheted off the barber pole and hit the car like shrapnel.

Just as they were loading Vito in, a breathless Sal Salerno came huffing and puffing down the street. He was ashen and soaked; his perspiration mixed with the rain and ice on his sickened face.

"Vito! My God . . . "

"He got stabbed, Pope," said Tommy. "It's bad."

"Get him to the hospital," yelled Sal.

There was no reply as Tommy got in the back seat and applied the towels to Vito's gushing wound. Winnie got behind the wheel shoeless; in his torn, bloodied and frozen black socks, he started the car. Sal was numb for a few seconds. He had just seen a murdered friend and a mortally wounded cousin in the space of ten minutes. He stood there as the car pulled away, being battered from above. Then, through the hail which sounded like a hundred gravel trucks dumping their loads, he heard his son screaming from within Scotti's.

Sal quickly made his way inside, through the crowd of gawkers. Joey was still wailing as his father saw the trail of blood left in Vito's wake. Biaggio had his arms around the panicked young man as Sal rushed over. Joey held tightly to the keys.

"It's okay, Joey. I'm here."

Biaggio stepped back as Sal clutched his son. From the back room came Rico and Johnny. They flanked the battered and detached woman like death row screws on execution day.

"She stabbed Vito," whispered Biaggio as he tightened the wrap on his injured hand.

Sal just watched as the boys marched her out the door and into the hail storm. The ice pummeled the large front window like a swarm of hungry locusts.

"Why?" Sal asked.

"She's Little Jimmy's daughter."

Now Sal had to wrap his mind around this concept. As he ran his hand through Joey's hair, the young man began to calm somewhat. It then dawned on Sal Salerno that in all the confusion of seeing his cousin dragged bloodied and lifeless through the storm, hearing his son screaming in horror, and watching the daughter of a friend dead for four decades be pulled from the barbershop a bloody mess, he hadn't informed Biaggio of what set him off scurrying through the squall in the first place. He arched his neck and whispered so that Joey wouldn't hear.

"Punch is dead."

CHAPTER TWENTY-EIGHT

V ITO SALERNO ALWAYS liked to consider himself as *consigliere* to Biaggio Falcone, though nobody had that official title in all the years that Falcone had been in power. Vito was as loyal and trustworthy as one could be, which was paramount in being the right hand of the boss, but he was a little too wild and unpredictable; though street-smart, he didn't possess the required intelligence to be what would amount to the third-highest position in the family. Still, Biaggio appreciated his devotion and tenure, and would have Vito assist in high-level affairs whenever feasible. Tommy Box o' Cookies was always Biaggio's main sounding board and advisor.

In the many years since Nicky the Zipper's incarceration, Tommy had been the underboss. Now, through nepotism, Rico Falcone had claimed that position—though most knew he was not deserving. Tommy was now basically a capo once again; he headed a crew of soldiers who would handle most of the low-level dirty work. Johnny the Beatnik also had a crew of his own, and plans were underway to give Carbone a shot at running one. Winnie, as Tommy's nephew, was being groomed as a driver for the boys, which was actually higher on the food chain than a common soldier. For instance, the soldiers would very rarely be permitted to even show their faces at Scotti's Barbershop for fear of drawing unwanted attention. Meetings involving them would be held at a rotation of varying places. Biaggio was very strict about such matters. Though hierarchy like Nicky and the late Staten Island Lou had found themselves convicted and sentenced on various charges, Biaggio, unlike several other family heads, had avoided prison altogether. It was crucial for a family to keep their boss out of the prison population to ensure continuity and general order. The combination of the barbershop and carpet businesses, and Falcone's cool and analytical mind had worked like a charm for years. In fact, nobody who was employed in the Falcone carpet operation had any ties whatsoever to the underworld family—except Rico.

Punch the Pedal enjoyed the driver position for years, and being the grandson of Luigi Scotti had put him on the fast track to acceptance. Punch had originated the convenient position of barber/driver for which Winnie was training.

Sal Salerno had none of these titles. He was not even officially in the family, so to speak. Biaggio created Sal's unique role out of his sense of guilt—warranted or not—over having indirectly caused Joey to be born with such tremendous physical and mental challenges. Sal did have a few younger men under him, though. Their roles were simply running numbers. That aspect of the family, though slowing with the advent of legal lotteries, was still more than one man could handle. Sal was in charge, but his role never involved any violence or even threats. A stranger could likely be somewhat intimidated by the former military man's size and confidence, but that trepidation would fade once you became his friend. He was peaceful and kind, but not a pushover—and you didn't want to be the rare joker to summon his dark side.

In much the same way that Sal's cousin Vito lacked certain traits required to be a true *consigliere*, the private doctor that Vito was rushed to while bleeding out like a hoisted slaughterhouse cow lacked almost everything required to save his life. It is doubtful he could have been saved by the best surgeon in the most modern emergency room, but the local mob physician had no chance. The code of secrecy, and the practice of having nothing on public record and nothing investigated by any official body, sealed Vito Salerno's fate. He died with the eternal honor of taking the knife that was honed to assassinate the head of the Campigotto crime family.

The days since the murders of Vito and Punch were quite hectic for the entire family. In the immediate chaos of it all, they left Biaggio at the barbershop with only Sal Salerno to protect him. Sal could obviously handle himself quite well, but he carried no weapon and had not been trained, or even sworn, to protect the don. Sal did clear the shop of all the onlookers just after Rico and Johnny left with the woman. They were told, directly by Biaggio and in no uncertain terms, that they saw nothing. Then Sal basically held the door as they filed out into the hail storm. The door was then locked until Biaggio's cleaners arrived simultaneously at the barbershop and Punch's apartment. Time was of the essence, and though there wasn't constant police surveillance outside of Scotti's, unmarked cars were a common sight, as were long camera lenses. The timing of the icy downpour may have actually been a godsend with regard to keeping the events of that day under wraps; there were no passersby and not a police vehicle to be seen.

Even though it was for no more than twenty minutes, Biaggio did not overlook the fact that Sal had stayed by his side, along with Joey, after all of the other fellas had left for the hospital or the doctor's office. There had been no discussion of the fact that Vito was not being sent to an emergency room. Sal assumed that's where he was taken, though if he'd given himself time to think about it, he'd know that was not the way these things played out. He had his hands full trying to calm Joey while finding a way to fill Biaggio in on the horror he'd witnessed at Punch the Pedal's residence.

There were many meetings—official and otherwise— following the twin murders. Was that crazy woman really Little Jimmy's daughter? She was. Did she also murder

Punch before she came to the barbershop? That seemed unlikely; Punch was obviously physically overpowered and bound to a chair.

It was assumed that Don Sacco, or at least his hot-headed deputy, Jackie Moose, was behind Punch's rubout, but did they also contract Jimmy's daughter to kill Biaggio? It didn't seem right. That's not the way things were done. Even if they were behind the woman, their goal would seem to have been to murder Rico, not Biaggio himself. The ramifications of these killings could be enormous. An all-out war between families could erupt. That was generally good for nobody. Lives would be lost. Income would suffer. Cops would clamp down on everyone. Biaggio needed to meet personally with Don Sacco. There would be no go-betweens or carrier pigeons. A meeting like this would take a few days to arrange to the satisfaction of all parties. In the meantime, Biaggio had two devoted men to bury. He used his connections in the funeral business to circumvent procedure and have them buried quickly and with dignity. He paid for every last detail, right down to the engraved headstones. After some brief discussion, it was decided that Vito's inscription would read: Vito "Bluesman" Salerno

⌒∞⌒

Sal sat in Peter and Kathy's living room staring at the television. Peter rented a video tape of *The Bridge on the River Kwai* for his father to enjoy since his parents had yet to purchase a VCR of their own. Sal took in the images of the film he had seen so many times before, but his thoughts were with Punch and especially Cousin Vito. Neither of them had any children and both were divorced, but they were loved by many. Sal told his wife what happened—leaving out the gory details—but most of the neighborhood whispered different variations of the truth. Police were sniffing around but were never told anything that related to the barbershop or Biaggio Falcone.

Mary understood Sal's pain, but she was furious that Joey

was present for Vito's murder. She warned Sal countless times that Scotti's was not a place for their son to be, shining shoes and palling around with mobsters. She always feared that her husband and son would be victims of stray bullets, caught in the middle of a mob war. Sal would have none of that talk. He hadn't seen any violence at the barbershop since the 1940s and was sure he kept himself, and especially Joey, isolated from that side of things. Joey had no friends of his own and took great delight in the camaraderie at Scotti's and in the occasional trip to Henley's bar with his father and the fellas. Even Peter would sometimes show up for a beer with his buddies.

Peter and Joey sat in the living room with their father, as did grandson Joseph. Kathy, Mary, and little Lisa prepared dinner in the kitchen. The plan of using the movie to take Sal's mind off things wasn't working too well. He attended two funerals in recent days, was briefly interviewed by police (whereby he supplied no answers), was repeatedly lambasted by his wife for putting Joey in harm's way—and for not insisting that Vito be brought to a real hospital—and knew it was time for him to tell Biaggio that he could no longer be involved with the family numbers racket. Salvatore Salerno's retirement wasn't shaping up as the sea of tranquility he had envisioned. His old job at the cola company had never raised his stress to the levels reached over the past few days. Joey had never seen real violence before, if one discounted the teaching methods of the school he was enrolled in as a child. Sal had never even permitted him to attend a wake, and that included Cousin Vito's, yet he had put Joey in a position to witness his murder.

"What's this movie about, Grandpa?" Young Joseph intruded on his grandfather's thoughts.

"Huh?"

"This movie on TV. What's it about? Soldiers?"

"Oh . . . yeah, Joseph. Soldiers in World War II."

"Like you?"

"Not really. These poor guys are prisoners. I was never a prisoner."

Peter rubbed his son's head as he added, "The Japanese colonel is using the prisoners to build a very important bridge. If he doesn't get it built on time, he will be shamed and considered a failure. Then he will have to kill himself."

Sal put his fingers to his lips to shush his son. No need to tell the child all that.

"Pop, he wants to know what it's about. He can handle it."

From the kitchen, Kathy beckoned. "Peter, can you come and slice the roast beef?"

As Peter started to leave his seat, his father waved for him to sit.

"That's always been my job," said Sal, smiling. "A retired guy isn't even good enough to cut meat anymore?"

He smiled, winked at his grandson, and headed for the kitchen.

"Thank you, Pop," smiled Kathy.

He gave her one of the few grins he'd been able to manage of late as he tugged on Lisa's ponytail. She gave her grandpa a big hug. Mary was somewhat distant as her husband bantered with the other most important females in his life.

"Looks delicious," he said as he positioned the cutting board to his satisfaction. His sons and grandson remained in the living room with the movie. Mary and Kathy were back and forth between the kitchen and dining room, bringing food in and having Lisa lay out the napkins.

Sal squinted to identify the grain of the roast, putting on the reading glasses that sat in his shirt pocket; then he stuck the two-pronged carving fork into it. He thought he had the direction of the grain correct, but it was still a little blurry, even with his glasses on. He raised his freshly sharpened carving knife, and then he could no longer feel it in his hand. It dropped to the floor with a clang. Mary turned to see her husband swaying as he reached to grab onto the table.

"Sal!"

Peter heard his mother's shriek and bounded into the kitchen. As his father was about to topple backward, Peter slid a chair under his large frame and steadied him into it. The carving fork remained impaled in the meat, the knife on the floor.

"Pop?" yelled Peter as his father's head dropped to one side, eyes shut.

"Sal," screamed Mary.

"Call an ambulance, Kathy," said Peter as he held his father in the chair.

As Mary and Peter comforted him in the chair, Sal's grandchildren stood quietly in the doorway, frightened and confused.

"It's okay, Pop," said Peter, hoping his father could hear him. "An ambulance is coming."

As Sal himself had done to Punch the Pedal just days earlier, Peter felt for a pulse on his father's neck. He thought he felt one. It was very slight, but it was there. He then noticed that his chest was not completely still. There was some shallow breathing.

It took Joey a while to get to his feet, but he ambled slowly toward the commotion as the black and white image of William Holden flickered on the television behind him. The prisoners of war were planting explosive charges on the prized Japanese bridge just as Joey reached the kitchen. He first saw the terrified faces of his niece and nephew. Then he saw Kathy hanging up the phone.

"They're on their way," she said.

He saw his mother and brother surrounding his seated father. Mary kissed and gently rubbed his forehead. He saw that his father's eyes were shut. He saw the knife on the kitchen tiles. Joey opened his mouth to scream. It was going to be an outcry even stronger and louder than the one he emitted when he saw a bloodied Vito being rushed from the barbershop.

But the sound never came.

The sick, injured, and downtrodden would converge on the emergency room each night like moths to a porch light. Peter and Mary sat there for hours. Kathy and a trusted neighbor remained at her house to care for Joey and the children. Peter tried to take his mind off his father's unknown condition by creating scenarios for the afflicted people who filled the ER waiting room. The little boy with his parents probably fell and hurt his arm or shoulder. The guy who kneeled on the floor, bent over a chair, probably had some gall bladder issues or maybe a kidney stone. The young, disheveled couple that kept nodding off together probably took too much of their favorite recreational drug. Then there were a few scattered people who appeared completely healthy. Maybe they had a hidden rash or something, or they could just be waiting for a loved one getting treatment within. Sure enough, one man stood anxiously as his wife walked out through the double doors sporting a temporary eye patch. They were free to leave. Peter envisioned his father walking out in much the same manner, but he knew that was not to be the case. The wait was killing him.

"My breath must be terrible," said Mary as she rubbed her thumb on her rosary beads.

"What?"

"Sitting here all this time. My mouth is all dried out."

"I can get you some coffee."

"That'll really do wonders for my breath."

He knew they had run out of distractions. Idle conversation and thumbing through magazines ran their course. They would soon hear something and they'd better be prepared to handle it.

"Mom, it's probably a good sign that nobody came out right away, you know."

"God knows."

"If it was, you know, the worst, they'd have come out

sooner. They're probably working hard to stabilize him and get him up and running again. Maybe he just fainted. People faint all the time."

"He didn't faint, Peter."

"He's been through a lot lately and . . . "

Peter stopped mid-sentence because he saw his mother stand. He turned to see a young nurse walking toward them. She was holding a plastic pouch. Peter could see that his father's wallet and the key ring that Joey always held on to were crammed inside the bag along with some other items: pens and Sal's numbers books. Peter Salerno's body went cold.

"Don't say it, nurse. Please," he pleaded as he grabbed his mother.

Then the young caregiver quietly uttered the unexpected. "He's alive."

Peter exhaled. Mary dropped back into her seat as her knees went weak.

"That's positive," said the nurse. "But the news isn't all good."

Mary squeezed her prayer beads.

"The doctor will be out soon," added the young woman. "But Mr. Salerno hasn't regained consciousness. He's stable, but he is in a coma."

Peter accepted the bag of his father's belongings but not the diagnosis.

"You sure? How do you know?"

"The doctors have tests. They've determined he is comatose. As I said, the doctor will be—"

"Can he come out of it?" asked Mary softly from her seat.

"I don't know much more than what I've told you. So sorry. Please wait for the doctor."

It was almost half an hour before the doctor appeared and went into more detail for Peter and Mary. He was professional and compassionate, using terms like "subarachnoid hemorrhage," "hemorrhagic stroke" and

"Glasgow Coma Scale." It was all quite confusing, but after all the talk, it meant that nobody knew if and when Sal Salerno would ever wake again. Nobody knew if he could hear those around him, but they suspected he could not. Nobody knew if he would lie comatose for twenty years, wake up tomorrow, or die tonight in his hospital room.

Mary had been up for most of the night in the sterile glare of the ER's lights. Peter finally drove her home before sunrise and kept Joey at his house for the night. She managed to sleep for a few hours, but set her new Panasonic angled-cube clock radio for 10 a.m. She didn't like the harshness of a buzzer and didn't want to be awakened by crass humor or loud rock 'n' roll. Finding a station that played American standards and big-band classics was getting harder all the time, but she would always find one to replace another that changed formats, though signal strength would vary.

She woke gently to the sound of Andy Williams vowing to one day cross a river in style. Her first instinct was to go to Joey's room and check on him, until she remembered that he wasn't there. Neither was her husband. Peter instructed her to call him so he could drive her back to Sal's hospital room, but she knew her son was worn out and wanted him to rest. Though there was an entire neighborhood that would be more than willing to help her—Brooklyn had always been known for that—Mary would call a car service after she showered.

⌘

The sun flickered in through Sal's window. The hospital corridor was busy, but his room was peaceful, save for the various beeps and murmurs of the monitors that were linked to him. He didn't appear to be in any pain; that's how his wife chose to deal with his condition as she sat at the edge of his bed.

"You ready to wake up, you loafer?" she asked in a voice more soothing than he'd be used to.

The machines continued their monotonous intonation.

"So this is your idea of retirement? To lie around and be waited on all day by pretty nurses?"

Beep. Beep. Beep.

"Joey wants to go to the bar. You know I'm not taking him to that place. He stayed at Peter's last night. Can you believe that? I can't remember the last time I didn't wake up and have Joey there. I didn't know what to do with myself. Oh, and the front door lock is sticking. You're gonna have to look at that."

She rubbed his hand. It didn't feel as big and strong as it had always been. It felt colder, too.

"You know, people are gonna be trying to give me those numbers if you're laid up here. Fat chance that I'm gonna get involved in all that. Next thing you know, those hoodlums are gonna send me to crack some guy's kneecaps. You want me involved in that stuff too?" Mary smiled.

Peter came walking in the door. His eyes were puffy and tired, but his walk was purposeful.

"How did you get here, Ma?"

"Hi, Peter. I took a car service."

"You should've told me. I called your house and got no answer. I went there and nobody answered the door. I went in there fearing the worst. You didn't even leave a note."

"I'm sorry. I should have told you. I'm not thinking clear." She turned to her husband. "You hear this, Sal? Your son is yelling at his mother. Set him straight, will ya?"

"I didn't know if you wanted me to bring Joey," said Peter.

"No. You crazy? The last thing we need here is your brother taking a fit."

"Maybe it'd wake Pop," said Peter.

"Very funny. Your father doesn't want Joey to see any stuff like this. You know that."

Peter marched toward the end table near his father's bed. He picked up the telephone receiver and put it to his ear.

"Good, it's on," he said.

"The phone? Does it cost more to have it on?"

Peter hung it up and reached around to his back pocket.

"No reason to pay more for the telephone. It's not like he's gonna be taking calls," said Mary.

Her son produced a rolled-up copy of the *Racing Form* and slid it gently under his father's hand.

"I once heard that music might be able to help bring people out of these things," he said.

He dialed the telephone and placed the receiver on his father's pillow, right by his ear.

"Well," he continued, "Pop's music is the horse racing hotline."

Peter went by his mother and placed his arm around her. He rubbed her shoulder as they viewed the man they loved so much—normally so strong and vibrant—solemnly reposed on the stark white bedding. The beeps and murmurs of the medical equipment almost provided a backbeat for the emotionless voice that resonated the harness racing results into Sal Salerno's auditory canal.

❧

Peter had been trying his racing-results method for several days. Each day had been just like last. No progression or regression. Just the same. Though yesterday, a nursing aide did shave the beard that emerged during Sal's slumber. Joey was showing signs of weakness and depression in his father's absence, and his brother thought he needed something more than the four walls of the past week.

The air was chilly, but Tommy Box o' Cookies sat atop a folding chair in front of Scotti's. His pullover was heavy and the sun was direct and warming. There was a second folding chair beside him, empty, as he thumbed through the *New York Post*.

"Joey's been wanting to come by and see you guys," said Peter, surprising Tommy.

"Hey!" replied the big man as he rose from his chair.

Tommy noticed that Joey, looking half of Peter's height,

held on tightly to his brother as he gazed down at the sidewalk. It wasn't the Joey he knew—the one who was always so excited to come to the barbershop.

"Anything new with Pope?"

"No," said Peter.

"How's it going, Joey?" Tommy smiled.

The young man didn't raise his head.

"Feel like givin' some shoeshines? Or how 'bout I give you one?"

"He's been having a little trouble bending," replied Peter.

"Well, how about going over to Henley's for a beer, Joey? You and the Beatnik can make bad Italian gestures at each other."

No response.

"Tommy, I think my father could use some visitors," said Peter.

"Sure! But your mother said—"

"I don't care what she said. I'm asking you guys to come see him. He needs that, I think."

"Then it's done. Come on, let's go inside."

The shop was dead quiet as Winnie cleaned some combs.

"Hello there!" said the barber as he saw Tommy escorting the Salerno brothers.

"Hello," responded Peter. He wasn't as familiar with Winnie as with some of his father's older friends.

"Joey, my pal!" said Winnie, smiling.

The whole place seemed different to Joey. It had the same antiseptic smell, but the absence of music—or even talk radio—altered the entire atmosphere. No radio. No Punch the Pedal. No Cousin Vito, and most importantly, no father for Joey to cling to on this lazy, cloudy Brooklyn afternoon.

"Is it okay to take him in the back to see Mr. Falcone?" asked Peter.

"My father ain't here." Rico coughed as he emerged from the back office with a cigar in his teeth. The heavy smoke wafted toward Peter and Joey, overpowering the gentle barbershop sting in the air. They could see Johnny the Beatnik waving from the office as he huddled with Carbone over Biaggio's desk.

"Oh," said Peter.

"How's the Pope?" asked Rico dutifully.

"Not so good," said Peter.

"Nnnnaahhh!"

Realizing his error, Peter rubbed his brother's hair. "He'll be fine, Joe. I mean that he needs a little time to get his strength back."

"You need something?" asked Rico in his usual tone of insincerity.

"No. Joey just wanted to see the guys. He likes your father a lot so—"

"I'll tell him yous were here."

Joey looked up at the silent radio on the shelf behind Winnie.

"Well, I guess we'll get on our way," said Peter as he helped his brother turn toward the door. The place seemed so cold, and Rico added an unwelcoming air that had never been present before. As they shuffled toward the door, Peter took some comfort in Tommy's smile. He had been there forever, and he made it all seem okay as he wrapped his big body around Joey and nuzzled him into the woolen safety of his sweater. Peter's thoughts danced around the fact that he and his brother were taking warmth and solace in the reassuring embrace of a fellow who had done God-knows-what to God-knows-how-many men in his lifetime.

"You tell Pope to get his ass ready," grinned Tommy. "We're coming."

✠

The hospital security staff, like most everyone else in the five boroughs, knew who Biaggio Falcone was. The combination of his celebrity, a handful of twenty-dollar bills, and a perceptible fear of all things unpleasant, granted him and his entourage entry to Sal Salerno's floor even though visiting hours had long passed.

They strode down the corridor as if they had built it. Biaggio, Tommy, Johnny the Beatnik, and Winnie. Scotti's was closed for the day, but Rico remained in the back room with Carbone and a couple of soldiers who were to be in his developing crew. Biaggio generally didn't like the idea of crew members congregating at the barbershop, but it was after hours, the shop was locked tight, and it was all part of his plan to help his son mature into a strong leader.

The three women at the nurse's station whispered and giggled as the band of neighborhood wiseguys reached the open door to Sal's room. Winnie carried an armful of flowers.

"You in here, Pope?" bellowed Tommy, not really expecting an answer.

The men entered gingerly as the monitors bleeped around them in the dim light.

"There you are," said Tommy as the boys saw their friend lying in his hospital bed. They continued to tiptoe around as Tommy laid a neatly tied box of cookies on Sal's table.

"All Italian. Seeds and nuts like you wouldn't believe. Just how you like 'em," he whispered to his longtime friend.

Not knowing what else to do, Johnny and Winnie tapped Sal's hand as they walked by. Biaggio stood in a corner of the room, below the hanging television, which was turned off. He ran a finger along his bristly eyebrow as he thought.

"What are we, a group of fucking monks?" he hollered, his voice echoing into the corridor.

The other three men flinched at the unexpected outburst. A nurse came scurrying to the edge of the doorway but said nothing.

"Turn that light on, Johnny."

The Beatnik lit up the room, and they all squinted in their fluorescent blindness.

"Sal," yelled Falcone. "Tommy's gonna open the cookies, we're gonna find something on this TV here, and you're gonna sit your lazy ass up and shoot the shit with us, *capisce*? I'd give you a cigar, but that nice nurse would probably break my arm."

The nurse gave an embarrassed smile and closed the door before going on her way.

"Nicky's gonna be out soon," said Tommy. "I know he's been wanting to play some bocce with you, Pope."

Nothing but the beeps from the machinery.

"These goons here," said Tommy, pointing at Johnny and Winnie, "they're gonna be outta control teaching more curses to Joey. I told them you'll lose a shoe in their asses, Pope."

Placing the flowers down, Winnie bent over with his hands on his buttocks.

"Right here, Pope," said Winnie. "Right up my shite pipe."

"I can't believe this *stronzo* is my sister's kid," said Tommy. "That's what it'd sound like if Shakespeare never went to school."

The boys laughed as Biaggio turned the TV on. He left the volume down as *Hill Street Blues* played out on the small screen.

"How am I gonna bet on football without your advice?" asked Falcone as he pulled a chair to Sal's bedside. "These guys here think Joe Montana is some jerkoff in the witness protection program."

"Winnie thinks the New York Sack Exchange is a gay bar in Manhattan," added Johnny.

"Yeah, that's where Johnny's father met his father," replied Winnie. They all chuckled.

Tommy opened the box of cookies as the laughter died down.

Beep. Beep. Beep.

"I, uh, I told Peter to let us know if Mary needs anything," said Biaggio. He spoke to Sal but looked directly at Tommy. "So you don't need to worry about that, Sal. We know you'll be back to your old self soon, but your wife and family will be taken care of, no matter what. I know you can hear me, so you can let that worry go, okay?"

The room was silent, save for the cold tonality of the surrounding apparatus. The bright light shone down on Sal

Salerno as his friends encircled his still frame. Tommy pulled the bed covers up a little higher on his buddy's neck.

"Winnie, why don't you ask that arm-breaking nurse where we can get some coffee to go with these cookies?" said Falcone.

"Sure."

Biaggio found the TV remote and pressed one of the four buttons on it to raise the sound.

"Turn off this bright light on your way out so we can watch television," continued Biaggio to his young driver. "Bring five coffees."

∽

Mary dried Joey off as he stood completely naked, the bathwater dripping to the floor of their bathroom. Though in his mid-thirties, this ritual had not changed at all since he was a toddler. The next step would be to completely dress him, then feed him breakfast. It was second nature to her, but it wasn't as easy anymore. She was older and weaker, though she'd never admit that to anyone. She counted on more help from her husband in his retirement since he'd have more hours to be with their son. She refused any nursing help for Joey; she'd long ago vowed to never again entrust his well-being to a stranger. Now, though Joey could do almost nothing for himself, he was actually blessed with more functionality than his father.

"No shave today," she said. "I'm feeling a little shaky and I don't wanna cut you again."

"Mmmm."

"Peter said when he gets off work he's gonna come over and watch the Knicks with you."

"Mmmmmmm," replied her son. When he projected his sounds for a longer time, she knew he did it for emphasis. He was pleased with what she told him. She knew it wasn't so much the basketball game, but the time he'd spend sitting with his brother. Joey would watch a test pattern if Peter was beside him, joking and helping him to enjoy a glass of soda.

She took his hand and led him, naked, to his bedroom closet. Though his shirts were nothing fancy, and all similar in style, they were different colors, and he took pleasure in deciding which one to wear each morning. It was decided that today would be blue.

∽∾

Lucy's battered face had healed somewhat since Rico pounded it and dumped her at the hospital. It was still quite bruised but not nearly as red and scabby as it had been. Her nose still sported an imposing bandage, but her eyes were almost fully open again. The cold night air felt good as she sucked it through her mouth and deep into her lungs. She was a tad dizzy, but that was understandable. Her dark-brown dress and blazer were impeccable, with still nary a wrinkle despite the flexure and contortions of moments before. Things were how she'd imagined them, though not perfectly so. The battery-operated cassette player was working from just inches behind her. It was playing "It Doesn't Matter Anymore"—a hit single for Buddy Holly just after his death in 1959—but much of the song was drowned out by the sounds of the cars and trucks rumbling by to her rear.

Nothing ever really goes exactly as planned.

That was the last thought she had before she closed her eyes tightly and, in the year of its centennial celebration, jumped headfirst to her death from the Brooklyn Bridge.

CHAPTER TWENTY-NINE

THE PIER JUTTED almost one thousand feet out into the clear blue Atlantic. The sun had barely risen but it was warm already. The tropical air was calm and salty.

"Don Sacco, Biaggio Falcone is here."

"Lenny Sheetrock" was what they called the head of Sacco's Florida security team. They were on a very public fishing pier, but nobody was permitted to enter the far tip of it this morning unless Lenny Sheetrock said so. Biaggio Falcone stood with Johnny the Beatnik about twenty yards from Sacco. There were three burly men between them and the end of the dock.

"Let him in. Just him. You stay back with the others, Lenny."

Don Sacco was out for some bluefish, as he was known to do several times per week. He found serenity with a rod in his hands and the crashing of the waves beneath the pier. Other times, he enjoyed going out on a boat for bigger fish. Arrangements were made to meet Biaggio here in a place that was quite public yet extended out just far enough from land and listening devices.

"Hello," was all Biaggio said as he walked up behind the rival family head.

"Biaggio. I'd stand, but I don't wanna spook the fish."

Sacco didn't look Falcone in the face, but his eyes slid to the side where Falcone came to rest in a beach chair that Lenny left open for him. Biaggio couldn't help but think that, with his sideways stare and his leathery, sun-damaged skin, Sacco was beginning to look very much like a fish himself. Maybe a pufferfish, given his portly physique.

"Nice weather down here," offered Falcone.

"Yes. Who can stay in New York in winter? You got Tommy with you here?" asked Sacco, never once moving his head.

"No. I brought Johnny with me."

Sacco thought for a moment.

"Johnny? You mean that hippie?"

"Yeah," replied Biaggio without expression.

"He doesn't seem like much protection for you. Not implying you need any protection from me, of course. You are my guest."

"Don't let his hair fool you. You have three guys with him back there. I'd bet he could convince two of them to fight each other while he slit the third one's throat. He trained under Nicky the Zipper."

"Oh. Say no more. Nicky was very respected."

"Was?"

"Is. Not was. Forgive me. He's been away a long time.

"Don Sacco, I must tell you that I need—"

"Whoa! Whoa!" exclaimed the fat family head as he rose to his feet. "I think I got one!"

He wrestled with his fishing rod as if he had an eight-hundred pound marlin on the line.

"Damn it! Lost him."

He sat back down, again shooting his sideways stare at Biaggio.

"I was saying," began Falcone, "I need you to put my mind at ease."

"Okay."

"With regard to our bunking heads a little. Did you give the order to kill my driver?"

"Well, when I am down here for the winter, many decisions are made by Jackie Musumeci. He's being groomed, you know."

"Don Sacco, you're not the kind of man to place blame."

"You didn't allow me to finish. Your driver, the one who

is now deceased, and your very own son—they brutally attacked two young associates of mine. Broken legs, lacerated liver, shattered teeth—very bad, Biaggio. Now, if they dusted it up with just any two guys, well then maybe things wouldn't have been so serious. I am godfather to one of those boys. I took a solemn vow in church to fulfill obligations to him. He goes through life knowing that Bruno Sacco is there for him, that people will respect him and no harm will come to him. So then I had a choice. Do I let this incident pass? Do I weaken everything my name stands for? Should all those who are close to me now worry that my protection means nothing? Should I be relegated to impotent laughing stock?"

"But you didn't respond in kind with their actions. My driver did not kill, yet he is dead. Murdered—not with dignity, but tortured slowly."

"And your son?" asked Sacco.

"What does that mean? I am here to talk about my son."

"Your son doesn't have a scratch on him. Have you noticed that, Don Falcone? Jackie Moose wanted to kill your driver and your son. It was I who put an immediate halt to that. We do not eliminate the son of a family head as if we are swatting a mosquito on our forearm. I knew that would lead to a wave of violence, and anger all the other families. So, what was I to do? I exceeded the punishment for your driver so that I might leave your son unharmed. I half thought that you might be coming here to thank me."

Falcone stared at Sacco's angular eyeball.

"I came to hear, from your lips, that my son is not in danger."

Sacco finally turned his head. Now Biaggio could see both of the fish eyes beneath his sun-scaled forehead.

"Much like the fatback that just eluded my bait," smiled Sacco, "your son is off the hook."

Biaggio put out a hand. Before Sacco removed his from the pole, he added, "For *this* incident, he's absolved. He needs to tread carefully in the future."

He then engulfed Biaggio's hand in his own cold, wet, crusty grip.

"Would you like to join me for some fishing?" asked Sacco.

"And just to be clear, you had nothing to do with the attempt on my life, and the death of my dear friend Vito Salerno?" responded Falcone.

"Of course not!" answered Sacco, still grasping Biaggio's hand. "The details of that incident are not clear, even to me. You kept a tight lid on that. I would have no reason to kill you, my friend. Nor would I bring harm to Salerno. I know he's been loyal to you for many, many years. I would look into the Verengia family. They've wanted him forever."

"No. That issue was resolved when Don Verengia passed on."

"Still, you never know. Maybe someone carried a grudge. I have a hothead in Jackie Moose. You've got a loose cannon in your son—forgive my frankness. Maybe they've got a blood-boiler in their family too. What happened to the rational thinking of years gone by?" said Sacco, his voice trailing off.

"I thank you, Don Sacco. Now, if you'll excuse me, I must return to New York."

"So fast? No time to enjoy the Florida sun?"

"Not this time," replied Biaggio.

He turned to walk back toward Johnny, who stood in awkward silence with Sacco's men.

"Biaggio," began Sacco, once again peering out of one eye, "what do you think would have happened had Jackie decided to, you know, neutralize your son?"

Falcone stopped for a moment, puzzled by the bizarre nature of the question.

"I wouldn't want to think about that, really. But since you asked, I'm quite sure Jackie would be in a wood chipper by now, and the bluefish would be in abundance at this pier."

Don Sacco's one visible eye blinked rapidly.

"Because," continued Falcone, "they'd be just below the surface, feeding on the bodies of you and Lenny Sheetrock."

Sacco emitted some combination of a cough and a chuckle as Biaggio smiled and went on his way.

Peter Salerno sat by his father's bedside, changing television channels. The sun was setting and visiting hours would soon be over. Sal had the *Racing Form* rolled up and stuffed into his left hand. The telephone receiver rested against his ear, but the results from Yonkers Raceway had long concluded.

"The kids both got good report cards," said Peter, surfing the channels for a movie. "Kathy's brother prays for you at mass every single day. So you got a priest in the family working hard for you. You got no excuse not to wake up, Pop."

He watched an unfamiliar film with the sound very low for a few moments.

"How 'bout these stupid movies? Someone is always having a bad dream and then they suddenly sit the fuck up in the bed like they were shot out of a cannon. You ever see anybody sit up in bed like that out of a dead sleep? Me neither."

Peter stood. He walked over, took the phone from his father's ear, and hung it up.

"Give that a try, Pop. Sit up like in the movies. Just jump straight the hell up so as I can tell people that shit like that really happens. Come on!"

Nothing.

Peter returned to his chair on the other side of the bed.

"What about 'See you in Hell'? Can one action movie not have somebody say, 'See you in Hell'? I hate that one. What about you?"

Beep. Beep. Beep.

"Then there's 'We got company.' Every moron driving a car that notices he's being followed has to say, 'We got company.' Please."

Peter changed the channel.

"What else, Pop? Lemme see. Oh yeah . . . the coroner eating a sandwich. How 'bout that one? Do you think people often eat their lunch while performing an autopsy? 'Look at me, I've opened so many bodies that I can down a can of Beefaroni while I pull out a lung.' "

Peter dabbed a little sweat off his forehead.

"A postmortem buffet, Pop? I just thought of another one. You know how when a TV cop enters a dark room with his gun out, he crisscrosses his gun hand with his flashlight hand and holds them both out in front of him? Looks cool, but it's bullshit. A detective once told me—Benny Crocetti's brother, in fact—that if there was a bad guy hiding in that room he'd instinctively shoot right at the flashlight and probably hit the cop dead center. So, cops who want to feel 'cool' might use that criss-cross method, but cops who want to go home at the end of their shift hold that flashlight as far out to the side of their body as their arm can reach. Let the bad guy shoot at the light, exposing where he is, and then empty your gun in that jackass."

He looked over at his father, hoping his monologue on movie clichés might strike a nerve.

Does he have a little more color in his cheeks? Maybe, but I'm probably seeing things again.

"I sold the old Caddy for twelve hundred bucks. I was thinking of laying a chunk of it on the Redskins over the Giants. Jimmy the Greek says . . . "

A noise.

The *Racing Form* in Sal's hand began to crumble in his grip.

"Holy Jesus!" gasped Peter as he leaped to his feet and the remote fell to the floor. He ran for the door.

"Nurse! Nurse!"

Though Peter half expected his father's squeezing of that racing newspaper to be quickly followed by laughter, conversation, and relief—it was an arduous process and a road measured in nuance that Sal took his loved ones on over the following days.

His eyes would open, only to quickly close again.

He would nod a response—or was it a response?

His hands would squeeze. Once for Yes, twice for No. But sometimes the responses would be wrong, or nonexistent.

There would be a grunt.

"Did he say 'Mary'?"

"Was it 'Mama'?"

Was it even a word at all?

Through it all, the doctors reassured the family that, whatever it was, it was indeed progress. There were no guarantees. There was no standard way for a person to emerge from a coma, and there was no standard expectation of their functional abilities after they had done so. Sal had been "gone" for two weeks, and there was no way to tell how much of him would return.

One cold evening, Peter sat by his father's bed as the gusts pounded their fifth-floor window.

"Bob Tarpinian! Mimi Brancone! Eddie O'Connor!"

Peter jumped as the names flew out of his father's mouth. They came dry as sand, but strong and in rapid succession. Sal's eyes were closed, but his fists were tight.

"Dan Haran! Ed White! James Willie Lomax!"

Peter wanted to get the doctors, but he was frozen.

Who are these people?

"Sam DeMeo! Harry Smith!"

"It's okay, Pop," yelled a startled Peter. "You're having a dream, is all. It's okay."

⚬⚬⚬

The lines of succession within the underworld were far from linear. The powers that be often frowned upon strict nepotism, but at the same time there was usually nobody more trustworthy than the son, or grandson, of a member. Many times the descendant had no interest in following in his father's activities. Many fathers didn't want their sons involved in the life they'd chosen. Rico Falcone always wanted to be like his father. He'd grown up watching the adoration and respect bestowed upon the man. He wanted that. Biaggio had reservations about it at first but hoped his son would develop into a level-headed leader. Olga, Biaggio's wife of many years, left him because Rico was accepted into the crime family—yet this woman enjoyed the life Biaggio supplied her to such an extent that she had little time for Frederico in his formative years.

Nicky the Zipper had two daughters, so he never had the chance to groom a son for the mob. Staten Island Lou had a boatload of kids, but none of them were privy to the secrets of his life, and none pursued a similar path. Tommy Box o' Cookies had one daughter and a son-in-law he didn't trust enough to bring to Biaggio, despite the young man's pleas. Punch the Pedal was grandson to Mr. Scotti, so he was one of those who skipped a generation, a surprisingly common occurrence. Johnny the Beatnik was a first-generation member, as was Carbone. Johnny came via Nicky, whom he had met at a boxing match. They struck up an unlikely friendship, and after years of building trust, he was awarded Nicky's endorsement. Carbone had been a great friend to Punch for a long time, indirectly helping out Biaggio in the process. That earned him his spot. Nephews were not uncommon within the families, Winnie being a perfect example.

Don Sacco had a son, but he died over two decades ago at the age of seventeen. He was driving home from high school, in the middle of the afternoon, when he was broadsided by a drunk driver in a pickup. The driver of the truck suffered only cuts and bruises but vanished from the face of the earth three weeks later.

∞

Don Sacco gathered Lenny Sheetrock and the boys around the television screen in his Florida apartment. This was different than his Florida home. His wife was in that house, playing cards with her friends. He was here at the apartment with his twenty-seven-year-old *comare*. He deemed it a fair exchange. For him, sex on demand with a beautiful young woman who'd never otherwise look twice at his plump sixty-five-year-old body; for her, money, jewelry, and fuel for her braggadocian rants. Sacco's men had a selection of girlfriends and/or prostitutes that would come and go as well. The women were not permitted in the locked den at the moment because Don Sacco wanted to show his boys a new videotape he had just received.

The twisted, broken paths of nepotism are evident in most aspects of society. Those who were not strictly members of a particular crime family were often free to work for multiple families, within certain guidelines. One such associate of the families died many years ago. He had no children, no wife, almost no family at all. There were a handful of people at his burial. His cause of death remained a mystery, but his body was found in his damp basement—a meal to his own dogs. What was left of him was buried, as per his written instructions, wrapped in his old, ragged cape.

He had one sister, several years his junior. She had three sons. One was a military man, one became an engineer, and one was a little different than the others. Always the family ne'er-do-well, it was he who came upon a long-forgotten box of his late uncle's belongings. It contained some notebooks, diagrams, diaries and musings. These items should have been turned over to the authorities or, at the very least, burned and consigned to oblivion, but instead, they gave some dubious direction to the life of a hounded misfit.

"Put the tape in, Steven," said Sacco to his short, fireplug bodyguard.

Steven put the small VHS-C cassette into its adapter and loaded the player. All manner of grain and horizontal lines danced on the television screen until the shaky picture came into view.

"I got a feeling we're gonna like this shit," laughed Sacco as the room grew thick with cigar smoke.

"What is it?" asked Lenny Sheetrock.

"Watch. You'll see."

The video was in color, but it almost seemed to be black and white. Maybe it was the lighting.

"Turn up the sound."

The tape was obviously recorded from a camera on a tripod, as the frame never changed. There was a man strapped into a chair. His eyes were wide; his brow covered in sweat. He was maybe thirty years old, with a receding hairline and large ears.

"Get me the fuck outta here!" he screamed, oblivious to the camera.

Scratchy, distorted circus music began to play as the bound man struggled to free himself. Barely audible beneath the jittery carnival melody came the clatter of squeaky wheels. A long table was being pushed into the camera's view, just in front of the victim.

"What the hell?" mumbled Lenny Sheetrock as Don Sacco coughed with laughter.

In full makeup and bright attire, a circus clown set the table in position. He then laid several empty, aluminum pie trays on the table as the man squirmed and hollered. The clown picked up the first round tray and walked toward the camera for his close-up. He smiled. The white makeup made his crooked teeth appear even more yellow than they were. Some of his red lipstick had smudged onto his incisors. Specks of lint were visible in his bristly orange wig.

Though the original was long gone and rotting in a grave on Long Island, Don Sacco and his boys were witnessing the return of the Diabolist—in the form of an unbalanced nephew who found direction and identity in his dead uncle's persona.

Advancing his case for lineage gone awry, the Diabolist filled the tray with whipped cream from a spray can, then stuck his white-gloved forefinger into it, covering it in the sugary fluff. He proceeded to lick it all off and smacked his crimson lips together. He pranced and twirled away from the camera and toward the bound man.

"Fuck you," screamed the victim.

Then he got a pie in the face.

"Don Sacco—" began Steven.

"Shhh," replied his boss.

The Diabolist went for the second aluminum tray on the table. He brought it toward the camera, grinning. As Sacco and the boys awaited the can of whipped cream to appear, the new Diabolist presented a dirty, jagged red brick. He placed the brick into the pie tray and then covered it all with whipped cream. He put a finger to his coagulating lipstick and winked at the camera.

"Oh, shit," mumbled Lenny Sheetrock as he sucked his cigar.

The dirty clown then skipped and hopped toward the confined man, who cursed through the cream that covered his face from the initial pie. The Diabolist grabbed a dishrag and wiped his victim's face nearly clean. The man spat on him. The evil jester turned toward the camera, brick pie in hand, and heaved his shoulders rapidly, as if in laughter. He took a step back from his victim and pulled his pie hand far behind him like a poorly-trained discus thrower. The carnival music blared as he slammed the second pie into the man's face. The victim's head was thrust much farther back than the first time. There was no cursing either, just the muffled grunt that came with a broken cheekbone. The man's head fell to the side. The whipped cream that covered his face began to turn pink, then red, as blood poured from his nose.

"Holy Christ," said Lenny. "Who is this freak?"

"You remember hearing about the Diabolist?" asked Sacco of his younger cohort.

The video continued as the victim's head moved. He was still conscious, though dazed and bleeding. The clown danced toward the camera with a third pie tray. He loaded it up with fistfuls of broken glass and covered it all with whipped cream. He pranced back toward his prey and wiped the bloody cream off with the rag. The man neither swore nor spat. The heartless harlequin then reached back and pounded the creamy glass shards into his captive's face as hard as he could.

"The Diabolist? Didn't that guy do this shit in the forties and fifties?"

"Yeah. Some of us would occasionally use him to make a point. Apparently, this is now a family business," laughed Sacco.

The tape went on as the torturer filled a final pie tray with a block of wood that had upwards of thirty, three-inch masonry nails spiking from it. He lathered it in whipped cream.

"Holy hell," mustered Steven as he lit another cigar for his don.

The Sacco crew watched the nail pie being driven into the victim's face. Then they saw the Diabolist finally conclude the proceedings with a bullet to the man's head. They viewed some additional scenes, recorded separately, of the costumed killer persecuting a man with slow-dripping acid, slicing off ever larger chunks of flesh and extremities, using various power tools, and so on. The Diaboloist's costume would sometimes change, but the recording would always culminate in a painful death. The tape ended as it began, with fuzz and horizontal lines. Don Sacco's smoky den was silent.

"What the hell was the point of all that? Who were those men who were killed, and why would any jackass record these? To give the cops irrefutable evidence against him?" asked Lenny Sheetrock in rapid succession.

"Lenny," replied the boss, "I have no clue who those men were, but they're not made—I can tell you that. What you saw was basically an audition tape. A business card. This guy wants to show that he has what the original had. He wants the legacy to continue."

"Legacy?"

"In his twisted mind it is. He's honoring his uncle or grandpa, or whoever the fuck the Diabolist was to him. He's telling the families that he's there if we need him. He included a phone number."

∽

After Peter's frantic phone call, Mary had a longtime neighbor drop her off at the hospital, once again leaving Joey with Kathy. Peter was excited during the call, rambling on about Pop talking and squeezing the newspaper. Mary was unsure what to expect when she arrived at Sal's room. Peter was standing there with a scribbled scrap of paper in his hand. Sal was there but appeared unchanged from what his wife had grown accustomed to. His eyes were closed and he was placid as a frozen pond. Peter breathlessly embraced his anxious mother.

"I know he looks the same now, Ma, but a little while ago he was rattling off names. The doctors saw it too. They checked him over and said it was a very, very good sign, of course."

She walked over toward her husband and clutched his hand as he slept.

"Don't get scared if he does it again," said Peter. "It comes outta nowhere. He just starts yelling. But he sounds strong."

Mary ran her hand along her husband's cheek.

"These names, Ma, I don't know who they are. I wrote some down. At least I think this is what he said," reported Peter as he fumbled with the paper.

She waited, hoping for Sal to tighten his grip on her hand.

"Ed White?" asked Peter. "Dan Haran? Eddie O'Connell?"

Mary raised her head as Peter continued. "Mimi Brancone? James Willie Lomax?"

She turned toward her son.

He carried on, "Bob Tarp . . . Bob Tarpeen . . ."

"Tarpinian," said his mother, softly. "And O'Connor—not O'Connell."

"You know these names?"

"I do."

"Who are they? They're not from the neighborhood. Not from work."

"They're soldiers, Peter."

He stood there in silence.

"Not the kind of soldiers from Biaggio's army. Real soldiers."

Peter walked toward his parents, setting the paper down.

"I haven't heard those names since you were a baby," she said. "They all fought beside your father. God knows if they're all still with us. He's lost touch with them."

Mary breathed deep and turned back toward her husband. Her heart stopped cold as she saw his big brown eyes wide open for the first time in what seemed like forever. They looked directly at her in a manner not cold or distant but warm and welcoming. His hand grew warm and strong as it contracted around hers. Peter knew it was time to get the doctors; as he was about to prepare his mother for Sal's clamorous roll call, the name that arose from his father's lips was delivered in a hush.

"Mary."

Chapter Thirty

THE DOCTORS WARNED of an arduous process, but Sal was up for the challenge. His whispered utterance of his wife's name was the first of many words, which later became sentences. The hand squeezing led to arm raising, which then begat the act of pulling himself up, a few inches at a time, from his hospital bed.

Weeks turned to months, but Sal persevered. Initially from within the confines of the hospital, but eventually, via trips from his home to the rehabilitation facility several times per week. It was a frustrating process and a firm invitation for depression, but when things seemed at their lowest point, Sal would remind himself of one fact: *My son has dealt with worse limitations for his entire life.*

By the time warm weather returned to New York, Salvatore Salerno was able to move about with the aid of a cane. His speech was slower with diminished enunciation, but he could be understood.

Joey responded well to his father's return home. He had not seen him in months, and his mother feared him viewing his lifelong pillar in such a state of fragility. Mary spent extra time preparing her son that morning. He even got his shave. He was dressed smartly as he waited beside his mother on the couch. Peter ushered his father in via wheelchair—his mode of transportation for the first several weeks of outpatient recovery. Joey smiled, not even acknowledging the wheelchair—a pleasant surprise to all concerned—and presented Sal with the key ring he harbored since the first night of his hospitalization.

Joey's manner usually paralleled his father's condition. After his initial rush of strength at Sal's homecoming, he regressed almost daily as he saw the struggles of rehabilitation wearing on his father. It did not go unnoticed by others that Joey appeared stalwart toward his own monumental challenges but couldn't bear to see Sal in any level of impairment. In time, and especially as the wheelchair skedaddled, Joey began to improve as well. He stood a little taller, ate more, smiled, and showed a renewed interest in music, shoeshines, and having an occasional spot of cold beer.

Mary spent more time at church than she had in the past. She'd bring Joey with her if Peter or Kathy were able to sit with Sal while they went. She prayed as she had for decades— for a miracle for her son— but now she also asked that Sal be returned to full strength.

Dear Lord, I don't believe I have the ability to care for the both of them.

An in-home nurse would be very costly, and medical insurance would only help so much. Peter and Kathy had two children of their own, and she couldn't expect them to be available on a moment's notice. Peter had a full-time job at the cola plant as well. Mary's sisters and brother helped as much as they could, but she really needed her husband to be self-sufficient again.

⁂

Sal's position as Biaggio Falcone's top numbers runner was secure, but since his stroke it had been farmed out to those junior to him. Things at the barbershop were quiet in the months following the deaths of Vito Salerno and Punch the Pedal. Biaggio had a long talk with his son about Don Sacco. He told Rico that he was safe, but his indiscretion had led to Punch's murder. Rico listened and kept his mouth shut, but although he believed his father's words, he had no such faith in the declarations of Don Sacco. He fumed internally over what was done to Punch, and was convinced that the Sacco family would make an attempt on his life when the time was right and their involvement wouldn't be as obvious. He kept these thoughts from his father.

Rico Falcone lived alone in a beautiful brick home on Shore Road. He had a majestic view of the Verrazano-Narrows Bridge. Though nobody in Brooklyn ever included the word "narrows" in its title—and a good percentage of them mispronounced it as the "VerraNzano"—Italians in the know were very proud that it was named after famed explorer Giovanni de Verrazzano; he was said to be the first European navigator to enter New York Harbor. There was also an ongoing debate as to why the bridge's title lacked the second "Z" featured in its revered namesake.

New York hates the Italians.

That was the most popular of the theories, fueled by the fact that it took nearly a decade and many a petition to get approval for the name. Even after its reluctant acceptance, it was very nearly changed at the last minute to be named after President John F. Kennedy, following his assassination in 1963. It took a personal request from the Italian Historical Society of America to United States Attorney General Robert F. Kennedy, who assured them that he would see to it that the bridge not be named after his slain brother, to keep the honor on track. John F. Kennedy would instead be memorialized by the renaming of Idlewild Airport on his behalf. An elderly next-door neighbor of Sal Salerno's—a man who came from Sicily to New York in 1902 as a knife grinder, and eventually ground his way to running a small chain of hardware stores—once wondered aloud as to what Giovanni de Verrazzano would have thought of the number of trunk-stuffed Italian corpses that were routinely hauled over his bridge to be deposited in the marshes of Staten Island and New Jersey.

Rico sipped his espresso from the front balcony of his home. He stared at the lights on the country's longest suspension bridge, as he had for many a night since he

271

purchased the home, but he never thought about, or knew anything of, the origin of its name. His girlfriend—the latest in a string of relationships that would last anywhere from a week to a season—had gone home hours ago. He had a busy day making plans for his crew, and he decided it would be nice to relax inside in front of his new Zenith rear-projection television. It was a modern marvel that would emerge from its wooden cabinet at the touch of a button.

He went inside and loaded his entertainment for the evening. It was the VHS-C tape that the new Diabolist sent out to all of New York's crime families. His father received the tape, said that the real Diabolist was long dead and that he had outgrown contracting someone like that many years ago. He regretted that he ever used him at all. Biaggio tossed it in the trash. Rico retrieved it. He was about to watch it on his Zenith. For the third time.

∽

Early Monday afternoon, Sal sat on his couch watching a game show that fought a losing battle to hold his interest. He was thrilled to be on the sofa, though. More couch, less bed. Joey sat beside him as Mary rattled around in the kitchen. The day was slightly overcast so Sal had the light on to help him read his *Racing Form*. Joey laughed at some of the contestants' antics on the quiz show.

"You like that, Joe?" asked his father, his speech slow and deliberate.

"Hmmmm."

All at once the television went black. Sal's reading light flickered, and Mary's electric opener stopped mid-can. Then, in unison, they resumed.

The doorbell rang.

"I bet that's Kathy," said Mary as she ambled past her men on the couch.

She opened the door to see a diminutive, dark-skinned African-American woman tapping on the bare porch light bulb.

"May I help you?" asked Mary as she tried to determine whether the woman was forty or sixty years of age.

"This bulb here was winkin'," said the woman, smiling. "Not sure why you have it on anyway. No need for this to be shinin' in broad daylight. You're throwing money away, ma'am."

Eyes still on the smiling visitor, Mary reached over to the light switch on the inside of the doorway and turned it off.

"Now there you go," said the stranger as she tucked a stray hair back under its clip.

"So . . . "

"Oh, how rude of me. So sorry. I'm Pearl Gholston," she said, extending her hand.

Mary grasped her hand, releasing quickly.

"If you're here to sell—"

"Lord, no," she replied. "Not selling perfume or cookies. Not here to change your religion, either." She produced an identification card that dangled from a lanyard.

"Who is it?" bellowed Sal from the room behind, slowly but with vigor.

"That must be Mr. Salerno," said the woman. "I can tell by the speech pattern. Then again, I don't suppose you'd likely have another man in there hollerin' at the doorway!"

Mary ignored both Sal and the visitor as she studied the ID card.

"You're a nurse?"

"Sure am."

"But I didn't call for a nurse."

"Well, not directly, maybe. You asked for me at church, I do believe."

"At church?"

"I work with my church, though not in this part of town. Mrs. Salerno, we're all part of one."

"I don't understand."

"Well let's say you asked a priest for help with your husband—"

"My daughter-in-law's brother is a priest, and I did mention—"

"You sure did. One priest asks another. That priest asks a monsignor who has lunch with a pastor who speaks with one of his clergy, and next thing you know, you got a little black lady on your stoop being stared at by the neighbors."

Pearl tilted her head just enough to lead Mary to see a curtain being quickly closed on her neighbor's basement door.

"Okay," replied Mary, trying to absorb it all. "But why didn't you call first?"

Cane in hand, Sal made his way to the doorway to investigate. He peered over his wife's shoulder at Pearl Gholston.

"That's why, right there," said the smiling nurse. "I haven't even been invited in yet, but I've gone and gotten your big bear outta hibernation. Hello there, Mr. Salerno."

As she had done many times before, Pearl talked her way in the door. She gave the Salernos a long list of references, interacted warmly with Joey, explained that she was not an expert in physical rehabilitation and that she was not there in an official capacity, nor was her visit endorsed by any hospital. She came via a wish that found its way through a loose network of churches. She didn't charge anywhere near the rate an on-the-books nurse would, and the compensation she would receive from the Salernos would be shared with both of their churches. This all sounded wonderful to Mary, but she'd first need to call some of Pearl's references and the church with which she claimed association.

Pearl left quietly after a cup of coffee in Mary's kitchen, bidding *adieu* to Sal and Joey as they housed themselves on the sofa.

"Maybe get someone to look at that wiring, Mr. Salerno," she said on the way out.

"Huh?"

"Those lights. The winkin' and blinkin'. Somethin' ain't up to snuff."

Mary knew she faced a long night of convincing her husband to spend just a couple of hours a day, a few days a week, with a complete stranger. After placing several phone calls to the woman's references, Mary was determined. Their guest was charming, professional, and brimming with energy and spirit. She was also affordable. Mary couldn't do this alone, and damned if her husband was going to vegetate before her eyes. Come hell or high water, Sal was going to give it a go with Nurse Gholston.

It was a warm, sunny Wednesday as Sal sat on his front stoop, cane in hand.

"Five-O," he said quietly.

"Not lettin' you off that easy," replied Pearl as she stood three steps below him, holding three fuzzy balls in her hand.

Sal looked around. He felt a little uneasy about it all.

"Hawaii Five-O," he replied.

"That's better. You tried to avoid the difficult word there. Not a good plan, Sal."

She thought for a moment.

"Say 'Zulu as Kono.' "

"What?"

"You heard me. 'Zulu as Kono,' " she repeated as she began to juggle the three fuzz balls.

He cleared his throat before trying.

"Zulu . . . as . . . Kana."

"Not Kana, Kono," she said. "Make your mouth like a Cheerio."

"Kono."

"Good. Say Kam Fong as Chin Ho."

"Oh, come on."

"You said you liked *Hawaii Five-O*. These were the dang credits to your show!"

"Kam Fong as Chinno."

"Chin Ho. Two words. Try again," she commanded, the balls were in flight before her.

275

"Chinno."

"Chin. Small silence. Ho."

"Chin Ho."

"Lots better! Hey, watch out!"

She tossed a fur ball that landed smack on his forehead.

"You gotta be faster than that, Sal Salerno. Catch that sucker next time."

⁓

The shadow cast upon the sidewalk could have been from years gone by. It could almost have been that of a swing-era street vendor nudging a fruit cart up the avenue. But this wasn't the 1940s and there was no produce to be had. Pearl Gholston was pushing Sal around the neighborhood in his wheelchair. Periodically, she would prompt him to stand and walk beside her with his cane and, if need be, her beanpole of an arm for support. They paused to watch a game of stick-ball that slowed traffic on the street beside them.

"Already sick of this chair," said Sal, taking time to enunciate.

"Yes, sir. I don't think you'll need it for much longer," she replied.

"Hey, Mr. Salerno," yelled one of the kids from the street game.

"Hi, Kevin. Hello, boys."

"Friends with the neighborhood kids, are you?" Pearl smiled.

"Most. Good kids. Play ball."

"Sal, you sound like the Frankenstein monster. You'll frighten those kids, is what you'll do."

He waved her off.

"Seriously, sprinkle a pronoun or preposition in here and there. Don't be lazy."

He looked into the distance as he prepared his sentence.

"There is . . . the church . . . where Mary and I . . . were married."

Pearl grinned.

"Nice. Let's say we walk on over there."

They sat on the parish steps, in the shadow of the steeple. Pearl set a slice of fresh pizza on each of their laps, just procured from the front window of a pizzeria that was on that avenue for thirty years.

"Have you been to this church lately? I mean inside."

"No," replied Sal. "Mary goes. Joey too."

"Why not you?"

"Not sure."

"Hot dang, this is some good pizza," yelled Pearl.

Sal took a measured bite of his slice.

"You thinkin' that maybe the Lord let you down a little? Maybe because Joey was born with his problems?"

"I dunno."

"Because if that's it, you could look at it another way too."

Sal glanced up from his pizza.

"Some folks can't have babies at all," she continued. "Now I know Joey brings a lot of baggage with him, but truth be told, aren't you glad he's here at all?"

"Of course."

"I know that. Just sayin'. You need help opening that soda?"

Sal struggled with the cap but managed to unscrew it.

"I remember when . . . we first delivered . . . the sodas with . . . the twist cap," he smiled.

"Whoo-hoo! That must've been like the moon landing for the cola industry!"

"Very funny," he replied, still grinning.

"So," she said, swallowing her pizza, "the Lord did send you a child—two, in fact. You can't say you were shortchanged too much."

No answer.

"Does that place make those calzones too?" she asked. "Boy, I love those things."

"Sure. Good ones, too."

He looked over at Pearl and his expression changed.

"I lost a lot of friends. My little cousin . . . got stabbed . . . in the heart."

"Oh. I'm sorry to hear that," she said solemnly. "Maybe you're wondering if there's a God at all then?"

He turned and took another bite of his slice.

"Well," she began, "I sure as heck can't tell you that there is."

He looked surprised.

"What?"

"Who am I to tell you that? I can tell you that you should try believing."

"Hard to believe sometimes. Want proof," he answered.

"Did you get that wiring looked at? Your winkin' lights?"

"No. Hasn't happened again."

She wiped the edges of her lips with a small napkin.

"Sal, just thinking of things like that electrical wiring in your house, would you say the human race has come a long way—technologically speaking—since the days of discovering fire and inventing the wheel?"

"Like the twist-off cap?" He smiled.

"Maybe, but more like the electricity in your home, the indoor plumbing, insulation, wooden structure, brickface, aluminum siding, and what have you."

"Yes. Many geniuses. You are going to say . . . that God . . . gave us those . . . geniuses."

"Not gonna say that. I believe that, but it's not what I'm gettin' at."

"Okay."

"If you saw a modern house, like any of these—with electricity, plumbing and all—built five thousand years ago, ten thousand years ago, what would you say?"

Sal laughed, "Show me that!"

She took a long drink of her fruit punch.

"The nerves that run throughout your body and mine, Sal, are our electrical system. Wanna talk plumbing? How 'bout veins and arteries? Would you call that indoor plumbing?

The structure that supports it all—the wood frame? Our skeletal system. Insulation? Fat. Though I could use a little more of that. Brickface or siding equals skin, Sal. Heck, we even have an advanced waste removal system in our *homes*. Don't even get me started on the topic of fancy filter systems. Our earthly bodies got 'em all over the place."

He rubbed the stubble on his chin.

"You have gas heat or oil?" she asked.

"Oh . . . oil."

"I knew that. Doesn't matter. You got a thermostat, right?"

"Sure."

"Well, so does your brain, Sal Salerno. You got a little doodad called the hypothalamus gland right at the bottom of your brain that keeps your body temperature steady as your home thermostat."

"Hmm."

"I'm just sayin' if there ain't no God above, then who or what came up with all this complicated stuff that took the human race thousands and millions of years to basically copy and then patent as inventions? It was all already here. Before you and I, and before the geniuses. I'm still waiting for them to come up with a fancy computer as fast and astounding as the human brain. Even yours."

Sal sat there and tapped his foot against the wheelchair that was parked in front of the church steps.

"Dang, this is some good pizza!" she said.

The passing days saw Sal grow more comfortable with Pearl as his New York skepticism waned and he began to accept that she was there to help him in any way she could. Her methods may not have come from medical books, but she got him moving and talking. One day she'd be blowing bubbles through a small plastic wand while big Salvatore Salerno swatted them from the air like a gorilla shooing jungle flies; two days later he'd find himself at a kiddie arcade playing a

Whac-A-Mole game with his nurse, the only adults in the place without juvenile accompaniment. Though initially quite embarrassed, two minutes into the battle he'd be hellbent on winning. Around the time of their third arcade visit, he did.

Sal hadn't been by the barbershop in months. He'd heard from Peter that the boys came to see him in the hospital, but he hadn't invited them to his home because he didn't want to rile up Mary—and, truth be told, he didn't want the fellas to see him in his current condition. He'd spoken to Pearl about his friends, but was careful to limit his revelations. On this day, their walk—more walk, less wheelchair—led them toward Scotti's. Pearl pushed the empty chair as Sal and his cane strode beside her.

"This here was my hangout for . . . almost forty years, Pearl."

"A barbershop? You ain't got enough hair to be spendin' all that time in there!"

"Nice bunch o' guys—once you know 'em," he said, his words clear and strong.

"They all barbers?"

"No."

He switched the cane to his other hand as he approached the old brick portion of the storefront. He ran his hand along the chipped and faded blocks, not far from the spinning barber pole.

"Wanna show you something. Come closer, Pearl."

His forefinger slid across several small holes in the facade.

"These are bullet holes."

"Are they now?"

"Some men tried to shoot a friend of mine right here."

"Lord! When was that, Sal?"

"Nineteen forty-six, I think."

"Say what? I know the hair-cutting business ain't so bad that they can't patch up some holes."

"Can't patch them. They're almost . . . a landmark . . . in this neighborhood."

"If you say so."

"Look behind you, Pearl. What's missing along the sidewalk?"

It took her a moment, but after studying the curb area of the sidewalk, she answered, "Looks to me like there's a tree about every thirty- or thirty-five feet along. 'Cept not in front of your barbershop. Why'd they skip a tree?"

"There was one there, but it was sick, so they took it out."

"When?"

"Same year as the bullet holes."

"Another landmark?"

"I'd say yes."

"So," she replied, "the city doesn't want a tree here?"

"The man who runs the barbershop doesn't want a tree here," he said, pausing to gather strength for a long sentence. "The city probably doesn't care because a tree would only help to block the view . . . from the police cameras."

Sal nodded toward the far street corner, where a long lens protruded from an unmarked car.

"Okay," she said. "Now I see. Am I gonna find my picture hangin' on the post office wall?"

He laughed. "No. You and I are okay, I think. You for sure."

"You wanna go in?" asked Pearl.

"I was thinking of it. You?"

"Well, with the police and the bullet holes and what have you, I'm thinking maybe not right now."

"It's okay. Maybe another time."

Sal sat back down in his wheelchair.

"Maybe you could wheel me back the way we came?" he asked. "This way we don't pass the front window."

⤳

The hot bath water was quite sympathetic to Sal's aching body. He was still quite uneasy that a woman other than his wife was in the same room with him as he bathed. Pearl helped him into the tub, and, though he had swim trunks on, he found it very unnerving. Now he was hidden behind a sheer shower curtain and was free to slip off his trunks. His nurse sat atop the closed toilet lid, and the bathroom door was open to lessen the discountenance. Mary had taken Joey for a visit with his niece and nephew at Peter's house. Sal could see a blurred image of Pearl through the curtain and vice versa.

"Maybe one day you'll come in the barbershop," he said, trying to minimize the situation through conversation.

"I could do that."

"They're really a nice bunch, Pearl."

"I understand that, but not too many nice bunches have the police stuck on them like a cheap toupee."

"I can't argue with that." He sighed.

"I wouldn't have pegged you for that, Sal."

"For what?" he asked as he grabbed a washcloth.

"You know, one of those types. Whatever you wanna call them."

"I don't do that stuff."

"Not my business, but if they trust you to be around them . . . "

"It's a long, complicated story," he said as he rubbed his aching leg.

"As I said, not my business, but if you ever want someone to talk to . . . "

"You're a nice lady, Pearl. You know how to help me walk and talk, but there are some things even you can't fix."

"Right as rain about that. You're the one who got yourself walkin' and talkin'. Not me. I'm just here to help. Help with your transition, I guess. Get you to believe in yourself."

"I've never hurt anybody."

"Good. Good for you. I heard stories about this neighborhood, though. My Lord. Not that mine is any different. I can't tell you how many young black men we've lost to gangs. Many of 'em gone because of a stray bullet.

Babies, too. I know your Italian gangs are a little different. More experienced. More money. 'They only kill their own' is what I've heard—as if that's an accolade. When they do kill their own, Sal, many of those dead men have families and children, too. Maybe those children didn't sign up for no brotherhood. Maybe they didn't sign up to lose their fathers."

Sal ran the soap across his chest. He looked at Pearl's blurred image through the curtain.

"I took a job with them to get help with Joey. I made it clear that I didn't want to get involved with any blood. I'm a hard-working man."

"How long ago was that?"

"When Joey was born."

Pearl looked at the curtain. She could see that Sal's head was bowed.

"All those years ago. Was there any point that you could've walked away as Joey got older?"

"Yes. They would allow that, I believe. Mine was a special case. The boss had a bond of sorts with Joey."

Sal swallowed hard. This was a lot of talking for him, in both measure and content.

There was silence, save for the light splash of soapy water. Pearl wanted relief for her patient, not depression, and this line of discussion could marshal him either way. Time for a curveball.

"I once heard that a mobster got on the Wonder Wheel at Coney Island with his mistress. They went around on the ferris wheel a few times, and when it came time to get off, their ride car came to a stop and they were both dead in their seat. Both somehow rubbed out while on the ride."

"I think that's another old wives' tale," said Sal with a smile.

"I don't know." Pearl laughed.

"There's another one that says a made guy's cheating wife was to meet her lover at a concert at Carnegie Hall. He was late, and she was nervous as the concert began."

Sal took a breath, as this was yet another longer set of words.

"When the performance started," he continued, "they had to stop because the piano was out of tune. Well, the short version is . . . right there on stage . . . they found her lover stuffed in the darn Steinway."

"You did not just say that!"

"I'm not even gonna tell you what part of him they found in the French horn."

They both had a good laugh as Sal soaped up his washcloth.

"That's just wrong!" said Pearl.

"Creative, I guess," he replied. "But surely not true."

He ran the cloth along his leg as his smile evaporated. He appreciated the compassionate listener beyond his shower curtain. He scrubbed hard on a spot below his knee, but it remained.

Probably a bruise.

"Pearl, if you ever hear a rumor about . . . a man being drowned in motor oil—"

"Oh, heavens," she said and laughed, maybe expecting yet another fabricated tale.

"—that one would be true," he said.

She halted her chuckle as she detected the change in Sal's voice.

"Is that so?"

"It is."

"Wanna tell me about it?"

"Not much to say. He was my friend. I found him like that."

"Dear. I'm very sorry."

"Thank you."

"Did you ever, you know, tell the police or anything?"

He peered at the curtain, fixing on her beclouded semblance.

"No, I didn't. I never said a word to anybody except the fellas."

"You okay with that?"

"I don't know, Pearl. I did what I was supposed to do."

"Supposed to do?"

"The police wouldn't have been much help in this case."

"Hmmm."

"Then, not ten minutes later, I saw my cousin . . . " He paused for a breath. "Saw my cousin bleeding to death, but . . . they didn't bring him to a hospital. Had to keep it quiet."

"That's a lot to digest, Sal."

"I kept that quiet, too. My own cousin. Even his family isn't quite sure what happened to him."

"No."

"They know he died, know he was murdered, but the circumstances . . . were never made clear."

"That's a whole lot to carry around with you."

"Eh, they all have their shady organizations, Pearl. The Irish, Russians, Asians. It's not an Italian thing."

"Now that came outta nowhere. Who said anything about the Italians?"

"Nobody," he said. "I told you that I never hurt anyone. That wasn't entirely true."

"Okay."

"I was in the war. Things got rough over there, you know. The rules weren't so clear."

"You might need to separate the two, Sal. What you did for your country, and for freedom, that's probably quite different than what the barbershop boys do. I'm not the judge of that, but common sense draws a line between the two."

"Sometimes that line gets blurry for me."

"You know that famous picture of the young anti-war protester putting a flower in the rifle barrel of a military officer?" she asked.

"Sure."

"Sometimes I feel as if I'm both of those people."

Sal let that thought linger as he began to stand in the tub, behind the curtain. He struggled hard, but asked for no assistance. He got to his feet as the water dripped from his body. Proud of his accomplishment, he called out to his nurse, "Can you hand me a towel, please?"

She brought him one—warm, fluffy, and white—and was about to pass it behind the curtain when he pulled the wet vinyl divider aside.

"Baths are a real pain lately, Pearl, but it's nice to feel clean," he said as he grabbed the towel and dried his broad shoulders.

She was proud and impressed that he stood on his own, but a tad embarrassed at his one glaring oversight.

"Good Lord, Sal, your trunks?"

He moved faster than he had in ages, frantically adjusting the towel to hide his nakedness.

∽

Mary was so impressed by Pearl's accomplishments with her husband that she insisted the woman come, after hours, for a small dinner party at the Salerno home. The invitation was extended for Pearl and a guest of her choosing, but the caregiver arrived alone. It was refreshing to behold her in a nice colorful ensemble, rather than wrapped in plain nursing garb. Mary had also gone out on a limb in suggesting to Sal that he invite Tommy Box o' Cookies and his wife Eleanor. In all her years in Brooklyn, Mary had occasionally seen, but never had a word from, Tommy's wife. Naturally, Peter, Kathy, and the kids were also in attendance, and of course, a revitalized Joey. Before dinner, he played his Beatles records for all—thrilled by the progress of his father. Tommy arrived at the door with two large cookie boxes and gave Sal a huge bear hug. He was on his best behavior in front of Mary, and she was especially warm toward his wife. Pearl Gholston arrived without food or drink but with a gift that Peter immediately hoisted in the living room.

A dart board.

"When Sal throws a dart, y'all better duck," she said to the merriment of all.

And throw a dart he did. Then another. They formed teams and battled as Joey's old records provided the soundtrack.

Peter helped Joey to participate, bringing him closer to the board and guiding his arm as he threw. One or two darts missed completely and lodged in the living room wall, but there was no concern.

"Don't think that I don't know what you're doing," Sal said to Pearl.

"What's that?" she responded, dart in hand.

"Even at a party, you got me doing therapy."

"Don't know what you're talking 'bout."

As others took their turn, Mary was able to get Pearl alone in the kitchen.

"You've done so much for him."

"Now, don't get all soft on me, Mary! He's done it for himself. He's fighting through his problems. Now he's feeling a little better."

Mary unfolded, then refolded a cloth napkin.

"Pearl, I . . . I don't want to get personal, but you didn't bring a guest."

"Nope."

"Do you . . . If I may, do you have a family? A husband? You're always helping us and we know so little about you."

Pearl took a breath and placed her left hand on Mary's. With her right hand, she pointed skyward.

"Oh. I'm so sorry," said Mary. "Forgive me."

"You're a sweet woman, Mary."

"Well, you're welcome here anytime. Thanksgiving, Christmas . . . "

"Thank you so. You might just find me grabbing at your turkey someday!"

Tommy's dart landed dead-center.

"Nice, big fella!" said Sal.

"I've been practicing on a picture of you at the barbershop!"

287

"Wise ass."

"You gonna come by?"

"I'll be by."

"Yeah?"

"Sure."

"The guys were wondering."

"I haven't exactly been playing Tiddlywinks this whole time, ya know."

"I know that. The guys just miss ya."

Sal picked up a dart. "Which guys, Tommy?"

"Come on. You know. Biaggio, Johnny, Carbone, Winnie . . . and Nicky'll be home soon."

"It seems so different to me. No Vito. No Punch."

"I won't argue there. It is different, but what are you gonna do? Life goes on, Pope."

Sal spotted Tommy's wife approaching, glass of wine in hand. He'd known her forever, and had often tried to convince Mary to befriend her, knowing they'd get along well if Mary could overlook the fact that she was married to a made guy. Eleanor was compassionate. She'd always been a great listener, a churchgoer, and was very kind to Joey.

"Eleanor, have you been taking good care of this guy?" Sal smiled.

"I try. Good luck trying to get him to walk a little. He needs to lose some weight."

"I'm big-boned," yelled Tommy.

"You've been doing a lot of walking, Sal. You need to take Tommy with you," she said.

"Any time."

"Tommy says you haven't been by Scotti's."

"That's true. Been busy with my new 'girlfriend' Pearl. Plus, Joey's been through a lot, lately. After seeing when Vito—"

Sal saw Tommy wave his hand to cut him off, so he changed gears.

"Seeing me in that condition," continued Sal, "wasn't

good for him. He seems better tonight with all of us here, but Mary and I aren't gettin' any younger."

Eleanor clutched Sal's arm. "I wanted to talk to you about Joey. You know Tommy and I love him the way an aunt and uncle would."

"Sure. He loves you guys."

Tommy interrupted, "Ellie, maybe now's not the time."

"What would be the time, then?"

"I dunno, maybe when it's just Sal and Mary here."

"I've only just spoken to Mary for the first time. I feel better telling Sal. He can run it by his wife if and when he feels like it."

"Hey, hey," said Sal, "it's fine. Just say what you gotta. I know yous want the best for Joey."

Eleanor took a small sip of wine before she spoke.

"There has been some talk around the church about a woman," she said, running a finger along the edge of her glass. "You might even remember her."

Chapter Thirty-one

After a fortnight of discussion and negotiation, and with the help of Pearl Gholston, Sal got Mary to go for it.

They strode along the avenue in the afternoon sun, just as they had countless times before. The pace was slower, but never had it been more determined. Sal was getting closer to his old self, at least with regard to posture and mobility, though he still required a cane. Mary grasped the arm that held his walking stick. At his insistence, his free arm carried a bag that contained meats, cheeses, and bread, fresh from the salumeria. They turned down a side street and continued walking a few blocks further than they'd normally go in that direction. The people were not as familiar, the homes, with some exceptions, were in various stages of disrepair, yet the postal zip code was the same as the Salerno home. They found the address they were given.

Finding no doorbell, Mary knocked.

A couple of dogs barked from within the home, then muffled voices could be heard as the canine sounds grew distant and, finally, silent.

The door opened. Mary took the bag of food from her husband's arm.

A handsome, chestnut-skinned woman in her fifties smiled at the Salernos.

"You are Mary and Sal," she said through a delicate Puerto Rican accent.

"Yes," smiled Mary. "You must be Vilma."

"I am. Please come in. Forgive my home."

As they entered, Sal wondered what exactly there was to forgive about the place. It was very neat and homey. Religious statues and crucifixes were proudly displayed in abundance. He wasn't sure what the aroma was, but it made him hungry. The barking resumed in the distance.

"My dogs," smiled Vilma, "you will not see them. My husband has taken them to a room."

"It's fine. We love animals," replied Mary as she presented her host with the grocery bag.

"Thank you. Please, come to the garden. She waits for you there. Please know that she may not take note of your presence. Kindly take no offense."

They continued through the kitchen and into the sun-splashed backyard. Flowers bloomed everywhere. The scent reminded Mary of a floral shop her mother would bring her to as a child. It reminded Sal of a funeral home. Sal took note of a healthy section of tomato plants on the side of the yard.

No, Sal, Italians don't own exclusive rights to tomato gardens.

He smiled, and almost chuckled at his thought until she came into view.

Her hair was light brown with touches of gray. She sat with her back to them, warmed by the summer sun. In her mid-forties now, she toiled without the velocity of bygone days. Her loose fitting clothing flapped in the mild botanic breeze.

"Sweetheart," said Vilma quietly. "Some nice people have come to see you."

Vilma turned to Sal. "I speak English to her today, so there are no secrets." Speaking again to the woman, she said, "Honey, you have visitors."

No response. Vilma led her guests closer.

"Annette?"

She turned slightly toward the Salernos. They saw most of her face. Lovely as always. Older and worn but, at the same time, youthful and smooth.

She lowered her pencil.

Neither Sal nor Mary had seen Annette since she was a teenager. They came to know her when she sat in the back of her grandfather's toy store, saying nothing but incessantly drawing the scenes that unfolded around her. Mary lost contact with her after the newly appointed Biaggio Falcone had her family's store burned to the ground for non-payment. Then she briefly reappeared in their life nearly a decade later when Sal found her among the mistreated children at the school they had chosen for Joey. Annette's family was exceedingly grateful to Sal for alerting them to the true conditions at that facility. That is likely the reason they acquiesced to this day's encounter. With her elders long deceased, Annette found a caring home with the family of her cousin Vilma.

Those born in Brooklyn during the first half of the twentieth century would rarely abandon their roots, and, though the situation was not entirely under her control, Annette was no exception.

"Do you remember Mr. and Mrs. Salerno, Annette?" asked her cousin.

The woman's head turned a little more. Sal didn't notice because he was searching for her artwork. He saw the pencils and some blank papers before her on a folding desk, but no evidence of a completed sketch. He was pleased to see the pencils, though. He'd often thought about the coal she was forced to use to express herself at the school, and the dark, foreboding illustrations she produced with it.

"Do you remember their young boy named Joey?"

Annette stared, but didn't turn away.

"They came to see you today, maybe to give them the strength . . . to believe?" Vilma concluded the sentence as a question, looking to Mary for approval.

Mary thought for a moment and smiled at Annette.

"We do believe, Annette. I don't really know why we came, other than to see you, because we remember you as the pretty little girl in the toy store, and when my husband heard . . . "

Annette turned away.

"I'm sorry," interrupted Vilma. "Sometimes too many words can confuse or agitate her. Please understand."

Annette's older cousin guided the Salernos a few feet away from the motionless woman.

"Maybe we should have lunch, that wonderful food you were so kind to bring. I will get my husband, Emilio. We will see Annette again later."

Vilma went to Annette's side and comforted her with a whisper. She caressed her shoulders and retrieved a fallen pencil from the ground.

They all retired to the kitchen where Vilma and Mary prepared thick sandwiches for all. Sal made small talk with Emilio, a friendly, hard-working plumber whom he saw around the neighborhood but with whom he had never exchanged more than a pleasant nod. He never knew the man was any relation to Annette, and frankly never knew what had become of the girl. Sal was shocked to hear she lived not two miles from him but rarely ventured beyond her home. After discussing the paths all of their lives had taken since the post-war years, and Vilma once again thanking Sal, on behalf of her family—living and dead—for rescuing Annette from the Dandridge School, thoughts returned to the matter at hand.

"Many years ago," said Sal, "I had a friend. A tough, but good-natured fella we called Staten Island Lou. We once tried to talk him into going to Lourdes. He had cancer."

"God bless," said Vilma as she crossed herself.

"He wouldn't go. I remember he said that he believed there was a miracle there, but it wasn't reserved for the likes of him."

Vilma took a sip of tea. "Maybe that miracle is waiting for Joey?" she asked.

Mary began to cry. Vilma went around the table to embrace her as Sal clutched her hand.

"We don't know," replied Sal. "But we heard through a friend that Annette had gone. That she had been to the baths."

"That is true," said Vilma as she steadied Mary.

"I don't know how to say this, Vilma, but since I'm from Brooklyn I can only be straight—God bless Annette, but has she improved at all since her pilgrimage?" asked Sal.

"If you ask me about her becoming like you and I, then the answer is no. She does not speak or take much care of herself."

"Oh."

"Sal, do you remember her drawings?" asked the woman.

"I do," he answered. "When she was in the toy store, she would draw the toys, the customers, her grandpa—all very nice. A very talented girl."

"And later?"

"Well, I do remember the ones from the school . . . "

"The coal," said Vilma.

"Yes. The pictures weren't happy then."

"You are very right, Sal. Between the loss of the toy store, then losing her Poppy, and then the experience at that place—her artwork became something else. Something very bad."

◆◆◆

Vilma opened the door to Annette's bedroom. It was dim, and her cousin could be seen through the sheer curtain on the second story window, still sketching in the yard. Emilio was downstairs clearing the kitchen table as his wife showed the room to Sal and Mary. Vilma turned on the light.

"Since our trip to the shrine at Lourdes, this is all that Annette creates."

She pointed at the wall behind the Salernos. They turned to see the entirety of it—floor to ceiling—covered in pencil renderings of the Virgin Mary.

"My God," whispered Mary Salerno.

In some drawings, the Blessed Mother stood in prayer. In others, she hovered as if in levitation. In some, she cried.

"That is the change in Annette," said Vilma. "She produces love. More so than even in her innocent childhood. Those vile, dark images that you saw in the school—she drew them for thirty years, day in, day out. Now she creates only one image, but one of immeasurable beauty."

⤫

Vilma led them back into Annette's fragrant garden. They could see she was immersed in her sketching. Their approach was cautious; Mary was still wiping her eyes.

"Sweetheart?" said Vilma.

The pencil went down quickly. Annette turned. She gazed without expression, but directly in Mary's eyes. Nothing moved, save the gentle breeze. Mary was thinking of something to say but decided that if Vilma was silent, that is how she should remain. She inhaled, the scents of the bloom returned her to the flower shop of her youth.

Then Annette reached out. She held a paper in her soft hand. It flapped like a white dove in the tender tempest.

"It is for you," said Vilma. "You may take it from her, Mary."

Mary approached Annette with a warm smile and a rapid heartbeat. She slowly accepted the paper.

"Thank you," she said quietly as her husband looked on, his mouth suddenly dry.

Mary stepped back as Annette glanced away. Turning the paper over, the Salernos saw Annette's latest vision. There, born from a number-two pencil, was an incredibly detailed depiction of the Mother of Jesus Christ, arms clutched around and clinging tightly to a young boy. The boy looked not like any known depiction of Jesus but almost exactly like Annette's schoolmate from 1955. Mary was certain that this was a young Joey Salerno, cradled in the arms of the Virgin.

⤫

Peter Salerno wanted to hear all about it. He knew he'd have to be involved in any pilgrimage his family would undertake because his father hadn't been on a plane since the war, and neither his mother, brother, wife, nor children had ever even considered setting foot in an aircraft of any kind.

Getting his parents to go out for any kind of nice meal at a restaurant was also a task of monumental proportions. There was, however, one place they always liked. It wasn't fancy or stuffy, it had been a cornerstone of Brooklyn since they were kids, the food was authentic and met with Mary's high standards—and it had been built from the ground up by hard-working Italian immigrants.

Spumoni Gardens was named for the delicious ices its owners began selling in 1939. They expanded to include pizza right around the time of Joey's troubles in the Dandridge school. In fact, the Salernos all remembered coming by for pizza as part of the calming process, to set Joey's mind at ease the day after Sal discovered him bound.

There had been countless trips since then, mostly in spring and summer, to eat in the friendly open-air courtyard, but not in recent years. Peter's friend Benny, though not a member of the family that had owned the establishment since day one, had been employed there for years—one of a small army of pizza makers required to keep such a hugely popular business running so smoothly.

Peter looked over at his parents, who sat patiently at the end of a long table. He stood in the outdoor line, waiting for his turn to order the food. He wished they could've brought Joey, but he had to leave his brother with Kathy so that he and his parents could freely discuss the whole Lourdes idea. It dawned on Peter that while they considered this journey, in an odd way, Spumoni Gardens was something of a pilgrimage site of its own. Tourists from the world over, and even natives from other parts of New York, would make a point of going out of their way to sample some world-class pizza.

"Benny!" said Peter as he reached the large window, the aroma of fresh sauce mixing with the heat of the ovens.

"Pete! How you been? How's the family?"

"Eh, you know, getting through."

"Kathy here?"

"No. I'm here with Mom and Pop. Takin' them to lunch."

"No Joey? That kid can eat his pizza!"

"That's something, Benny. 'That kid' you call him. He's older than both of us."

"You're right. I know. He's just innocent."

"I had to leave him home today. I'll bring him by, maybe next week."

From the rear of the kitchen came a yell. "Martin, we need more squares over here."

"Got it," replied Benny.

Peter didn't know who or what the Martin reference was about, but went ahead with his order, telling Benny he'd speak to him later.

The Sicilian slices were smoking when Peter got them to the table. They were the specialty of the house. Hot, thick, and chewy, with the tasty sauce on top of the cheese.

"Remember when we'd all come out here to 86th street for Christmas shopping?"

"Sure," said his father as he allowed his memory to the forefront.

Sal recalled how the four of them would visit many of the shops on the street, be it down by 4th Avenue, up past 25th Avenue near Spumoni Gardens or anywhere in between. The Christmas lights would be aglow and the music would echo through the winter evenings.

"Oooh," said Mary. "The squares are as good as ever! Try it, Sal."

"Delicious," said her husband, wiping sauce from his lips.

"Was Benny working?" asked Mary.

"He's in there," said Peter. "I'm sure he'll come out if he gets a minute."

"So your mother told you about the trip we're thinking of?" asked Sal, knowing the answer.

"Yep. That's all good, but it's gonna cost a lot of money,

Pop. Plus, I don't know how good Joey could handle a trip like that. A long flight, then maybe a train or whatever."

"Yeah, but maybe coming back he could fly the damn plane himself," smiled Sal.

"I'm serious," said Peter. "This is a big decision."

Mary put down her pizza.

"You didn't see Annette," she said.

"You're right, I didn't. But you said she still didn't talk or nothin'."

"The pictures, Peter," said Mary. "The beautiful pictures."

"I understand all that, but alls I'm sayin' is that a few pictures doesn't mean that she had some vision or contact with any saint or angel."

"The Madonna," said Mary. "Not an angel."

"Ma, none of us have been to Lourdes, but I'll bet my house that everywhere you turn over there somebody is sellin' a painting, a T-shirt, maybe even a freakin' bobblehead of the Virgin Mary."

"You'd better ask for forgiveness for saying something like that," snapped his mother.

"I just meant that maybe Annette's mind was so filled with seeing those images everywhere she turned that she became obsessed with drawing the same things."

"No, Peter. She drew your brother cradled in her arms," said Mary as she kissed the medal that dangled from her neck.

Peter sprinkled some oregano.

"Can you pass me that garlic?" asked Sal.

"Many, many people have gone to Lourdes," continued Peter. "Almost nobody gets some miraculous cure. I just want yous to understand that."

"Why did you use the term '*almost*'?" asked his father as he accepted the powdered garlic.

"Well, on rare occasions you might hear something happened there, but that's maybe once every—I don't even know how long. They get hundreds of sick people every day over there, all of them looking for a miracle."

"If there is just one cure left in those waters, why shouldn't it belong to Joey?" asked Sal.

"I just want you to think it through, Pop. It won't be an easy trip. You're doing much better, but it's a lot of travel, and between you and Joey, plus Ma is afraid to fly. Not to mention the cost—"

"We have a little money saved."

"Yeah, but that's for your retirement."

"Good, because I'm actually *in* my retirement."

"I'm not tryin' to talk yous out of it, Pop. I'm just giving you all the facts to help you make an informed decision. Just think about it before you invest money in something that's very unlikely to happen."

Sal gulped down his cold soda.

"Pete, for forty years I've been going around our neighborhood collecting money based on that very premise."

He put down his plastic cup.

"And I've seen my share of winners."

Sensing a losing battle, Peter just smiled. "So you're gonna play that number, I guess."

Sal felt two hands on his shoulders. He turned to see Benny standing behind him in his sauce-covered apron.

"If you're gonna play a number, stick with the neighborhood policy," said Peter's friend. "The one the state runs takes 50 percent!"

Benny was smiling as he rubbed Sal's neck.

"You're looking good, Sal," he said. "And you, beautiful as always, Mary."

"Benny!" they said in unison.

"How's the pizza? We still doing okay?"

"Delicious," replied Mary. "How's the family?"

"Very good. My boy is in the Marines now. Can you believe it?"

"Good for him," said Sal.

"God bless him," added Mary.

From the takeout window came a yell. "Martin! Martin, get back here. C'mon, it's freakin' lunch hour over here!"

"Okay, I'm coming! Jeez," he yelled before turning back to the Salerno family. "If I was a smoker I'd get a cigarette break right now. No habit, no break, I guess."

"Benny," said Peter, "I gotta ask, what's with all the Martin stuff these guys keep saying?"

His buddy laughed. "These fellas here. Pete, what's my full name?"

"Your full name? Benito Crocetti."

"Exactly. You know who Dino Crocetti is?"

"No."

"I do," yelled Mary. "That's Dean Martin. That's his real name. Did you see him in that *Cannonball Run* picture? He's still so good-lookin'."

"I saw it, Mary," replied Benny. "Very funny. They're doing another one of those, I heard. Anyway, Dino got his named changed to Martin, so these guys did the same to me. Just for laughs, Pete."

"Martin, please!" came the yell.

"I'm comin'!" he barked. "Great to see you all again. Please bring Joey next time. I know he likes when I toss the dough in the air."

"We will," said a grinning Sal as Benny waved and headed back toward the ovens.

"He's a nice fella," said Mary. "I always liked Benny. Nice that his boy joined the service."

Sal put a salt shaker on top of his paper plate. He'd finished his pizza and didn't want the breeze to launch his dish.

"Pete, maybe later this week I'll need a ride from you—if you have time. Otherwise I'll take a taxi."

"Where to?" asked his son, digging into his second slice.

"Eh, I'm gonna go see the fellas."

Mary looked over at her husband.

"A ride?" asked Peter. "You ain't up to walkin' there?"

Sal moved the salt shaker between his fingers, tapping it on the paper plate.

"You know what I want?" he said.

Peter glanced at his mother.

"You know what I really want?" continued Sal. "I want a nice cold lemon ice before we leave."

⤢

That Saturday afternoon, as promised, Peter gave his father a ride. They pulled up across the street from a club. Sal's cane rested between his legs in the front passenger seat.

"Maybe I should make a U-turn and pull you up right in front," said Peter.

"No. I want it this way. You wanna come in for a minute to say hello?" he asked.

"No, Pop. It's okay. You go. Call me when you want me to pick you up."

Sal looked at his reflection in the side-view mirror.

"I haven't seen them in so long."

"You look great, Pop. Strong and healthy."

Sal unlocked the door.

"Want me to help you out?"

"I guess I don't look that strong and healthy," said Sal with a grin. "I can get out myself. Thanks."

His cane touched the blacktop and he leaned on it as he stood. He was diagonally across from his destination, but there wasn't much traffic to negotiate. He'd be able to cross the street on his own.

"You sure you're okay?" yelled Peter through the open car window as the door closed between them.

"No problems at all," he answered. "I'll see you later. Thanks again for the lift."

He looked both ways, allowed a delivery truck to pass, and headed across the street. When he reached the sidewalk, he faced left and marched slowly toward his destination.

A small handful of men were out front. Their faces became clearer as he neared, but they weren't looking in his direction as they interacted. Getting closer he recognized two of them, at least he was reasonably sure he did. He remembered one as a determined altruist who dreamed of one day adopting disadvantaged children. The other he recalled as a charming singer who'd melt the female heart with a smile and a song—he had a collection of souvenir hair clippings to prove it.

He hadn't seen Bob Tarpinian or James Willie Lomax since the war ended, but there they were in front of the Veterans of Foreign Wars hall, along with some vets he had never met before. Yes, he was sure it was them. They weren't exactly the pillars of virility from their days in Europe, but neither was he.

Hell, they look a little like Orville Redenbacher and Uncle Ben, but I'm probably gonna look like Cap'n Crunch to them.

Sal was nervous but very happy that he'd looked up his old friends. He'd found a couple who lived in or around New York, agreed to meet at the VFW hall, and asked his son to drive him to Queens for the occasion. The vets glanced his way. Their conversation stopped.

"Yeah, it's me. Who wants to go a few rounds?" Sal smiled. As he raised his cane like a weapon.

"Sal," they yelled simultaneously.

As he embraced his friends, he thought about all that had transpired in his life since they last spoke. He hoped they had contact information for more of the old platoon and company, which had been comprised of men from most every region of the country. Mostly, he hoped that somehow, they were all still alive.

∽∞∽

While Sal spent Saturday with his old friends at the VFW hall, Mary took Joey out for some shopping along the avenue. She arranged to meet up with her new friend, Eleanor DiRocco, as she wanted to thank Tommy's wife for suggesting to Sal that they pay a visit to Annette. With Joey holding onto her arm, Mary chatted with Eleanor in the heavy afternoon sun.

"When Annette gave me the picture she made, I could barely talk at all."

"That's a wonderful story," said Eleanor.

Joey appeared to pay no mind to their conversation as he eyed the storefronts that they passed and also took note of the shine, or lack thereof, on the shoes of the locals.

"Joey's been doing much better since Sal has improved, too. But we're thinkin' of making that trip to France. Sal's set on it, I think. I'm gonna need a sleeping pill on that plane, though." Mary laughed.

"It will be great. Don't worry about the plane. They're very safe and comfortable. Tommy and I went to Italy two years ago and it was fine. You don't even feel like you're moving most of the time."

They passed a neighborhood record store.

"Mmmmmm," said Joey, pointing.

"You and those records. Eleanor don't want to spend the day in some dusty record store. I'll take you later, okay?"

Joey didn't respond as he stared at the colorful posters in the store window. Between large banners advertising new releases from Bruce Springsteen and Tina Turner, there was a picture of the late Bob Marley gazing pensively at something off-camera, his face—framed by his long dreadlocks—almost resting on his hand.

Legend: the Best of Bob Marley and the Wailers.

The store window also contained a sign proudly announcing that they carried select titles in the new format known as the "compact disc." Joey couldn't read, so that visual was meaningless to him. He did, however, continue to wonder just what it was that drew the stare of the long-haired Jamaican fellow. He would ponder it for the entire day.

"I've been trying to get Tommy to get a check-up," said Eleanor. "I told him to look at what happened to Sal. A big, strong guy like Sal. It's like talking to a brick wall."

"He should be careful. Has he been feeling sick?"

"He won't tell me anything, but I know he's been a little weak. He never goes to a doctor."

"Sal was that way too. They think they're indestructible."

Joey knew they were getting closer to Scotti's Barbershop.

"Hmmmm. Hmmmm," he pointed ahead.

"He wants to go to the barbershop," said Mary. "I guess we could stop in for a minute, for Joey's sake. I already said no to the record store."

"I was going to stop and see my husband anyway, if it was all right with you," said Eleanor.

There were two folding chairs in front of Scotti's, next to the red-and-white barber pole. A folded newspaper rested on one, the other was empty. Eleanor opened the door. There was Winnie, giving a haircut. A father and son sat nearby, awaiting their turns in the barber chair.

"How d'ya want your lambchops?" asked Winnie of his customer.

"Huh?"

"You know, the sideburns," replied Winnie.

"Oh. Short."

"Well, well!" said Winnie as he saw the two women enter with Joey.

"Hello, Winnie," said Eleanor.

"My favorite Auntie! Hello, Mrs. Salerno. Is my pal Joey ready for a haircut?"

"Not yet, thanks. He just wanted to stop by."

Winnie grinned at Joey as he put his scissors down and headed for the closed backroom door.

"They're all in the back. Private stuff, I guess. Let me just tabhang here for a minute," he said in his thick Brooklynese, leaning his ear against the door.

"Tabhang?" Mary whispered to Eleanor.

"He's my own blood and I don't know what he's saying half the time."

After a moment, Winnie knocked on the door and

returned to his customer. Tommy opened and saw the visitors. He emerged from the same doorway that a dying Vito Salerno had been carried through not even a full year before. He kissed Eleanor and Mary, and took Joey by the hand.

"Where's Pope?"

"He's seeing some old friends today," said Mary.

"Old friends? You mean there's people older than us?" Tommy Box o' Cookies asked with a smile.

"Hard to believe, eh?" said Mary.

"Did he go with Pearl?" asked Tommy.

"No. Peter drove him, but he's there all by his lonesome."

"Good for him. How is Pearl doin'? She's a nice lady."

"To be honest, we haven't heard from her in a while. We miss her."

"She's all done with Pope?"

"Well, that's pretty much what she said. She feels her job is done, I think."

"And it was some job that she did, am I right?" said Tommy.

"You're very right."

"Now I know you two ladies probably don't wanna come in the back room. There's some smokin' and swearin' underway at the moment."

"Hmmmmmmm," grinned Joey.

"Exactly, kid," said Tommy. "Mary, could I bring him back there for a couple minutes? I know the fellas would love to see him, and he always likes to look at Biaggio's fish."

"Sure, Tommy," said Mary. "Maybe I'll drag your wife next door for a cup of coffee."

"Sounds good to me," said Eleanor, giving her husband another peck on the cheek.

"Don't let him breathe in that cigar smoke," said Mary as she watched Tommy slowly guide her smiling son into the hazy shadows of the back room.

∞

Mary and Eleanor enjoyed their coffee and conversation. Joey felt comfortable and content with Tommy, Biaggio, and the boys. He spent a lot of time studying the fish in Biaggio's colorful aquarium and thinking about the image of the Jamaican fellow with the fixed stare in the music store window.

Sal had a bittersweet time with the men at the VFW hall. They had always remained youthful in his mind's eye, but reality was not as kind. It hurt him to learn that some of them had passed on or become very ill. Pearl Ghoslton had helped him to feel much stronger, yet today he suddenly felt like an old man, maybe for the first time. Still, he was happy he went and had vowed to stay in touch with those vets, both old friends and new.

⌒∞⌒

That night, hours after being dropped home by Peter, Sal sat on his sofa, right beside his wife. Joey went to bed and Sal took the opportunity to soak his feet in a plastic tub while Eddie Murphy and Joe Piscopo clowned around on a *Saturday Night Live* rerun.

"I'm so happy you went," said Mary as she rested her head on her husband's sturdy shoulder.

"Me too. I can't believe you took Joey to Scotti's without me. That's gotta be a first."

"Oh, it is. Well, I was with Eleanor, and Joey wanted to see those guys."

"Thank you. Despite everything, he likes it there. He's got no friends of his own."

"I was thinking," said Mary, "maybe we could get him his own little fish tank. Not a big one like at the barbershop, but a little one of his own."

"Hmm. I'll look into it. It's a lot of work changing water and all—and he can't do it. That would be more for us to do."

"No, they got filters and heaters."

"Believe me, sweetheart, even with filters you have to change part of the water every week or so. I've seen Biaggio do it, and his son too. That's why so many kids get those tropical fish and they die right away. The kids count on the filter system. It's not enough, I promise you."

She kissed his stubbly cheek.

"You're always thinking, Sal. Trying to do everything just right. You wanna come to bed or are you gonna watch this show? I gotta get up for church with Joey."

"This show? I liked the original group with John Belushi."

"Good, then. Let me dry off your feet."

Mary knelt on the carpet and dabbed her husband's calloused feet with a bath towel.

"Sorry," she added, "but that goofy-looking clock radio you bought me is gonna wake you up, along with me, in the morning. You can go back to sleep, though."

"Go 'head! Goofy-looking? You kidding me? That thing is space-age. A cube that's balanced on its corner? It looks like the future, but then it goes off and you got some old big-band radio station programmed to play out of it."

"What, you want me to set it for some punk rock or—what do they call it—new wave?"

They both laughed as Sal stood. They left the little tub in the living room, its salty water just returning to a state of calm, as they headed to the bedroom, arm in arm.

"Who knows?" he said. "Could be I'll even hop out of bed with you when Benny Goodman gives us that wake-up call. Maybe I can walk over to church with you and Joe."

⌒

Unbeknownst to his father, Rico Falcone had a late night meeting in a damp Canarsie warehouse. He'd decided he wanted to meet the new Diabolist. Seems there was a certain auto-dealership finance manager—not connected to any family—who had jerked off a good friend of Rico's; the friend was an employee from the carpet business, also not officially connected. Apparently, the fast-talking financier sold the man a fancy pile of nothing in worthless warranties and extras, but refused to rescind them the following day after the customer had a chance to study his contract. Rico even called the dealership on behalf of the aggrieved party but was dismissed by the salesman, who was obviously either quite brave or exceedingly foolish.

He told Rico to take him to court.

This was obviously a job that Rico could handle himself, but given the fact that it might lead to an unwanted crossover between the carpeting business and his other, more secretive activities, Rico decided not to give this job to anyone directly connected with the Campigotto family.

Plus, his father would be completely against it.

And he desperately wanted to see the Diabolist perform in person.

The good news for the finance manager was that Rico determined this job was not to go the whole nine yards. In other words, the victim would be allowed to live.

The bad news for the finance manager was that he was going to be in a humid garage with the Diabolist; he would be bound flat on the floor, a wheel-less car chassis (the same make that he peddled) would be jacked high above him, and then dropped onto his legs.

It mattered not to Rico that the cost of the scenario was greater than the amount of the extras originally bilked by the dealership. Rico footed the entire bill because, to him, this was a full audition for the Diabolist.

Within a week, Rico's friend would receive a full refund, be permitted to keep all the extras, and be gifted with something relatively new to North America—a new minivan for his wife.

CHAPTER THIRTY-TWO

IN THE DREAM, Peter Salerno might be seated in the stands, or the broadcast booth, or as a member of the grounds crew. He was almost never an actual member of the team. This night's dream was a little different. Joey was the shortstop for the Brooklyn Dodgers, as he always was; no matter that the Dodgers had resided in California for over a quarter century. Joey stood between second and third, pounding his glove. His body was anything but fragile and tilted; he was strong, lean, and waiting to devour any ball that should come his way. Sal was the manager—as usual— knee on the dugout steps. His baggy, blue-and-white uniform flapped in the breeze as he spat tobacco juice on the edge of the infield. Mary never appeared in the baseball dreams.

Peter was a member of the team this night. He was seated in the bullpen with the other relief pitchers. He kept looking down as if to make sure he was really clothed in Dodger blue. He was, but as in all prior variations of this REM scenario, he recalled carrying a large case of soda to his seat—not to drink, but the same type he delivered at work. In each dream, he dropped the heavy crate, spilling the pop all over his seat. Without reason, he sat on the sticky residue, which then effectively glued him to the seat. Didn't matter if it was a spectator, broadcast, grounds crew, or bullpen seat—Peter couldn't free himself from it. He saw Joey turn his head from his position on the edge of the infield grass. He was looking out into the bullpen. Looking for Peter.

The bullpen phone rang.

He could see that the manager—his father—was on the

dugout phone, calling to the bullpen to get a relief pitcher ready.

"Peter, get up," barked the bullpen coach.

They want me in the game? They want me to get up and start throwin'?

He looked down the row of pitchers to find the bullpen coach.

In full Brooklyn Dodger uniform, holding the phone receiver, was his wife Kathy.

"Peter, get up," she yelled.

He tried to stand.

That damned soda. Stuck to the seat again.

He woke from his dream to see Kathy standing beside the bed, nightstand telephone in hand.

"Peter, get up," she said, shaking his shoulder.

The stillness and his wife's filmy, creviced gaze told him it was the middle of the night.

"Your mother's on the phone. They just rushed Pop to the hospital."

Not again. Not again.

That was the mantra that rang in Peter Salerno's head as he made his frantic, pre-dawn drive to the hospital. His father worked so hard to rehabilitate his mind and body. All the work with Pearl. All the sweat and all the prayers.

Not again.

He hadn't had time to even speak with his mother. She told Kathy that Sal was unresponsive, but the ambulance crew told her he was alive. He had grunted loudly in his sleep, appeared to nearly sit up, but collapsed back onto the bed. Peter told Kathy to tell his mother he would come for her later, drop Joey with Kathy, and take her to the hospital—but he had to get there first and find out what was going on.

Upon his arrival, it was another waiting game. It hadn't been a full year since the last eternity spent in wait for a report on his stricken father. It felt like it was yesterday.

The hours rolled on.

Not again.

As the sun grew stronger in the sky and crept through the hospital blinds, he finally got some news.

No stroke.

His father had a heart attack and was rushed into surgery because it was determined that he required a pacemaker to save his life.

How big of a setback would this be? Would he be bedridden? Would he even survive?

Peter wouldn't receive a definitive answer to any of his questions this day.

He left that afternoon without being able to see his father; he was told there was a good chance he could see him the following afternoon, if all went well. He went to his mother's house to comfort her and Joey. He called some family and friends, helped to bathe and dress his brother and took him and their mother over to his house to occupy their time. He distracted them as best he could and alleviated one worry from his list by having them both in plain sight.

⤫

The next afternoon Peter brought his mother to the hospital. They were told they could spend a little time with Sal but that he'd likely be tired and might drift in and out of sleep. When they first entered the room he was indeed asleep. The machines were humming just as they did many months before. There were different ones this time. A thatch of wires connected Sal's chest to a continuous EKG. He appeared pale but peaceful. Peter and Mary sat in silence, hoping for a chance to speak to the most important man in their lives. Mary hated the waiting and, after ninety minutes, decided she wanted to take a trip down to the first floor for a sip of coffee and a change of scenery.

Ten minutes later, as Peter thumbed through some magazine he'd normally never touch, he heard it.

"I got a ticker in me now," were his father's first words. They came in a garbled struggle.

"I know, Pop," he anxiously replied as he stood. "They told me."

"Where's your mother and Joey?"

"Ma is here. She's downstairs. Joey's with Kathy."

Sal breathed deeply. He tried to clear his throat.

"Peter. It's no fun dying piece by piece," he smiled.

"Cut that shit out, Pop. Nobody's dying here. First you had a stroke and you beat that. Now you got dealt a heart attack and you whipped that too. You're invincible."

"I used to think Rocky Marciano was invincible. But that was only in the ring. His time came too, Pete."

"I bet you're home within a week. I think the stroke was worse. You can move your arms and legs—"

"Do me a favor. Look out in the hallway and see if your mother is coming."

Peter did as he was told.

"No, Pop. She's not there."

"Good. I wanna tell you something—"

His words were interrupted by several coughs and his hand went to his chest.

"You okay?" asked his son, nervously.

"Just some soreness. Listen, you remember Staten Island Lou?"

"Sure."

"When he was in the hospital, in his final days—"

"Enough with this. What final days?"

"He told me that the worst part was that he'd fall asleep and dream he went to Heaven. He'd reunite with all those who'd gone before. It was beautiful and peaceful. He was happy and relieved. Then he'd awake in pain in his dark hospital room. He'd curse those dreams because they taunted him. He'd think he made it to the other side only to realize he was still suffering on his deathbed."

"You need to relax and rest."

"I just had that dream, Peter."

His son didn't know how to respond.

"Well, you woke up and saw me," smiled Peter. "You tellin' me that's bad?"

"I need you to do a couple of things," he said, not making eye contact.

"I'm on it. I'm gonna call Pearl—"

"There's a gun at the back of my sock drawer. I want you to take it out of the house. You can keep it or give it to Tommy or—"

"Please."

"And about Joey—"

"Pop, he knows you're here again. I'm gonna get your keys—"

"No. I think maybe this time you shouldn't give him my keys."

Peter swallowed hard.

"I brought you a diet soda," came the voice from the doorway.

Mary walked in to see her husband awake. His gaze immediately turned toward her. He managed a warm smile.

"Nothing for me?" he said.

She rushed to his side.

"Hey, I'm gettin' tired of this. I know you got a girlfriend in this hospital."

"More than one," he grinned.

She wanted to wrap her arms around him, but those damned wires were everywhere.

"You know what, sweetheart?" he said. "I'm hungry. Maybe tomorrow you sneak me in some decent food?"

Peter wondered if he really was hungry or if he was saying that to ease Mary's nerves. He also knew that he wouldn't be able to come to the hospital the following day because they were very shorthanded at work and he'd already used up most of his accrued time caring for his family over the past year. He needed to support his own wife and children.

"Pete, maybe we should think about letting Joey come up and see me here," said Sal as he held Mary's warm hand.

Oh, no.

This was a first. Now Peter was really concerned.

"Maybe, Pop. Talk it over with Ma. I'm not sure it would be a great idea. Joey could wig out if he saw those wires and all. Maybe he should see you when you're home."

Mary squeezed her husband's hand. Gone was the strength that had always been found in its grasp. The Sal she knew would never ask to have Joey see him this way.

She rested her head on the very edge of his shoulder, just away from the wires, brushing his thinning hair as she spoke. "You wanna dance, soldier?"

❧

Peter was up early for work the next day. Joey was going to spend the day with Kathy while Mary would be at the hospital with her sister. Peter's mind raced as he blindly went through with his deliveries. He called everyone he knew to alert them of his father's condition.

Should they be permitted to visit him? Is he too frail for it?

Should Joey be brought to Pop's side? Would that do more harm than good for the both of them?

Mostly, his mind pondered the pacemaker situation. He knew almost nothing about them. There was an appointment coming up to have his questions answered, but his father needed it to save his life, so there was no debate involved. He had one now, and it would keep him alive—or so they hoped. He remembered hearing a story once about a young boy who received such a device while his parents were informed that a second procedure would bring certain death. They knew that once the battery died, so would their child.

That story probably ain't true.

True or not, there was no mention of such a situation with his father, so that was a bit of good news.

I hope that story ain't true. Poor kid. Pop's actually lucky, in a way.

❧

314

Peter was exhausted when he got home. He called his mother and she told him that Sal slept most of the day. She smuggled in a light sandwich as he'd requested, but he didn't touch it. He'd asked about Joey again. Peter told his mother that he'd asked about leaving work a little early the next day and was given permission to do so if nobody called in sick. Peter bitched about the fact that both he and his father gave so many years to that company, yet getting time off to see Sal was like pulling teeth. His mother reminded him of all the time they'd granted him after Sal's stroke.

"They got a business to run," she said.

"You stay with Joey tomorrow, Ma. He needs you too. I'm gonna see Pop in the afternoon. He'll probably sleep all morning anyways."

Peter rushed through his deliveries the following day. Numerous times the older shopkeepers inquired about his father's condition, remembering him fondly for both his professional, well-mannered soda deliveries and his trustworthy numbers sales. Every few stops he'd borrow a store phone from an owner he knew well and give his mother a call to see if she'd gotten any updates and to see how Joey was holding up. This was all in addition to the normal concerns a typical man has about his own wife and children, keeping the bills paid, keeping his job in focus, and managing finances for today and tomorrow. In Peter's mind, these woes were manifesting themselves as dark eye bags and weight gain. Kathy suggested he might want to have his thyroid and kidneys checked, but he chalked it all up to stress and lack of sleep. No doctors for him.

After leaving work early, Peter went directly to the hospital. As he entered the cold elevator, he wondered if his father would even be awake. One way or another, he'd have to address the subject of Joey coming to visit. His mind wandered away toward work once again. Would he get that promotion to indoor work as his father had earned years before? The excessive time off was surely hurting his chances. How much longer would he be able to handle the physicality of deliveries? That was a younger man's job. As the elevator door opened to his father's floor, he remembered that his uncle once worked as an elevator operator in Manhattan.

There's a job that's almost extinct.

The corridor was brightly lit as always. Then there was that odd aroma of disinfectant, mingling with some type of meat gravy. Maybe some applesauce too.

There was some bustling going on down the hall.

Is that by Pop's room?

Peter's steps grew longer and faster.

I think Pop's room is farther down.

He was into a trot now.

Shit. That is by his room.

Hospital personnel fluttered around the doorway like bees to a hive. Some equipment was being quickly wheeled away. Peter wasn't sure if these were doctors, nurses, therapists, or some combination of all. There was at least one man in a suit walking away from the room writing something onto a clipboard.

As Peter just about reached the room, he was intercepted by a young nurse that he recognized.

"Mr. Salerno, we've been trying to reach you. We called your work number . . . "

He nearly walked through her as he bounded for the room.

There he was.

Salvatore Salerno was lying in his bed, eyes shut. The room was silent. There were no wires. No beeps. Nothing.

He was gone.

Kneeling at his bedside in prayer—their backs to Peter— were Biaggio Falcone, Tommy Box o'Cookies, Johnny the Beatnik, and Winnie. At the foot of the bed knelt Pearl Gholston.

Peter wanted to cry out. He wanted to scream. He did

neither, standing there and watching his father's friends pray in silence. He grabbed for the wall as his knees shook. He felt the sweat coming on.

Pearl spotted him in the doorway, blessed herself, and approached.

"Peter," she said softly as Sal's kneeling friends turned their heads. "He went peacefully. Surrounded by friends."

She took Peter's hand. His mind was racing.

"Come and pray with us. Help us to smooth his journey."

Pearl led him to Sal's bedside. The fellas remained in prayer, saying nothing. She rubbed Peter's back as he stared at his father's ashen face.

"I'd been here for two hours, then these gentlemen came later. We were all able to speak with him a little, then he just went to sleep."

Peter took the time to pray as best he could. He dreaded telling his mother, his children, and especially his brother. He cursed his job for keeping him from his father on his last day. He cursed himself for not bringing Joey to the hospital immediately after his father's request.

Biaggio and the boys began to get to their feet. Peter finally absorbed the odd premise of Pearl Gholston spending any length of time with the barbershop crew.

Tommy couldn't stand.

"You okay, Tommy?" asked Peter.

The big man was in tears as Peter and Winnie went to his side.

"I'm good, boys. Very sorry, Peter."

He had difficulty standing, even with the aid of the others.

"Just some foot problems." He smiled as he wiped his eyes. "Gettin' old is no picnic."

Tommy finally got to his feet and wrapped his big arms around Peter.

"Well," he said, "Heaven's got another Pope now, I guess."

∽

Lisa and Joseph were deep in a game of Battleship on the living room floor as Kathy fried some pork chops for their dinner on the kitchen stove.

"D-5," said Lisa.

"Crap," yelled her younger brother. "You hit my submarine."

Joseph quickly covered his mouth and they both giggled, hoping their mom hadn't heard the bad word.

"F-7," offered the young boy in return.

The telephone rang.

Kathy left the stove to grab the kitchen receiver from the wall, hoping it was Peter.

It was.

He stood alone at a bank of pay phones on the hospital's first floor. He'd just dropped two dimes to make the call he'd been dreading.

"He's gone, Kathy," was all he could say. They weren't the eloquent words he'd rehearsed on the elevator down.

She stood there—stunned—as the meat sizzled behind her.

"They said he just went to sleep. Pearl was with him, and Tommy and some of his friends—"

"God. I'm so sorry," she whispered, well aware of the super hearing her kids seemed to possess at all the worst times.

"Don't say nothin' to Ma or the kids. I'll handle all that," he said.

"Okay," she answered, not sure what else to say.

"You sunk my sub!" Joseph said from the living room.

"I don't know when I'll be home," said her husband through the crackling phone connection. "I guess there's some stuff I'll need to take care of here, then I'll go to Ma's house and break it to her and Joey."

"Maybe I should go with you—"

"No. I can handle it. I want you and the kids there for me when I get home. I might wind up bringin' Ma and Joey with me to the house tonight."

Kathy's attention was drawn by Lisa, who came hopping up from the living room.

"I sunk two ships so far!" she boasted with a smile.

As Kathy tried to return one in kind, Lisa pointed past her mother, eyes wide.

"Mom, look," she screamed.

Kathy turned to see a burgeoning grease fire from her pan of burnt pork chops.

"I gotta go," she yelled, dropping the phone.

She almost ran to get a pot of water, but remembered that Sal once told her to use baking soda on a grease fire.

Water makes it worse, she recalled him saying in that confident voice of his.

She grabbed a box of baking soda as Lisa picked up the dangling telephone receiver. Joseph remained in the living room, likely rearranging the toy ships while his big sister was away, or at least taking a peek at hers.

What now?

Peter held onto the pay phone, trying to imagine what crisis was taking place in his house while he stood helpless in a cold hospital. He felt the sweat rolling down between his shoulder blades.

Kathy dumped the entire box of powder on the flaming pan, standing as far back as she could, holding the baking soda container with the very tips of her fingers. Soon the fire was out, replaced by thick, black smoke.

"Daddy?" said Lisa into the phone.

Kathy began waving a towel to clear the smoke. She pressed the exhaust-fan button on the new range hood that Peter bought her at Sears.

"Hey, sweetie," said Peter nervously. "Is everything okay there?"

"I think so," answered Lisa as the fan sucked out the smoke with a loud hum. "Mommy's stopping a fire."

"A fire?"

The exhaust fan did its job admirably and the choking

black smoke was drawn out into the warm Brooklyn evening, toward the heavens.

∞

The funeral home foyer was expansive and elegant, yet warm and comforting in its serenity. The antique sofas and chairs were occupied by what appeared to be all of Brooklyn. The rest stood, chatting quietly and choosing to recall happier times, rather than dwell on the loss of Sal Salerno. It was after dinner and the sun began to fade. There had been a two-hour viewing that afternoon, and Peter decided it would be best to bring his brother between the two public sessions. Even Mary and Kathy had not been at the midday viewing; instead they dressed and prepared Joey for his early evening journey. The guests in the packed lobby waited patiently behind the closed door. Peter Salerno was inside with his mother, brother, and wife. Young Lisa and Joseph were to arrive shortly in the care of Mary's sisters. Peter would deal with that later. He had this hurdle first.

Tucked into the back of his suit pants, hidden by his black jacket, was his father's dusty Smith & Wesson snub-nose revolver. It irritated Peter's lower back to no end, and he now wished he'd left it under the seat of his car. He'd remembered his father's wish to have it removed from the house just as he was helping his mother and brother into the car.

I shoulda left it for another time. Too much on my brain.

In his state of mind, he'd just wanted to do what his father asked of him right then and there. He'd let him down by not bringing Joey to the hospital, so he was going to at least do this. Now he felt foolish carrying a gun at his father's wake. As soon as he got home, he would just hide it at the back of his own sock drawer. He'd probably keep it, since it did belong to his Pop. It could be used to protect his family from a burglar. That was why his father kept it. It was never carried in public. Not until tonight, anyway.

Stupid. I gotta put this in the car later. It's diggin' right into my back.

As he had done when they'd first arrived, Peter took Joey by the hand and led him toward their father's richly stained, sycamore casket.

"Let's go up one last time, okay?"

Joey didn't respond, but neither did he resist. Mary, eyes red and skin pale, sat beside a comforting Kathy in the only two occupied seats among the many empty rows. They'd soon be filled by the masses congregating in the foyer just behind the locked door.

As they approached Sal's body—dressed handsomely in a dark-gray pinstriped suit—the floral scent grew stronger. Beautifully-crafted arrangements framed the entire scene in vivid color. American flags were everywhere. Peter knew Joey would have great difficulty in kneeling, so he stood there beside him, his arm around Joey's tilted shoulders.

"Pop would need us—you and me—to be strong for Ma now, Joey."

"Hmm."

"We all have something in us called adrenaline. It's like when Popeye eats his spinach; if we use our adrenaline, we can get stronger. Pop taught me that."

Joey moved one of his perfectly shined shoes slowly from side to side.

"You think you can dig a little deep and be strong for Ma?"

He stared at the hollow expression on his father's face, absorbing the fact that his skin appeared smooth and powdery. He didn't respond to Peter.

"You okay?"

Nothing. Peter held his brother closer.

"This here is not really Pop, if you know what I mean. Pop's spirit is gone from his body. That's why he looks a little different. His spirit has gone up to Heaven, where we'll all go someday. Now he's with his parents, some of his friends, and Cousin Vito too."

Joey began to raise his left arm. He pinched his thumb

321

and forefinger together and pointed away from his body. It wasn't the signal to take him for a drink. Peter thought for a moment, wondering if this was a new spin on one of his brother's regular signs.

"If I'm right about what you're asking, then yes, Pop is with John Lennon, too."

Joey looked at the row of shiny buttons on his father's burial suit. His head now almost rested on Peter's side. He lowered his pointing left hand. His arm found its way around Peter's back, pressing against the gun hidden beneath his brother's suit jacket.

"Hmmmm."

CHAPTER THIRTY-THREE

ITH THE BURIAL of Salvatore Salerno, the world continued to turn, though Mary had thoughts that it might not. Military buglers were a dying breed, but they had one on hand to play "Taps" for Sal. As the small—yet striking—honor guard crisply folded a flag and presented it to Mary, she recalled the day in 1945 when she was first permitted to hold Joey. She had been handed him, snug in his blanket, weeks after his birth. Weeks after being told he was unlikely to survive. This American flag in her hands felt heavier than her son had.

In the distance, well beyond the gates of the graveyard and across the rumbling waters of the East River, stood the Manhattan skyline. Peter Salerno imagined that if one were to erase the Empire State Building from that landscape, it might help to convey the state of his family without the man who epitomized it.

The world continued to turn. Ronald Reagan won a second term in a landslide. Mary Salerno woke each morning to an old song on the fancy, cubed clock radio that her husband had called "space-aged." She had to be sure to be up before Joey. Peter did all he could to assist, but Sal was the tent pole for Mary and Joey, and Peter had a tent of his own to nurture. Mary's sisters helped, as did Pearl on occasion. Kathy was as fine a daughter-in-law as one could ask for, but she had two children fast approaching their teen years and a part-time job to help with the bills. Joey grew a little slower, despite what appeared to be a genuine attempt to utilize his adrenaline for his mother as Peter had asked. Just as Joey's birth defects had worn on his family over the years, likely aging them all prematurely through sadness and strain, the loss of his father delivered him a shocking blow that drained away even the simple pleasures he'd known. All talk of the Lourdes trip had seemingly been buried with Sal. Mary's faith had taken another hit, and she no longer sat in a pew on Sunday.

But she did pray.

Biaggio Falcone offered his help on more than one occasion, but it was politely declined. He even offered Peter the chance to work in the numbers business—not as the head man that Sal was, but as one of the lower level runners. It would bring much-needed additional income and could enable Kathy to stay home. Peter was as respectful as could be but managed to avoid a direct answer. Truth be told, he was torn. In tribute to Sal, Biaggio let the offer stand, never insisting on a final answer. He had problems of his own; his passion for the family businesses—carpeting and otherwise—began to wane. Rico desperately wanted to run things, he deemed himself ready, and wanted to take the family to heights once thought unreachable.

But there was still Don Sacco.

In Frederico's mind, the aging Sacco would rather he just disappear than become a new family head. There had been some serious turmoil regarding one of the larger New York families. Sparks flew outside a New York City steak house, leaving two very prominent figures in a bullet-ridden, early-evening heap. That event caused a chain reaction of upheaval, violence, and clandestine meetings. Though the event was found to be the culmination of a struggle within that particular family, hairs were raised and paranoia festered.

Rico obsessed on the thought that Don Sacco would have him killed at the first hint of his ascension, but he dared not tell his father, who had made that Florida trip to receive Sacco's solemn promise that Rico was in no danger.

He'd have to be patient.

It was almost noon one chilly morning, when a game show Joey was watching was interrupted by a breaking news update.

Joey rubbed his fingers together as he watched the Space Shuttle Challenger disintegrate in midair. His mother was in the kitchen, sewing a knee patch on his jeans. Joey saw the way pride turned quickly to bewilderment, then immediately to horror, on the faces of the onlookers on the grandstand. Many turned away and just stared into the distance. He wondered if they were looking at anything in particular. He recalled the photo of Bob Marley on the record store poster.

He'd didn't recognize the term used by mission control that day, which was broadcast in monotone for the world to hear as they watched the shuttle fall in pieces to the earth below. He knew he didn't want to ever hear it again.

Obviously a major malfunction.

It wasn't long after that Rico Falcone found himself glued to his television set, along with thirty million others. His girlfriend-of-the-month sat on his lap as they anxiously awaited the opening of a newly discovered secret vault buried deep in a tunnel beneath an old Chicago hotel. The dusty depository reportedly belonged to an idol of Rico's—infamous gangster Al Capone. After much conjecture about how many dead bodies and how much money was going to be discovered on live television, it seemed that Scarface's vault contained a couple of empty liquor bottles and a stop sign.

The world continued to turn as Mary or Peter would sometimes take Joey down to visit the fellas at Scotti's. It wasn't the same without Sal, Vito, or Punch, and even Tommy wasn't there as much anymore. New men were appearing. And soon it was more likely that Peter would take Joey out for an occasional beer with his friends from either work or the neighborhood. A special time for the brothers took place around Joey's fortieth birthday. Peter and his friends arranged for an overnight bus trip to Atlantic City. Joey's spirits were certainly raised by the excursion, and he actually moved around better than he had in the two years since he lost his father. He smiled as he pulled the slot machine levers, and even put chips down at the roulette wheel. Peter cared for all of his brother's needs, be they feeding, bathing, or bathroom issues.

The entire group of nearly twenty gathered around the television in one of their rented suites to watch game six of the 1986 World Series. Peter had placed a wager on the New York Mets.

They trailed the Boston Red Sox three games to two and were one loss from elimination. In this odd situation, even most Yankees fans were rooting for their cross-town rivals because, to them, anything was better than a Boston world championship.

A gloom hung over the hotel suite as the Mets had fallen behind by two runs and had come to bat in the bottom of the tenth inning. It was their last chance.

One out.

Peter and the boys were hoping for maybe a walk and a home run to tie the game. Joey sat in the seat of honor, right in front of the screen. Peter helped him to some potato chips.

Two outs.

Shea Stadium grew quiet, so did the hotel suite. The Mets had no base runners and were down to their final out. NBC ran an image of Boston's Marty Barrett, naming him player of the game.

Strike one.

The Red Sox dugout was jubilant, the Mets' silent.

Strike two.

Through some quick-fingered error, Shea Stadium's scoreboard briefly showed a slightly premature message:

Congratulations, Boston Red Sox, 1986 World Champions.

Peter looked over at Joey sitting quietly in the blue Mets cap he'd bought him for the occasion. His expression gave no clue as to the status of the game. While others mumbled and cursed, Joey deliberately chewed his chips and rubbed his fingers together.

The Mets got a single, and there was a small ripple of applause in both suite and stadium. Then they got another single, and another. The mood changed quickly. The suite was alive, the stadium rocking. Joey chewed his potato chips. The Red Sox threw a wild pitch, then let a ground ball through their legs and it was over. The Mets won. Down to their final strike with nary a man on base, they somehow won the game. The NBC announcers said nothing for over three minutes, letting the Shea Stadium crowd do the talking. Peter had never seen anything like it in all his years of watching baseball. Events such as this never even happened in his recurring baseball dreams, with Joey at shortstop and he glued to his seat. There was a word that kept circulating around the hotel, and later down on the casino floor. It glided from mouths, through cigar smoke and whiskey breath. The word echoed throughout New York even as the seventh and final game had yet to be played. That game was a mere afterthought; the world knew the Mets would win it, and they surely did. The word lingered on the lips of New Yorkers for what seemed an eternity.

Miracle.

Peter kept that word in the back of his mind. He wasn't sure if he'd seen a true miracle—probably not. But he wondered what types of improbable outcomes, and what types of sudden reversals, could occur in some kind of perfect storm, and what role hope and belief might play in it all.

Maybe he should talk to his mother about the Lourdes trip again.

∽

The new year brought more sports-related joy to the city, but with a touch of sadness for Peter. The New York Giants, his father's beloved football team, won the first Super Bowl in their history. They beat the Denver Broncos in front of over one hundred thousand fans at the Rose Bowl in Pasadena, California. Peter wondered if any of those hundred thousand were bigger fans than his Pop had been. How many had braved the cold to watch those Giants lose countless games in the Polo Grounds and Yankee Stadium?

Though Joey seemed to enjoy the game, his gaze would wander from the television screen to focus on nothing in particular. The spirit and vigor he'd displayed on the Atlantic City trip had long since subsided. There was talk of getting him a walker.

That summer, the walker arrived. Joey wanted no part of it at first, but he came to understand its necessity. At least things were looking better financially as Peter's modest investments flourished. The Dow reached new highs, and his children's small college funds blossomed. The plan of funneling some money from Kathy's part-time work toward the kids' future brought some slight joy to Peter as he continued to lug those heavy soda crates. His mother's home was fully paid for due to his late father's relentless work ethic, and he was hoping to be on a similar path.

The world turned on, and summer slipped into autumn. Joey would navigate the streets of Brooklyn with his mother by his side and the rattling walker in front of him. Mary Salerno was closing in on her seventieth year, yet still performed all the duties of a new young mother. She did this despite a growing shortness of breath, and aches that were previously nonexistent. Not a night passed that she didn't thank God for the genes of her ninety-year-old mother, but Mama never had to raise an eternal child, and Mary began to believe her mother would outlive her.

Right around Joey's forty-first birthday, the stock market crashed. Along with countless others, Peter was dealt a devastating blow. In one day, his savings were decimated. He'd always laughed at his mother's warnings about the stock market, joking that if her mattress burned she'd be penniless. She'd been right once again.

Just after Joey's forty-second birthday, George H.W. Bush won the presidential election. Word began to spread through the neighborhood that Scotti's Barbershop, which had stood unchanged since before Mary was born, was about to go through a major remodeling. Some heard that it might even be torn down.

Peter, Kathy, and the kids were helping to decorate Mary and Joey's Christmas tree when they learned that a Pan Am flight headed to New York from London exploded over Scotland, killing all on board and several in the safety of their own homes below, the falling chunks of aircraft vaporizing anything in their path. Later reports concluded that anti-American terrorists hid an explosive device within a radio cassette player. Among the murdered were high-ranking officials from the Volkswagen automobile company. Somehow, this sent Peter's thoughts back to the day, nearly eighteen years before, when Punch the Pedal smuggled Cousin Vito into his wedding via the old, rusty VW van with the peace sign stuck to its grill.

He was going to spend some time this Christmas reminding his mother about Lourdes.

Peter enjoyed his own fortieth birthday, but without the hoopla and expense he'd showered upon his brother. There was no Atlantic City trip and no miraculous baseball game. He enjoyed a home-cooked meal and blew out his candles with the newly teenaged Lisa, and young Joseph, beside him. His mother seemed to be gathering the resolve to attempt the journey to France. If nothing else, she knew that Sal would have wanted her to try.

Serious construction was ongoing at the barbershop. Some of the surrounding businesses were shuttered as well. Peter hadn't seen Tommy Box o' Cookies in some time, and nobody else was willing to reveal much. Mary lost touch with Tommy's wife as she and Joey spent more time indoors. It was easier on their legs.

Protesters filled the streets of Brooklyn after an African-American teenager, who'd ventured into the wrong neighborhood with the innocent hope of buying a car, was brutally beaten by a bat-wielding Caucasian mob. He was then murdered with two bullets to the chest. Not long before, a white woman jogging in Central Park was beaten and raped by at least one black man. Speculation at the time suggested she was attacked by a group of wilding African-American youths. The Central Park jogger nearly bled to death from her multiple lacerations and internal wounds. Her skull had been fractured so badly that her left eye was dislodged from its socket.

Mary wondered what kind of world her grandchildren had inherited. Why was it that the worst animals of one race always seemed to descend upon the innocent of another? Always in search of the weak, the outnumbered, and the helpless? Maybe these vultures should just meet up and settle their differences on level ground.

Even she noticed how, three years earlier, Mets and Yankees fans alike had bonded in their mission to deprive Boston of a World Series title. That had her thinking that anything might be possible.

Maybe not.

The world could indeed be a very sad and evil place, but it continued to turn.

OCTOBER 1989

Chapter Thirty-Four

CONNECTIONS ARE EVERYTHING. Zoning laws and permits could be squashed like a gnat on the back of a neck.

It was roughly the time of Joey Salerno's forty-third birthday when it opened. Scotti's Barbershop was gone, as were the neighborhood establishments to its immediate north and south. Rico Falcone got what he wanted, despite the mild protests of his father—who seemed to care less with each passing day.

It was called "The Bullet Hole," and it said so in neon. Only one small portion of the old façade remained. The section of Scotti's front bricks that was struck by the bullets intended for Biaggio in 1946 remained. It was illuminated by colorful lights, giving it the look of either a museum piece, or possibly, a sideshow attraction.

It was the nightclub that Rico dreamed of. Five times the size of the old barbershop, with large, secure offices in the back. Steel doors and soundproof rooms. Better to hinder a police raid or, more likely, a hit team sent by Don Sacco, Rico reasoned. During the massive renovation project, Biaggio's main concern appeared to be his freshwater aquarium, which had been temporarily relocated to the offices of his carpet business. It was now back where it had always been. Two fish died shortly after being transported, and this weighed heavily on him, causing him to curse the day he acquiesced to his son's wishes.

With no hair to cut, Winnie made use of his hobby and became a prominent disc jockey at The Bullet Hole. He continued to be Biaggio's driver, though he found himself chauffeuring Rico around more often than not.

They, along with more fellas than had ever been permitted in Scotti's, sat by the large screen television in the club's back room to watch the third game of the 1989 World Series. Rico's statuesque new girlfriend, Georgiana, sat on his lap as the pregame show from San Francisco's Candlestick Park was interrupted by a 6.9-magnitude earthquake. The stadium rocked in a much more serious manner than Shea Stadium had three years earlier. The game, and entire series, would be postponed for ten days as the Bay Area tried to recover from a disaster that chose to strike just as its two local teams, the San Francisco Giants and Oakland Athletics, were to battle for the championship for the first time in history. The bridge that connected the two cities suffered a partial collapse during the quake and would remain closed for a month.

The Giants had once hailed from New York but lost a legion of old fans when they turned their backs on their original home. They would eventually lose the series to Oakland without winning a single game.

<hr />

With the game postponed, Rico decided he'd take Georgiana out for dinner. He had completely fallen for the tall blonde, and the revolving door of girlfriends ceased to spin. He didn't let on to the fellas about how he felt, other than one initial comment, "I'd give my right nut for her to suck on the left one."

Not exactly greeting-card material, but he did seem to go out of his way to please her. She was a huge fan of Billy Joel, the popular musician and Long Island native, and, when she discovered that he was to be the musical guest on *Saturday Night Live*, she made Rico promise to watch the show with her. It wasn't a program that he found particularly enjoyable, but he called in a favor and secured two tickets for them to be in the studio audience for the performance. Georgiana was floored, and Rico got to keep his right nut after all.

❧

In 1917, three children in Fatima, Portugal reported seeing a woman who was brighter than the sun. The youngsters said the woman called herself The Lady of the Rosary and appeared before them on the thirteenth day of six consecutive months. These claims led to the children being questioned, threatened, and even jailed. They said the Mother of God told them three secrets which they refused to reveal at the time. They also said that the Lady would perform a miracle for all to see on the thirteenth of October, 1917. A crowd estimated at over seventy thousand gathered that day to see for themselves. There were many photographers and journalists among the assemblage. One of the children, a ten-year-old named Lucia, called out for the crowd to look at the sun. It was reported in many newspapers at the time that the clouds parted and the sun changed colors and danced in the sky. These claims were made by thousands upon thousands of people who were there that afternoon. Some say the sun rotated like a wheel, and some say they saw nothing.

❧

Rico and Georgiana waited patiently in their seats for *Saturday Night Live* to begin its live broadcast. The guest host was to be actress Kathleen Turner, but it was Billy Joel that drew them to the show. Rico knew a few of his songs such as, "Piano Man" and "Just the Way You Are" but didn't count himself as much of a fan. He kept looking back at two men who entered the studio after them. They sat about four rows back and just to Rico's right. They looked hard-nosed but well groomed. Rico wondered what would cause two men to attend a show without female accompaniment.

Those two ain't no queers. That's for sure.

Georgiana knew it wasn't likely that Billy would sing her favorite song, "Only The Good Die Young," since it was a dozen years old, but she crossed her fingers anyway. She'd always loved the way that song touched on the struggle between Catholic virtue and lust.

The show went live with an opening sketch that parodied the legend of the 1917 miracle in Portugal.

The Miracle of Fatima '89.

The bizarre skit replaced the Virgin Mary with an American Flag in a commentary on a recent United States Supreme Court ruling that upheld the rights of flag burners. Rico didn't find it funny or even understand most of it. He'd heard of Fatima but always confused it with the story of Lourdes. He knew it was believed that Mother Mary appeared, and he knew that plans were in the works to take Joey Salerno to the site in hopes of a miracle.

Is Joey going to Fatima or Lourdes?

He kept looking back at the two men.

The skits that followed didn't entertain him much, though Georgiana was laughing. He knew he should have packed his weapon, but there were metal detectors at the entrance to the Rockefeller Plaza elevator bank that audience members were required to pass through on the way up to studio 8H.

They must be Sacco's men.

Winnie was armed, but he dropped the couple off outside and had been told not to return until 1:15 a.m. Rico wondered if the men planned to kill him right in Rockefeller Center as the crowd spilled out, just like that very public hit outside the steakhouse. Would they steep so low as to do it while he was with a woman? Would they kill her as well?

Who did they pay off to get in with guns? They wanna whack me on fuckin' live television.

Georgiana let out a screech when Billy Joel launched into his recent hit single "We Didn't Start the Fire." He sped through forty years of history in less than five minutes, calling out Harry Truman, Doris Day, Buddy Holly, Mickey Mantle, *The Bridge on the River Kwai*, the Mafia, Beatlemania, Pope Paul, and dozens of other people and events before finally concluding with a reference to the celebrity advertising wars between the major American soda companies.

Rico's beautiful date loved every second of it, but he was itching to leave.

As the show dragged on, Rico envisioned different ways that the hit might go down. He stared back at the men, trying to strike fear and alert them that he knew.

Another odd skit was presented whereby Kathleen Turner portrayed a frustrated woman who confided in a talking Easter egg. She told the egg man that she feared her son was being led toward Satan worship by the loud music he enjoyed. There was talk of pentagrams, an altar, and animal sacrifices. This led Rico's racing mind to entertain thoughts of a colleague.

The Diabolist.

Rico knew if he made it out of Manhattan alive, he was calling the Diabolist.

Before long, Billy Joel was back on stage. He performed a new song about a fisherman struggling to earn a living and keep his boat. Georgiana liked it well enough, but it wasn't "Only the Good Die Young."

Rico told his date that he was going to leave and that she should wait until the show's conclusion and meet Winnie by the car.

"Get in the car and tell Winnie to pick me up outside the 21 Club."

He knew this would alarm her, but there'd be no need to have her involved if the two men left with him. Rico was aware that the NBC staff didn't want audience members getting up to leave during the show, and he would stand out if he left at that point. There would also be no way the two hoodlums would be able to follow him out without exposing themselves.

He kissed Georgiana's cheek and stood. The two men looked at him. So did most everyone else, but he didn't take note of that. He put the tips of his fingers inside his suit jacket to make the men wonder if he was carrying. He stared into their eyes as he walked up the aisle, only to be intercepted by a flustered young NBC page. The fresh-faced usher tried to lead Rico out the door as quickly and quietly as possible.

Nobody followed.

He handed the page a couple of twenties and had him go back in and get Georgiana.

Nobody followed.

As the two of them entered the elevator, she appeared quite shaken. He told her all was well, convinced as he was that he'd exposed and foiled a clumsy attempt on his life.

That old fuck, Don Sacco. Pulling strings while he hides in Florida like some roasting pig.

Morte.

∞

Though reasonably certain, nobody was 100 percent sure if they had ever heard the Diabolist speak. If you had his business card, as all of the New York families presumably did, and had ever dialed the number on it, an intelligent-sounding man would answer the phone. After leading the caller through a few hoops, he'd refer to the Diabolist as his superior and arrange an appointment to meet. Surely this crazed architect of orchestrated torture didn't have a male secretary? Most suspected the killer and the receptionist to be one and the same, but the Diabolist never uttered a word in person. He'd just nod or scribble a note.

Rico Falcone drove himself to the meeting. It was a rundown apartment in the Alphabet City section of lower Manhattan. He parked his car by a fire hydrant and emerged with two guns secreted in his waistband and one on his ankle. Rico had no fear of the nocturnal drug dealers and graffiti spreaders who littered the sidewalk.

Nobody from the family knew of this meeting. It was Frederico's plan.

As instructed, he rang the bell in the specific pattern, and entered when the buzzer sounded. Making his way up the creaky stairs, he couldn't believe the stench of the dim hallway. Mildewed vomit.

How do people live like this?

A snatch of light seeped through the cracked door on the second floor. He'd been told to just walk in, which he did. Rico kept a hand near one of his guns, but he kept telling himself he had nothing to fear from the Diabolist. He was paying him, after all.

The upper corner of the peeling door frame almost seemed to move.

Upon closer inspection, it was just a cockroach. But it was large. So big that Rico could hear it scurrying.

The apartment was small and dark. There was no furniture in sight. It was cold. Rico hit the wall switch, but the light remained off. This couldn't be where this guy actually lived.

There was some type of illumination dancing in an adjacent room. It seemed to move across the darkness from side to side. Then he smelled it.

A candle.

He was being signaled.

He followed the wavering light to find him seated behind a small card table. There was an empty folding chair awaiting Rico. The Diabolist sat with an open notebook before him. The same book you'd find in the possession of any school kid. He placed the candle back on the table and its glow flashed off of the shiny fountain pen that rested in his other gloved hand. Rico had seen pens like that before. They were built like guns. Probably Swiss. He figured the pen to be worth about five hundred dollars, the notebook fifty cents.

This freak stole that pen.

The flamboyant killer appeared to be in a casual mood this night. There was no makeup, no elaborate headdress or glorified Halloween costume. Just a knit cap pulled down below his eyebrows and a black scarf wrapped across the bridge of his nose and everything below.

He motioned for Rico to sit.

Other than the notebook and candle, the tabletop held

only one other item. It appeared to be a brown rabbit's foot, not a totally uncommon good luck charm.

Except this one still had blood on it.

The Diabolist removed the black leather glove from his right hand and reached out across the table. Rico shook his hand, and the glove went back on. The theatrical butcher sat back in his wobbly chair and folded his arms. Rico knew it was time to speak.

"This is gonna be a big one, my friend. You up for it?"

His gloved right forefinger began to twitch and he gave a slight nod.

"I need to send a message to every family. We will not be intimidated or shit upon any longer. I need you to do something for me that I can't do my usual way. There are only two people on this planet that will know about this. You and me."

Rico could hear his associate breathing heavier. Another big roach—maybe the same big roach—stumbled slowly across the floor.

"I want this to be videotaped and sent out to a list of people that I will provide you. I'll also need you to travel, but you'll be paid handsomely for your time."

Rico quickly pictured this guy strolling onto an airplane and stowing a case in the overhead bin, though his thoughts were soon back on track.

"I know you don't get hired as much as your predecessor did. I also know that, if and when a family uses you, it's to get rid of some low-level asshole, but with a message attached. That is your most precious asset—the ability to send a message."

The Diabolist's hand crawled toward his pricey pen. The roach on the floor began to wobble before toppling over onto its back.

Maybe that pen ain't Swiss. Could be Italian like me, or German, like the roach.

"I assume you know who Don Sacco is."

The pen was headed toward the clean, white page when it suddenly stopped. The roach's legs waged a furious battle, kicking and swinging in a vain attempt to right itself.

Is that even a rabbit's foot?

A nod indicated that he certainly knew of Don Sacco.

"Nothing too elaborate. No fancy props and junk. I just want you to cut his fucking head off and send a video of it to the other families."

There was no movement of any kind, save for the dying cockroach.

After several seconds, the eccentric executioner put pen to paper. He tore off the sheet and handed it to Rico. The numerical figure almost seemed to bend in the dancing shadows of the candle flame.

"Agreed," said Rico.

The Diabolist quickly retrieved the paper and jotted down some more. He slid it back across the table. Rico picked it up again and read the scribble:

Half pay before—half after.

"No problem."

The paper was taken back again and set ablaze in the candlelight.

Rico then went into greater detail as his hired hand listened attentively, never saying a word.

They would meet in Florida. The Diabolist would not be involved in the capture of Don Sacco. Rico had a detailed plan involving the pre-placement of an explosive on Sacco's favorite fishing pier. After driving himself to Florida and scouting the area, Rico would know just where to place the explosive so as to kill the three or four men who would normally guard Sacco from a distance. He could then do away with Lenny Sheetrock, or whoever stood nearest to the don, with a spray of bullets. Then the bastard would be his. Reeled in like a prized tuna and ready to be gutted.

The glove was removed again for a second handshake. Rico stood and headed for the door. He sidestepped the dying cockroach so as not to soil his shoes—they were Salvatore Ferragamo. The Diabolist rose and retrieved the furry foot from the table. He pocketed it with his pricey pen, and closed his notebook. He snuffed out the candle and then the roach.

His shoes were Thom McAn.

THANKSGIVING DAY-1989

CHAPTER THIRTY-FIVE

THE SNOW CONTINUED to hit the windows of Mary Salerno's home. Kathy dried off the freezing metal of the walker that her mother-in-law had thrown down the front steps of the house. Why his mother insisted on embarking on the Lourdes trip on Thanksgiving haunted Peter to no end. He'd tried to have her choose another date—any other date—but she insisted. He'd told her that it was the busiest time for air travel; she'd replied that though the days just before and after the holiday were busy, the day itself would be fine for travel. He finally gave in for the sake of tranquility and the fear that they'd never go at all if he upset the apple cart.

He couldn't imagine a Thanksgiving without his wife and children, but there would be plenty more they could celebrate together, and they'd have a nice time at his aunt's house this afternoon. Plus, Kathy would get a break from preparing the big meal. Lisa and Joseph had already spent the night at Mary's sister's home, baking cookies and playing in the snow. Their mother would soon join them there. Never mind that Peter wouldn't get to watch the Cowboys–Eagles game, or even the Lions–Browns. His thoughts were more in tune with hoping that their flight would actually take off in this weather. It snowed all night. He was about to take a transatlantic flight with his weakened mother and a physically challenged brother—neither of whom had ever set foot on an airplane before—yet he was more worried about Kathy's return drive from the airport on those icy roads. He'd wanted to take an airport shuttle, but that was another argument he'd lost to a determined female.

345

The credits rolled on the old cartoon playing in the living room. Peter made his way in to find his brother seated under a blanket in the warm glow of the space heater.

"How 'bout we hit the bathroom before we go, Joey?"

"Hmmm."

"It's gonna be a lot of fun. You're gonna love the plane ride. Remember how fast Punch used to drive us around? We're gonna go way faster than that! But you won't hardly feel it."

He helped his brother struggle to his feet and turned off the television.

Alls I gotta do is hope for a miracle.

∽

Biaggio Falcone hoped to spend Thanksgiving with his son. But he told his father he was going away with friends. Who these friends were or where they were going was never made clear. Biaggio would be carving the turkey at the home of Tommy and Eleanor.

There was no snow for Rico to deal with in Florida. He staked out Don Sacco's fishing pier for two days, hidden behind binoculars in the safety of a rented van. The night before, he enjoyed a fresh fish dinner, lost a load of cash betting Jai-Alai, and made a trip to a toy store. He purchased a plastic kiddie swimming pool. It was white with blue trim, and it had several smiling dolphin caricatures going nose to tail around its outer shell.

It would be the tub in which Don Sacco's headless body would be dismembered on Black Friday.

∽

The total airport delay was less than two hours. The snow had tapered to flurries. Peter had a window seat on the plane, as his mother wanted nothing to do with any views. She sat by the aisle, with Joey between them. As they waited on the JFK runway for their turn to take off, Peter decided it might be better if he distracted Joey from the upcoming flight crew safety demonstration. He set Joey up with a portable CD player, gently slipping the headphones over his ears. He'd brought a couple of compact discs, but didn't have any Beatles. He thought his brother might appreciate his personal favorite: Ultimate Rascals. Once they were airborne they would be shown the movie *Turner & Hooch*, a buddy comedy featuring Tom Hanks and a big, sloppy French Mastiff, or Dogue de Bordeaux. As Peter pushed the button to play his CD for Joey, his mother mentioned—yet again— the reason she insisted on heading to Lourdes in the off-season.

"No crowds. Less people to stare at my son."

"I know, Ma. You told me."

"Sorry. It's just my nerves. You know, Glenn Miller was flying to France and they never found him."

Peter hoped that the music drowned that out. Not something for Joey to hear. He could faintly recognize the sound of "I Ain't Gonna Eat Out My Heart Anymore" coming from the headphones, so Joey hadn't heard his mother's reference to an airplane disaster. Bad enough that Peter was looking for radio cassette players that might be concealing a bomb.

The aircraft took flight without incident, and Joey seemed calm. The music distracted him from the safety instructions, and he'd heard neither the pilot's nor his mother's announcements. Peter's friend, Benny Crocetti, gave him a book on the miracles of Lourdes and he looked forward to this flight as a brief window of calm that would give him the chance to read it. Just thumbing through it, he came upon the fact that over sixty unexplained cures had been officially declared as miracles by the Catholic Church. He read a chapter on the Lourdes Medical Bureau, an investigative body that had been in existence for over a century. It was the duty of this board of doctors to weed out and dismiss any claims that could not pass a rigorous examination. A subject's original diagnosis must be confirmed as valid and medically incurable. The apparent cure must occur immediately in conjunction with a visit to Lourdes, and must be complete and permanent. If the medical bureau finds all of these conditions met, it may deem that the cure is medically inexplicable. Upon that determination, it is then up to the church to investigate whether the cure is indeed a miracle. That process can take more than a decade.

Miracles ain't easy.

Thousands upon thousands have deemed themselves cured after visiting the shrine and being caressed by her waters, yet of that group, less than seventy have so puzzled the discerning eyes of the scientific world, and made it through the scrutiny of a team of doctors whose sole job is to poke holes in the claim that they may be referred to as miracles.

Peter quickly leafed through the pages, absorbing the stories of inoperable cancers that suddenly vanished, of multiple sclerosis gone without a trace, heart disease completely reversed, tuberculosis healed, eyesight restored to the blind, and the paralyzed rising to their feet to walk.

Peter looked over at his brother who was trying to remove the headphones. He helped to take them off. Joey leaned over to look out the window. He saw the clouds but showed little interest. Mary's pills were kicking in and she was dozing off.

"They're gonna show a movie soon," Peter said to his brother.

He wondered if there might be a cure in store for Joey. Didn't have to be any kind of confirmed miracle. One of the thousands of cures that get denied by the bureau would probably be just fine.

But only sixty or so *official* miracles? So many people go to Lourdes. If there was a study of all the sick who happened to go to, say, Shea Stadium since it was built, would there also be sixty or seventy miracle cures among them as well?

Joey ran his finger along the plastic clasp that held his tray table upright against the seat in front of him. Peter was lost in his thoughts.

There's always the thousands who feel they got a cure, but didn't pass the miracle test. There must be something to that. We don't really need no official miracle.

Crackling static signaled that the pilot was about to speak over the plane's loudspeakers. The pilot probably said that there would be an in-flight movie on the way, or he may have mentioned something about the altitude or air speed, but the calm, almost robotic sound of his voice, the coldness of the audio transmission, and the image in Joey's mind of the clouds he saw out his window, all caused him to hear something different than everyone else.

Obviously a major malfunction.

The scream and the kick came together. Joey launched his foot into the seat in front of him The tray table came crashing down. Mary's heart raced as her son's shrieking dragged her from her slumber.

"Nnnnnaaaaaayyyyyhhhhh!"

"What's wrong?" yelled Peter, dropping his book.

Joey continued to kick. He grabbed at his seatbelt. He felt like he had when he'd been strapped down at the school. Peter wrapped his arms around him.

"It's okay, Joey. Nothing's wrong."

Mary looked at all the neck-craning passengers.

"Don't worry. He won't hurt you," she offered bitterly.

They all looked away.

Joey lurched back and forth in his seat, saliva dripping from his mouth. Two flight attendants headed to Mary's side. She told them all would be fine and they could return to their normal duties. Peter held his brother tightly, still not sure of what set him off.

"It's all good, Joey. Everything is okay. I want you to calm down and take some deep breaths. We're gonna watch a funny movie and then we are gonna land very softly and get to see a beautiful country that we ain't seen before."

Joey's screams turned to whimpers. His breathing slowed. He felt safe with his brother. Peter's arms felt almost like his father's.

⚬⚬⚬

The flight took eight hours. Peter was sure that Charles Lindbergh's trip had been faster. He spent much of the journey wishing he had the money to afford tickets on the Concorde. With the time difference it was well past midnight, and Peter herded his mother, brother, wheelchair, and luggage directly from Charles de Gaulle airport to their nearby hotel. He hoped they'd be able to at least get a glimpse of the Eiffel Tower, but he was told it was a twenty-minute ride from the hotel to the city of Paris. It was time for a quick bite, a long sleep, and then a five-hour train ride to Lourdes.

I wonder if they got any Thanksgiving turkey in the hotel restaurant?

⚬⚬⚬

In 1858, Bernadette Soubirous, a fourteen-year-old girl, was out gathering firewood when she claimed she saw the first of many visions of a white figure in dazzling light. She said this apparition later identified itself as the Immaculate Conception and instructed Bernadette to uncover a spring, which she did by digging through dirt and mud with her bare hands. She said the holy vision also asked her to have local priests build a chapel at the site. In March of that year, a crowd of townspeople—including the local physician, Dr. Pierre Romaine Dozous—watched during one of Bernadette's visions; the candle she held burnt down so far as to have the open flame in direct contact with her bare skin for over fifteen minutes. Bernadette suffered no pain or injury, according to the doctor's documents.

The initial trickle of water that Bernadette uncovered with her hands now drew up to five million pilgrims a year to the town of Lourdes. Most wished to drink of it, or bathe in it, to cleanse their souls. Some came in hope of a miracle.

⚬⚬⚬

The train ride was tedious, but an improvement over the air-travel experience. The Salernos checked into their Lourdes hotel, freshened up, and ate lunch. Then it was time to head to the baths. Mary was all business. There might be time to sightsee later, but her son was getting in that water without delay. Exhaustion be damned.

The day was overcast and the air chilled. Peter heard some mumbling about eight degrees, but that was Celsius. It felt like forty-five to fifty degrees to him. Due to the walking distance, Joey was in the wheelchair. The walker wouldn't cut it today. Peter guided his brother's chair along as Mary ambled slowly beside them, her arm wrapped within her stronger son's.

Gift shops. Everywhere.

"Do they let you leave this place with a dollar?" she grumbled.

Peter studied the souvenir stands. Key chains, magnets, pens, snow globes.

All featuring the Mother of God.

Mostly he saw the bottles. Large and small, and in all shapes. Made for those who wanted to return home with some of the blessed water of Lourdes. All featuring the Mother of God.

"Not what I expected," said Mary.

"Well," replied Peter, "these shops wouldn't be here without the demand. People want this stuff, Ma."

Those were the words he spoke. What he almost said was: *If animals carried cash, some dogs would charge others a fee to sniff their asses.*

Mary shivered as the brisk breeze intensified. Peter now understood why this little French town of fifteen thousand residents was second only to Paris in the number of hotels per square kilometer.

Joey liked the snow globes.

❧

Que Soy Era Immaculada Concepciou.

Those words, the ones said to be spoken by Our Lady to Bernadette, were imprinted on the statue at the grotto. It was a beautiful and peaceful oasis with no sign of a souvenir shop.

The blessed spring at the rear of the grotto was illuminated beneath protective glass. Many stood in awe, and most in prayer. Some took photos and relished the occasional droplet of water that would land upon them from the rocks above. As Peter studied the way people would stare at and photograph the lighted water hole, his thoughts took him back to Brooklyn, and the reverence shown to the bullet holes in the brick face of what used to be Scotti's Barbershop. They too were often photographed, and now they were illuminated as well. What Peter found most interesting, and what his mother almost refused to look at, were the canes and crutches.

Hundreds of them.

They hung everywhere. Presumably abandoned and left as a testament to the power of faith.

Souvenirs from the cured.

The line for the baths wasn't too long this time of year, and the men's line was always shorter than the women's. There were a lot of wheelchairs. It seemed as though most every language on Earth was being spoken by someone or another in the queues. Prayers were plentiful, rosary beads essential, and many of the pilgrims sang "Ave Maria." After about thirty minutes of inching closer, passing several different statues of the Virgin, it was time.

Mary waited outside while Peter went in with Joey. She didn't expect much, but she allowed a small part of her to wonder if Joey would come walking back out to her standing tall and unhindered.

They were greeted by three smiling, sturdy *brancardiers*. After determining that Peter and Joey were American, one of them began to speak his best English.

"You bathe too?" he asked Peter.

"Oh, no thank you. Just my brother today."

"Yes. Bless you."

They guided the Salernos to a small, cold room.

"He must be without clothing. We can help you."

Peter understood, but he asked to be alone with his brother for a moment. His request was granted and a blue curtain was pulled across the room.

"It's just gonna be a little bath like at home," he told Joey as he undressed him. "But it will be much, much faster. It's gonna be cold, though. You can tough it out for Ma. I know you can. This is what Pop wanted for you. You can think about him when you're in the water. Talk to him in your mind."

When Joey was ready, the *brancardiers* returned. Peter hung his brother's clothes on a peg of wood. The men produced a damp white sheet that felt as if it had been stored at the North Pole.

"He wear this for the bath."

After all the years of talk, after the promises made and broken, here they were on the day after Thanksgiving, in the foothills of the Pyrenees, putting their faith in waters unearthed beneath the muddy fingernails of a teenage girl from the time of Abraham Lincoln.

Joey shivered but held strong within the frigid sheet. Peter stood to the side as the three strong volunteers carried his brother toward the stone pool. He shivered but didn't resist.

"He go all under or up to the neck?"

Peter wasn't prepared for the question.

All under?

"Maybe just to the neck, please. I want him as calm as possible."

"What prayer do you choose?"

Another zinger.

"Um . . . m-maybe the Hail Mary?" stuttered Peter.

He looked at the statue of Mary that stood near the base of the cold tub. The men began to pray as they lowered Joey toward the water. Peter considered the thought that, upon completion, his brother could possibly emerge from the water under his own power. Might he even speak Peter's name for the first time?

The water rushed up his nose and down his throat. It was biting and frothy, but most of all, salty. It woke him up, and he began thrashing like a hooked mackerel, knocking his submerged head against something. He finally managed to solve the mystery of up from down. Fighting for the surface, his eyes burned as he choked. He was tethered to something and could feel it wrapped around his bare chest. Breaking the surface for the first time, he was blinded by the glare of the morning sun. This was when he realized he'd smacked his head against the slick, briny underside of a fishing boat.

Rico Falcone was tossed into the Atlantic Ocean by Don Sacco. Though the actual overboard heave had been done by the two men now laughing at Rico as he flopped in the pounding waves, Don Sacco had given the order from his captain's chair. As the water cleared from Rico's eyes, he was able to get his feet against the starboard side of Sacco's private vessel. He was wrapped tightly in some kind of heavy-duty fishing line which kept him hooked to something or other on the boat's deck. He couldn't see up into the boat, but he could see Lenny Sheetrock and some other big goon looking down at him through shit-eating grins. It was then that he began to feel the stinging on his forehead as the salt water rummaged through an open wound he didn't know he had. His eyes were nearly closed, swollen from the beating he had taken. He remembered none of it. His last memory was of being under Sacco's favorite pier in the middle of the night, hours before the don was to be there. He'd been rigging the explosive charge that he'd paid good money for in Newark.

As the disorientation subsided, the pain took over. Rico's face felt as though it had been used as the knee kicker he wielded in his carpet business. He didn't know it, but his nose was broken, his eye sockets cracked, and he'd lost a handful of teeth.

The waves smacked against his swollen face, forcing

water into his ears. The fishing lines kept him afloat. They prevented him from drowning, but he knew that wasn't a good thing.

Then he saw Don Sacco's fat head lean over the edge of the boat. The wide brim of the old man's hat partially blocked the sun from taunting Rico's inflamed eyes.

"So, you was gonna kill me?" came Sacco's words on a cloud of cigar smoke.

Rico wondered where his plan went wrong. Something slimy brushed against his leg as it dangled below the surface.

"I will give you credit for having balls. He does still have balls, right Lenny?"

The burly lackey laughed as he tugged on the lines that kept Falcone afloat.

"Yeah, I wouldn't let them take your balls, kid," said Sacco. "I know you're a real ladies' man. I like that. I bet that in my day I got more snatch than you, though. I was a legend back when things was good, ya know."

Rico tried desperately to think of a way to free himself and swim away. Though even if he could get loose, there was no land in sight. They'd just shoot him as he swam.

"I had so many dames that I have actually fucked two with the same name," said Sacco. "I know, you're thinking, 'big fucking deal.' You're thinking, 'lots of guys have had two Maries or two Theresas'."

Sacco drew deeply on his thick cigar. "I banged two women with the same full name. Completely by chance. That's how you know you've had a lot of ass."

At this point Rico was finally able to see that the water around him was becoming chunky and red. He could smell it now, too.

Blood.

"Give it some more," bellowed Sacco to someone on his boat.

Another monkey came into view and began chucking some bloody mess into the water all around Rico. It was Jackie Moose. All the way from New York.

Fish guts.

"Did you really think you could just hop down to Florida and dispose of the leader of a family? An explosive under my pier? You watch too many old war movies, Falcone."

Sacco turned and spoke to someone else who was not in Rico's view.

"Come here my friend. You'd appreciate this."

Wearing a big hat very similar to Sacco's, and holding a full wine glass, the Diabolist appeared before Rico. His face was painted white, but it could have been sunscreen. He gazed over the side of the boat, peering down with a lifeless stare. He took a gentle sip of the Barolo Monfortino that Sacco poured for him—vintage 1955.

∞

Joey's body vibrated in the cold stone tub. The *brancardiers* held him down, but with his head safely above water. The prayers continued as Joey shook. He groaned a little, but his gyrations seemed more a reaction to the temperature than any attempt to fight the process.

With the final Amens, they lifted him from the bath. They invoked the names of Mary and Bernadette, but they were said quickly and Peter didn't catch it all. One of them gently offered Joey a sip from a fresh cup of Lourdes water, which he managed to swallow with a cough.

Peter watched for any sign of a miracle.

The men gave Joey no opportunity to stand. They quickly carried him to the dressing room.

Mary sat on a wooden bench awaiting the return of her sons. She'd seen several people emerge from the baths. Almost all were smiling or in prayer. Nobody discarded a walking stick.

Then they came.

Peter was pushing his brother in the wheelchair.

"Did they make you leave through a gift shop?" she asked dryly.

"Don't be like that," replied Peter. "I was very proud of Joey in there. He's one tough customer."

The clouds were growing darker.

"I thought maybe I'd see him carrying you outta there," she answered.

Wrapping her arms around Joey, she asked, "Was that good? How did it make you feel?"

She was hoping he'd say 'Great' or 'Miraculous.' Even 'Shitty' would have been more than acceptable.

He said, "Hmmm."

Peter was still intrigued by something he'd noticed in the baths. By the time Joey was lifted from the pool and carried to the changing room, he had completely dried off. There was no towel used and the time elapsed was surely no more than a minute. He brought that to the attention of the *brancardiers*.

"Yes," was their only reply.

⸺

"I have never laid a hand on you. I let you go around unscathed after you brutally assaulted my men. All of this I did out of respect for your father," said Don Sacco.

Rico thrashed about in the water, trying to free himself so that he could drown.

"But now," continued the boss as he looked out onto the blue horizon, "now you hire this man to decapitate me so that it can be played on television?"

The Diabolist took another sip of wine.

"The world should think we are some kind of terrorists?" yelled Sacco. "We should behead people and capture it on video? Oh, I'm gonna give that kiddie pool to my grandson. Thanks."

The don's attention was drawn by something farther out in the Atlantic.

"Is it? Is it, Jackie? Is it?" he asked like an excited schoolboy.

Jackie Moose grabbed a set of binoculars, maybe the ones they found on Rico. He peered out over the sea.

"Can't tell."

"More chum. More chum!" the boss said excitedly.

His underling obeyed, filling the waves around Rico with another bloody helping of mangled fish flesh.

Rico desperately tried to look around, hoping for any sign of a boat, but his feet would slip off the side of Sacco's vessel and he'd be under water again, only to be dragged up by the cords that led up to his persecutors.

"I would've done away with you in a respectful fashion if I hadn't heard of your ugly plans for me and my severed head. But now, Rico, fuck you. We're gonna enjoy ourselves."

The don's head sat in a fog of cigar smoke. It lingered beneath the brim of his hat.

"This devil here," he said, pointing to the Diabolist. "He's too smart to ruin his livelihood by assassinating the head of a family. He even brought the money you paid him and handed it to me as a tribute. He's an odd sort, but he's got brains. He'll be respected by all the families if and when they learn of his loyalty."

They tossed chum for over a half hour and had Rico in the water for fifteen minutes when they finally confirmed a sighting.

"Hell yes," yelled Sacco.

His men cheered the way the Romans must have when they welcomed a hungry lion into the arena to stalk the *bestiarii*.

Rico twisted his bleeding head to see it approach. It looked blue from a distance but seemed almost green as it drew closer.

It was at least twelve feet long and certainly weighed over a thousand pounds.

Galeocerdo cuvier. Tiger shark.

Rico braced himself.

Fuck me. Stay still.

Sacco and his men were nearly jumping up and down. The Diabolist stood peacefully but may have had an erection.

It swam past Rico. Some of the floating fish entrails

briefly adhered to the tip of its dorsal fin. It rotated in the bloody surf and submerged. Rico considered asking Don Sacco to shoot him, but he knew the request wouldn't be granted, so why give the old fuck the pleasure? He continued his silence.

God, how the Diabolist wanted to capture this all on film, but he knew not to defy the don's orders.

Rico felt it below. It almost raised him out of the water.

He had been hit by the shark's wedged head. It prodded him with its snout but again moved away.

Where the fuck is it?

He knew he shouldn't move, but it already found him. The best method of defense would be to punch it in the snout or poke at its eyes. He'd heard that over the years, but it didn't do him any good as his arms were bound to his sides. He'd have to try kicking it, but then he'd have no balance at all and would likely just flop around like a helpless tuna.

His thoughts briefly went to Georgiana. Then he thought of his father. Would he ever know what happened to his son?

"Please . . . " said Rico through his shattered teeth.

"Huh?" replied the don, momentarily pausing his celebration above. "Shhh," he said to his minions. "He's talking!"

"Please," he said again, spitting out the salty, bloody water.

"You say 'please'? You wanna ask me for mercy?"

Rico mustered all his remaining energy. "Please tell my father that I am dead."

Then he turned to await the shark.

"Hail Mary, full of grace. The Lord is with thee . . . " He paused as he saw it. Midway through its slow approach, the shark found another gear. Like a jet on takeoff it launched itself toward its bound prey. Rico saw its planed head rise to the surface. He saw its eye. Black like an inkblot. It was neutral and passionless, like the eye of the old stuffed lamb toy he disposed of at Vito Salerno's murder scene. He watched as the eye rolled up like the wheel of a tired slot machine. The Diabolist's eyes rolled at the very same time. The shark opened wide to reveal its rows of jagged and twisted teeth, each one a dagger in itself.

" . . . blessed art thou . . . "

It tore into his left shoulder.

Sacco and his boys watched intently as the shark pulled Rico's arm away, shredding through his heavy bone as though it were the shell of a sea turtle. It ripped the limb from both Rico and the binding cords. He screamed as his blood mixed with that of the disemboweled bait fish. As the predator swallowed arm, Rolex, and pinky ring, another fin breached the crimson surface.

A second tiger shark arrived.

Aboard Sacco's boat, the fellas drank and smoked as the pair of man-eaters divvied up Rico's body in a flurried twist. Within a minute, almost nothing remained.

Only blood.

Nobody spoke as the blood spread, fading from red to pink as it diluted with the sea. The fins could no longer be seen. Lenny cut the lines that held Rico, and they fell to the winds.

"One thing about that guy," said Sacco. "He was as dumb as an anchor, but he went out like a man."

He turned to the Diabolist. His white grease paint was thinning in the Florida sun.

"You did the right thing. You basically had two choices and you chose the honorable. I want you to know that I am grateful to you with all my heart."

Don Sacco embraced the pernicious punchinello, though as not to get too close to his face or crotch.

The sea water was returning to blue as the don concluded his bear hug.

"Would you like more wine?"

The clown gave a slight shake of the head.

"Okay. Again, on behalf of my wife and family, I give you my heartfelt thanks."

Sacco gave a nod to Jackie Moose, who stood to the rear of the jester. Moose took a wide step to the left and put a bullet through the Diabolist's head.

His pale face hit the deck with a crack; blood poured from his skull and oozed toward the drain hole.

"What a shame," said Sacco to no one in particular. "He was in a catch-22. We couldn't let him walk away."

Jackie and the boys lifted the body before too much blood soiled the deck. Don Sacco refilled his wine glass.

"What could this circus clown know of *omerta*?"

The fellas tossed the Diabolist's remains over the side of the forty-seven-foot Buddy Davis sport boat. It made quite the splash as one of the boys got to cleaning up the bloody deck. Don Sacco took the wheel and began the long haul toward the coast. They headed away from the sun as the soggy body of the hellish prankster was left for the creatures of the brine. It drifted slowly in the general direction of the Bermuda Triangle.

∽

Now what?

That was the sole thought that filled Peter Salerno's mind. He stood there in a darkening, windy French town known for its miracles, but he hadn't found one. His mother was surely disappointed, but he knew she wouldn't let on. Now he'd have to wheel Joey back toward the hotel while his mother framed her sadness in wisecracks.

"It looks like it's gonna pour," he said. "Let's get Joey to the hotel before he comes down with pneumonia."

"Maybe it'll be walking pneumonia," replied his frustrated mother.

Peter was about to remind Mary about being positive, maybe mention the word "faith," when the rain began.

"Damn it," said Peter as he wheeled the chair under a small overhang, "You and Joey wait here. I'm gonna run up that hill to the souvenir stands and get us some umbrellas."

"We can go with you."

361

"Ma, I'll be much faster by myself. Stay here. It'll keep yous dry."

As Peter began to jog toward the hill, his mother called from behind. "If the umbrellas got the Virgin's picture on them, they're gonna charge you more."

She started to rub Joey's shoulders. He just looked off into the distance. People were moving about briskly—at least those who could. The rain came harder, and since the afternoon hours at the baths were coming to a close, the entire area emptied out quickly.

Peter had long vanished over the hill when Mary spotted an empty bench under an overhead shelter, maybe fifty feet from where she stood.

I can get us over there and get off my feet.

"Joey, can we make a break for it through these drops? We can get over there where it's more comfortable and your old Ma can sit."

"Hmmmm."

After about four steps she realized that pushing Joey's chair up even a slight incline in the rain might not have been the best idea. Sometimes her mind thought her body was about twenty years younger than it was. Still, Mary Salerno was no quitter.

"You getting fat?" she said, laughing at her son as they were showered with rainwater. She had the chair picking up a little speed and was approaching the halfway point. She was beginning to think about ways to put a positive spin on this long journey that produced spiritual solace but nothing along the lines of what they'd—perhaps foolishly—hoped for.

My son cleansed his soul in there.

That thought lingered with her as her foot landed awkwardly on something she hadn't noticed.

A tree branch.

Nothing too big, maybe actually more of a glorified twig, but it seemingly had fallen from the centuries-old poplar tree during the windstorm and landed in Mary's sloped path.

However it got there, it was enough to impair her balance and send her hard to the ground. She lost her grip on Joey's wheelchair and all she feared was that it would roll backwards down the incline with him still in it. She managed to get her left foot behind one of the wheels, but her right ankle twisted, and now it began to hurt.

Where the hell is everybody?

There were no people in sight. Just rain. It crossed Mary's mind that the crowds at Lourdes traversed country and continent for the chance to be submerged in its waters, yet they scattered as it fell from the heavens. Joey heard the whimper that she tried to muffle. She turned face down for a moment, still keeping her foot against the wheel, in an attempt to push herself to her feet. Her hands were wet and muddy, as were Bernadette's some 131 years before. She gave it her all, but there was no way she could bring herself to stand with one injured ankle and another foot occupied as a wheelchair brake.

Mary felt the chair move.

She turned to look up; she saw her son Joey standing above her, his head framed by a black sky. His hand was outstretched, offering to help her to her feet.

Okay, don't get carried away. He could always stand.

She reached for the familiar weakness of his grip, knowing he wouldn't have the physical strength to pull her up.

His grip felt strong. She still refused to trust it, not wanting to pull her sickly boy down on top of her. She adjusted her left leg so as to get to one knee. This action freed the wheelchair, which began a slow, backwards descent, gaining speed until it collided with a wrought-iron fence. Maybe it was the sound of the metal-on-metal collision, but finally, two women appeared just down the hill and began to hurry through the rain towards Mary and her son. It was then that Joey began to pull. His grip felt like Sal's as he elevated his mother from the ground to her feet. Her mouth was wide as she tried to keep her weight off the injured foot. She half expected to hear him speak her name, but he said nothing. He was still tilted to one side and hadn't acquired the body of an Olympian, but something was very different.

By the time the women reached them, Peter could be seen hurrying down the hill toward his family. The women spoke French, but Mary understood the gist of their words.

"We're fine. Thank you very, very much," she smiled.

One of them hurried to reclaim the lost wheelchair just as Peter arrived with the umbrellas.

"What happened, Ma?" asked Peter nervously as he opened what Winnie might call a "brolly." It was not adorned with any caricatures, just plain black, like the sky above. He handed it to his mother and opened the second for his brother.

"I fell, Peter. Then your brother got out of his chair and pulled me to my feet."

He studied his brother there in the downpour, while holding out the second umbrella to shield Joey from the rain. Quite matter-of-factly, Joey reached out and grasped the handle.

He held it on his own.

The French lady returned with the chair. Peter thanked her and told his brother to sit in it.

"Nnaayyhhh."

Joey looked at his mother as she balanced on her good foot. He pointed her toward the chair.

Mary made the sign of the cross, quickly mirrored by the two women, though they weren't entirely sure why.

"Mmmmm."

Mary followed Joey's command and took a seat in the wet wheelchair. She closed her eyes tightly, so as not to cry. The women headed whence they came and Peter called out behind them. "Thank you. God bless you."

Peter took hold of the chair and began to slowly push his mother toward the pathway to their hotel. He kept a keen eye on his brother, who walked slowly beside them under his new black umbrella. Mary half expected a parting of the clouds, maybe even the appearance of a spinning sun. That was not to be, but her sons did walk together, all the way back to the hotel.

⟡

The rest of the day, Peter watched his brother closely, especially at dinner.

Will he feed himself?

He did not. However, he walked throughout the hotel under his own power, never stopping for a rest, despite Peter's insistence. He made the effort to use a spoon on his own, though he didn't fare too well. Peter tried to pace himself, but he peppered Joey with questions.

"You feelin' okay?"

"You hungry?"

"You tired?"

"How 'bout a sip of Kronenbourg?"

He wondered if one of the questions might be answered with a true word. Just a simple yes would wipe away the years of anguish and toil.

"Hmmmm."

Still, there was the walking. No wheelchair. No walker.

Where did the strength come from?

Peter's thoughts turned to adrenaline. Joey witnessed his mother's fall. There was nobody else to help her. He'd often asked his brother to be strong in the absence of their father. He considered that the adrenal burst might subside overnight, their last before returning to Paris. He'd heard the stories of a single human being able to lift a car to save a child trapped beneath. Maybe this was Joey's version.

⟡

The next morning, the sun returned to Lourdes. It fought through the blinds and woke Peter, warming his face. Joey slept beside his mother in the other bed. Peter rubbed his eyes and looked forward to finally taking his family to see the

Eiffel Tower and the Louvre Museum. He showed Joey a photograph of the Mona Lisa in a book several weeks before, and he knew his brother liked it because he studied it for the better part of an hour.

What he didn't know was that the ambiguity of her expression, and the depth of her stare, led Joey to once again consider the poster he saw of Bob Marley gazing yonder.

Peter wondered about his mother's sore ankle as he saw her sleeping soundly. He got his feet to the floor and stood to check on his brother, who would be on the far side of their mother.

He wasn't there.

Just as panic was about to rear its ugly head, he heard a sound from the bathroom. He rushed there to find his brother standing beside the sink. It was dark; he hadn't turned on the bathroom light. Joey was shirtless, but his loose-fitting jeans were on.

For the first time in his forty-three years, Joey Salerno put on his own pants.

The Salernos postponed their trip to Paris. The museum and the tower could wait. They wanted to spend the remaining days of their trip in Lourdes. Mary cited her ankle as a factor, but truth be told, she wanted to spend time at the Basilica. It contained two churches and a crypt. There would be several masses to attend. Yesterday seemed so rushed. Mary wanted her son taken into the baths as soon as they arrived. Now she wanted to take her time and give thanks. She wanted to experience the full meaning of Lourdes with her grown children. The sun hovered bright in the sky this day, though she did have a newfound respect for the subtlety of rain.

Mary wanted to pause and take in the many beautiful statues that they'd hurried past the prior afternoon.

She especially wanted to see the one of the young Bernadette Soubirous and her lambs.

Chapter Thirty-Six

O N THE FLIGHT home from France, there was nary a mention of the Louvre or the Eiffel Tower. The days spent in the hills of Bernadette filled the Salernos with a kind of peace they had not known before. Joey's apparent adrenal surge showed no signs of subsiding, and there would be no fearful outburst on this return flight. He sat calmly through takeoff, safety demonstration, and all manner of pilot transmissions. Mary's ankle was feeling much better, and Peter brought home about a dozen small souvenir bottles filled with the waters that had washed over his brother. These were to be bestowed upon close family and Pearl Gholston.

∽

The nightclub that was once Scotti's Barbershop was not open to the public during the day, but the offices in back were most busy during those hours. There were a lot of men buzzing about as Rico had not been heard from in almost a week.

Both Carbone and Johnny the Beatnik no longer had their long hair and beards. These styles had always been frowned upon by Rico, and as his ascension seemed inevitable, both men conformed to the short, slicked back look that was prevalent among the families. Though Biaggio had long permitted the two to present themselves as they liked, provided they were clean and respectful (to him they were honoring the image of Jesus Christ) they decided together to morph into something that Rico would be more comfortable with.

367

Dedicated soldiers.

Newer men were also rising through the ranks. Mario Campigotto, the great-great-grandson of the revered Don Campigotto, made the most of his interview with Biaggio on that stormy day years ago, when both Punch the Pedal and Vito Salerno lost their lives. He'd returned with his father in tow—as per Falcone's request—a month later, and found Biaggio in a wistful mood. Arrangements were soon made for him to pledge his oath and get his button, with his pedigree greasing the wheels.

There was another young fella, a wiry sort with jet black hair named Pancrazio. Biaggio loved that name but hated that the junior men insisted on calling the kid "Scarface." There was no hint of a scar on this guy's comely kisser— which could be solid grounds for such a nickname. It was his slight resemblance to Al Pacino's character in the film *Scarface* that induced the younger mobsters to rename him.

Biaggio knew that the real Scarface was indeed an Al, but it wasn't Pacino.

Deep in the back offices, they sat together, just the two of them. Tommy Box o' Cookies was spending too much time in his wheelchair. He found it quite ironic that his losing battle wasn't at the wrong end of a shotgun, and he wasn't being put through a shredder in some New Jersey warehouse. The cigars hadn't rotted his mouth with cancer and the booze hadn't ravaged his liver.

With a lifetime of whacking and limb breaking behind him, with decades of drinking, smoking, and whoring haunting his quietest moments, Tommy DiRocco was being done in by his cookies.

He'd lost his right foot to diabetic rot.

He knew he was probably going to die piece by piece and that his wife was wasting her time getting all excited over something called a Seattle Foot. She was sure it would have him upright soon enough, as soon as his doctor said it was ready to be fitted.

After all, he had lost over forty pounds.

All of that was for Eleanor and her peace of mind. He was going to spend much of whatever time he had left with his old friend Biaggio.

The don sat just to Tommy's left. His aquarium bubbled and hummed behind him. Its colorful vibrancy embraced the fishes within, but had little effect on the surrounding room— on this day, at least.

Biaggio Falcone didn't want to open the package that sat on his desk, but he knew he must. He'd wanted his most trusted colleague beside him and called for Tommy as soon as the messenger dropped it off. More accurately, as soon as he'd seen that it came from Florida.

<hr />

Weekday evening or not, Mary Salerno's family was coming over tonight to welcome her home, see Joey, and help them put up their Christmas tree.

Peter and Kathy brought the kids; Mary's mother, and her sisters and brother came with their families. Lourdes' water was handed out to all. They marveled at the story Peter told them. The improvements Joey made were obvious. He shuffled from room to room without the walker. He lifted from his chair under his own power. His smile came more frequently than it had in years, at least since his father had been stricken for the first time. Mary took note of that, and her thoughts focused on Pearl.

"I should call Pearl. She should be here tonight."

Mary dialed her number, but all she heard was the hollow sound of ringing through the earpiece.

No answer.

"Not home, I guess. I have to give her some of the Lourdes' water. What would we have done without her?"

Mary smiled as her grandchildren decorated the Christmas tree. It wasn't yet a week since Thanksgiving; heck, it wouldn't even be December until the weekend, and Mary's tree was going up. She had always put her tree up on

Christmas Eve, but things do change. Her teenage grandkids wanted the tree up, so there it was. Young Joseph pulled one particular decoration from the strewn boxes and turned to his father.

"Look at this one, Pop," he laughed.

Peter walked over and his son placed the small plate in his hand.

Peter starts first grade—1955.

He remembered the day rather clearly. His father ironed his shirt. He had a Lone Ranger lunch box. He could still hear the words his mother uttered to Sal on that September morning.

There'll come a day you and I won't be here for Joey. Who'll care for him then?

Peter gave his boy a friendly elbow and hung the plate on the tree.

Mary went and sat beside her daughter-in-law.

"Where would we be without you, Kathy?"

Kathy brushed it off, but this was not something that Mary would normally say. She was never one to verbalize such things. You'd know she loved you, but more from her deeds than her words.

"I mean it," continued Mary. "I thank God for the day my son met you."

Kathy could only respond with a warm embrace. She was almost overwhelmed.

"I want you to give a bottle of this water to your brother," said Mary of the family priest. "I know he can make holy water on his own, but this stuff is top shelf!"

They laughed, and Kathy thanked her.

"Without your brother, we'd have never found Pearl. Him getting the word around the parish that Sal needed help—"

Kathy interrupted. She'd known this for a while, but something told her not to tell Mary. Her mother-in-law had always been one to conjure up theories and cast a discerning eye. She didn't want any question and answer session between Mary and her brother. Maybe now was the time.

"You know, Ma, I've talked to my brother about that," she began. Mary smiled as Kathy went on. "He told me that he doesn't remember saying anything to anyone at the church about Pop's condition before Pearl came to your door."

Mary sat there for a moment, trying to figure out how Pearl might have known to come calling on them if she somehow hadn't heard it through the channels of the church.

"Ain't that somethin'?" was all she said.

Kathy breathed a sigh of relief just as Joey approached her. He hadn't seen the Mona Lisa in person, but that was okay. Everyone had their own version of that five hundred-year-old masterpiece. For Peter, it might be watching a perfect game thrown by Don Larsen or Sandy Koufax. Sal might have chosen the sight of Secretariat shattering numerous records en route to a stunning Triple Crown triumph.

Joey held his personal masterpiece in his hands as he sidled up to Kathy. She gave it to him as a Christmas gift shortly after they'd first been introduced, and he wanted to hear it now.

Sgt. Pepper's Lonely Hearts Club Band.

She remembered the gift that she bought him at Woolworth's all too well, and helped him to play it, as well as his other Beatles records, many times over. She stood to bring the album over to Joey's record player. Mary gently placed a hand on her arm.

Kathy remained in stillness as Joey ambled across the living room, past his niece, nephew, and grandmother. He slowly knelt down and put the record on by himself.

That was Mary's masterpiece.

༄

The rectangular box sitting on Biaggio's desk was wrapped in brown shipping paper. There was no detailed address of the sender. Just the word "Florida."

He made sure the office door was locked so only he and Tommy would be there for the opening. The pumps hummed by the fish tank as he pulled away the outer paper. He took a blade from his desk and sliced through the packing tape they way he'd seen more than one throat slit on his way up through the ranks.

The first thing he saw as he gingerly lifted the flaps of the box was his only son's New York State driver's license. He needed no further proof. In the circles in which he ran, with their unique forms of communication, this told him that his boy was dead. He feared it might be a finger or even an entire hand. Thankfully, this was less gruesome, but it also prevented full closure. At least Biaggio could bury a hand.

Paperclipped behind the license was a postcard. There was no handwritten message, but the front of it featured a picture of the sun, the word "Florida" emblazoned in bright orange, and a wide, gleaming view of the Atlantic Ocean.

The rest of the box was filled with money. Thousands of dollars stacked and bound together. The full amount that Rico Falcone gave to the Diabolist, who, in turn, handed it over to Don Sacco, was forwarded on to Rico's father.

Biaggio couldn't piece together all the details, but he was wise enough to assume that his son took his final breath in, or near, the waters off the east coast of the Sunshine State. He knew in his heart that Don Sacco was involved, obviously because of the location but also because of the amount of money in front of him. What that money was, or how it was connected to his son was still unclear, but he believed the fact that it was brought to his doorstep exuded a rare type of honor that most men would never bear.

For as long as Biaggio Falcone would walk the face of the Earth, he would never discover that his son and only heir left this world in the jaws of a shark.

Tommy saw the contents of the package but said nothing. From his wheelchair, he placed his hand on Biaggio's shoulder. They both understood that Rico had likely sealed his own fate through his arrogance and irrationalism. Whereas most would certainly preserve the box and its contents for a full police investigation, Biaggio would keep the license and the money but burn the box and the postcard.

They sat there in silence. None of the other men dared to even knock on the door; they saw the package delivered, saw Biaggio make two quick phone calls, and watched as Winnie wheeled Tommy in shortly thereafter.

Biaggio ran his fingers along the picture on Rico's license.

"Tommy, you know why I've always been so particular about my aquarium?" he asked.

This wasn't along the lines of what Tommy expected to hear, but if that's what his lifelong friend wanted to talk about, so be it.

Biaggio continued, "When I was young—no more than seven maybe—I had a little fish tank. I'd begged my father for one. Every Christmas, all I wanted was a fish tank. So, he finally got me one. Nothing fancy, of course. Just goldfish—they don't need no heater or nothing, just clean water. But I had four goldfish. Valentino and Chaney, I named after the actors. They were the big stars back then. Tunney, I christened him after the fighter, of course. Then there was Mussolini. My father named that one."

Tommy found himself staring at the elaborate aquarium that his friend now had. He could only imagine the rudimentary setup he must have fawned over in the 1920s.

"I took good care of those fish. Didn't feed them too much. Changed the water without fail. They grew nicely. Especially Tunney."

Biaggio managed a slight smile as he recalled a goldfish he cared for over sixty years earlier.

"Even my father complimented me on how committed I was to my four fish. *Dedicare* he used to say. *Dedicare*."

He placed his hand over Tommy's, which still rested on his shoulder.

"You ever hear that joke about the two goldfish who were talking about God?" asked Biaggio.

"No," replied Tommy quietly.

"One fish says to the other, 'I don't care what you say, there ain't no such thing as God.' So the other one looks him in the eye and says, 'Then who feeds us?' "

Tommy nodded his approval.

"Let me pour us both a drink," he said.

"Not for me, Tom."

As Tommy wheeled himself over to the liquor cabinet, Biaggio continued his story.

"So, one night I was sittin' alone in the kitchen eating the macaronis that my mother made for me. I heard a ruckus coming from my parents' bedroom and I went to investigate. I see my father standing there with his back to me. He didn't have no shirt on, but he did have my mother by the throat. She was pushed up against the wall, trying to get away from him. I ran and tried to jump on his back, but he just tossed me aside. I hurried back into the kitchen, and by the time I got back to their room, he was beating my mother with his belt. With all the strength I could muster, I drove my macaroni fork into that bastard's back."

Tommy poured his drink but never put it to his lips.

"I drew blood, but I don't think it hurt him too much. The fork bent on the way in. Then he came after me, but he left my mother alone. I tell you Tommy, he beat the livin' shit outta me. Go on, take your drink."

Tommy took a sip, then put the glass between his legs and rolled back toward his boss.

"The beating was one thing," continued Biaggio, "but then he decided to teach me a lesson. He gathered my four goldfish into a soup bowl and brought them into the back yard. It was the middle of summer. Probably still ninety degrees at dinner time. He had a chair out there and he ordered me to sit in it. He told me if I tried to get up, or if I even blinked, he would punish my mother in a manner so fierce her sisters wouldn't recognize her. He forced me to watch as he dumped my fish out onto the hot stone walkway. The four of them started flopping about, their mouths open wide. At first they were in a little puddle from the water that fell with them from the soup bowl, but then the puddle evaporated in the hot sun. They moved a little slower as each minute passed. One of them, I think it was Chaney, flipped into the dirt near the tomato plants. He got all covered in the soil. It stuck to him like breading."

Biaggio glanced at the fish in his current tank.

"I don't know how long they baked there in the sun. I could see them drying out and shrinking. It seemed like they lasted much longer than I ever expected. Tunney lasted the longest. He suffered the most but lasted the longest. He truly was a fighter. When it was all done and Tunney stopped moving, my father put his hand under my chin. I fought hard not to cry in his presence. He lifted my face so that he could look me in the eyes. All he said was, 'They died because you lack respect. Now you may bury them.' "

Tommy downed the rest of his drink, knowing his wife would crucify him if she saw a glass of booze in his hand.

"Now," said Biaggio, "I have to call the undertaker to bury my son."

He was holding up the driver's license.

"Regardless, he will have a funeral and a gravesite."

"Whatever we can do to help," was all Tommy could say.

"I know. You're a good friend, Tom."

"I have to ask you—will there be any answer from us to Don Sacco?"

Biaggio sat for a moment, but he already knew his reply.

"No. It's obvious he didn't seek out my son. Rico went after him."

Tommy felt some relief. A war wouldn't be good. Especially now, with the hierarchy growing old, the successor gone, and the future of the family in doubt. It would be good to end it right where it was. He did have a question about another ending, though.

"Biaggio, if I may ask, did your father continue to, um, mistreat your mother?"

"Hell yes. She endured another ten or twelve years of it. I couldn't stop him. It continued until the day I walked into Scotti's and pledged myself to Don Campigotto. Then it stopped."

There came a loud knock on the office door. Apparently, somebody wasn't afraid to interrupt.

The truck came to a rattling stop in front of the newly remodeled club. Biaggio himself walked out alone to meet them. They mentioned on the phone that it would be better to wait until spring, but Biaggio would have none of that. He was honoring a wish from an old friend.

Say a prayer for my Joey. Put a new tree out in front of the barbershop. Pope said it many years ago. Biaggio had done the first request often, and now, as he held out his hand, he was pleased to finally be doing the latter.

He didn't know it, but he was shaking hands with the grandnephew of the man who had pulled his truck up to the same spot more than forty years before. Nepotism wasn't only flourishing in Biaggio's business.

One Two Tree-Tree Service

They came, at Biaggio's personal request, with a huge concrete saw and a young, strong and healthy sycamore tree.

And this time we'll nurture it, Baggio thought.

CHAPTER THIRTY-SEVEN

RICO'S FUNERAL SERVICE was discreet and small. According to the world in general, he wasn't even dead. He was a missing person, though Georgiana was the only one to file such a report. The police were around asking questions, but, of course, they got nothing.

There were many meetings about the status and future of the Campigotto crime family. It was understood within the family that Biaggio was losing interest, especially now with the death of his son. This fact was not disclosed to anyone from the outside, or the other families. It was nearly time to restructure. Johnny the Beatnik would gain power, as would Carbone. Tommy could still advise, but his health problems were a concern. His nephew Winnie was loyal and well-respected, but his lack of a certain aura would prove to be a ceiling against his advancement. Mario Campigotto was a superstar. He had the right blood in his veins, and many could see the day when a true Campigotto might once again head the family. Probably not for a while though. Still young, Scarface Pancrazio was another one to watch. Young and ambitious but maybe with a little too much Rico in his heart.

∽

Just before the holidays, Peter Salerno got home early from work to find his son Joseph digging around the house looking for hidden Christmas gifts. The teen was hoping to find some new video games for his Sega Genesis system, but Peter found him sitting on his parents' bed holding the loaded revolver that Peter kept at the back of his sock drawer. Peter's heart may have actually stopped when he saw the weapon in his boy's hands.

Despite the fact that the gun had long belonged to his father, Peter decided it would be best to bring it over to give to Tommy or Biaggio. It was on this visit that Peter learned of Rico's disappearance.

Biaggio spent quite a while with the Pope's son that day. He had many questions about Joey and the trip to Lourdes. Word spread through the neighborhood that the Salerno boy received a miracle. Peter was quick to dispel any miraculous talk. He explained the detailed process involved in having the church recognize a miracle. He told Biaggio that Joey hadn't had a full recovery by any means. He didn't even know if his improvement would last. The Lourdes Medical Bureau would certainly dismiss Joey's case within minutes.

Peter's detailed explanation was interrupted by Biaggio only once. "Peter, I've been around a long time. Seen a lot of stuff. Good and bad. I'm pretty sure they'll never let me run the Vatican, but this old guy says your brother was hit square in the face by a miracle."

Peter knew better than to protest.

"Is he still shinin' shoes?" asked Tommy.

"You know it!"

"Well, you tell him I only pay half now as I only got one fuckin' shoe."

Peter laughed, but in reality he prayed for Tommy's recovery each night, and hoped that the prosthetic foot he was awaiting would prove to be a godsend.

It was then that Biaggio returned to his longstanding offer.

"I still could use someone to help with the numbers. Men who can be trusted with money aren't easy to come by. Your mother won't be able to care for Joey forever, and your wife shouldn't be expected to dedicate her life to that, Peter. You could earn some extra money to pay for a nurse for your brother."

It also crossed Biaggio's mind that maybe Peter would have more interest in deeper family business than his father ever did. Salvatore Salerno was one of a kind. In this time of upheaval, Peter could be making a smart move if he decided to pledge himself. But let him start with the numbers.

Peter looked at the gun that he gave to Biaggio. It sat there on his desk, which is where his father probably got it from in the first place. There was still a little lint on it. He wondered if that lint came from his sock drawer or if it was still there from his father's. He knew that his mother wouldn't be around forever and that she was getting too old to care for Joey anyway, despite the fact that he put his own pants on every morning and was getting better at handling his own bathroom needs. He also knew that his mother's home was paid in full and they could borrow from it, or if, God forbid, she passed on, they could sell it and use the proceeds to pay for his brother's care. He also still had Pearl Gholston's phone number.

"No, thank you, sir," was his reply to Biaggio Falcone. Looking in his eyes, Peter could see the older man's love and respect for Sal Salerno—the Pope—and his sons.

Christmas 1989 came and went. Joseph got his video games. The Salerno family enjoyed the holidays more than any time since Sal died. Among other things, Peter bought his brother a baseball glove. Nobody expected Joey to start shagging fly balls, and he didn't, but Peter took him outside—weather be damned—and had him picking up balls that he rolled to him. Just seeing Joey bend like that made it all worthwhile. He didn't get them all, but when he did come up with one in his new glove, he didn't look much different than a real shortstop.

The whispers around the neighborhood just after the ringing in of 1990 were that maybe Biaggio Falcone wasn't running the family anymore. He was still seen at the club, but folks heard that maybe he was just a figurehead, someone there to take the heat off the new boss—whoever that was.

∞

It was an unseasonably warm January afternoon when Peter, his son, and his brother were out front of Mary's home throwing and rolling the baseball around. Mary watched from her second-floor window, rooting Joey on in his attempts to scoop up the slowly rolled balls. Her grandson Joseph swallowed the last gulp from his soda bottle. His father still brought home lots of cola.

They were interrupted by the rattling of an old shopping cart. Here came the old man looking for empties. As always, he was tucked inside his worn Yankees jacket. Peter hadn't seen him since the snowy Thanksgiving morning when he and Kathy came to gather up Mary and Joey for the drive to the airport. He walked by without expression, headed for the trash can on the corner.

"Give him your bottle," said Peter to his son.

"Mr. Notoro," yelled Joseph.

No answer.

Peter gave it a try. "Mr. Notoro, we have a bottle for you!"

The old man continued toward the trash.

Mary had no patience for this. "Don't play deaf! My grandson's got a bottle for you. Turn around, Nicky."

He stopped. As he slowly turned his head, they all saw the familiar scar that zagged down the left side of his face.

Joseph handed his empty bottle to Nicky the Zipper.

"Grazie. Dio vi benedica."

As Nicky added the bottle to his cart, he looked up at Mary in the window. He gently kissed the tip of his finger and pointed it skyward. There may have been just the hint of a smile before he moved on. He enjoyed walking his streets after spending nearly twenty years in prison.

"Poor old guy," said Peter to his son. "He used to practically own this neighborhood. Now look at him. He probably can't spell his own name."

Mary sipped a cup of coffee at her window perch.

"That's just what he'd want you to think," she mumbled under her breath.

⤜⤠

Mary Salerno had been feeling tired. Too much holiday excitement, she figured. Peter volunteered to take care of his brother for a few days at his house so that his mother could rest. She'd go to bed early each night after watching a little television, but she always set her alarm clock for the next day as she never liked sleeping too late. A coffee and a newspaper were a great way for her to start the day.

Marcus Brown was a nine-year-old African-American boy who lived with his parents in an area that was a short subway ride from the Salernos' Brooklyn neighborhood. He was especially excited this morning as his mother dressed him in a fancy new suit she'd bought on Fulton Street. It felt important against his skinny body. His family heard about Joey Salerno's story through whispers in their church pews. Mrs. Brown managed to get a message through to Kathy, and after speaking with Mary and Peter, Kathy agreed to have the Browns come over and meet Joey. He'd been in a great mood during his little vacation at her and Peter's home.

Little Marcus was deaf and blind. His mother thought a journey to Lourdes might hold something positive for him.

⤜⤠

The shopping cart clattered and bounced as bottles mixed with cans. It came to a halt at the front door of the club. Never lifting his head, Nicky took a key from the pocket of his old baseball jacket and let himself in. As the door closed behind him, one could see a crude, handwritten sign taped to the glass.

Coming soon—Scotti's Barbershop.

Inside, Baggio Falcone, Tommy Box o' Cookies, Mario Campigotto, and Nicky the Zipper discussed the future of the family. Although the Salernos didn't know it yet, Baggio Falcone already set forth standing orders concerning Joey

Salerno. The Miracle Man would not only always be welcome at the club, he would have a space of his own and an honest job doing what he loved. Shining shoes for his family's friends. Earning money on his own, being his own man.

❧

Little Christmas, or the Epiphany, is on the sixth day of January. In Italy, many children open their Christmas gifts on this day as they are told that the presents were left overnight by La Befana, a witch who is said to ride her broomstick in an endless search to find the baby Jesus. This day marks the end of the Christmas season, and Kathy thought it would be the perfect time for young Marcus to meet Joey.

That meeting took place at Kathy's house; although extremely exhausted, Mary joined them for a short while and gave Marcus and his mother great hope. After seeing Peter and Joey together the last few days, she knew her sons were going to be okay. Mary spent the rest of the day watching her television shows and reading. She was saddened to see that the Leaning Tower of Pisa, the beautiful bell tower that stood in Italy for over eight hundred years, would now be closed to the public due to fears of a pending collapse.

She fell asleep that night wondering how the powers that be could have allowed that situation to occur.

We have walked on the moon, for Heaven's sake.

❧

January seventh began with an old tree branch tapping on Mary's bedroom window. Today would be windy, and maybe a little colder than earlier in the week. The sun's rays seeped through the trees and slid through the venetian blinds. They beamed across Mary's room and settled on a framed photo that was taken nearly half a century before. It showed her husband in full military regalia. Not far from Sal's photograph hung another frame. It contained the drawing that Annette made showing Joey in the arms of the Virgin.

As it had every day, the cubed, futuristic clock radio

jumped to life. It was tuned, as always, to Mary's favorite oldies station, and today it didn't disappoint.

There was over a minute of soothing instrumentation from the Les Brown Orchestra before any singing was to be offered, but Mary didn't budge. The sun caressed her face as she lay there beneath her warm blankets.

Doris Day began to sing.

There was neither gesture nor shift. Not a twitch.

Not even a breath.

Neither sun nor song would interrupt her enduring repose. She drifted away thinking first of Pisa, then of her two sons, healthy and able to take care of themselves. Finally, as she went to her dreams, there stood Sal in full uniform, as in the photo. His strong hand was open, inviting her for a dance.

My dreams are getting better all the time.

And even her dreams were in Brooklynese.

About the Authors

Daniel O'Connor was born in Brooklyn, NY. He lost his mother when he was four years of age, and then his father two years later. He lived with his grandmother until she passed when Dan was ten. Rather than purchase a clown mask and a chainsaw, he kept the demons at bay through books, movies, music—and writing. Upon completion of a decorated Suffolk County, NY police career, Daniel moved to the southwest with his wife and two daughters. It is there that he wrote, using characters and scenarios developed with his cousin Peter Randazzo, the dark love letter to old Brooklyn: *Sons of the Pope*. He is currently at work on his second novel.

His upcoming 2013 short stories: "The Binding" from the anthology *Blood Rites*, and "Between Catskill and Cooperstown" from the anthology *Serial Killers 2*.

Daniel's blog: PrimalScreaming.Wordpress.com

Twitter: @DanOVegas

Contact Daniel: AuthorDanO@aol.com

Peter Louis Randazzo was born, lived, and left us way too soon, in Brooklyn, NY. A graduate of John Jay High School, Peter would tell you he wasn't really a writer. He was, however, a master story-teller. He would mesmerize with his tales of the characters, from all sides of the law, that weaved in and out of his hard-working life on the streets of Brooklyn. The names were always changed to protect the innocent—and they all claimed innocence till they took their last breaths. Peter was a wonderful husband, father and grandfather, and his memory is cherished by enough people to fill New York City. One thing is certain: Without Peter Randazzo, there would be no *Sons of the Pope*.

Made in United States
North Haven, CT
24 November 2022

27183358R00231